STORM TRACK

STORM TRACK

a novel by
Ron Terpening

Walker and Company
New York

To
my mother, Darlene,
my brothers, Larry and Bill,
and my sister, Mary

First published in the United States of America in 1989 by the Walker Publishing Company, Inc.

Published simultaneously in Canada by Thomas Allen & Son Canada, Limited, Markham, Ontario.

Library of Congress Cataloging-in-Publication Data

Terpening, Ron, 1946–
   Storm track / Ron Terpening.
      p.   cm.
   ISBN 0-8027-1069-7
   I. Title.
PS3570.E6767S76   1989
813′.54—dc19   88-26786
                                      CIP

Printed in the United States of America

10 9 8 7 6 5 4 3 2 1

1

(SATURDAY, APRIL 26)

On Saturday afternoon I went down to 165 feet, on an inspection dive that was supposed to last fifteen minutes. The pumping station on the mainland had reported a loss of pressure and wondered if our drilling activities might have damaged the pipeline.

I was working for PetroCanada, a subsidiary of the Canadian Petroleum Development Corporation, and had been assigned for the last six months to Al-Qabisi, one of the cantilevered jackups built by Marathon LeTorneau for the National Drilling Company of Abu Dhabi, and later sold to Libyan Oil.

PetroCanada was due to pull out by the end of May, and I was anxious for the time to pass. The company had agreed to Canadian demands to withdraw support from Libya as part of a government deal to obtain free-trade concessions from Washington. I was proud of the company. We were pulling out well before the American corporations with holdings on the mainland.

The triangular-shaped platform, rising above lattice legs, was anchored in 150 feet of water just off Libya and Tunisia in the Gulf of Gabes. We weren't far from the islands of Djerba, Ashtart, and Kerkennah, and I'd often thought of our rig as one small island among many. To the north we had the Italian island of Lampedusa, to the east Malta and Gozo, and further north, off Cape Bon, Pantelleria.

The water was shallow enough for an experienced

diver to go down with scuba, but a nearby pipeline I was inspecting dropped into a valley before leveling out near the coast, so I went down with a Kirby-Morgan mask and an umbilical cable with a phone line and diving hose hooked up to the Quincy compressor.

Before the dive even began I'd been apprehensive. Jake, my tender, a Texan with the weathered face and inveterate drawl of a seasoned cowboy, had broken his arm the day before when the crane operator near our diving station had nodded off and dropped an anchor the last ten feet to the platform. The anchor's fluke caught Jake near the elbow. He'd been in a lot of pain before they flew him out, but he still took the trouble to warn me.

"Derek, I'm tellin' ya, buddy, watch out for this guy." He shook his head and a grimace twisted one side of his face, deepening the creases. I wanted to tell him not to worry, that everything would be okay, but he grabbed my arm before I could speak and focused his steel gray eyes on me.

I could see the pain there, and for a moment he dropped his head to hide it and then looked back up. "Next thing ya know he'll run the crane over the air hose when you're down under. I'd keep my eye on him if I was you. You can't trust these fucking Arabs anymore."

I nodded. I'd never heard Jake swear before. He was as religious a man as I'd ever met. But I shared his sentiment. Even though I'm Canadian, I hadn't felt safe since we'd heard the U.S. 48th Tactical Fighter Wing had bombed Libyan targets two weeks earlier. We knew something big was up before it ever hit Radio Malta, our preferred English-language station, broadcasting strong at 93.7 MH$_z$ VHF/FM.

We'd been awakened by the F-111s screaming over us at two hundred feet on their final approach to their targets. From where we sat, you could just see the light of the explosions near Tripoli and catch the far-off, thunderlike rumble of the anti-aircraft guns that continued to boom for hours.

Since then, the few foreigners on the jackup had been tense. The Italians didn't seem to mind, but most of the Canadians were jumpy. I'd told Jake I was planning on leaving as soon as my next break came, which was about when we had to pull out anyway. At the time, Jake had been noncommittal; he'd even hinted he might stay on.

Now, with his injury, I guessed everything had changed for him. "Jake," I said, "you were pretty damn smart. Made me think you wanted to stay and then got yourself a private flight out of here."

He tried to grin, his eyes hooded. "I'll trade this busted elbow with ya, if you're in a hurry, pal."

I laughed and patted him on the back. "It'll be okay, Jake. You just worry about yourself now."

He nodded, closed his eyes for a moment, and then said in a soft voice, "Good luck to you and Wanda."

"Thanks, Jake." I sensed the longing in his voice and felt lucky. Wanda was my wife. Jake had been my best man at the wedding five months earlier. It wasn't until then that I learned he had hopes of someday marrying a girl back in Houston. Once he had enough money, I knew he'd say good-bye to foreign operations and go back home where he belonged. But now it was just too hard to find work in the Gulf of Mexico.

On the incoming flight that Friday evening after the accident—in one of the company's new Westland/Aerospatiale Pumas—they sent a tender to replace Jake, a tall, blond-haired, muscular kid barely in his twenties. One
of those body-beautiful California types, first time on a rig and, as my granddad back at Moose Jaw would've said, green as elk piss.

Saturday, when the kid and I started going over the

check sheet, right off we had problems. Communication problems. I felt like the father I'd never wanted to be.

I told him, "You see this air hose? It's laid so the crane operator can't run over it. But he can always drop a load on it. Or on you. Keep your eyes on the bastard."

The kid shrugged. "Don't worry about me. I can take care of myself."

It was me I was worried about, not him.

"You familiar with the Galeazzi chamber?"

He stared at me for ten seconds, his jaw wired shut. When his nod came, you'd have thought he was balancing a jug on his head. His head gave one of those almost imperceptible twitches you measure with millimeters. The Galeazzi decompression chamber sat just behind the diving station, which was near the northwestern leg of the jackup.

I'd given the kid a tour of the rig before the dive. Between us and the opposite leg to the east with its matching crane, sat the shaker tank, drawworks, and rising above all, the derrick. To the south, just beyond the racking platform, were the crew quarters and above them the control room. The kid had arrived on the helipad, which jutted out from the platform deck to the east of the crew quarters.

"I don't want any slack on the air hose when I'm down," I said. "Got that? And keep the hose at an angle at least four meters from the down line." I hoped the kid understood metric and then thought I'd better make sure. "No closer than twelve feet."

He scowled.

I pointed at his chest. "We nearly lost a diver once. His tender let him spiral around the down line."

"You want me to dive for you?" he said.

I didn't like his tone and was about to tell him so, when I managed to restrain myself. I didn't want to anger the guy who'd be tending my air hose.

4

I handed him my log. "Decompression tables are in the back. Keep good track of the times and depths. I want to stay out of the chamber if I can." I pointed to the hang-off bar. I'd made it myself from a two-foot length of 3-inch pipe. Welded a U-bolt from a cable clip to the middle for the line. It was simple but saved a lot of energy during ascent. Depending on my down time, I figured I'd have several decompression stops and a total ascent time of close to an hour. It'd be nice to have something to sit on.

"When you figure out the stops, send that down."

He nodded curtly.

While he hooked me up, I warned him of a few other hazards. He started saying, "No problem, man," to everything. If he'd had dreadlocks, I'd have thought he was Jamaican. By the time I was ready to go neither of us was too happy.

I started out carrying a reserve two-tank pack that I tied off at one hundred feet for a dive on scuba I planned on taking later that day. I was thinking ahead and feeling good about it.

Ten minutes into the dive, I was at the site, engrossed in tracing a crack in the pipeline. The break was more extensive than I'd thought. It ran over twenty feet, half the length of a pipe joint, and ended up near a crossover line. Part of the weight coat, a shell of concrete laid over the pipe to neutralize its buoyancy, had fallen away, and the dope coat was badly scraped. We'd have to wire-brush the area and seal it with Splash Zone.

It didn't much matter but it looked like the trench had settled due to our drilling nearby. Nothing I could do about that. Repair the line and hope for the best.

The job was going to require a saturation dive, and I was estimating the welder's time and needs when a nagging pain at the back of my head became a full-fledged headache I couldn't ignore. And then I noticed the air. A strange smell. *Ammonia?*

"Bad air," I screamed into the phone. "Get me up!" I jerked the air hose four times and reached for my weight belt.

Before I could find the quick release buckle, an upwelling of nausea overcame me and I doubled up in pain. My mask banged against the pipe, the blow disorienting me.

Still no pull on the air hose. What'n hell was the tender doing? He should've been hauling me up hand over hand by now. Was the hose fouled up? Had I circled the jackup's leg going down?

I was on the verge of blacking out and I started to panic. The weight belt slid from my hand and caught on one of my fins. I'd been too dizzy to drop it far enough from my body. I thought I started screaming then, but it may have been only in my head, a bad dream that soon faded into a silent fog.

I woke up at the diver's station when they hooked me up to some pure oxygen. Then they rushed me to the decompression chamber, where I lay in a daze trying to analyze what had really happened. The tender's embarrassed explanation was the last thing I remembered, his words swirling down my eardrums like a whirlpool of vertigo. Something about a galley hand sloshing an ammonia-saturated platform wash around the compressor; about how the hose got tangled with a broken cable from an anchor winch.

What in hell was a galley hand doing near our station? And where in the hell had the dogman for the crane operator been? He should've kept the anchor cable clear.

First Jake, injured by an incompetent crane operator, and now me. I lay there, trying to stay awake like you're supposed to in the chamber, wondering what the next disaster would be.

After a while, I started thinking about Wanda. We were an unusual couple, an Italian and a Canadian, a cultural attaché and a commercial diver.

I'm probably the only commercial oil-field diver who met his wife at a reception for an ambassador, in my case the new Italian ambassador to Tripoli. I was present as a company representative, albeit reluctantly. It wasn't my idea of a fun time.

A functionary of the Italian Cultural Mission to Libya accompanied the ambassador—Wanda Donati. I learned later that her distinctly American forename was chosen by her parents in the period when Italians, like Americans, were enamored of foreign names. Two of the Italian favorites were Walter and Wanda. I don't think I ever met a Wanda in Canada or the U.S. But there was one in Tripoli, a dark-haired beauty with bangs cut just above her eyes, a pert nose, cheeks that looked as if skimmed by the first rosy blush of a ripening peach, and lips that were luminous.

She laughed when I asked her when she celebrated her *giorno onomastico*. Was there a Saint's Day for Wanda?

She was a natural beauty, best of all unselfconsciously so, a young woman who didn't need makeup. Her inner contentment shone on her face. And her cheerfulness, I soon learned, was not a social grace; it too came naturally.

I found her *joie de vivre* contagious, and she must have seen something attractive in me. She said later that I stood out from the rest. I said it was because I didn't belong there; she said it was because I wasn't affected by *snobismo*. It's pretty hard to be a snob when you're a hired hand among aristocrats. At the time, I was making over forty thousand American dollars a year, nearly sixty thousand Canadian, but next to these folks I was white trash, as Jake would have put it.

I'd lasted just over forty-four years as a bachelor and I was married within a month of meeting Wanda.

When I'd mentioned the possibility of her coming out to the rig on her vacation, she'd been delighted. We finagled her on as a kitchen hand. I told her jokingly that not every woman had a chance to go from a cultural attaché to a cook's assistant. I could see she didn't mind. She wanted us to be together more than anything. Even though absences made our reunions that much more sensually intense, both of us were tired of our desperate passion. We'd been married barely five months and of those five had probably spent only two together. We were devouring each other too frantically. We wanted time to get used to each other. To become friends as well as lovers.

About then the kid told me my time was up. I climbed out of the chamber, thought about lecturing him so he'd learn something from the accident, and decided I was too tired to go through the hassle. A wave of exhaustion washed over me at the thought. Save it for tomorrow. He had enough to do now, and I needed sleep more than an angry confrontation.

I asked the kid to clean up the chamber and was getting ready to telephone Wanda when suddenly my stomach dropped like a quick dip in the highway. Before I could move, the platform shuddered violently. A ripple surged up the legs and flowed over the platform surface, followed by the whining of metal under strain.

A moment of eerie silence, seconds long.

And then a muted concussion and a slow vibration that rapidly increased in intensity. My eyes opened wide. No more than ten seconds had passed from the initial dip. No doubt about it—that was a blast. A gigantic blast!

"Underwater explosion!" I screamed. "Hang on!"

Almost instantly, a geyser shot up near the jacket, drenching us with its spray.

Shit! The leg was collapsing! I grabbed the tender for support, my nausea upwelling again as the platform swayed. The steel beams supporting the hull were snapping like metallic buttons. As the platform began to tip slowly, the kid yelled in panic, jerked from my grasp, and took off running toward the racking platform in the center of the tripod.

I was struggling to overcome the sickening sensation, when a series of explosions rocked the platform near the shale shaker. The concussion slammed me against a railing and I fell to my knees, the wind knocked out of me. I looked back to where the shaker tank had stood. Fragments of scorched metal drifted through the air below a black cloud that rapidly billowed upward. If fire spread from the tank, the bottle racks would go next. I didn't want to be near when that happened.

I gasped for a breath of air and took off in the direction of the crew quarters, running at a slant up the platform, which was tilting at a crazy angle.

Either the hull would rip off near our leg or the pressure would snap the other legs and everybody'd be lost.

I heard another explosion and then a terrible shriek of metal under strain. I turned just in time to see the derrick start its slow, awkward topple. I had a sickening vision of the derrick man, a Canadian national I'd talked to once or twice. He'd be at the fourble board, some ninety feet above the derrick floor. Seconds later, the derrick picked up momentum and thundered down, hitting the control room and crashing on the racking platform. The hull of the platform bent like a trampoline, surged up and then down, and then vibrated with palsy.

I could hear screams from the direction of the dog-house now. Sheets of orange fire rose in waves, crinkled at the edges, and turned black. A cloud of toxic gas from the underwater explosion wafted over the edge of the platform, burning my eyes.

How could I have been so stupid—bringing Wanda out here?

I couldn't blame the new tender for this. I'd bent company rules to do it.

As I approached the crew quarters, I could see fire. An off-duty derrick man rushed by me, his face blackened with soot. He was trying to get to the drawworks to rescue his friends, and I was heading the other way to rescue Wanda.

A Libyan roustabout appeared at the door of a storage shed. His eyes were wild and I saw a Russian-made submachine gun in his hand. He was shouting in Arabic, the closest equivalent something like, "Death to the American bastards! The camel-sucking CIA! Attack!"

I tried to shout back in Arabic that it was an accident. That people needed help. That the whole structure might collapse into the sea. But the man's ears were deaf.

He pressed his finger to the trigger, firing into the air. I hit the deck and crawled for protection behind a lifeboat stanchion. The boat itself dangled by one cable over the side.

I looked back the way I'd come to a scene of devastation. The crane near the diving station was gone, lying now somewhere on the bottom. A group of Libyan roughnecks and roustabouts had gathered near the main-engine heat exchangers and were firing weapons toward the doghouse, which from where I crouched seemed engulfed in flames.

A crazy paranoia gripped the Libyans. They were firing guns when they should have been looking for fire extinguishers. The roustabout who'd blocked my route had disappeared. I stood and ran toward the southern leg. The door to the kitchen area was in sight now. Was Wanda inside or had she tried to get out? The crown block from the top of the derrick had crushed the dining room just beyond.

And then I saw the flames near the wire-line logging unit. If the fire spread uncontrolled to the high-explosives storage area, I knew all of us were finished. The last shipment of supplies had contained ten boxes of 60 percent straight dynamite and five 50-pound cases of 90 percent gelatin dynamite for multiple charges. The straight dynamite alone would create a tremendous explosion, probably enough to destroy the entire rig. Each box contained 105 eight-inch sticks.

And I'd lost count of the number of canisters of blasting agents in a separate storage magazine near the gear units by the southernmost leg. They'd go next. And the spools of Primacord, a high-velocity detonating cord. And the Detasheets, olive-drab colored sheets of a flexible high explosive made by DuPont. I felt sick. The Detasheets were a potent mixture of PETN and an elastomeric binder. All in all we had nearly a ton of explosives on site.

The acetylene tanks blew then. The back of the living quarters imploded, as if under a direct hit by a bomb. The hot air scorched my lungs and brought tears to my eyes.

Wanda! My God! If she were hurt, I'd get vengeance on them all—Libyans and Americans.

I reached the door to the kitchen area just as a dark-skinned man, his black hair glistening with shards of glass, crawled out of a pile of rubble from the ruins of the control tower, an automatic pistol gripped in his left hand. He screamed in Arabic and pulled the trigger. The slug slammed into the metal door at head level and a fragment of the bullet caught me in the neck. I stood there for a second stunned into immobility. And then a second shell ripped by my head and I fell through the door.

Screaming myself now, I scrambled on hands and knees toward the inner door that led to the galley.

"I'm Canadian, you bastards, I'm Canadian," I was screaming in Arabic.

Wanda was near the stove, caught beneath a fallen metal exhaust duct. As I ripped the material away, I could feel the growing heat. One of the propane tanks that fed the kitchen had gone up and the dining room was an inferno.

I had to get her outside and to a lifeboat.

When I pulled her free, her head fell at a grotesque angle and I had to struggle to control myself. As a diver I'd learned to put a lid on fear, but this wasn't my own life at stake, it was my wife's. I hadn't prepared myself to face that.

I put my ear to her mouth and thought I felt a light waft of air. She was still breathing at least.

And then I turned her on her back to give her some air and saw what remained of her chest.

I was sick, then. Wanda hadn't been crushed by the exhaust duct. No, something else had done this. A weapon. Someone had shot her at close range.

Her eyes fluttered open and I watched her lips quiver. Each painful movement was a stab in my heart.

"Derek," she whispered, her eyes unable to focus on my face.

"I'm here," I said. "I love you." I tried to shield her head from the overheated air rushing past.

She struggled to speak again and I bent to kiss her lips, to quiet her, to tell her she didn't need to speak.

But she tried to avert her head and whispered, "No, Derek. Listen!" A surge of life momentarily animated her face, but her eyes were swinging wildly.

"It was *me* . . . the ambassador. *Mio* . . . Stop them!"

And just as quickly the energy dissipated like the last flicker of a dying candle.

12

Mio. She'd reverted to Italian. *Mine*. But my what?

I bent over her, waiting, my cheek and ear brushing her lips.

Waiting . . . but there was no breath there now.

It was useless to drag her to the boat. Tears welled up, but wouldn't fall. A cold rage seized me. And then I looked again at her lifeless features—twisted in pain—and bent over in agony, oblivious to the flames that were spreading from the dining room to the kitchen.

And then there was only one thought in my mind, all other pain, all danger far away outside me.

Someone, somewhere, would pay for this. Nothing else mattered now.

2

THE FIRST PLACE I touched down, after coming off the oil rig, was As Sukhayrah, in Tunisia. The company maintained installations at two provincial capitals, Gabes and Sfax, and had an office further north in the capital city of Tunis. I spent all of May going from one to the other trying to find out what had destroyed the jackup. The company engineers said the Libyans were handling the investigation; any claims would have to be made in their courts. I said I wasn't interested in claims. I wanted to know what caused the accident. The only responses I got were shrugs of indifference or frowns of annoyance.

The heat that summer made every task, every effort to get information, that much harder. By mid-May the daytime temperatures had soared to a hundred degrees Fahrenheit, and by the end of the month they hovered above a hundred and ten. The papers all said we were in for one of the hottest summers in recent memory.

At first, the nights brought some relief. A light sea breeze sweeping in from the Mediterranean. A mountain draft flowing down the Dorsale range of the Atlas Mountains and spreading over the littoral like a cool tidal current. But soon even these faded away.

In June, the company put me in touch with a Libyan oil official in Tripoli. We spoke over the telephone in Arabic. When I told him my wife had died in the confusion following the explosions, that she'd been shot by a Libyan national, that his government was responsible, he replied with a heated denial that ended in a high-pitched tirade. I only caught about half of what he said but the gist was clear. The blame lay with others. With foreigners. The officials in Tripoli were as paranoid as those on the rig at sea. All they could think about were enemies of the state and plots to destroy the government.

"So you deny involvement in what happened," I said.

"The government has come to the conclusion that the American CIA was responsible. A terrorist attack."

"But it was an accident—an underwater explosion."

"Saboteurs. U.S. Navy frogmen. They killed your wife."

"The shooting was all done by *your* people."

"In self-defense. Without their heroic efforts, all would have died."

"Bullshit!" I said and hung up.

I went through the company again and asked if the president of the parent corporation in Toronto could learn anything from the Canadian government.

A week later they told me that both the Canadian Security Intelligence Service—the SIS—and the American CIA denied involvement. Neither organization had launched an attack on an oil rig.

The infernal heat made the lack of news harder to take. By the end of June, the temperatures exceeded the limits of even the most hardened Berber. Sixteen hours of incandescent daytime heat, not a shade cloud in sight for weeks on end.

In the cities of the Sahel—the narrow coastal strip of western Tunisia running south from Bizerte to Zarzis—the heat persisted throughout the night, radiating from paved and packed-dirt roads, from old, stone buildings and new, high-rise concrete hotels, from phosphate refineries and chemical plants.

The tourist hotels were nearly deserted; on Djerba island, the Dar Jerba, Africa's largest hotel, with 2,450 beds, laid off most of its staff. The few tourists who came to the island spent their time indoors or in the water. Northern Europeans, like pots in a kiln, turned from gray to pink after barely fifteen minutes of exposure.

In the old cities, the crenellated walls and battlements of the *medinas,* the caparisoned stalls of the carpet sellers, the stacked apartment houses, all became fiery crucibles stoked by a relentless sun. The interiors of cars and trucks were deadly ovens, each piece of metal, plastic, or hardened rubber—a door handle, emergency brake, steering wheel, gear stick, or seat covering—all impossible to touch.

I didn't give up. I wasn't going to let the heat defeat me. I tried to get in touch with a fellow named Hansen. I'd worked with him years before on a project to help the Canadian government, but the SIS wouldn't tell me where he was stationed or even if he was still with them.

The same lack of information characterized the Italian Embassy and the Cultural Mission in Tripoli. When I telephoned to learn more about what Wanda did, a first secretary at the embassy told me her duties were entirely educational. She had no connection to the ambassador, other than serving as a translator at certain government social functions.

"Did she have any contacts with the Italian secret service?"

There was a moment's silence at the other end of the line and then the first secretary's voice came back cold and precise.

"Sir, none of the personnel of either the embassy or the cultural mission have any contacts with the intelligence service."

"Bullshit," I said and hung up on him too. It didn't seem to matter if the officials I spoke to were Libyans or Italians. No one was involved. No one knew anything.

That summer's agony extended into July. The desert

winds began to pick up strength, moved north from the dune belts of the Sahara's Grand Erg, swept over the barren *hammadas*—the rock wastes of the Tunisian steppe—and into the central plains. The daily papers reported that the boundaries of the great salt lakes— Chott Djerid and Chott el Rharsa—were slowly contracting. In the inland basins, the dry winds scorched the tufts of esparto grass, forcing the nomadic tribes to drive their sheep and goats into the higher plateaus. And finally, thrust eastward by the Tebessa Mountains, the hot, dry air began to sear the more fertile, coastal land.

The shade trees, standing like sentinels along the esplanades of the larger cities, began to suffer. Small fig trees in protected courtyards shriveled; the leaves of the carob and citrus trees in the groves along the coast curled under the stress. To the untrained eye, only the olive trees and date palms stood indomitable, hiding their distress from all but the attentive eye of the farmer.

I wasn't as strong. By mid-July I was worn out. My days were filled with frustrated inquiries, my nights with nightmares. My psychic wounds were festering under the hot African sun. I'd spent seven or eight weeks trying in vain to pry information from company and government officials. In the end, I gave up.

I wired my bank in Toronto and had most of my funds, nearly forty thousand Canadian dollars, transferred to a small account I kept open in Rome at the Banca Commerciale, while another five thousand was sent to me in Tunis.

Heading west, never staying more than a day in one place, I must have hit every night club in Northern Africa, and when those were exhausted, I did the circuit of Southern Europe.

And always the twice-a-week calls for more information, and the same answers.

At a certain point, tired of fleeing from myself, I

managed to make a turnaround. I spent a week in Italy, drying out and looking for something. For what, I wasn't sure. Perhaps the simplicity of isolated villages, the tranquillity of lake shores unfrequented by tourists, the desolation of high-elevation Apennine meadows. Silence after so much empty noise. Coolness after so much heat.

None of it lessened the turmoil inside, the horrible visions of what had happened on the jackup.

Finally, on the tenth of August, I headed for Rome, Wanda's city.

I knew I'd been avoiding her family. I'd always felt uncomfortable with them. During my only visit to her parents' home, her father, a professor of medieval history at the university, had spent over an hour showing me the various items of antique furniture acquired by the family over the centuries. We moved through rooms of marble and rosewood paneling, through a waiting area dominated by full-length mirrors with gold frames, through a gallery of sculptural fragments.

There were high-backed chairs with brocaded seats from the early Renaissance, a wedding chest from the sixteenth century, baroque wardrobes with ornate arches, upholstered wing chairs and settees that might have graced a salon in the eighteenth century, ceramic vases from Arezzo over a century old, and floor-to-ceiling bookcases with leaded-glass doors protecting old editions of the classics.

At a certain point I wondered if the tour was meant to show me how little I fit in with the family, how different I was from them. Not only a foreigner, but a common laborer. My topics of conversation seemed alien in that setting. I felt I should have been discussing classical music with her father rather than the depressed oil market. And her mother was quiet to the point of severity. Wanda's cheerfulness, I figured, must have sprung from some recessive gene.

18

So this time, I came to Rome with reluctance and stayed a few days, hesitating the while, wondering if I should see her folks and trying to figure out why.

Finally I gave up on that, too. I preferred to think of Wanda as I knew her, not as her family did.

The day before I planned to leave, I made my customary call to the PetroCanada agent in Tunis. I telephoned as a matter of course, expecting the usual lack of help. To the company the accident was old news. Something they'd just as soon forget. Any day now and I'd be back in Tunisia myself with nothing to show for my efforts.

It took me a moment to realize the fellow was saying he had information.

It was all I could do to ask him what it was.

"Derek, you're in luck. Not that I think it'll do you much good."

I gripped the phone and felt my heart skip a beat.

"Hansen has turned up in Rome."

"Where is he?"

"He's working with the *Ministero degli Affari Esteri*."

That was the Italian Ministry of Foreign Affairs, and I wondered why he was working there and not out of the Canadian Embassy or a commercial front.

"What's he doing for them?"

"Something to do with the Department for Development Cooperation. They attract students from developing countries. Give them scholarships to go to Italian universities."

"He's recruiting agents?"

The company man ignored me.

"Anyway, that's all we have from here," he said breezily. "Where are you now, anyway? Let us know when you're ready to start working again and we'll line you up with a job."

I thanked him and hung up, my mind on Hansen and what I'd done for him. I'd been well paid for helping him out, but I figured the guy owed me at least one favor. He'd taken the credit for my work. And I didn't think he'd forget that, even after fifteen years. Stopping Carlo Spugna was probably the high point of Hansen's career.

It took me some time to locate Hansen, and when I did he wasn't too happy about talking over the telephone. We set up a meeting for seven that night at a small *caffè* just south of Piazza Colonna.

When Hansen arrived, precisely at seven, we took a small table at the back of the room, away from the hubbub. The *caffé,* sandwiched between an apartment house and a toy store, was long and narrow, with an espresso machine and pastry case situated toward the front to attract those passing by. At that hour, the street was packed with Italians hurrying home and with tourists out for their evening stroll. Most avoided the tables in the back, where service was slow and more expensive, in favor of the chrome counter near the espresso machine.

"Coffee, Stone?"

I shook my head. "I'm not sleeping well. I'll have a Branca Menta. Over ice."

The drink, a liqueur that combined Branca Fernet, a foul-tasting digestive, with crème de menthe, was one I often ordered when I had time to kill. It usually took me a half hour to get through a glass.

Hansen nodded and, when the waiter came, ordered two of them.

Hansen was a strange man. He'd never divulged his first name, and never used mine. It was a practice I didn't much care for. I'd always felt it was a tactic he used in an effort to keep distance between us.

His hair had gone gray, not light but dark, and the dull hue made him look ill. He'd aged badly and it seemed from his gaunt face that he'd lost a lot of weight recently. I wondered for a moment if he had cancer.

20

He must have seen my appraising glance because he smiled tightly and said, "Don't look so good, do I?"

I shrugged and said I probably looked the worse for wear, too.

He appeared not to hear me. "I got back from Kam-wala just over a month ago."

I shook my head. I didn't know the place.

His smile had disappeared.

"A prison," he said quietly. "'In Lusaka, Zambia. Just a mile from the president's statehouse, but one hell of a distance in level of comfort. I went from one to the other like that." And he snapped his fingers.

I wanted to ask why, but the waiter was there with our drinks and when he left Hansen didn't seem interested in small talk.

He asked me straight out what I needed, and I told him about the jackup and what had happened to Wanda. "I thought you might be able to help," I said when I'd finished. "Maybe provide some information. Everyone seems pretty tight-lipped about this and I don't know why. The government wouldn't even tell me where you were."

His eyes tightened. "Maybe they couldn't find me in the computer. You know how that is."

I sat back and made a noncommittal gesture. I knew he hated the guys behind the desks. "It's not just the service," I said. "Everything's gone high-tech these days."

Hansen stared over my head blankly for a moment and then, a half smile on his face, said "I can't tell a micro-chip from a potato chip, can you? Never will understand those machines."

I tried to grin at his dumb joke but it was hard. I said, "I'm not worried about trying to figure out a computer—I'm having a hard enough time trying to understand myself."

I was glad he didn't say anything. I didn't want to talk about the pain inside. I'd worked too hard trying to forget who I was, trying to go on as someone new—and not succeeding. I couldn't take any more probing.

"How'd the government get you out of Kamwala prison?" I said, trying to get back to the SIS and what they could do for me.

He snorted. "They didn't. My own team paid to get me out. A private deal." He paused and stroked the loose skin hanging from his sunken cheeks. "So you see, I don't know what's been going on in your area. I'm afraid I can't help either."

"I don't want much. Just a name. Someone who knows what's going on."

His lips curled at the corners. "You don't want much? You want everything you mean. Names are hard to come by."

"You have contacts with the Italians. Ask around. Find someone working with the Libyans."

He stared at me reflectively. "Stone, you can't bring her back."

My eyes were locked on his and neither of us moved for a moment. Finally, I nodded. "I know. But put yourself in my position." It was a lame statement, but I didn't know what else to say.

He hadn't touched his drink. The ice in the tall glass was melting. Suddenly he dropped his eyes, lifted the glass, and drained the Branca Menta in one long swallow. I waited for the shudder, which never came.

"Give me two days," he said and stood abruptly.

Before I could get to my feet to shake his hand, he walked out without looking back.

The call came Tuesday night at eleven. He wasted no time.

22

"Stone, this is Hansen. The name you want is Dalmoro."

"Dalmoro," I repeated. "Where can I find him?"

"Messina."

"Messina. In Sicily?"

"He'll meet you tomorrow night. Eight o'clock. Be in the second-class waiting room at the central train station. I've described you to him and he'll find you."

"What's he look like?"

"I don't know. Never met the man."

I didn't like being left in the air, but I was grateful for what he'd done. After an awkward pause, I said, "Thanks Hansen. I appreciate it."

"Stone?"

"Yes."

"You're on your own."

"I know," I said quickly.

"No, listen to what I'm saying. You don't know me and I don't know you."

"Okay," I said, fighting the testiness in my voice. "I did you a favor once, you've done me one. We're even." I felt trite saying it, but it was the truth, and he knew it too.

"Just so you understand how it is," he said, and I heard the phone go dead as he hung up.

He hadn't said good-bye, he never did, so I was used to that, but this time I got the feeling one of us had just died.

3

I COULDN'T GET booked on a *Rapido,* so I caught an early morning *Diretto* from Rome's Stazione Termini, with a connection to the ferry at Villa San Giovanni, arriving in Messina just after five that evening. I didn't bother leaving the station. I'd seen the city before and other than the cathedral I didn't like much of it. So I bought a copy of the local paper and a recent issue of *Gente,* a magazine focusing on the glamorous, the scandalous, and the bizarre—with just enough nudity to whet the appetite for more—and sat for nearly three hours in the second-class waiting room on a wooden bench that had unpadded armrests every few feet to keep people from lying down.

Travelers came and went at irregular intervals, and when seven forty-five rolled around, I began glancing at each new arrival, waiting for a sign of recognition.

An elderly gentleman with a cane worked his way toward me and sat two seats away on my left. He fumbled in the pocket of his suitcoat and suddenly leaned over as if to speak.

I stared at him expectantly.

"Mind if I smoke?" he said in Italian.

Was this some code?

I cleared my throat. "Smoking's prohibited here," I said, and pointed across the room. "But you can smoke on that side."

The man grumbled something in dialect, put his cigarettes away, and struggled awkwardly to his feet.

I was shrugging apologetically when I felt a hand on my shoulder.

"Signor Stone?"

"Yes," I said, looking up to see a short man, very thin, with a face darkened by years of exposure to the sun.

"I'm Lucio Dalmoro," he said. He reached for my suitcase. "Come with me. I have a car outside."

Bad teeth, a voice that rasped, an accent that seemed Venetian. But he'd smiled pleasantly enough.

I followed him out of the station, his shoulders bowed, small head barely visible, black hair curling at the nape of his neck. Not a thug, but there'd been something in his eyes—a crafty glint—that reminded me of a Greek I'd worked with once, a wily fellow who'd succeeded through one scheme or another in conning most of the Arab roustabouts out of a good portion of their weekly paychecks.

Once in the car, Dalmoro switched to English and hissed, "We go eat," his pronunciation so bad that I responded in Italian.

We didn't speak much in the car; I was intent on the route, not wanting to be lost in case I had to make my own way back.

Dalmoro drove to a restaurant along the waterfront, not far from the station, a modest *trattoria* frequented by lower-class stevedores and fishermen. The small parking lot, lit by a single arc lamp, overlooked a scrap yard for freighters. Operations had stopped for the night, but in the sultry air I could still smell the diesel of the track-mounted, salvage cranes.

In the restaurant, Dalmoro ate quickly, answering my first question with an abrupt, "We eat now," and not saying another word until he'd finished a plate of spaghetti and a *quarto* of red table wine. I found myself gulping my own pasta as if I had to keep pace with him.

Five minutes into the meal, he tore his *panino* in two, wiped the plate clean with one piece, stuffed the bread in his mouth, and then looked up at me, his head and shoulders still hunched over the plate.

"I'm just back from Libya. Two days ago. Can't get enough of this pasta." He smacked his lips appreciatively, but his black eyes gave no hint of animation.

I nodded. "What were you doing in Libya?"

He pointed his finger at my chest. "The question is, what are you Americans doing? Your people are up to something."

I frowned. "I'm not American," I said. "I'm Canadian."

"You work with Hansen? He said something about a company liaison."

He not only thought I was American, he thought I was with the CIA.

I shook my head in answer to the second statement and then said, "I worked with him once. Years ago."

He nodded. "Me too. He told me you wanted information about the Italian woman."

I stared at him. Didn't he know I was the Italian woman's husband?

He paused. "The Libyans are worried about what's going on. A big affair. The woman might have been involved."

"Involved with what?" I could smell his bad breath across the table.

He paused again and his head bobbed reflectively. "That's what bothers me. I've been told not to follow up on that affair."

"Told by whom?"

"By my people."

I wanted to ask who that was but thought better of it. I supposed that meant the Italians. He was being evasive, and I wanted to save my probing for what really mattered.

Dalmoro's eyes narrowed and he tapped his empty wineglass. "I don't like being told to drop this." His voice had fallen as if he were speaking to himself and with the rasp in it I had a hard time understanding him.

He lifted his eyes suddenly and caught mine, his gaze opaque, unreadable. "I can't do anything about it but you can." His voice was measured, the tone matter-of-fact.

"How?" I was willing to do anything if it brought me closer to the people responsible for Wanda's death.

"I can put you in touch with an agent who knows the American principal in this affair. Gene Harrell."

"That's the agent?"

"That's the American. The agent's a contact he uses. Someone we know about and use occasionally too. A Maltese national who married a Sicilian girl. We call him Rocco. Only one thing. I can't be tied to any of this. If you need help, you get it elsewhere—from your own people."

My lips tightened. I was getting tired of secretive bastards like Hansen and his parrot Dalmoro. No one wanted to take responsibility for anything.

"What am I supposed to do if I learn something you might want to know?" Then it hit me. "Damn it, that's why you're sending me out, right?" I could feel my brow furrow. "And what is this 'affair' you keep mentioning."

He didn't raise his voice, the tone as flat as before. "You learn something along the way of interest to us, you walk into any police station or government office and tell them. A formal contact. And don't bother mentioning me because they won't know me."

He shoved his plate away and reached for the bottle of mineral water I'd ordered along with my wine. "*Posso?*"

I nodded. "Go ahead."

He poured a small amount in his wineglass, swirled it around, drank it in one swallow, and then, after touching up my glass, filled his own. I waited him out without saying anything.

"This Gene Harrell, the American, he's a diver. Like you."

My head snapped back. I hadn't told him I was a diver.

Dalmoro grinned. "Nice NATO file on you. Maybe what you did for the Canadians, Gene Harrell does for the Americans."

I frowned. "I don't get you. I worked as a temporary once. It was a special situation. They needed my expertise. What's this Harrell doing?"

Dalmoro pursed his cheeks. "It's very confusing actually. If I knew I'd tell you. You'll have to find out from Rocco. He can put you in contact with Harrell."

I wasn't happy about being shuttled from one person to the next. Dalmoro wasn't saying much, and I knew he had to know more than he was letting on.

"Just a minute," I said carefully. "You work in Libya. You knew about Wanda Donati. You even knew she was my wife, right?"

Dalmoro laughed. "So what?"

I didn't like him laughing. I said harshly, "So I want to know what she was doing."

He didn't say anything and I took a wild guess. "What'd this Harrell have to do with her?"

He shrugged. "Nothing, probably. Look, I can tell you this. Your wife worked with us because she had friends in Libya who were involved with certain activities of interest to NATO intelligence."

I interrupted him. "What activities?"

"Varied activities. Matters of intelligence."

I reached out and grabbed his wrist. "What in the fuck are you talking about?"

Dalmoro's eyes went icy and he reached over with his

28

free hand and pried my fingers loose. "Don't you ever touch me again," he said. "You want answers, talk to your own people."

I looked around the restaurant in frustration. Most of the diners had left, and our waiter, I saw, was hovering discreetly in the distance. Dalmoro affected a disinterested air, swirling his glass over the drops of water beading the table. I shook my head and raised both hands. "Listen, I can't get any answers from *my* people. I'm not working with the Canadians. I'm working alone. If you know something, just tell me, damn it. It won't go beyond me. I don't have anyone I could tell it to, anyway."

Dalmoro stared at me for a few moments and then looked away. He gestured toward the waiter. "*Un altro quarto di vino rosso e mezzo litro di acqua minerale.*"

"*Gassata?*" the waiter asked, looking at me rather than Dalmoro, and I nodded. I'd been drinking the carbonated mineral water.

We waited until the waiter brought the small carafe of wine and a bottle of San Pellegrino.

Dalmoro poured himself a glass of wine and took a few sips before speaking.

"About three months ago we heard something about the Libyans plotting a theft. Of what, we weren't sure. Only that it was to be in Italy. And something technical. My guess was military equipment—maybe American. Maybe from one of the NATO bases. But we couldn't find out for sure." He paused and carefully straightened the silverware on the table. "Your wife was in touch with some of the people involved in the planning. We were trying to find out more when she died in the accident."

"The accident." The Italian word for accident was *incidente,* and I repeated the word dumbly, my mind suddenly swirling with everything the Libyans had told me—that it wasn't an accident, that the Americans were responsible.

I stared at Dalmoro and said, "This Gene Harrell. Was he connected with the plan?"

Dalmoro rubbed his whiskers thoughtfully.

"I don't think so. Not with the planning at any rate. But he may be connected with the theft. Or with an attempt to recover whatever's missing. I think the Libyans pulled it off. I know something happened to upset the government. There was quite a furor a week ago. The science and technology boys looked like they were on pogo sticks, jumping up and down and throwing tantrums, screaming about a VLSI processing board. You know what that means?"

I could see he didn't expect me to know, so I said, "Vaguely. It's an integrated circuit. Very-large-scale integration. A microprocessor with a large number of gates and other logic circuits and their interconnections." My courses in engineering hadn't been an entire waste.

He stared at me as if I were speaking Greek. "Don't try to explain that," he said. "It drives me crazy."

I thought of Hansen and his aversion to computers—it was hard to be left behind by the modern world.

"What happened then?" I said.

"I tried to find out what had been stolen, who was responsible. I had contacts in Libya who said the Libyans had nothing to do with anything going on in Italy. Not that I believed them." He shrugged. "And then I was told by my superiors to forget it. To stop pursuing the matter. That we'd risk an American operation."

"The recovery attempt?"

His head wavered. "Could be. That's when I learned something from Rocco. That this Gene Harrell was involved somehow. That Harrell had contacted him for help."

"With what?"

"A boat."

I frowned. "That's it? The guy asks for a boat and you think he's connected with a theft in Italy?"

Dalmoro ignored my sarcasm. "Apparently there's more to it. I asked Rocco why the guy wanted a boat and he said Harrell was supposed to meet three other Americans on an island just north of here."

Dalmoro was still holding something back, and I was getting frustrated at having to work so hard to find out what. "Just a minute," I said, and then stopped to think.

Somehow Dalmoro knew that either Gene Harrell or the three Americans were directly involved with the theft. There had to be a connection. An intelligence service—maybe the Italians themselves, maybe the Americans, maybe even the Libyans for all I knew—had provided information to put Dalmoro onto Harrell.

"These three Americans you mentioned—" I was struggling to understand their role. "Why is Harrell interested in them?"

Dalmoro shrugged. "That I don't know. They may be a go-between. They may be people helping him." He waved his hands in a gesture of impotence. "I didn't have time to pursue the matter. And now I can't. Officially, at least."

I was thinking hard and not getting anywhere myself.

A go-between. Between who? I rubbed my forehead and squinted at Dalmoro. "Let me get this straight. Are you suggesting the Americans are helping the Libyans?"

Dalmoro snorted. "Your guess is as good as mine."

"That doesn't make any sense." I paused and frowned, trying to figure it out, thinking that, no, it didn't make sense unless . . . unless they were arms merchants. Hadn't Dalmoro hinted as much? That the plan might have been to steal American weapons? Perhaps something technologically advanced.

But I was still confused. Arms merchants didn't usually steal weapons. They bought and sold them. And in this case would an arms merchant put money above the direct interests of his country? I hoped not, but I supposed anything was possible.

My mind went blank for a moment, and when I looked up I caught Dalmoro staring at me. That look of craftiness again. There for an instant and then gone. Hansen's sly grin came swimming back before my eyes—that dumb comment on computer chips. Both Hansen and Dalmoro knew more than they were letting on.

Suddenly my eyes opened wide and I said, "Or is it the Italians helping the Libyans? That's what you want me to find out, isn't it?" I almost choked on the words in my hurry. "You're wondering why your government called you off. Are you guys working against the Americans?"

He exhaled slowly, a pained expression flitting over his features. "Look, don't overanalyze it. I agreed to meet you and help *you. Capito?*" He saw my instant skepticism and sighed tiredly. "Okay, I'm helping because I think the results will be mutually beneficial. I can't pursue this matter without compromising myself or the service. You can. How many times do I have to say it?"

I stared at him, trying to read something behind his words, trying to catch a glimpse of the crafty look I'd seen before. Was it just my imagination? Or was it the tone? *Mutually beneficial.* For some reason—coming from his mouth—the words rang false.

I looked down at the table and then rubbed my eyes in exhaustion. I was losing sight of why I'd come to see this fellow. I wanted information about Wanda, and everything he told me seemed to lead away from her, not toward her. But still, it was the only tie-in I had. Wanda had been in touch with someone involved in the same deal as the American, this Gene Harrell. He was at the other end of the rope, and if I followed it, somewhere along the line I might find out why Wanda was killed and who did it.

I cleared my throat. "Okay," I told him. "If this agent you mentioned—"

"Rocco."

"Right. If he can put me in touch with Harrell, I'll see what I can find out. But I'm doing it for myself. Not for you or your country."

He dipped his head in a placating gesture. "That's fine."

I waited until his eyes found mine again and then I said, "You said Gene Harrell was a diver like me. How'd you know that about him?"

"Rocco. It was a bit garbled but he mentioned something about Harrell saying he was an underwater-salvage expert. Rocco got the impression that the three Americans Harrell was supposed to meet needed his services. That didn't make a lot of sense, but you'll have to find out from Harrell what's going on."

"None of this makes much sense," I said dryly. I started counting on my fingers. "Three Americans who need a salvage expert. Gene Harrell, working for who knows whom. A theft. Of what, who knows? A Libyan connection." And Wanda, I said to myself, not feeling like mentioning her aloud. I went on. "Italians. What in the hell they're doing you don't know and neither do I. Rocco." I paused. "And who else only God knows."

Dalmoro had a wry look on his face when I finished.

"Did I leave somebody out?"

He grinned. "Don't forget yourself," he said.

— — —

4

— — —

THE RENDEZVOUS WITH ROCCO was set for ten o'clock the next night at the Bar Alfieri in Milazzo, a small town of about thirty thousand inhabitants, just west of Messina. I stayed the night in Messina in a hotel on Via Primo di Settembre, the street leading from the train station to the cathedral, and caught a bus in the morning for Milazzo.

As I climbed the hill stretching up from the harbor in Milazzo, the coppery sun struck me on the side of the face like a branding iron. Another sweltering August day. Before long, my short-sleeved shirt clung to my body, drenched in sweat. In my left hand I was carrying a small twenty-four-hour flight bag and over my right shoulder a sport coat. My passport case in the inside breast pocket of my coat thumped me on the back with each step.

The salty air, heavy and moist, made breathing difficult. I had to stop for rest every fifteen minutes or so. My body, once hard, had grown soft over the summer.

About noon, I checked into a small *locanda* overlooking the harbor. I had a lot of time to pass, and I made the mistake of buying a bottle of Stock-brand whiskey—it had taken me a good two weeks to dry out from my last months-long binge—and when I tried to stop drinking, halfway through the bottle, I couldn't.

The light cascading in the window began to hurt my eyes, so I closed the shutters and sat in muted darkness. The two pears and a roll I'd bought for lunch lay untouched on a small table near the washbasin. I could smell the pears, just a hint of their fragrance, but I'd lost my appetite; I felt like vomiting at the thought of eating. There was a knot in my stomach even whiskey couldn't untie.

Around six, I set out from the *locanda,* making my way unsteadily down a winding road toward the lower city and the harbor. In an attempt to sober up, I walked for nearly an hour along the *lungomare,* and then found the Bar Alfieri and sat down to wait.

I was over two hours early and I started drinking again, trying to go slow but carried along by a feeling of uneasiness, upset then that the alcohol failed to settle my nerves and angry finally that I had nerves to fight in the first place. The nerves of steel I'd prided myself on for so many years were gone.

Rocco failed to show at ten and I waited another hour, the passing of time beginning to get hazy. Two hours. My anger turned to sullenness. I'd been in the bar too long, drunk too much. The bottle of whiskey in front of me was nearly empty, a half-inch of golden liquid at the bottom. Could I have drunk that much by myself? I was too confused to remember.

I waited another half hour, gripping my glass and trying to resist the temptation to fill it with the last of the whiskey. It was late and I'd have to make it back to the *locanda* on my own. I tried to remember the route. Damn! I couldn't even remember the name of the place!

Fresh air. I needed to get out. I pushed back the chair and stumbled for the door.

The street near the bar was dark and I turned to my right, moving toward the light of a cross street in the distance. My right hand scraped the rough surface of the buildings along the way. Apartment houses or businesses, I couldn't tell. Not a sign of life in any.

I tried to think of what I'd do now, but I was too tired and too drunk to formulate a plan. That bastard Rocco!

Dalmoro had promised me he'd be there. No way to find—what was his name? I couldn't even remember it. The American.

A moment of panic. His name? How could I find him without a name? I was forgetting everything.

A shadow to my left.

Instinctively I threw up an arm. Someone was there, but my eyes wouldn't focus.

"Signor Stone?"

I lowered my arm, suddenly nauseous, my breathing ragged.

"Who is it?" I asked in Italian.

"Rocco."

He stepped toward me and took my left arm. I still couldn't see his face.

"I take you to see Signor Harrell. I couldn't come in bar. People there who know me. Too dangerous." He tugged on my arm. "You come with me. To harbor. We row out to meet him."

"At sea?"

"An island. Hurry. We have not much time."

Time. I shook my head. Time had lost all meaning. I looked up, trying to find stars, a constellation to orient myself. The moon. Some sign of order, some indication of time and place. But before I could focus on anything, Rocco grabbed my arm and pulled me after him, and for a good while afterward everything became a blur.

Cocker spaniels. That's all I'd been seeing in Italy the last two weeks, from Cremona south. There was one that night, pattering along by himself on a narrow jetty north of Milazzo near the cape and the lighthouse. Big floppy ears, a swinging gait, moving somewhere, and fast.

Made me think of the farm near Regina. Pheasant hunting in the wheat fields. The old Australian wolfhound we kept around but never fed much. He had to scrounge for a living and did a good job of it. Even ate frogs and was nearly as good as a cat at catching birds.

I think I tried to call after the cocker. Rocco, a hard-faced, mustached man dressed in a black pullover shirt and frayed cotton pants, jerked my arm and told me to shut up. I glared down at the top of his head, which only came up to my shoulder.

"Here, carry this," he said, thrusting a package that felt like a bottle in a plastic sack into my hand.

We'd reached a short, wooden dock that projected into the harbor from the jetty. The dock appeared abandoned, the planks rotting away. As we moved along it, Rocco's hand under my arm, I could hear the waves sucking at the boards from below and lapping around the splintered edges. At the far end, Rocco knelt and unlocked a chain that ran from a rubber tire on the dock to the bow ring of a rusted-out launch. About a fourteen-foot boat with a mole-battered pontoon hull and two outboard motors at the stern, one missing the cowling and both grimy with oil.

I made my way to the rowing thwart in the middle—the oars were stored along both sides—and sat facing Rocco, who was trying to start the motors. He had some unkind words to say, but he said them in dialect. About all I could make out was that the boat was a rental. A pretty cheap one at that. I could see the oars might come in handy.

Once we were underway, Rocco asked for the package, and I found it beneath my feet, where I'd let it drop. Rocco snatched the thing from me before I could drop it again, and pulled out a bottle with a twist-off cap. "Grappa," he said. He broke the seal, unscrewed the metal cap, and then took a quick swallow. I heard the gasp of breath.

He put the cap in his shirt pocket, handed the bottle

to me, and said, "Drink. Rough sea beyond the lighthouse."

The grappa burned a path down my chest, and I felt like my breath was being sucked out by a pump. Harsh stuff, burning the gullet, starting a fire in my stomach. I felt him lifting the bottle to my lips. More fire. Pain that brought tears to the eyes. I knocked the bottle away, heard it hit metal, gurgling as the liquor spilled from the tight neck. A sudden dulling of the senses. A tremendous weight pressing down on the top of my head. I gave in to it and passed out.

Swells—a smooth running sea. The soft lapping of waves. A cradle's lullaby. No sound of motors. A smell so briny that for a moment I felt like an olive curing in a vat.

And then dizziness.

I was lying in the stern, my feet jammed against the transom, the boat's central rib digging into my back. I could hear oars, squeaking in the sockets, and then feel them as they rhythmically banged into the side of the boat. My head shook with each thud.

In a daze, I struggled to sit up. The boat swayed and I grabbed for the gunwale. The grappa had not yet lost its harsh taste, but the jagged edges of reality were returning. I could smell my acrid perspiration. When I wiped my mouth, the rough whiskers of my chin scraped the back of my hand. Even my throat seemed raw, as if from a nagging summer cold.

I tried to call for Rocco, my voice a hoarse whisper. I couldn't get the words out of my throat. I turned, straining to see. A figure in the bow with a light. A signal.

As I shifted my weight, the rocking of the boat, the roller coaster dips and rises of the swells, the lapping of waves suddenly changed from a lullaby to a nightmare's dizzying carnival ride.

And then a wave of nausea rose over my whole body and I began to vomit. I grabbed for the gunwale, trying to keep my head outside the boat, a primitive instinct for cleanliness somehow directing my thoughts.

And then finally, gratefully, I lost consciousness again.

Angels. A brightness whiter than the sun, their faces blazing with a light so pure and incandescent that it washed over me like the cooling waves of the sea. They were talking, their words indecipherable. The syllables struck me like thunderclaps from high above.

The voices . . . Something was dreadfully wrong! A scream of horror! Was it my own or someone else's?

That was the last thing I remember before the light began to dim and I began a long fall into darkness.

The first sounds came from far away, like the slow approach of distant thunder. And then, without warning, like the first heavy drops of a summer storm, soothing coolness followed by the burn of salt in a raw wound.

I was lying on a shingle beach, the stones sharp and uncomfortable. Worse yet, my head felt as if a bullet had exploded inside, fragments exiting through my eye sockets and a colander's worth of holes near my temples. Dazzling sunlight. Eyes squinting in the glare.

I was looking at my head lying on the beach!

Looking at my body from above. Hair matted with blood. I reached out, saw my own hand, and found the bullet holes in the skull. Dead!

I closed my eyes, confused. Bullet holes. I could feel them. If I were dead, how come I could feel?

I took a deep breath and about then, as my head began to clear, I opened my eyes again and finally realized that *I* was alive, but that the fellow lying near me wasn't. I was in too much pain at first to care. The arm I'd stretched out to touch him with was too sore to retract.

My skin felt like Chinese sugar paper; it was ready to crinkle and dissolve.

I tried to pull myself further up the beach—the salt water was eating at my skin like acid—but I was too weak to make any progress. The sun, burning from above, scorched its way through layers of peeling skin.

The man on the beach—I couldn't get beyond observation, couldn't ask the necessary questions. I stared at the slack face, at the water lapping into his mouth and around the open eyes that seemed black stones. With each gentle ebb, blood seeped from the clots in his hair. His body surged and bobbed when mine did. The thought was weird but I couldn't help thinking it: he was a picture of total relaxation.

I searched him and found a wallet in the back pocket of his slacks. He looked to be in his fifties, his face lined with creases so deep they were still visible despite the puffing of the skin. I couldn't tell if he'd been beaten before being shot or if the salt water had just gotten to him. He didn't look at all like Rocco.

I couldn't find my own wallet. My pockets were empty. I looked at my clothes as if they belonged to someone else. Hell, hadn't I been carrying my sportcoat? I couldn't remember. No ID.

I looked at the dead man's wallet clutched in my swollen fingers. I didn't have any ID, but this fellow did. All that was left of his life was right there in my hands. With my swollen fingers it took me a moment to unsnap the flap over the card case and find the identification.

Gene Harrell.

Gene Harrell!

The name hit me like a blow on the head and I dropped the wallet, a wave of darkness blotting out the light. I tried to think. What had happened to Rocco? And to me? Where was I?

There were no answers. No memories. Only Rocco in the boat. The dazzling light—and then darkness.

I thought about Harrell. He was a diver, like me. He was a link to the three Americans Dalmoro had mentioned. He might even have known Wanda. Might have known who murdered her. But he couldn't tell me now.

Or could he?

I could use him. I could do what Gene Harrell was supposed to do. He wouldn't mind—he was dead. *I was Harrell!* And so, in a way, he was alive and Derek Stone was dead. That was the way it had to be. That's what I'd wanted for all those months anyway. And perhaps the terrible memories of the past would die with me.

I was too mixed up at the moment to realize that just changing names wouldn't change who I really was or what my past had been. But no matter—I was thinking about the future now, and assuming Harrell's identity seemed like a good idea.

I crawled further up the beach and gratefully fell asleep.

It was the heat of the sun that woke me, the smell of rotting seaweed strong. A hot breeze wafting over me, dying and falling. My head was clearer and I looked inland, hoping to find trees for shelter from the sun. Barely fifty feet away, I saw the massive wall of a limestone cliff that stretched up from the narrow strand. To the left it was heavily fissured and scrub brush had taken hold.

I looked around for Harrell. The least I could do would be to drag him out of the water. And then what? Hide him? Bury the body? I didn't think I had the strength. But I didn't want anyone to find him too soon and start wondering who he was.

I couldn't find the body.

I tried to stand up and fell to my knees. The pain in

my head was excruciating. I sat down on the shingles and squeezed my temples between the palms of both hands, trying to suppress the jolts that left me dizzy. I wanted to lose consciousness then, but couldn't.

The body. Had it all been a dream? A nightmare caused by an excess of sun and alcohol?

No, I was sitting on a hard object—his wallet. *My wallet!* I got to my knees again and clutched the damp leather. My swollen fingers felt like miniature cannons. I could no longer unsnap the flap protecting the photo case. The edge of one card stuck up from the credit card slots—a simple but elegant, five-orbed crown the only mark visible.

I had to get out of the sun. Look through the wallet later when I could think. Ice-pick stabs of light off the sea pierced my eyes. I tried to fend off the blows and saw my arms. I'd been wearing a short-sleeve shirt and the skin, where it showed, looked like a leper's. The pain of being alive—the physical pain—was almost too much for me. I found some larger rocks near the edge of the shingle beach and crouched in the shade.

Strange, how much I'd wanted to kill myself. Trying to drown in alcohol. Trying to forget Wanda at the same time I was looking for her killers. And I'd taken Gene Harrell's identity with a kind of wild joy—with the mad laugh of the successful suicide.

From somewhere above me I heard a car, coming downhill, the muffler backfiring, the sound of the motor—geared down—first strong then weak. Curves. There had to be a road winding down from the top of the cliff. The fissure I'd seen earlier cutting inland probably gave way to a valley. I couldn't stay on the beach forever. I had to find the road.

The sun had dropped halfway between its meridian and the horizon, the air heavy and sultry. I scrambled over the rocks, breathing heavily, my shoes scraping as

I slid and stumbled. The breeze had died and the roar of the cicadas was now louder than the sound of the waves lapping at the rocky shoreline. The electric buzzing reverberated in my head like a chain saw ripping through the metallic strings of a harp. I was on fire. And where I wasn't burning, I was itching.

When I twisted my head to crack the neck muscles in a vain attempt to relieve tension, a light sifting of sand filtered down from my hair. I took stock of myself. Except for my shoes and the cuffs of my slacks, I was dry at least. My clothes, surprisingly, were none the worse for wear. My body had done all the suffering.

I couldn't tell if I'd been washed back to the Sicilian coast or if I'd come ashore on one of the islands to the north. As far as I could see there was nothing but rugged shoreline, steep craggy hills, a few scattered pine and little other vegetation. It took me several minutes to find the road. I finally located it by listening for the car. Whoever was driving had rounded the fissure and was coming straight toward me. From above. Dropping toward the shoreline.

Five painful minutes later, after a brain-lacerating scramble up a rocky slope where the escarpment had collapsed, I was standing at the side of the pockmarked pavement. My head felt as if a bomb had gone off inside. Each pulse of the blood through my temples struck a sledgehammer's blow.

I tried to run my fingers through my tangled hair, found a lump at the back of the head. But the pain was most intense behind the eyes. I rubbed them, then gingerly touched my face. At least a two-day's growth of beard.

A car swung around a curve, and as it came into sight began to pick up speed. A stocky Fiat. Looked like a silver-blue, four-door sedan. I stepped onto the pavement. There was barely room for the car and a small cart. I wasn't going to let them get around me.

The driver skidded to a stop ten feet away. A kid in his twenties, beside him a young woman.

The kid gripped the steering wheel with both hands. He was wearing tan driving gloves. The woman had braced herself with one hand on the dashboard, the other on the door. I saw her right elbow depress the lock even though both windows were wide open.

I walked toward the driver's side. The air was hot, the breeze, which had picked up again as I clambered up the slope, still too light to provide much cooling.

The Italian nodded and I said *"Buona sera"* and tried to smile.

What to tell them? As near the truth as possible. Out sailing, fell overboard, lost the boat. Something. My mind was working in slow motion.

Before I could organize the words, the Italian spoke. "It's going to be a rather hot evening. Can we give you a lift?" His intonation denoted good manners and culture. He was wearing a white dress shirt, open at the neck. Casual, but a young man of education.

I tried to smile. *"Per favore."* I looked down at my arms. "I've been out all day. Lost." I put both hands to my temples. "I . . . "

But the Italian had already turned to the woman. "Donata," he said, "help him get in the back."

Instead she came around and led me to the front. "You can sit by my brother," she said. "The front seat's more comfortable."

When I was inside, she gently closed the door and got in behind me. I tried to turn to thank her but gasped as the effort brought tears to my eyes. The back of my neck felt like . . . the words *pepperoni pizza* came to mind, and I think I tried to grin. That was a mistake. When the pain hit me this time there was nothing to compare it to.

The woman leaned forward and pulled the shirt collar away from my neck. She whistled softly.

"Giacomo, he needs help."

Needs help. I closed my eyes and slumped forward in the seat. It wasn't until I heard those words that the effort of making it up to the road and into the car hit me. I let myself go then, slipping down like a diver into watery silence.

I couldn't have been out for more than twenty minutes. When I woke, we were still on the road. Climbing into the hills now, the light less intense. In a few hours it would be twilight.

The two Italians were talking quietly. I stirred and the woman put her hand on my shoulder.

"A few more minutes," she said. "We'll stop at a *taverna*." She shook her head in sympathy. "You're dehydrated. You need water. And then we'll take you to the clinic at Mirabella. Another half hour."

I mumbled thanks. How would I ever be able to repay them?

And then I realized the woman had asked me something. "*Cosa?*" I whispered.

"What's your name?"

And almost without thinking, as if from somewhere deep inside, I said, "Gene Harrell."

5

IT WAS DIFFICULT to talk after that. My mind was running over too many confusing events. I kept coming back to the oars. I was sure that wasn't a dream. I could hear them thump into the side of the boat. Had the motors died? What was Rocco doing with the signal light? Asking for help? Or looking for Gene Harrell? And what had happened to us all? Rocco missing, me washed ashore, Harrell next to me. I didn't like it.

Harrell had been dressed in a business suit, and his wallet had the expensive look of pinseal leather. I still hadn't counted how much money he carried, but I'd seen the upper edge of a sheaf of bills. So he hadn't been murdered by local *briganti*—or at least not for his money.

I rubbed my chin and felt the whiskers. That was another problem nagging at the back of my head. I was sure I'd lost a day somehow. But what was one day when I'd lost so many over the preceding months? It shouldn't have mattered, but for some strange reason it did. Finally I put it down to forgetfulness. I'd left Messina early, had started drinking in the *locanda* in Milazzo. Forgot to shave.

The woman asked me a few questions, and I tried to explain what had happened, sticking as close to the truth as possible. I blamed my catastrophe on a wave that caught me by surprise and flipped the boat—and then had to lie about my lack of ability as a seaman. She might have wondered what I was doing that far out at sea by myself, but if so she was too polite to ask. Foreigners did the craziest things. Maybe I was out on a quest to hook the big one.

I knew she was trying to help, but it was all I could do just to keep my eyes open. It wasn't for lack of effort. She had features that caught the eye. And what had her brother called her? Donata? She reminded me of Wanda. Not that they resembled each other, but Wanda's last name was Donati, and both women had a quality that, judging from my past experience, I thought most men would recognize instantly. An attraction that's hard to resist and yet hard to explain.

I had always wondered about that. How did one define that particular quality? It wasn't beauty. I'd met many women who were beautiful but who aroused nothing more than aesthetic appreciation. When I was younger, I'd thought it was only my own peculiar tastes at play. But then I noticed that certain women—and Wanda was one of them—captivated almost everyone they met.

Donata had asked another question and my head jerked up. It was easier to doze off than to think. "I'm sorry," I mumbled. "I didn't catch what you said."

"Sorry. I should let you rest. You look like you're burning up." She reached over the seat with her left hand and felt my forehead.

Her hand was cool and I reached up and held it there, shutting my eyes. And then, a minute later, she reversed her hand and laid the back of it on my cheek.

"Lie back if you can," she said, and I did as I was told, easing gently into the velour-upholstered seat. I wondered how many layers of skin I'd lose on the back of my neck. It felt like a mass of boiled pork fat.

Her brother's voice interrupted my thoughts. "Just a few minutes and we'll be out of these curves." He shifted down as we crested a hill and then seconds later moved back up into third. We were crossing a long narrow

valley, mottled, army green scrub brush the only vegetation. In the distance, just where the road swung around
a hill, I could see the gnarled trunks of a few scattered
olive trees.

"The road climbs again out of the valley and then
drops to the harbor," he said. "The *taverna*'s near the
top of the hill. We'll have a few rough curves and then
it'll be over."

"Giacomo, let him rest."

I closed my eyes and tried to picture Wanda. It wasn't
easy. A moment of panic hit me when I realized I was
seeing a fusion of Wanda and the young woman in the
car. I had only one photo of Wanda. A picture taken by
me at a garden restaurant on the outskirts of Tripoli
halfway up a hill overlooking the gulf. What had I done
with my own wallet—and my passport? I was too confused to remember if I'd left them in my sport coat or
had lost them at sea.

Giacomo had said something to his sister and I listened
to her reply, finding it easier to picture her in my mind.
The facility with which I did so bothered me. But hell,
I'd just seen her. And all I had to do was open my eyes
and I'd see her again. Wanda was . . .

I stopped myself short, surprised at feeling guilty. I
was barely able to formulate rational thought—what with
the dull ache in my head—and I was worried about being
attracted to another woman! But that wasn't the first of
my stupidities. I'd been in a fog for three months. It felt
good to feel alive again. Even if alive meant in pain.

Hearing her voice, I gave in to the vision. She was a
good-looking woman. In her late twenties or early thirties, I guessed. Shoulder-length chestnut chair, lightly
mussed by the wind. Bare shoulders. She was wearing a
white cotton camisole top with a delicate floral pattern
along the border. It went with her complexion. Her

cheeks gave off a summer-evening glow, and even with my eyes shut I could see her eyes.

I've never been one to notice the color of people's eyes, but it was different with this woman. She had eyes like emeralds laid out on gray satin, a shadowy halo surrounding the translucent green like rocks around a tropical pool. I knew the metaphors were excessive, but she had that effect on me.

For a moment I confused her with the angels I'd seen in my vision at sea. She had the same soothing effect, her voice gentle, her manner full of care.

Her brother, who I judged to be younger, was less talkative. He was letting Donata handle most of the conversation.

They weren't Sicilians, I decided. Not southerners either. Probably northerners on vacation in the islands. Maybe from Lombardy. I couldn't place the accent any better than that, although Italian, along with Arabic, was one of the languages I spoke best. I'd had occasion to learn it while working in the country—and being married to Wanda had helped.

Most working Italians had the whole month of August free. For someone from North America, it was a strange system. I'd never been able to figure out why the Italians all wanted to be on vacation at the same time, why they couldn't spread out their time off over the course of the year. The big cities died in August; the beaches and islands flourished.

I sat up and rubbed my temples again. We'd crossed a good part of the valley. The pain behind my eyes was easing. Or shifting. I could feel the lump at the back of my head. I'd hit something hard. But it was getting easier and easier to think.

The two had lapsed into silence. I turned with effort and asked where they were from, if they were on vacation.

Giacomo looked in the rearview mirror at his sister and then said, "We live here. In Leporetto."

I shook my head; I'd never heard of the place.

"A little village back in the hills."

It still wasn't enough. I wanted to know where I was.

I touched my forehead. "I'm a bit confused. What island is this?"

"Vignetti," Giacomo said. "Just east of Lipari."

So the currents north of Sicily had carried me toward the mainland.

"It's a small island," Donata added. "The population swells in the summer to a couple thousand, but the rest of the time there are only shepherds, fishermen, a few artisans, and shopkeepers. Barely two hundred people. Most belong to one of two families. Ours—the Pellico—and the Mancini. Unfortunately, we're not too friendly. We try to avoid them if possible."

Giacomo wrinkled his nose in disgust. "They're thieves."

"Not all of them, Giacomo."

I looked over at the kid. Both his and his sister's voices had been sharp. He was frowning, his jaws clenched. A moment later, to break the silence, he said to Donata, "It doesn't matter. You're leaving tomorrow."

I pondered that in the silence that settled once again between them. A love affair that went against the family interests?

I'd never liked people who pried into the personal lives of strangers. But she'd asked several questions of me. And both she and her brother, despite his laconic manner, seemed to have an open air of European cosmopolitanism about them. They weren't as closed in as the Sicilians I was used to dealing with on various oil rigs. Perhaps, as a foreigner, I could consider myself exempt. So I asked what I wanted to know.

50

"Going to the mainland to study?"

She laughed and shook her head. "I finished the university six years ago. Giacomo's the student. He's studying law in the *Facoltà di Legge* at the University of Rome. I'm going to Malta. I have a tutoring job with a family there. On Gozo. Nine months a year. I've just been home for the summer."

"What do you tutor?"

She laughed. "Everything. I teach *Zi'* Carlo's kids what they'd learn in school. He's the most powerful man on Gozo. Has a beautiful villa just outside San Lawrenz."

I'd been on Gozo, the second largest island of the Republic of Malta, but had never made it out to San Lawrenz. I tried to place the village in my mind.

"Isn't that out near San Dimitri Point?"

She pursed her lips and wobbled her hand back and forth to show I was only a little off.

"That's a bit further north. If you go due west from San Lawrenz you reach Dwejra Point. So you've been to Gozo?"

Giacomo broke in before I could reply. "She works for the guy who owns Malta Independent Oil." He had a note of pride in his voice. "Spugna's one of the richest guys in the Mediterranean. He's made MIO one of the biggest private oil companies in Europe."

My breath caught in my throat. *Spugna!* Zi' Carlo she'd said. Carlo Spugna. Damn! I hadn't been paying attention. And what had the kid said? MIO. Malta Independent Oil. Only he'd pronounced it like a word—like *mio*. That was what Wanda had said! Only I'd thought she'd been speaking Italian, saying *mine*.

I was stunned. Carlo Spugna had started a company called MIO. I knew Spugna well but I'd never heard that name for his company.

The implications were overwhelming. I stared at Giacomo in shock. "MIO," I said.

Giacomo glanced at me and then looked back at the road. We were on a gentle curve near the end of the valley. Olive trees struggled out of the rocky terrain to our left, while to our right newly planted vines spread their tendrils along rows that became ever shorter as they progressed up the terraced hillside.

Giacomo raised his eyebrows. "You know the company? Not many foreigners have heard of it."

Donata laughed, following her own train of thought. "*Zi'* Carlo always says the happiest rich man is the unknown rich man."

I was too upset to respond to either. My mind was racing. I hadn't known about MIO but I knew Spugna all right. Only I'd thought he didn't know me.

The underwater explosion. Shit! I'd carried the explosives. The tanks. The new kid. I'd tied them off at one hundred feet, but he'd prepared—

And then I stopped in horror. The kid hadn't prepared anything. Jake had! Jake! I couldn't believe it. But the conclusion was inescapable. He'd planted explosives with the tanks and around the platform, set the timed detonator, arranged to get injured and off the jackup before the explosion occurred. Hell, maybe he even faked the injury. And then the payoff. Carlo Spugna or his henchmen would be responsible for that. I was sick. It wasn't the Libyans who'd killed Wanda. *I had!*

And it was all because of Spugna's company. That had to be over fifteen years ago. What had he called it then? Spugna Oil Exploration. No one ever told me he'd changed the name. Or if they did I hadn't paid attention.

Had Spugna found out what I'd done to thwart his company's efforts to control oil exploration off the coast of Malta? If so, it had taken him a long time to track me down.

As a result of my sabotage efforts—many considered natural disasters—the first offshore wells near Malta were abandoned by Spugna Oil in 1972. I'd done that as a favor for the Canadian government. Or rather for the SIS. Hansen was my contact. At the time he was assigned as liaison to British Intelligence. Malta was an independent republic but part of the Commonwealth, and the Royal Navy still anchored in its harbors—the Maltese wouldn't see the last of the fleet until 1979, when Rear Admiral Cecil pulled out of Grand Harbour on the destroyer *London*—so British interests in the area were high.

In the early seventies, Spugna Oil was suspected of financing much of the underworld drug traffic that passed through the Mediterranean. And the company was also just beginning to get involved in arms smuggling. Spugna Oil had set itself up as an intermediary between the West and those countries of the Middle East who couldn't deal directly with the U.S. or Europe, but who wanted the West's weapons. In an effort to harm Spugna's business in general, the intelligence community decided to make sure the company's oil exploration was unsuccessful.

Encouraged by discoveries in Sicily and off the coasts of Libya and Tunisia, Spugna Oil was exploring the area both to the north and the south of Malta. In 1953, an Italian company had discovered an accumulation of oil in the Ragusa anticline in southeastern Sicily. And three years later, the nearby Gela field was opened for mining. Smaller volumes of oil continued to be discovered in the fields of Ponte Dirillo to the east of Gela, and then farther north at Cammarata-Pozzillo. Spugna's agents had informed the company's management that within five years the Sicilian fields would account for over ninety percent of the overall Italian output. Spugna was determined to do as well off Malta.

The company I worked for belonged to a rival consortium. At the time—in 1971—I was employed by an underwater maintenance group providing full-service diving to the sheikdom of Qatar. We specialized in inspection and underwater welding—wet and dry hyperbaric—and worked off Idd el Shargi, Maydan-Mahzam, and Bul Hanine, the latter discovered in 1970 and put into production in 1972. The state of Qatar was seventeenth in the world league of offshore oil producers, pumping about 190,000 barrels a day.

I was in charge of a fairly large crew then, responsible for such things as modification of offshore structures, hot taps, replacement of risers, and all manner of other underwater repair jobs, including work on subsea pipelines. I'd been only too happy to do my part to see that the work of Spugna's men was sabotaged. The consortium was planning on moving into the Mediterranean north of Africa once we got the Persian Gulf's production running smoothly.

But despite my hand in Spugna Oil's failures I found it hard to believe that anyone in the company knew who I was. I'd covered my tracks well. Or thought I had. Could Spugna have tracked me down through Wanda? Or had there been a leak from NATO intelligence—perhaps through the Italians, perhaps even the SIS. Damn! The explosion—maybe that was meant for both of us!

When I looked up again, the twilight had deepened and Giacomo had turned on the Fiat's headlights. As we climbed, the high beams flickered across the pavement and illuminated a stone wall running alongside the road. Behind the stone wall stood an orange grove, and the scent, heady as perfume, soon filled the car.

The lack of direct sunlight was a relief to my head, which still throbbed. I shut my eyes to avoid the glare of the headlights, but then quickly opened them. It was better to see the curves than to feel them only. My head felt like the sea with its own tides.

Giacomo spoke. "So how do you know Spugna?"

I struggled to compose myself. He must have asked the question five times.

"I don't, really. But I know what his company does." I couldn't restrain myself. "They're one step short of being terrorists in my book."

Giacomo laughed. "Agreed. But he pays well."

Donata let out an exasperated sound. "Pays the family," she said. "I get an allowance. Barely enough to clothe myself."

Her brother snorted. "What do you need money for? He feeds you, your room is free."

Donata said nothing.

Spugna was one of the local tyrants, known to all but rarely seen. The type to leave the running of his commercial interests to intermediaries on the pretext that he was involved with more important things. Concerned with self-protection. Hiring a private tutor for his children fit the pattern. Security for himself and his family above all else. He was probably afraid of kidnappers. Wouldn't even let his kids attend a public school.

I broke the silence. "How many children does he have?"

"Just two," Donata said. "Vanni's only five and Franca's eight. They're both good kids."

I couldn't help myself. "Not like their father, huh?"

She didn't respond and I turned slowly to look at her. I hadn't meant her to take it as criticism of herself.

She refused to look at me, but I could see her brows were furrowed. I was just about to speak—to try to excuse or explain my tone—when the Fiat left the road and bounced over some ruts. I glanced back quickly to the front, grimacing, as Giacomo applied the brakes. Apparently we'd arrived at our destination.

The *taverna* was a square, country farmhouse-style building set off the side of the road in a small clearing.

Nothing else in sight. Smoke rose from a chimney at the back. The kitchen. Whoever ran the place probably lived in it too. A dusty mongrel lay spread-eagled near the open door.

Donata helped me out of the car, and with head bent and an awkward shuffle I followed her and Giacomo to the entrance. I had to duck to miss the wood-beam lintel. Inside, in the subdued light, I noticed that the floor was packed dirt. I heard talk to my left and then a sudden burst of laughter. When I looked in that direction, three old men glanced back. Had they laughed at me? Their faces showed no humor.

And then, hearing the sound of clinking bottles, I caught sight of two young guys in the corner beyond the old men. Staring at us also, sneering. So they were the ones who'd laughed. Creeps.

Giacomo grabbed my left arm, not noticing the wince that crossed my face, and led me to a table near the bar, which ran along the back of the room. The furnishings were simple and bare, no candles on the tables, no cushions on the crude wood chairs, one bottle of corked red wine per table. Overhead, four scattered lightbulbs of weak wattage illuminated the room.

After we sat down, I noticed a massive stone hearth to my right. With the summer heat, no fire had been lit, but wood was stacked nearby. The scent of pine was strong.

We ordered, Giacomo a beer, Donata a soft drink, and I a *caffelatte* with a glass of *acqua gassata*.

"Bring us three *panini imbottiti* also," Giacomo said.

The innkeeper, a gaunt man who looked like he was recovering from a long illness, nodded and left.

I looked again around the *taverna,* which seemed unnaturally quiet. The three old men, their skin roughened by years of working in the fields, were playing cards. Their bottle of red wine stood nearly empty.

The other two men, in their early twenties, were drinking beer and smoking. Both were unshaven and in need of haircuts. They wore faded western jeans and white T-shirts that were stained with sweat below the armpits. The one on the left had a tattoo on his right arm where the sleeve was rolled up to hold a pack of cigarettes. Unsavory characters at best. Trying hard to imitate the hoods in American-made, B-grade gangster movies.

Donata tugged at Giacomo's shirt. "Those are Pietro's cousins—Cecco and Beppe."

"Mancinis," he sneered. "So what?"

"So I'm going to go say hello."

"You stay here. You know what *papà* will do if he hears."

Donata's eyes flashed with anger. She leaned over the table and whispered something in dialect. Giacomo's face grew red, but he said nothing.

I tried to distract Donata by asking how she got to Malta. Did Vignetti have an airstrip or a commercial boat service? I needed to know myself if I was going to get off the island.

Donata looked at me with a distracted air. "I go by boat," she said slowly. "From here to Messina and then to Valletta."

I was about to ask her why Valletta, when I saw both guys get up and head our way. Giacomo had his back to them, but he saw Donata's head rise and turned to look. The taller of the two guys had a knife out and was cleaning his thumbnail as he moved toward us. His belt strap hung down a good ten inches beyond the buckle like a tail—or was it supposed to be a phallic symbol?

Giacomo pushed back his chair and Donata reached for his hand.

"No," she said. "Don't say anything."

"Leave it to me," I said, in an attempt at humor. "I'll take care of it."

No one laughed.

The taller kid spoke first, as if Giacomo weren't there. "Ciao, Donata."

She nodded pleasantly. "Ciao, Cecco. *Come va?*"

"*Bene,*" he said and then came right to the point. "Pietro couldn't make it."

Giacomo's face was livid. He turned on his sister. "*Puttana!* You had this all arranged."

I didn't like him calling his sister a whore. I tried to keep my voice level. "I suppose she arranged my being picked up."

No one looked at me. I didn't belong. I was a foreigner, and worse yet one too dumb to shut up when something didn't concern him.

But it wasn't dumbness. It was an instinct I have for calling trouble down on myself to spare others. I didn't want a fight to break out. If I could get them to concentrate on me—an outsider—maybe they'd feel less bitterness toward each other.

But the shorter creep, spitting between gat teeth toward Giacomo, raised his right fist, slapped the inside of his elbow with his left hand, and, not content with the gesture, reinforced the insult by swearing, "*Va fan culo, stronzo.*"

Oh shit! I thought. Either one of those epithets was enough for a fight. Despite the flow of adrenaline, I didn't have the strength to put up with angry words, let alone physical blows.

By this time, everyone except me was standing. I decided to join the crowd. A mediator was needed. I put my hands on the table to shove my chair back and suddenly, as if that was the signal they were waiting for, all hell broke loose before I could get to my feet.

The tall guy, knife blade slashing, lunged toward Giacomo. Donata thrust out her arm and screamed, "No, Cecco!"

Giacomo took a step back and looked for help. I could see no one was going to bother. He was on his own.

Cecco shoved Donata aside. She tripped and fell back on the table. I reached for her arm, knocking over the bottle of wine. Before I could get it, her hand closed around the neck of the bottle.

Beppe, the shorter fellow, aware of her intention, grabbed for her skirt, and I chopped his arm with the best karate blow I could manage. I think it hurt me more than him, but he let go. That was all Donata needed. She took one step and brought the bottle down on Cecco's head.

The force of the blow, which shattered the bottle, startled all of us. Wine and shards of glass splattered, and Cecco went out like a gnat flying through flame.

I stared in shock at the puddle that I hoped was red wine and not blood, pain overridden now by the influx of adrenaline.

Beppe, perhaps realizing he had no chance against the Pellicos by himself, turned on me. Before I could move, he shoved the table into my stomach. I struggled, trying to slide the chair away so I could get to my feet, but its wooden legs dug into the packed earth and I started to tip over backward.

Just before my head hit the ground and I joined Cecco, a crazy thought passed through my mind. If the sea couldn't kill me, maybe the land would. Earlier it might not have mattered so much—I would have joined Wanda in the sea—but now it suddenly did. And why? Well, I didn't have a lot of time to think about that but deep inside I knew.

———

6

———

To WAKE UP in a place you've never seen is disconcerting. Worse yet when the first thing you notice is that the windows have bars. The only thing familiar was my headache, although that was less painful. Still, I was beginning to wonder if it was a permanent fixture.

I was in a small but clean room, more accurately a cell, with walls freshly whitewashed. New construction, I thought. A smell of wet cement still hung in the air.

About ten feet from the floor, on the back wall and on the side facing what I thought was east, there were two small windows, barely a foot square, double-barred. These provided the only illumination, but at the moment, with the sun high, the air shimmered with a light so brilliant that my eyes hurt. I could hear the ecstatic buzz of summer insects, the occasional call of birds. A childhood vision of freedom—kites flying in the wind—came to mind and then died slowly away. I was no longer a child and no longer free.

I looked down from the windows and the white walls.

A stylish ceramic toilet, also white and the best of modern Italian design, sat in the corner near a small sink. Above the sink hung a mirror made of reflective metal. There was no furniture other than the bed, which was bolted to the floor.

For a moment I wondered if I was in a clinic. Perhaps an asylum. That would be one step better than a jail.

I sat up with effort. I was getting tired of living in a mental world that bordered on endless gray.

I was also hungry. I hadn't even gotten to eat my *panini* before those idiots attacked us. It took a crazy man to laugh at my situation, but I did. Back on the beach I'd felt like dying, and ever since failing I was trying harder to live than I ever had before.

Perhaps it was the sense of freedom that came with giving up one identity for another. A fresh start, as it were—except for the memories. My head had been battered enough to count for a lobotomy, but apparently it was made of iron. I couldn't forget Wanda—and the words she'd uttered before dying.

I heard a voice in the hall, one shout and then silence. I strained my ears. There was the sound of metal slamming.

So, there were other cells. Donata and Giacomo? Or those creeps?

A moment later, a one-foot-wide judas gate slid open and a metal tray appeared at the end of a dark hairy hand. There was a bowl on the tray and two rolls.

Food. I could smell it already. The aroma of soup. It cleared my head for the first time since I'd left the *locanda* in Milazzo.

The *panini* had been slit and one stuffed with a slice of white provolone cheese, the other with a thin sheet of prosciutto. And the soup was a delicious *risotto in brodo*.

My jailer had left the judas gate open. When I finished eating, I set the tray by the opening and lay down to see what I could make out. A narrow hall, lit again by external light from windows high up on the walls. No sign of people.

It was time to start sorting things out before anyone disturbed me. I got up and moved over to the mirror. Reflective metal is not the greatest surface for catching detail, but the vision that appeared almost made me laugh. I saw the original savage, hair sticking out like the quills of a frazzled porcupine, a bristle of grizzled whiskers, eyes that looked like blue grottos on a stormy day. With both hands resting on the sink for support, I brought my face closer. Just who was this Gene Harrell staring back at me?

What in hell was going on, and what could I do to see that things turned out okay?

Obviously I was in trouble. I'd been in a fight. I was a foreigner. Hell, a foreigner without a passport. And they'd confiscated Gene Harrell's wallet. It wasn't in my pants. Did they already know I was an impostor?

I wondered again what had happened to my sport coat with the handcrafted Florentine leather *portfoglio* carrying my documents. Either back in Milazzo, where it would disappear when I didn't show up, deep underwater with Rocco, or floating in an abandoned boat somewhere in the Tyrrhenian sea. Derek Stone existed only on paper now.

And what about Gene Harrell? I had to learn more. Had to try and find the three Americans. Wherever they were. Go in Harrell's place and see what the Americans had to do with Wanda. Learn what I could before they discovered I was someone else.

Harrell's death bothered me. Someone had hated him enough to murder him. Maybe it would've been better to remain Derek Stone. I'd done some bad things in my time—most of which I could rationalize by saying they were done in the service of my country—and I'd been smart enough to stay off anyone's wanted list. Or at least I thought I had—until now. Until I'd opened my big mouth to Jake. And then it hit me. Jake must have told Spugna about me.

The guard returned then for the tray and soup bowl. I tried to question him. Asked him what was going on. It was hard. I could only see his hand. He had a gruff voice. Said I'd have to wait. I'd see a magistrate soon enough.

The mention of a judge caused my heart to pick up a

beat. Funny how that happens. If he'd said I'd be seeing a firing squad or a torture chamber, I'd have probably been calmer, my fate more certain. I sat down to wait with a heart that was beating like the drums of an African night.

They came for me a few hours later. Two uniformed police officials. Both very crisp and efficient. I was walked in silence to a courtyard and placed in a blue police van with the word *Carabinieri* splayed across the side in large, white letters. I didn't like that. *Vigili Urbani* would have been more soothing. The military police were concerned with everything from clandestine activities and terrorism to drug smuggling and international crime. What were they doing on this speck of land?

We drove for about five minutes at the most, less than two kilometers, one officer in the back with me, the other at the wheel.

I didn't have time to ask what was going on.

When the driver opened the back of the van, we were in a small village, parked before a one-story building with the words *Municipio di Mirabella* painted in black above the keystone of the single entrance arch. The air was humid, the temperature at least ninety degrees Fahrenheit. I was happy to get out of the glare and into the building.

Inside, rooms opened up to the left and right off a central flagstone-paved hallway. A series of framed scenic paintings was hung between the doorways, depicting what I supposed were the major touristic attractions of the island. We passed by two doors, each framed with strips of mottled marble, one for the *Questura*, the other an *Ufficio d'Informazione Turistica,* and stopped before an opaque-glass door with the faded word *Pretura*.

The young policeman at my left opened the door and said, "*Avanti.*"

I walked in to find a legalistic-looking man seated behind a desk, head down as he perused a sheaf of papers. He was dressed in a dark blue business suit, with an equally dark, thin tie that made him look pale and cold. Under the artificial light his sharp features seemed harsh and officious. The air had that metaphysical tang that my Italian friends would have called the *puzzo d'avvocato*—the stench of lawyers. An odor perceptible only to those about to be judged and condemned. I thought of what my father used to say. "A fox smells his own hole first." I guess that meant that the stench came from the prisoner not the judge.

I looked around for support. There was no one else in the room. Wasn't I going to have the right of attorney?

The room contained no benches for spectators. Merely two small tables in front of the judge's desk, each with two unpadded wooden chairs.

After a few minutes, the man looked up, nodded, told the policemen they could wait outside, and turned back to his papers.

He frowned as he read one page and then, almost impatiently, looked up, gestured toward a seat at a table to my left, and said, "Sit down."

He picked up the sheaf of papers, straightened them, slid them in a file folder, and stared at me.

"Your name?"

I swallowed hard. The moment of truth. My mouth was suddenly dry.

The man's dark eyes were locked on mine. I could feel my forehead begin to perspire.

"Harrell, Gene," I said in the Italian fashion.

"Date of birth?"

I stared. Date of birth? I didn't have the slightest idea. I cleared my throat. Stumbled over the words as I tried to choose what I was going to say. I started talking about an accident, about the injury to my head. The judge interrupted.

"It says here, September 2, 1937."

I dropped my head, shook it as if to say, "Of course, how stupid of me," and managed to mutter "*Giusto.*" I made an awkward gesture toward my head. "*Sono ancora mezzo stordito.*" Half-stunned was only part of it. I was scared to say anything now.

My mind was in a whirl. I'd just aged four years.

As Derek Stone, I was born March 28, 1941, in Regina, Saskatchewan—the closest city to our farm large enough to have a hospital. I grew up pretty much in isolation. Had no brothers or sisters. When chores were done, I spent my time wandering through the fields, exploring the scattered plots of trees on our property, hunting, catching polliwogs in the summer in the year-round pond behind the barn, living in nature. But when I graduated from high school in '59, I was tired of the life we led on the farm, tired of chores, tired of my father telling me what to do. I joined the Maritime Command of the Royal Canadian Armed Forces, and went from the tyranny of my father to that of the military. But I learned how to dive. The rest of the time I spent waiting for freedom, and when I got out didn't know what I wanted to do in life.

I'd made one friend in the military. A fellow by the name of Chuck Alyea. When he said he was going to study engineering in Montana, I decided to do the same. In '63 I enrolled at the Montana College of Mineral Science and Technology in Butte. I chose industrial engineering with a specialty in mining and oil exploration. Got my degree in '67 and went to work for a Texas company involved with offshore exploration in the Gulf of Mexico. But that was only the first of many companies. I believed in individual freedom, in taking the initiative, in being frank and direct. It didn't take much to make me angry, and I was fairly blunt about it. All traits the business world happened not to prize.

Sometime in the early seventies, I wound up working for a subsidiary of All-Europe Oil Exploration and Development Corporation, a company providing technical assistance to the sheikdom of Qatar. When the North-West Dome was discovered in the Gulf in '76, I left All-Europe Oil to work directly with the National Drilling Company of Abu Dhabi. Abu Dhabi, one of the United Arab Emirates, was developing Bunduq with the state of Qatar's help.

For a while I worked on a diving crew, first off Al Ittihad, a jackup, and then off different production platforms in the Gulf of Persia. And then came a series of other jobs that led to my position as head diver for PetroCanada, which was helping Libya develop the Gulf of Gabes. Somehow, one job had gotten strung on after the other, like links in a chain, and I'd never really taken the time to step back and analyze if I was doing what I wanted to.

The man behind the desk in the courtroom was speaking. I stared at him, wondering if I looked as wild-eyed as I felt. His voice, toneless and bureaucratic, slowly penetrated my skull.

"What's the purpose of your visit to our island?"

I raised my head and made an effort to get control of myself. What else would my aim be? "Tourism," I said. I tried to smile pleasantly.

The man's beady eyes never wavered. "How did you arrive?"

"By boat."

"By commercial boat?"

I hesitated. Lie or tell the truth?

The judge didn't wait for my answer.

"Why do you have no passport?"

I coughed and licked my lips. "I was in an accident . . . in a rental boat. I lost it at sea. I haven't had a chance to get in touch with the Canadian Consulate in Palermo yet."

The man frowned. "Why would you go to the Canadian Consulate?"

I stared at him, my eyes wide. What was wrong? Shit! Gene Harrell was American!

The judge tapped the file of papers. "There's an Australian Consulate in Palermo. And the High Commission in Rome."

Australian? That made no sense. Was Harrell Australian? In confusion, I struggled for words.

"I didn't know. I thought maybe the Canadian Consulate could help."

The man stared at me without saying anything. A minute passed, while he thumped a pencil on the desk and looked at me.

Finally, he sighed. "Signor Harrell, today is Saturday. We have been unable to contact the people we need to verify your identity in either Rome or Palermo. Our *pretore* is on vacation. I'm the *vice-pretore onorario*—the honorary vice-prefect, a common citizen. Nothing can be done until the *pretore* returns on the twenty-third."

All this and the guy wasn't a judge. It was my turn to frown. "The twenty-third?"

"Yes. A week from today."

"But what am I being charged with? Why is there no attorney to represent me?"

The man looked surprised. "Charging you? We are not charging you with anything. There is no penal magistrate on Vignetti. The police are holding you as a simple preventive measure. Have you committed a crime?"

I quickly shook my head. "Why am I being kept in

jail? Can't I be released to a *pensione?* This is a small island. There's no place to go.''

"There are many places to go. Ferries, boats for hire, hiding places in the hills. We know nothing about you. You were found unconscious. You had only an expired driver's license issued in Perth. No passport. Before we can let you go, we need to check with officials in Rome.''

"A week," I said slowly. I was thinking hard. Seven days minimum in that whitewashed cell with nothing to do but think. I didn't like it. "Can't I do anything to speed up the process?''

The *vice-pretore onorario* reached for a large envelope with a string tie-around clasp. He undid the flap and an object slid on to his desk.

He picked it up and opened it. "Is this yours?''

I started to shake my head and then realized he was holding Gene Harrell's wallet. It looked different when dry. I nodded. "That's my wallet.''

The assistant laid the wallet on the desk and folded his hands under his chin. "Your wallet contains only sixty thousand lire. Is that what you had when you came here?''

I lifted my shoulders and hands in a gesture of uncertainty. "I'm not sure. That sounds about right." I didn't want to suggest the police had stolen any.

"Do you have other money to support yourself?''

I paused. Sixty thousand. That was barely forty American dollars. I did have the hefty *conto corrente* under my real name in the Banca Commerciale at Rome, and some funds—about two million lire, which sounded like a lot but amounted to less than fifteen hundred dollars— tied up in the Banca Nazionale del Lavoro in Milan from the days when I used to invest in the *Borsa Valori,* the Italian stock market.

But how to get at either with no ID?

I had to say something. The man was waiting.

I nodded vigorously. "I have a bank account . . . in an Italian bank." I cleared my throat. "In Milan. *Più di due millioni di lire.*" I didn't want to mention the large account in Rome. "And more in . . . Australia."

I'd nearly slipped and said Canada again. I couldn't get over the fact that Harrell was Australian. Hadn't Dalmoro told me he was American?

The man behind the desk nodded. "Okay. Here's your wallet. You should arrange to see that sufficient funds are transferred here. Your expenses while in our custody will be paid by you. If everything checks out, you should be released early next week."

I nodded, trying to suppress the anxiety I felt, and stepped forward to pick up the wallet. I wanted to get back to the cell and see what was in it. "Thanks," I said briskly. "I'm sure there'll be no problem."

The *vice-pretore onorario* pushed a buzzer on his desk and turned back to his sheaf of papers. A moment later the two police officers stepped into the room. "That's all," the man said without looking up. "Take him back. We'll know more next week."

Next week. I thought about his words on the trip back. And the thought was not comforting. Unless I could get out of the cell on my own, I might be in for a rough time. They already knew more about Gene Harrell than I did. And what else would they find out?

—————

7

—————

I MUST HAVE slept a good twelve hours in a state of exhaustion, waking only once early in the morning to go to the bathroom. The small triptych of sunlight from the east window was just beginning to spread itself in an unfocused glow near the ceiling of the opposite wall. When I finished urinating and lay back down on the narrow bed, I dropped back immediately into a seamless state of unconsciousness.

Hours later, I heard voices, indistinct at first and then raised in volume. I sat up feeling groggy. The room blazed with incandescence and the cotton padding on the bed was soaked with sweat. Suddenly a burst of laughter rolled down the corridor, dying out in my cell with a hollow echo.

A friendly dispute? I recognized the voice of my jailer, a short, middle-aged, asthmatic Italian, at least thirty pounds overweight. We'd spoken for nearly five minutes the night before when he brought me a dinner of soup, fried fish, and salad. I'd tried to ask if there were any Americans on the island, but he claimed he didn't know. He was more intent on explaining that the food I ate was purchased from my own funds at a nearby *rosticceria*.

The laughter I'd heard came from someone else. Whoever was speaking was using what sounded like a dialect, and I found it hard to make out the words.

They were walking toward my cell. I moved over to the judas gate and crouched with my ear to the metal plate.

"Come on, Luigi, it's only for today." The voice was cajoling, the language now standard Italian. "I'll bring him back tonight. No one'll know."

That was Giacomo Pellico. No doubt about it. Speaking to the jailor Luigi. *Bring him back!* It was me they were discussing.

I stood and walked away from the door, my heart beating. The key was being turned in the lock. The door swung open and Giacomo's smiling face greeted me, peering over the shoulder of the jailer. I squinted at both of them.

"Luigi's my uncle," Giacomo exclaimed gleefully. "He's agreed to a Sunday excursion."

I stared at him suspiciously. I sensed a note of false bonhomie that I didn't like. "Where to?"

"To a *festa,* Signor Harrell. A good-bye party for Donata. Five hours and we'll have you back."

I looked askance at the jailer. I didn't want trouble. I'd already given up thoughts of escaping. It was stupid to risk a warrant for my arrest when I had nothing to fear—at least, I didn't think I did, anyway. I didn't know enough about Gene Harrell to be certain.

Giacomo grabbed my arm and I winced.

"Sorry, Signor Harrell. Forgot about your sunburn." He released his grip and then smiled triumphantly. "Luigi's one of the family. He's a Pellico. The police are all off-duty today. No one will come until tomorrow morning. It's a Sunday. We want you to join our celebration. Donata asked for you."

My eyes widened. He was probably a good liar, but I made up my mind instantly. Freedom. A day outdoors. The rest of the week would pass that much faster.

I nodded. "Okay." I was still wearing the clothes I'd been washed to shore in, but the police had taken Gene Harrell's wallet before I could look through it. I turned to the jailer.

"*Il mio portafoglio*," I said. "I need it just for today."

Giacomo said, "No, no, Signor Harrell. That's not necessary. You're a guest of my relatives."

Damn. I wanted a look at what was in that wallet. Anything to give me an advantage the next time I was taken to the *Pretura*.

"*Per favore, signore*," I said to the jailer. "I want to buy a gift for Giacomo's sister. In thanks for saving me."

"I have it in the front desk," he said. "I'll give you some money. But we've already spent sixteen thousand lire on your meals. Save some of the rest. It'll take several days to get money transferred from the mainland."

I'd told the police I would arrange for a withdrawal on Monday, when the banks opened, although I hadn't figured out how to handle that. Would they believe me if I told them the account in Milan was in another name? It wouldn't look too good. Only criminals or people with something to hide used more than one name. Maybe Giacomo could handle it for me without letting the police know the details.

At the front desk, the jailer opened my wallet and rifled through the money compartment.

I held out my hand. "I'll bring it back." I figured he was worried I'd skip out if I had my wallet. "I can't go anywhere without a passport. I want to look through my photos."

Luigi, breathing heavily, wiped slobber from the corner of his mouth. "Photos?" He frowned. "There are none."

"What? Let's see." I reached out and grabbed the wallet. The photo compartment was empty, the driver's license no longer there, but two cards were stuffed into the credit card slots on the other flap. Before I could get them out, Luigi yanked back the wallet.

"Police property until you're released," he said. He

handed me two ten-thousand-lire notes. "That'll have to do."

Donata was waiting outside at the wheel of the Fiat sedan with the motor running. Giacomo opened the back door, told me to get in, and then slammed the door behind me.

He bent quickly to the open window. "Sorry. Forgot about your head."

He wasn't remembering much I thought, but I told him it was okay. "My head's better today."

He climbed in the front and slammed his own door. "*Presto, andiamo!*" he shouted, and then looked back.

"You'd better lie down on the seat," he said. "Just for a few minutes while we're going through the town. Nothing to worry about. I just don't want anyone to see you." He shrugged. "For Luigi's sake."

Giacomo was too nervous for me. Did he think this was a jailbreak? "Where are we going?" I asked.

"To my cousin's house. And then to a restaurant."

We lapsed into silence for the next several minutes while Donata drove through Mirabella. The pavement radiated heat under the noon-time sun, and I could smell the rising fumes of asphalt. The municipality had recently repaved the roadway stretching along the harbor. From there we started climbing and Giacomo told me I could sit up. The road, which wound uphill in a series of switchbacks, was deserted.

At one point, more to peeve his sister than to inform me, Giacomo said, "Signor Harrell, you're lucky Luigi's a Pellico and not a Mancini."

I nodded once, expecting Donata to get angry, but neither she nor I said anything in reply.

The house of their relatives sat on the edge of a rugged cliff overlooking a small fishing village on the western side of the island. We swung off the road, and Donata parked between a sporty, fire red Alfa Romeo Spider, the top down, and a rusty three-wheeled truck with an immense fifty-liter wine jug in the open bed.

A parapet overlooked the house, with a footpath leading down from the parking area. Before taking the path, we stood for a minute at the edge of the cliff, which was lined with a small hedge of prickly pear cactus. A warm breeze off the sea wafted past us toward the east, and I breathed deeply, appreciating the fresh air and the open spaces. I knew when I returned to the cell the heat would be unbearable.

Giacomo pointed to a small indentation in the shoreline far below. "Porto Metello," he said. "We'll eat at the Ristorante Metello, named after the unfortunate nephew of Augustus. The one Virgil wrote about in the Fourth Eclogue."

Today Giacomo seemed to be the talkative one, while Donata appeared withdrawn and preoccupied. I wondered if she was thinking about her boyfriend or about leaving her family. Given the obvious animosity between the Pellicos and the Mancinis, I couldn't imagine her wanting to stay.

I looked down with a sense of longing at the small port. It lacked the facilities of the larger harbor at Mirabella. There was no quay and no breakwater. The fishing boats were drawn up on the narrow shingle beach that stretched no more than three hundred feet in length before the cliffs took over again. I imagined I could smell the briny nets hung up on poles to dry just beyond the boats.

To get the day's catch from the port to the village on the hillside, the fishermen had built a series of concrete steps that cut back and forth up the crumbling cliffside. I could see a young woman toiling slowly up the steps toward the village. The village itself consisted of a single street with buildings clustered along the inland side of the road.

From the parking area, we walked down a footpath that led beneath wild rosemary—the shrub's purple flowers gave off a bee-enticing fragrance—and then circled around a small hill. On the leeward side, a grove of eucalyptus trees surrounded a two-story block farmhouse. The resinous scent of the eucalyptus oil was overpowering. The aromas of summer hung in the heat and humidity and made my heart beat wildly with hope. I wondered if my giddiness was a result of illness or renewed life. It had been too long since I'd felt this good.

And then I figured out that my sense of smell was so strong because I was hungry. I'd missed the breakfast call at the jail—if there'd been one. I could see Luigi pocketing a few thousand lire and giving me nothing. Thoughts of food made my stomach growl. I was famished, *una fame da lupo* as the Italians would say.

After I'd been introduced to two sets of cousins, and various aunts and uncles, and forgotten who was who, we all piled into the vehicles and drove down to the restaurant at Porto Metello.

The Ristorante Metello, Giacomo told me, despite its humble appearance from the outside, was the finest the island of Vignetti had to offer and one of the best in all the Italian islands.

The family was ushered to a large room at the back, near a large brick oven where whole chickens were roasting over the fire. The long refectory table was covered with a pink tablecloth, the settings were of silver, the wineglasses of crystal. Individual cloth napkins were artfully arranged in the goblets. Unexpected elegance. *Expensive* written in every detail.

I felt Gene Harrell's money in my shirt pocket, with a strange mixture of worry and curiosity. I was worried about the expense of the upcoming meal and curious as to what else was in the man's wallet. Damn the jailer for not letting me bring it.

No one came to take our orders. Instead, the *capo di famiglia* ordered for everyone—("Don't worry," Giacomo told me again, "you're a guest of the family")—first an assortment of appetizers, then a delightful first course of *tortellini alla panna* followed by two main courses of fish and chicken, with side dishes of roast potatoes, peas, golden baked fennel, and tomatoes *alla Siciliana*. A simple salad with a mustard-flavored dressing came next, and then cheese and fruit. And all was accompanied by large bottles of red wine ranging from local table wines to a light Grumello and a more generous Gattinara.

The meal was a culinary delight—or as Giacomo academically put it, "A Lucullean feast." Each bite was like a tonic, soothing both the mind and body.

Despite my maneuverings, I'd been placed at the table between two cousins of Donata and Giacomo, a young man named Rafaello, still in the *liceo,* and an older married woman who asked me to call her Silvia. I'd hoped to sit next to Donata or Giacomo. I had too many questions I wanted to ask.

Everyone addressed me as "Signor" Harrell, despite my requests to use Gene. I was plied with questions about the accident at sea and had to speak to the group as a whole. It was all very awkward and I was happy when the conversation became general and I could relax and withdraw into myself.

The pleasures of the meal were undermining my resolve to wait out the week in jail. For a moment, I pondered ways of slipping off and making my way to the port at Mirabella, where I could hire a boat to take me to another island or the mainland. Two small details held me back. One, I didn't have enough money to hire anything. Two, I couldn't leave Giacomo and Donata holding the bag for my escape.

When the coffee came, the kids left the table and went

behind the restaurant, where an outdoor, cement-paved patio, strung with festive paper and colored lights, provided room to dance. Apparently they'd brought their own tapes to use in the restaurant's amplified tape deck. Rafaello and two of his sisters argued over who to play first. The sisters won out and inserted a recent cassette of Adriano Celetano.

I kept my eye on Donata. If I could get her alone, I wanted to work the conversation around to Carlo Spugna and MIO. I had to find out more about him and his various operations. Anything that would help me later. His company had to be what Wanda was referring to. Nothing else made sense.

But Donata was still surrounded by family, all talking animatedly. It would be rude to insert myself. I looked around and spotted Giacomo coming out of a *gabinetto*. I caught his eyes, flicked my head, and he walked over to me.

"*Bella festa, eh?*" he said, and I smiled.

"*Magnifica.*"

I paused, looking for an opening. A casual comment about tourists or foreign yachts. Were there any Americans on the island? A group of three perhaps?

Before I could find the right words, Giacomo dropped his voice. His tone was serious.

"I'm sorry to hear about what happened with the *vice-pretore onorario*. The man is a fool—and a friend of the Mancini family. He treats all foreigners as if they were terrorists. But don't worry. We'll help you like you helped us."

I stared at Giacomo, puzzled.

"In the *taverna*. I saw what you did to Beppe's arm. You helped save my life." He paused and then said, "You should be free now. The *vice-pretore onorario* is afraid to do anything when the *pretore* is gone."

I shrugged. "He didn't look afraid."

"He hides his cowardice behind a show of bravado. Do you know your Latin theater? The braggart Spanish captain? That's him."

I smiled. Giacomo was testing me. Most educated Italians I'd ever met, including Wanda, considered their educational system vastly superior to that of the New World. I wasn't about to get into a contest of classical allusions.

"I spent all day yesterday trying to help you," Giacomo went on. "Reading law books."

I looked at him in surprise, and he said, "A matter of student curiosity."

I didn't know if I liked my predicament being a matter of someone else's curiosity—whether student or professional lawyer.

He spread his hands, palms up, and shrugged. "In recent years, the government's given the police expanded powers. Because of the terrorist threat. You're being held under one of the new preventive measures. A *misura di prevenzione*. Doesn't take a judge. The police can do it on their own. The *vice-pretore* was afraid to countermand it."

I nodded. "Thanks for your efforts anyway."

He pursed his cheeks. "I went through most of the *Codice di procedura penale*—five volumes. The fifth deals with the jurisdictional rapport between our system and foreign authorities. Six hundred seventy-five articles just for that."

I could see the frustration in his eyes. "You'd have been better off if they exercised the *divieto di soggiorno*—just kicked you off the island and forbade you to return."

I was about to say that would've been all right with me, and then thought better of it. The Pellico family had been too nice a host.

Giacomo pursed his lips. "All the guy did to Cecco

and Beppe was fine them for disturbing the peace and let them go.''

I shook my head. ''They got away with a fine?''

''You would have too if you'd been Italian.''

I nodded and then looked around, trying to find an excuse to slip away. I didn't want to discuss the Italian penal system with Giacomo. I was in jail and it looked like I'd stay there until word came from the Australian High Commission in Rome. And what could they say? That, yes, a Gene Harrell existed, that he had an Australian passport. No one had bothered to take my fingerprints. And I doubted the Australian government had prints for Gene Harrell. That is, unless he had a criminal record. So how could they prove or disprove my claim?

My breath caught in my throat. Something strange was going on. Why didn't I see it before? I looked at Giacomo. ''I think the *vice-pretore* is just holding me until the *pretore* himself returns. They aren't checking out my ID with the High Commission. You're right. He's just afraid of doing anything on his own. They don't have any reason to hold me. They should be helping me.''

Giacomo's brow furrowed in thought. ''I'm not so sure. Perhaps they are helping you. Perhaps they've simply requested a duplicate passport.''

''Mmm, I doubt it. I think I'd have to go directly to the embassy myself. I'm not sure how they handle that.'' I paused, thinking. ''Unless they sent my driver's license to Rome.''

Over Giacomo's shoulder, I saw Donata make her way toward the outdoor patio with one of the other girls.

''Why don't we go outside for a breath of fresh air?'' I said to Giacomo. ''I'll be enclosed soon enough.''

In the patio, it took me ten minutes to get Donata alone, and I had to agree to dance with her first. She wouldn't take my battered body as an excuse. It wasn't that I minded dancing with her. I was just more eager to talk—and talking was impossible while we danced. The music was too loud.

When the song was over, I asked if she'd mind taking a walk along the harbor. "There're some things I want to talk about," I said.

She looked at me enigmatically and then nodded. "Okay, but let me leave first. It wouldn't look too good to walk out together. I don't want everyone talking."

She saw my look of surprise and hastily added, "It's a small island and some people are still in the dark ages."

Her concern provided an opening for conversation, and when we were alone, walking along the road near the beach, I asked her about her boyfriend.

She kept her head down, the soft waves of her hair hiding her face, and tugged at her skirt with both hands.

"It's over," she said brusquely and quickened her pace. A moment later I saw her wipe away a tear.

I felt sorry for having upset her and kept my curiosity in check. It wasn't the opening I'd thought it would be. We walked in silence.

But a few minutes later, she gritted her teeth and spoke. "I just can't take it anymore. Pietro's just like Giacomo. All either can talk about is how much they hate the other."

She raised her head and looked at me, her eyes now clear. "I should have realized it was over when I came back this summer. Everything had changed. Pietro was different, I was different. We went through the motions but—" She shook her head. "It was too late."

I listened without responding, unsure of what to say. Consolation from a stranger didn't seem appropriate.

We were already at the end of the harbor. "I think we'd better return," Donata said, and I nodded. We stood for a minute facing the sun, which was an hour or two from setting. Near the point, the wind was stronger.

80

Donata's skirt and blouse outlined the form of her body, and her hair streamed over her shoulders.

"You look like the tragic heroine of a nineteenth-century French romance," I said, wondering afterward if she'd realized I meant that as a compliment. I didn't really know what French romances were like—I just wanted to say she was beautiful.

She laughed, and then said, "We may have a storm tonight. We need some rain." And then she slipped her arm through mine.

No need to explain. I took a deep breath, trying to absorb as many sensations of the moment as possible. Dull green waves smashed on the rocks and the wind picked up the salty spray, showering us with a light mist. When the heavier gusts came, dabs of froth were tossed from rock to rock. The boats drawn up on the beach were creaking in the wind, their multicolored hulls laid keel-up by the provident fishermen. Towering thunderclouds loomed on the horizon far to the west.

We turned and headed back the way we'd come. I slowed my pace while my mind rushed over what I had to say. I didn't have much time now to ask about Carlo Spugna.

"Working should help you forget Pietro," I said, by way of transition. "You'll be busy. Time will pass."

She managed a smile. "And we all know the saying, right? Time heals all wounds."

A moment of sadness overcame me. Ask about Spugna, my brain said, but my heart was locked on the proverb. Time. That was something Wanda hadn't had enough of. I tried to harden my heart. Spugna was still alive and Wanda was dead. He had all the time in the world. I was going to have to change that. I couldn't let myself wallow in self-pity. I couldn't give in to the feelings that Donata aroused in my heart.

I cleared my throat. "You said the other day you liked your job. Do you have much contact with Spugna?"

"With Carlo?" She nodded. "He's a very busy man, but he loves his children. He tries to make it out to the villa every night. The main office is in Valletta, and he stays in the family house there sometimes. But only when he has to."

"He travels by ferry?" I knew the trip from the island of Malta to that of Gozo didn't take long.

"Sometimes. If he wants time to think. Otherwise he flies his own helicopter. From the airport at Luqa. But it's not much faster."

I tried to keep my tone casual. "What's the villa like? It must be nice." The curiosity of the traveler.

"You'd love it, Gene. It's very beautiful. You should come and visit."

For the first time, she'd addressed me by Gene rather than Signor Harrell, and it felt good—even though it wasn't my real name.

She looked at me, her green eyes glistening with excitement. "I could show you around San Lawrenz and the island. On a weekend. I'm free every Saturday and Sunday. You could stay with us at the villa. There's always a guest room available."

"I'd like that," I said. "What's this Carlo like? I've heard some bad things about him."

"Lies," she said emphatically. "His enemies tell lies about him. *Zi'* Carlo is very nice. You'd like him too. Maybe he could even help you find a job."

Zi' Carlo. I'd heard her say that the other day. *Zi'*. *Zio!* Was that just a term of affection?

I stopped and then caught her eyes as she swung around to face me. We'd reached the restaurant and I had to ask before we got inside. "You said, *'Zi' Carlo.'* Spugna . . . is he your—"

"My uncle," she said. "*Mamma* is his sister."

I walked into the restaurant, feeling a sense of dismay. And then I saw Giacomo standing in the anteroom with two police officers. My heart fell. We'd been caught. It was my fault. I never should have left the jail. Now Giacomo and his uncle Luigi were in trouble. The irony of the sudden realization that my jailer was related to Carlo Spugna left me dumbfounded.

Giacomo stepped forward, his face grim.

"What's the matter?" Donata asked, frightened.

Giacomo's dark eyes darted around the room. He didn't want to look at me.

"What is it, Giacomo?" I said. "Don't worry. It's my fault, not yours."

His eyes locked on mine. "They've come to arrest you for murder," he said.

8

The interrogation began in a cramped room that smelled as if a rat had died in the ventilation system. I'd expected a simple whitewashed cell; instead the room was jammed with cabinets, medical paraphernalia, an examination table, and other accoutrements of a small clinic. What I thought was a primitive lie-detector machine, looking like an instrument of torture, rested ominously on a stainless-steel trolley near the sink.

My clothes lay in a disheveled pile near the door, and I was seated in a metal chair against the only bare wall. The arresting officers had gone off duty and I was being questioned by two men, a thin pale fellow with glasses and slicked-back greasy hair—I called him Signor Occhiali to myself—and an older, balding man with a shiny nose and puffy cheeks. Him I addressed silently as Signor Paffuto. The names helped lessen my fear.

Two hours into the interrogation, as night fell, they brought a table-clamped lamp into the room and directed the beam into my face. After a while, a headache began to build behind my eyes. When I closed them, the lamp glared white through the eyelids, like the headlight of a locomotive.

Sometime in the night, they turned on a wall-set air conditioner that blew cold air over my naked body. I tried to relax into the chill, imagining the breeze as an ice pack for my aching head, but soon I was shivering violently. My head continued to burn with fever.

They wouldn't let me sleep. The two men rotated in

and out of the room, their shifts lasting for what I imagined to be two or three hours. The voices changed but the questions and accusations were always the same.

"Who is he?"

"Who's who?"

"The man you killed."

"I don't know. I didn't kill anyone."

"Why'd you do it?"

"Why'd I do what?"

"Why'd you kill him?"

"I didn't. I don't know who the guy is."

"You two rented a boat. Why?"

"I rented it by myself. I was alone. Ask the guy at the boat rental in Milazzo, he'll remember."

"You expect us to believe you just fell out of a boat all by yourself?"

"I was drunk."

"So you killed him in an argument."

"He wasn't on the boat, damn it."

"You were both drunk, fighting. You shot him. Before he died he grabbed you, knocked you overboard."

I shook my head adamantly. "No. I went out by myself. I don't know who he is."

They'd taken me to see the body. It was the real Gene Harrell all right, the same suit, the same build, but the features on his face had lost their last touch with reality. I couldn't even imagine what he'd looked like when alive.

At first, I'd thought of telling the truth. But I was afraid they wouldn't believe me. And then, once I'd started to lie, the truth became impossible. I thought of Carlo Spugna. He had to know who Derek Stone was—at least by name. But he wouldn't know Gene Harrell. I'd assumed Harrell's identity and I wanted to keep it as long as it was useful to me. And I had to find the three Americans Harrell was supposed to meet.

Either way, whether I claimed to be Derek Stone or

Gene Harrell, the police would think I'd killed the man whose body had washed back to shore with the incoming tide. They'd asked me over and over again why I thought the body had ended up near the same beach where the Pellicos had found me. Coincidence, I said. And wasn't that as close to the truth as anything? Except that whoever killed Gene Harrell had tried to kill me too. No, that wasn't a coincidence. But I couldn't let the police know.

The dead-rat smell was overpowering and my headache grew worse. The questions continued to batter my ears.

"Where did you meet him?"

"I'm feeling sick."

"Why'd you kill him? Was it an accident? You were drunk, right?"

"I'm sick, I tell you. Dizzy. I'm going to throw up."

"Who is he?"

Damn the assholes. I slumped forward and puked.

"*Porca Madonna!*"

I heard his voice as if through a muted trumpet. The sound reverberated in my head like a timpani drum and I vomited again. I was on my hands and knees. My festa was now his. Despite my dizziness, there was a certain amount of grim satisfaction at the thought.

And then another wave of nausea crested and crashed over me. I retched until I felt as if I were turning inside out, and then rolled to the side, my nude body collapsing onto the cold floor. I took a shallow breath and tried to sink into the pain, focusing on it until there was nothing else.

I was in the launch again, heard the voices from far away, couldn't make out the words. I started to shake. I didn't want to see the demons. Didn't want to see Gene Harrell's head with the bullet holes. That was *my* head now.

I struggled from the grasp of the horrifying vision.

Better to feel the body's pain than the mind's. My stomach, in slow motion, took one last somersault. A series of dry heaves wrenched my lungs and left me weak and breathless. My chest felt like a washcloth wrung out by a strong-fisted washerwoman. "Kill me," I think I screamed. "*Uccidimi!*" If I'd had a gun I'd have done it myself.

They carried me to another room and left me lying under a cold shower while they cleaned up the mess. I tried not to think. I'd never felt such pain in my head. My mind screamed to die. I didn't think I could take much more before I'd dash my brains out on the cement floor.

For a moment, panic seized me. There was a bullet lodged in my brain. I should be in a hospital not a jail. I should be under a surgeon's knife. What was happening to me? I moaned and forced myself to breathe slowly and deeply. I'd gone a lifetime without headaches and now the damn things were getting even.

Sometime later, both men returned and led me in a crouch back to my original cell. They threw my clothes on the floor. I lay down on the bed. I was too exhausted to get dressed, the heat in the cell too oppressive. What seemed hours of torment later, after a futile search for a position that would ease the pain, I finally fell asleep.

I came out of the blackness to find someone shaking me. The back of my head was numb. I'd fallen asleep on my back, with my neck crimped over the edge of the bed. My head was too heavy to lift without the help of a hand.

"Hurry, Signor Harrell." Another rough shaking. I looked up, trying to focus on the figure leaning over me. It was Giacomo, his hair backlit by the light streaming in the window high up on the east wall.

"Get dressed. We've only got a minute."

I stared at him numbly.

"*Un minuto?*"

"*Sì, sbrigati.* Hurry!" He handed me my clothes. "Donata's at the restaurant, talking to *Zio* Luigi."

Zio Luigi? I rubbed my head and then saw the keys in his hand. My eyes widened. *Zio* Luigi was on duty.

The keys! I had a chance to get out!

Giacomo looked anxiously toward the open door.

"Hurry! Luigi'll be bringing the food back. We have to get out of here."

I had my pants and shoes on and slipped my arms through the shirt. Giacomo grabbed my arm and pulled me toward the door. "Let's go! We've come to help you, just like I promised."

We ran up the corridor toward the jailer's office. I stopped. "My wallet."

Giacomo looked out the door and then turned. "I've already got it. Come on, the car's down the road."

I followed him out the door, squinting against the harsh glare, and we ran to the right over the rough cobblestones.

The car was parked at a side street next to a still-shuttered pharmacy. In the window a smiling, cardboard woman held a box of Bayer's *aspirina* in one hand and two white tablets in the other. "*L'analgesico che scaccia il mal di testa,*" the logo said.

I felt like jumping through the window and grabbing the cardboard aspirin.

Giacomo didn't wait for Donata. He gunned the motor, popped the clutch, and turned the corner, tires squealing. My head fought the pull of gravity, but I didn't feel like complaining.

"Where're the police?" I asked.

"Eating breakfast."

"What about Donata?"

He shrugged. "She can take care of herself."

He avoided my stare and added, "She's innocent. What can they do to her?"

"Innocent? She was supposed to leave the island last night."

"Don't worry about her. She missed the ferry. She'll leave tonight." He glanced in the rearview mirror. "There'll be no problem."

I didn't like that but I said nothing. The car picked up speed. We were on the same road they'd brought me to Mirabella on.

"Where are we going?"

"To Leporetto. And then the hills."

The hills. How long would it be before the police tracked me down?

As if reading my mind, Giacomo said, "No one'll find you there. You can stay with the family that watches my father's flocks."

We lapsed into silence. Giacomo concentrated on the road and the rearview mirror. I spent my time fighting the pull of gravity on curves and the jolts that threatened to snap my neck every time we hit a pothole, and thought about all they'd done for me. Was it just gratitude, as Giacomo said, or hatred of the Mancinis?

At one point Giacomo reached into his back pocket and handed me Gene Harrell's wallet. I held it like an icon. It was finally mine to keep.

"Let me see if everything's here," I said and opened the wallet.

The credit card slots held two cards. The one with the five-orbed crown was a business card identifying Gene Harrell as a management consultant for the Australian Transportation Corporation. The title and company didn't tell me much, but it was a start. The guy might have been working for the CIA but he wasn't American.

The second card was a credit card for the Commonwealth Bank of Australia.

I opened the photo case. The jailer'd been right. The plastic windows were empty. Strange. For a so-called business man far from home, Harrell had been carrying the bare minimum. I counted the currency. There were six bills, three notes of ten thousand lire and three of one thousand.

I was putting back the bills when I noticed the ink below the picture of Michelangelo on one of the larger bills. The bank note was an older, 1962 issue, one of the bills replaced in 1976 with a note of different design and smaller dimensions. I looked closer. There were a series of numbers with small dots above each, ending in letters. For a moment I was puzzled until I realized what the dots were. They were mathematical symbols. The numbers were geodetic coordinates, stated in degrees, minutes, and tenths of a minute. I wasn't a navigator, but I knew the latter represented a precision of approximately a tenth of a nautical mile or better. A precise location. The numbers themselves—36° 12′ 47″ N, 13° 39′ 20″ E— meant nothing to me, but I made up my mind to find someone who could tell me. It was the first piece of luck I'd had since Wanda's death. Thank God, the bill was unwieldy and the jailer hadn't spent it. I could just see the restaurant owner waving both hands and telling the jailer he wanted one of the *normal* bills.

"Everything there?"

I looked up at Giacomo and nodded. "Except the driver's license. And I guess some of my money was spent for food, but everything else is okay."

"I noticed the business card. You work in transportation?"

I needed time to think, so I said I hadn't realized he read English. He said he'd studied it in school, but couldn't really speak it. He wanted to go to England some day to improve his fluency.

"That's how I learned Italian," I said. "Living in

Italy. I was married to an Italian for a while." I put the wallet in my back left pocket. "The card's an old one. I've worked a lot of jobs. Most recently I've been working as a commercial oil-field diver. My training's in oil-field engineering."

"That's how you'd heard of Carlo Spugna?"

I nodded. It would've been a good time to ask more about MIO's operations, but I was too tired to carry on a lengthy conversation. And I had to find out about the other Americans.

"There must be other foreigners on the island, right? Tourists?" I asked.

He shrugged. "Occasionally. Why?"

"I need to get in touch with some people. Three Americans." I looked away from him, following the road with my eyes, trying to sound casual. "I don't know who they are, but I heard they're looking for a diver."

He shook his head. "Haven't heard of anyone. But I'll keep my ears open. Let you know if they show up."

"I really need the job," I said, and then managed a grin. "Good way to get me off the island, too."

We drove for over an hour, climbing, dropping down around hairpin turns, and then climbing again. The sun, which struck us from the left through the open windows at the start, slowly moved higher until finally it was straight overhead and the front seat was in shade. Summer blazed through the windows, the wind hot and humid. My shirt was drenched with sweat.

At one point, seeing my slitted eyes and the grimace on my face, Giacomo loaned me his sunglasses. I lay back and tried to sleep, but the tension in my body kept me in a state of vibration. I felt as if I'd drunk five cups of coffee on an empty stomach. I was too tired and too wound up to sleep.

The village of Leporetto sat on the southwestern tip of the island, on a flat, limestone plateau overlooking a precipitous drop to the sea. In the distance, in the direction of Sicily, we could see strips of dirty clouds, the pollution-tinged effluvia of Etna that later in the day would darken and thicken as the *scirocco* winds drove them to the east. Leporetto itself was surrounded by steep, stony fields that gave way to a rugged mountainous terrain with Laricio pines, sumac, and other Mediterranean vegetation struggling for existence in the cracks and crevices.

Giacomo bought two bottles of *acqua minerale,* four rosette *panini,* and two hectograms of prosciutto, and we started to climb, following a narrow path that twisted steadily upward. The air grew cooler as we ascended, and soon we were high enough to see the dusty red haze building up over Sicily. The strips of clouds had massed into a thick fleece and the hot angry wind was already beginning to push the particle-laden air into small but expanding bulbs of cumulonimbus.

We climbed without speaking, our breath coming in short harsh gasps as the air thinned. A peregrine falcon, drifting on the rising air currents, followed our ascent for a while and then disappeared. The path itself was littered with dried sheep dung, and I could see where the flocks had eaten the lower leaves on the scrubby holm oaks and myrtle bushes.

Near four o'clock in the afternoon we stopped and rested beneath an immense granite boulder that sheltered a patch of blue lupins.

"Let's eat," Giacomo said. He pulled the crumpled package of prosciutto from the sack and handed me one of the *panini.*

"Just a minute," he said. "I've got a knife you can cut it with."

I sliced the loaf and stuffed it with prosciutto. "You take this one," I said. "I'll fix another for myself." When I finished the second loaf, I gave him his knife, asked, "Where's the pasta and wine?" and we both managed to laugh.

"Wine wouldn't help your headache any," Giacomo pointed out, and I nodded.

"It's getting better. I just need some good sleep." I grinned. "I thought I'd got rid of it once, but it keeps coming back."

Giacomo looked up the trail that wound to our left around the boulder. "It's not far now," he said. "We'll eat better tonight with Pino and Mirra. Bread, cheese, wine, roast lamb, milk if you want. It'll be another feast like yesterday."

"Hmm." I didn't know how ready I'd be for that. Yesterday's feast had ended up on a cement floor.

I finished my sandwich and asked how often the shepherds came down to Leporetto.

"Not for months. In May they pack in whatever they'll need for the summer. Flour, wine, spices, pasta. There's plenty of milk and meat from the flock."

"I thought I heard a dog barking a while ago when we came out on that ledge," I said. "Are we getting close?"

Giacomo nodded. "Another hour maybe. I'm not sure where the flock is. Probably in the meadows near Punta Rossa. That's one of the tallest peaks in the island. Pino and Mirra usually set up house in a cave below the peak. You'll like it."

"What are these shepherds like?"

Giacomo laughed. "They're kids, barely in their twenties—but they've got three children of their own. Two twin boys and a girl. I guess the boys—Astolfo and Lando—must be about five now, and Nina's a couple years younger. They'll be a little shy around you."

I'd been thinking about this hideout and I had a few questions. We'd finished the snack and got up to move on. "How long do you think I should stay up here? I'd like to get off the island as soon as I can."

"It's dangerous right now. The police will have the harbors watched. It was the Mancinis who accused you of murder." He shook his head, scoffing. "Just trying to get back at us. Donata said you weren't a murderer. I'll keep an eye out and come back for you when things look okay. You're safe up here. Pino's dogs will let him know we're coming long before we see them. And they'll do the same if the police come after you. Pino knows these mountains better than anyone on the island. With his help, no one'll ever find you."

The sun was at the horizon—glinting below storm clouds—when we arrived at the upper-elevation meadows and found the flock. I hung back while Giacomo talked to Pino, a skin-and-bones kid with hollow eyes and long black hair. It was hard to imagine he was a father. While they talked quietly in dialect, two of Pino's sheep dogs sniffed me over and then lay down by their master. Bocca and Rugo, he'd called them. In a minute he gave them a signal and the two tore off around the flock.

Giacomo turned. "Come with me, Signor Harrell, and I'll introduce you to Mirra and the kids. They're in the cave."

He clapped Pino on the back. "I'll tell her you're coming. *Pensaci! Una festa stasera!*"

Mirra was sitting outside the cave, tending a fire under a spit that held a lamb shank. A pot of boiling water hung from a tripod over the flames. I could see the bundle of spaghetti that would go in once Pino arrived.

A rooster and three hens pecked the ground, cautiously watching a little girl, who every few seconds would giggle and then make an awkward spurt in an attempt to catch them. The boys were not in sight.

Giacomo called to announce our presence, and Mirra poked the fire once and then stood. She wore an ankle-length heavy cotton sheath, and I was surprised to see she was pregnant. She didn't look over twenty, a pretty creature with dark eyes, delicate features, and long black hair that was braided on both sides but not in the back.

She smiled at Giacomo and then called her daughter, who came over and hid behind her legs.

Giacomo pushed me forward.

"Nina, questo è Zio Gino."

I couldn't help grinning. At least he hadn't introduced me as *Nonno*. Better to be an uncle than a grandfather. And then the irony of the matter hit me. I was just like Carlo Spugna. He was an uncle too.

I spent three days in the mountains. In the day I went with Pino to herd the flocks and at night I played with the boys, Astolfo and Lando, and with Nina. Mirra and Pino would watch with amusement as the kids clambered over me. It wasn't often that an uncle who was willing to play showed up out of nowhere.

On Friday, August 22 by my calculation, Giacomo showed up late in the afternoon. He met me and Pino where the flock was grazing and drew me aside.

"Good news," he said. "I've found the people you mentioned."

"Where? You sure?"

He was surprised by my questions. "Well, they're American and they need a crew member for a salvage operation. A diver. That's what you said, right? They've anchored in Mirabella harbor. They don't speak Italian, so they want someone who's bilingual."

"Great," I said. "How'd you find out?"

"The harbormaster posted a notice asking for help."

I nodded thoughtfully, trying to mask my curiosity. "Did you talk to them? Where's the salvage job?"

"They wouldn't say, except it's not near the island." He grinned. "I made sure of that. So, what are they after? Maybe buried treasure, eh?" He laughed and poked me in the arm. "I told them I'd bring you tonight."

"You're sure they're Americans? Three of them?" I don't know why I asked. If they were looking for a diver, they had to be the people Harrell was supposed to meet. Giacomo was going to start wondering why it mattered so much.

But he simply nodded and said, "Two men and a woman. I spoke with the captain, Signor Blike, a big man, gray beard down to here." He held his hand across his collar bone. "I told him you were perfect for the job. Just what he was looking for. He said they'd be in port until tomorrow morning and if you weren't there they'd leave without you. But don't worry, there's plenty of time. We'll leave when it gets dark."

Giacomo stayed for dinner. The kids cried when he told them *Zio* Gino had to leave. I wanted to tell them I'd return, that I'd come back next time with gifts. Give them an illusion, some hope. But I couldn't. I didn't know where I was going and I doubted I'd ever return.

9

"Flashlights," I said.

We stopped and looked down across the slope.

Giacomo extinguished his own light. "Where?"

I grabbed his arm in the darkness and pointed. "Along that ridge."

A waning half-moon shed a glimmer of light through a layer of scattered clouds. The path was barely visible, the trees and shrubs dark masses against the rock.

"I don't see them," Giacomo said.

I strained my eyes, trying to find the spot where I'd seen the beams. "Maybe they've gone around a bend. I'm sure they were flashlights. Two, I think."

"*Merda.*"

We stood in silence, waiting.

After a few minutes, Giacomo whispered, "There's another way down, but it's rugged. It'd take a rope and grapnel to manage it." He paused. "Or we could go up. Come down when they've gone."

"I want to get out of the mountains. I need to get off the island. We don't have that much time."

"Shh." Giacomo pulled me to a crouch. "There. Below that overhang. They've stopped."

"I see them." One of the flashlights was suddenly extinguished, the other played weakly over the boulders along the path. "Maybe they're resting."

Giacomo nodded, and then the features on his face suddenly dissolved into shadows as the moon slid behind a cloud. With his dark slacks and green dress shirt he blended into the shifting layers of darkness.

"My shirt's too light," I said. "They'll see me a mile off."

"Take mine."

"No. I couldn't. *Grazie lo stesso*. What would you wear?"

He didn't respond.

I wanted to move in some direction. Giacomo seemed paralyzed, lost in thought.

"Can we get by them?" I asked.

"Possibly. If we could find a good hiding place off the path. Did you see if they had a dog?"

Shit, I hadn't even thought of dogs. "I'm not sure. But if they have dogs and we go higher, they'll find us."

"No. We go through the sheep and then up rocks. A dog would be worthless."

The shot caught us by surprise, first a metallic zing and then, nearly instantaneous, the sharp crack of a rifle. Behind us the rock splintered.

I hit the ground and scrambled for a boulder toward the left. Giacomo had lunged for the base of the cliff, away from the line of fire below us.

"You okay, Giacomo?" My voice came out with a shaky hiss.

"*Sì, sì*. Stay down."

He scrambled over to me. "They tricked us, the bastards!" His voice was harsh and strained. "I know them. That's not the police. That's the Mancinis. Pietro blames me for Donata. They left one guy with the light and the others moved up in darkness. They're after me, not you."

What? How'd he know that? "Maybe the police organized the villagers to look for us."

He lowered his voice, calmer now. "It doesn't matter.

At night they can't tell who's who. They'll shoot at either of us. We've got to get back to Pino.''

I hesitated. "Giacomo, I'm not going back. They split up to trick us, we should do the same.''

Giacomo peered over the edge of the slope. "I don't like it.'' He paused, and then said vehemently, "We're safe in the mountains.''

"I have to get to that boat tonight.''

"We don't have time to argue.'' His voice was cool. "Whoever shot at us is working higher.''

"Go then. When you're out of the line of fire, make some noise. It'll help me if they think we're both moving up.''

I felt Giacomo's hand reach for mine. "Good luck,'' he said, his voice softening. I felt something cold pressed into my palm, a set of keys. "If you make it to Leporetto, the Fiat is parked by the church on the central square. Make sure it's not watched before you use it.''

He pressed my hand and then began to move off in a crouch. "Thanks, Giacomo,'' I called quietly after him. I wanted to tell him I appreciated everything he'd done for me, but he'd already slipped into the darkness.

I looked up at the sky. The clouds, under the impetus of a strong breeze, appeared to be thinning. If the moon came out, I'd be a sitting duck.

I tried to remember the location of the shot. How far away was it? The echo in the hills had distorted my perceptions. It had to have come from one of the ridges below us. But I couldn't remember how the path went at that point.

To my right, a sheer cliff face provided no easy access. Below me, to the left, the mountain fell away at an angle, but the slope was strewn with shattered rock and desert-like vegetation. If I moved that way, they'd hear every step.

I had no choice. I got to my feet and began running

down the trail, racing toward the man who'd fired the rifle, seeking a cleft in the rock wall, a mass of boulders, some place to hide. I tried to muffle the sound of my feet. The path was packed dirt, covered with pine needles from the trees at the crown of the hill. The crunch of my feet came to me like the hard panting of a dog.

It happened so fast, so unexpectedly, that I had no time to think. The figure of a man rose up in the middle of the path. In instinctive defense, I raised both arms, screamed, and plowed square into the man. My forearm caught him in the collarbone and his head snapped foward with an audible crack as his trunk went backward. We went down together and I slammed into his chest, his breath bursting out of him with a sharp smell of garlic.

I was too stunned to think of hitting him again. And then I realized I didn't have to. His body jerked once, gave way to a palsied shaking, and fell limp. I put my ear to his mouth. He was unconscious but alive, his breathing shallow. I was afraid I'd broken his neck.

I rolled off the man and crawled around on my hands and knees, looking for the rifle. I couldn't find it—it must have slid somewhere down the slope among the rocks. I swore softly. I didn't want to kill anyone, but in a tight pinch a bullet over my pursuers' heads might have slowed them down. No help now.

I got to my feet and than a sharp pain in my ribs doubled me over. Damn! I eased back up, gritting my teeth. I didn't have time to be self-indulgent. The next shot could end all my pain.

Holding my left arm across my chest, I worked my way down the trail. In a few minutes, I came to a small grove of oak trees, where shepherds and flocks bedded down for the night on their spring migration into the upper elevation plateaus. The next stretch, I remembered, consisted of a series of cutbacks. The route, with its hairpin turns, would be dangerous. The narrow path

100

twisted along a massive outcropping of granite that protruded out of the mountain like the muscular shoulder of a giant and plummeted a good two hundred feet before it crumbled away into a more gentle slope.

I couldn't risk meeting armed men with no chance of cover. I headed into the cluster of trees. The moon illuminated the clearing with a weak half-light.

And then, barely fifty feet away, back toward the path, I heard voices. Two men speaking in dialect. Islanders. I slipped behind one of the scrawny oak trees and looked up, considering a climb, but the leaves weren't thick enough to offer sufficient protection. I lay flat on the ground and tried to calm my pounding heart. The voices drifted toward me softly, camouflaged in part by the rustling of the leaves.

"Fermiamoci qui."

Shit! They were stopping. The two figures were clearly silhouetted against the skyline, both armed with rifles. The shorter fellow was breathing heavily. He sat down on the path and laid the rifle against a rock.

"Ne vuoi?" The taller figure, still standing, offered something to his companion.

"Certo." The man took the wine pouch and drank deeply. He wiped his lips, handed the pouch back, and said, "You think Dario has them pinned down?"

The other man grunted. "Who knows? Let's just hope he's smart enough to know it's us coming. If they've run, he'll be after them."

"Eh già!" The tired man sighed. "You may have to go on alone, Sergio. I can't take this pace. Dario may need help."

"They're trapped. They can only go up. If we get Pino's wife, she'll tell us where they are."

"She won't talk."

"Point a gun at her little girl's head and she will."

They stood for a moment without speaking. Finally

the tall one slung the pouch over his shoulder and cleared his throat.

"You rest here. Watch the trail. But don't shoot unless you're sure it's not us. I'll try to catch up with Dario."

"*Va bene.*"

"If we're not back by daylight, go on back down. We'll meet you later at the farm."

The asthmatic fellow lay back with his head against a rock, and the man he'd called Sergio disappeared around the corner. I stared at the dim form of the bulky Italian. I could hear the rasp of his breath from where I lay. He didn't sound too good. If I could get close enough, he'd be no match for me. But I had to wait long enough for his friend to be out of earshot.

I waited for what seemed a half hour, trying to ignore the mosquitoes that swarmed around my sweating face, and then crawled toward the down side of the clearing. The distance from the edge of the grove to the path was at least twenty-five feet, too much to cover surreptitiously. So I planned to get below the man as much as possible and come up along the cliff face rather than straight out of the trees. Maybe I could make him think I was one of his friends.

I inched my way over the rough ground, and ten minutes later I'd reached the point where I was going to have to come out in the open. I hesitated and then got slowly to my feet, my back sliding up the side of the cliff. Every time I straightened my frame I could feel a twinge of pain in my left rib cage. I'd either bruised or broken some ribs.

The fat man didn't stir. I made it upright, took a deep breath, and was about to step forward casually, when I heard a snort and saw his body twitch.

My heart thudded in my chest and I froze. My eyes and ears strained to pick up the slightest impulse. And

102

then the fellow snored loudly and I saw his head jerk and slowly loll to the side.

The guy was asleep!

Step by step, holding my breath, my body tense, I moved toward him in the dim light, praying I wouldn't stumble and wake him. When I was about five feet away, close enough to attack if necessary, he stirred and I froze again. I could hear the blood pounding through the veins in my temples. The moonlight struck his face and my eyes widened. It was my jailer, Luigi. Giacomo's uncle! This wasn't one of the Mancinis, it was the police.

Luigi grunted like a pig, and the breeze wafted the smell of wine to my nostrils. The guy was dead to the world.

I looked at his rifle and saw that his right arm lay across the butt. I didn't want to wake him. Why wake a man if it meant you might have to kill him? And I didn't really need a weapon. Better to sneak by and have them think I was still in the mountains. I stepped over the recumbent form and moved down the trail, slowly at first, and then, as I rounded a bend, faster.

Damn! I thought. I'd done it! I'd gotten away. It felt as good as striking a gusher.

The Fiat was parked beneath an ash tree near one of the square's two ornate lamps that shed a warm yellow glow on the cobblestones. I stopped near a phone booth and scoured the vehicles parked around the square. There were only seven cars. Probably the village's total. The *piazza* was deserted, the only sound the cooing of pigeons nesting on the ledge of the building behind the booth.

The center of the square held a small octagonal fountain. Water trickled out of the mouth of a pudgy cupid sitting on a large sphere in the middle. The water had a stale taste, as if it had set out in the sun for a day or two, but I took a drink and then washed my face.

The car started easily. I circled halfway around the square and pulled onto the road leading to Mirabella. A sigh of tiredness, tinged with relief, eased from me. The road was deserted.

I drove with the windows open, listening to the pleasant whine of the tires. The warm breeze ruffled my hair and I ran my hand over my face. Another couple of days and I'd have a good beard started. I turned on the convenience light and looked in the rearview mirror. A grizzled face stared back at me. What a sight! So that was Gene Harrell. I almost laughed. He was getting worse every day, but I didn't care.

"Nice to know you, kid," I said aloud and shut off the light.

10

I HAD A long drive ahead of me and two things I was hoping for: one, that the police weren't organized enough to set up roadblocks; and two, that it would still be dark when I reached Mirabella and the harbor. If I didn't get there before dawn, I fugured slipping undetected through Mirabella would be damn risky, if not impossible.

I didn't have much time to think, since the terrain was rugged and the drive unfamiliar, but whenever I hit a straight stretch and could relax, an undercurrent of worry flowed just below the level of consciousness. It took nearly the whole trip for the nagging thought to surface, and it was only when I cut the motor and lights two kilometers outside Mirabella and started thinking about where to leave the car that it really took shape in my mind.

Why were the Pellicos so hell bent on helping me? Sure, Giacomo said I'd helped save his life, but I hadn't really done much. Or at least not enough to merit what they were doing for me. As far as they knew I didn't have any money to repay the favors. But then again they didn't seem to need money. Was it just Italian hospitality?

Figuring out the answer was about as hard as picking up a wet grapefruit seed off a waxed linoleum floor, so I gave up and put it down to simple generosity and a desire to help the underdog. I guess once they'd saved me the first time, I became their charge. Things would have been different if they knew what I'd done to harm their uncle and Malta Independent Oil.

I coasted to a stop just short of the village and left the car at the side of the road. There wasn't a sign of the police. Probably all in the hills by now.

I made my way down a cobblestone lane that skirted the cemetery on one side and the backs of a row of small businesses on the other.

From a distance, the harbor glistened like a string of pearls. As I drew closer I saw that most of the fishing boats had already put out to sea, but the slips along the five short docks at the western end near the harbormaster's office were filled with pleasure craft of all sizes and sorts.

By the time I reached the jetty it was nearly dawn. A small light burned outside the *capitaneria di porto* but the door was locked. I walked over to a phone booth at one corner of the building and looked at the bulletin board.

The notice was written in English on the ship's stationery.

Seeking English-speaking diver with knowledge of salvage operations. Short-term job with excellent pay. Must be willing to serve as a general deckhand when underway. Contact Preston Blike, Captain. The Nerina.

Giacomo hadn't told me what size boat we were dealing with, so I walked up and down three of the five docks before I saw the ship anchored with the bigger yachts out in the harbor. The *Nerina* was a long-range, pilothouse trawler that looked to be nearly eighty feet in length with a beam close to eighteen. She looked impressively sleek and powerful, with her steel hull painted white.

I found an old sailor with a fourteen foot outboard who was willing to take me out for three thousand lire. We approached off the starboard side, where a small

106

inflated rubber dinghy was tied up to an aluminum accommodation ladder. I hailed the ship twice and gave up when no one answered. No reason to antagonize a possible employer with a wake-up call at dawn.

I grabbed one of the dinghy's painters trailing from the bow and told the old sailor I'd wait in the tender. "I guess they weren't expecting me until eight or so," I said. "Let them sleep in."

He didn't care. I'd already handed over the three bills. I watched as the fishing boat chugged away, the old sailor sitting in the stern with his left hand on the tiller, and then I climbed the ladder. I'd have liked to look around, but I didn't want to take a chance of having one of the crew catch me at it. From the top of the ladder, what I could see of the ship looked spotless.

I lay down in the dinghy, nursing my sore ribs, and tried to think. What had Lucio Dalmoro told me in Messina?

A wave of exhaustion swept over me. I couldn't remember. The alcohol, the blow to the head—my recent past was slipping away into a haze of confusion. I felt a twinge of fear. Did the Americans know Gene Harrell or was he just a name to them? Or not even that. Maybe he was looking for them and they merely wanted a diver. Who were they expecting to show up?

At some point, before I could figure out an answer, I fell asleep.

"What the fuck is this?"

I woke to a rough voice and looked up, shading my eyes from the sun. It had to be late in the morning since the sun had risen above the headlands.

The voice belonged to a red-haired man with a face corrugated by a host of scars, pimples, and lumpy boils. Scraggly whiskers, looking like a sow's bristles, sprang out between the blue lumps on his chin, and several large sores festered on his cheeks and forehead. His blue eyes looked faded and bleak. I'd never seen a man so ravaged by skin infections.

I got to my feet, grabbed the ladder for support, and saw the gun in his hand.

"It's okay," I said. "I came out last night and didn't want to wake you. Are you Preston Blike? I'm here to hire on as a diver, if you still need one. I'm a professional with experience in underwater salvage."

"Come aboard," he said, moving away from the rail.

I climbed on deck and saw that he'd stuck the gun under his shirt. He wore a long-sleeved flannel shirt, faded jeans, and canvas rubber-soled shoes. Every piece of skin that showed—on his face, neck, wrists, and ankles—pustulated with bumps.

He gestured toward the large, open aft deck with its built-in seating and nearby davit. There was enough room to park a car on deck. "Wait here. I'll get the captain."

When he disappeared down the port companionway, I frowned. I hadn't liked seeing the gun. Someone was too damn paranoid. But then I thought of all the stories I'd read of yacht hijacking, drug running, smuggling, and what have you. But didn't most of that take place in the Bahamas—on the cocaine route from South America to Florida?

The red-haired guy returned in ten minutes with the captain—a stocky, barrel-chested man in his fifties with a thick shock of salt-and-pepper hair, a gray beard, calm eyes, and distinguished-looking features. In a suit, he'd have looked like a Wall Street investment broker. He was dressed in white cotton slacks, with a green pullover yachting shirt and matching deck shoes.

Once on deck, he strode toward me, hand outstretched, and said in a genial manner, "Preston Blike. Pleased to meet you."

108

I smiled, said, "Gene Harrell," watching his face for a glimmer of recognition that never came, and then shook hands. He had a grip of iron and I tried to return it.

Out of the corner of my eye I thought I saw the red-haired guy stare at me with an odd cast to his face, but when I looked his way, he averted his eyes and then abruptly turned and sauntered toward the companionway.

Preston Blike called him back. "Billy Wayne, let me introduce you before you leave."

"I was just going to get Diane," he said, his voice sullen.

"She's not up yet. Let her sleep. We'll take Gene on a tour and then he can get his gear aboard." He turned to me and grinned. "If you couldn't tell, by the way, you're hired. First thing Billy Wayne said was you were a professional diver. We just lost our salvage expert. Family problems. Had to return to the States. Done any salvage?"

Before I could answer, he patted me on the back and said, "Billy Wayne Henderson's our shipwright and mechanic. He pretty much runs the ship. You'll be working under him."

I didn't like the smirk that crossed Henderson's florid face. He kept both hands on his hips.

Preston Blike turned to me, his features kind in contrast. "You can discuss your salary with Billy Wayne. We go on a first name basis, so feel free to call me Preston." He grinned. "Captain Preston, if it makes you feel better."

Preston Blike had a deprecating sense of humor that I appreciated. I wondered where he ever found Billy Wayne. They didn't seem a likely pair.

Preston jerked his head toward Billy Wayne and said, "Let's take Gene on a tour of the boat and then let him get his gear. Once that's on board, we'll ship out." He turned to me. "I'll explain the situation once we're underway, Gene." He winked. "Have to be rather secretive about salvage operations or we'll have a fleet of Italian scavengers following us."

I cleared my throat and said, "I don't have any gear. I'm ready to go anytime you are."

Preston raised his eyebrows. "No gear?"

I sighed. "Didn't Giacomo Pellico tell you about what happened to me?" I'd thought over my story before falling asleep. I'd do my best to integrate it with whatever Giacomo had said, hoping to mitigate the seriousness of my situation.

Preston frowned. "Pellico? . . . Oh, the kid. So that's his name. He just said he knew someone who could help us out and I said send him on down. That was pretty much it. I left the communicating to Billy Wayne." He grinned and turned to Henderson. "Billy Wayne, what'd the kid tell you?"

Billy Wayne scowled. "These dagos are fucking illiterate. Can't speak English worth shit. I couldn't understand a word."

Preston made a vain effort to smother his grin. "You'll have to excuse Billy Wayne. None of us speaks Italian. That includes my ex-wife, Diane. She's a professor of French, so she understands a little—the romance cognates—but we've had it rough in Italian ports ever since we left Marseilles. It's quite a chore just to get fuel, let alone water and provisions."

I nodded. "I can help you there, too. I speak Italian."

"Great. You'll like that, won't you, Billy Wayne?"

With an implacable cast to his face, Billy Wayne said, "So what happened to your gear?"

I stared at him amiably. "To make a long story short, someone stole it, along with everything else I own." I shrugged. "When I went to report it to the police, they held me for not having papers." I shook my head. "I've been working as a yacht bum, and the people I was with pulled out without me. You believe that?'' I manufactured what I hoped was a look of dumb amazement. ''Hired a sixteen-year old kid and left me stuck here.''

I looked both men in the eyes, one after the other. I had to make this sound convincing. ''Giacomo Pellico was helping me with the legal problems.''

Preston Blike pulled at his beard. ''So did you get everything straightened out?''

I hesitated. ''Well, not entirely—but I'm losing too much time here waiting for documents to arrive. If I can get off the island, I can take care of myself.'' I grinned. ''The authorities here would probably prefer that.''

Preston Blike listened to my story, his face serious, and then nodded in sympathy when I finished. ''I hope it works out for you. As long as you're on board the *Nerina,* you'll have no problems. I'll just add you to the crew list.''

They took me on a tour of the boat then, which was one of the nicest laid out I'd ever seen. The pilothouse, its control console gleaming with dials, contained the best in advanced electronic gear—a Furuno forty-eight-mile radar, SSB and VHF radios, a depth recorder, Wagner autopilot, and a fully automatic Loran LC-90 that computed courses, speeds, ranges, bearings, and times. The padded helm seat was upholstered in dark leather.

''Just like a pilot,'' I said. ''Not much to do once you get it in the air.''

Preston Blike grinned and put his hand on the wheel. ''It's the easiest watch you'll ever stand. You could watch TV if you could pick up a good channel.''

Preston moved over by the navigator's table against the starboard side of the wheelhouse and stood in front of the chart. He took a deep breath. ''Feel that cool air?'' He grinned. ''Cruiseair reverse-cycle air conditioning. Muggy as hell outside and just like the Rockies inside."

I nodded appreciation.

"Let's go below and see the accommodations," he said cheerfully.

We went down the port companionway to the cabin and turned up the left waterway, starting our tour in the bow.

Just behind me, Preston Blike said, "We can accommodate eight in comfort. The two modest staterooms forward are for the crew."

Blike had a different definition for modest than I did. The rooms were luxurious by most standards.

"The two staterooms aft are a bit more sumptuous," he went on. "We won't bother Diane now. You can take a look later if you like. The master stateroom has a queen berth and a bath with jacuzzi."

We moved aft of the forward staterooms and stood in a well-appointed galley with a dinette area just beyond.

I looked at the appliances. "Nice," I said simply. I was thinking it must have cost a bundle. It wasn't your typical salvage ship, that's for sure.

Preston Blike must have read my mind because he said, "The company I work for spared no expense."

He was right. The main saloon was furnished in hand-rubbed cherry and included a lower helm station, entertainment area, and wet bar. The boat reeked of executive perks.

"We've got three heads," Blike boasted. "Two with showers."

I nodded. This wasn't going to be a hardship cruise. "Where's the dive gear?"

Blike led me to a locker near the starboard companionway. "It's all here, everything you'll need."

I took a look. Right off I didn't like the buoyancy

compensators. They were the older, horsecollar BCs with oral inflaters.

I tossed the three BCs aside. "These won't do," I said. I knew I couldn't be picky, but I drew the line at archaic BCs. "I'll only dive with a vest jacket that has an auto inflater."

Preston Blike waved his hands nonchalantly. "We'll be stopping in Syracuse. You can pick up anything you need at company expense. How's the rest?"

I shrugged. "No problem with the weight belts. The tanks look fine."

There were six aluminum tanks manufactured in the United States, each holding eighty cubic feet and stamped for three thousand pounds working pressure. They'd been hydrostatically tested four months previously.

"Where do you hail from?" I asked, curious to see if they'd made an Atlantic crossing.

"The *Nerina*'s usually moored in Marseilles or Viareggio. The company just bought it two years ago. In Florida. But it was built by de Vries Lentsch of Holland in the late seventies."

Two years ago? But the tanks looked like they'd been inspected in the States. Four months earlier. In April. When Wanda died.

"Tanks come with the boat?"

"No, we flew them in when we came."

That explained the date, but not what Preston Blike and his crew had been doing for four months.

"Been here long?" I asked.

Preston Blike looked at me intently. "Not really. Not this trip. But Billy Wayne and I've been out a few times putting the boat through its paces."

Better shut up, I told myself. You'll make the guy suspicious.

I bent over and scrounged through a large plastic

garbage bucket holding fins. "Let me try on the fins. Got big feet. Wear a size twelve shoe."

I sat on a locker and tried on a pair. The fins, even with the adjustable heel straps loosened as far as they'd go, still pinched my toes. I pursed my lips and then shook my head slowly. "We'll need a larger pair," I said.

When I saw the speed with which Preston Blike agreed, I added, "Might as well get a good regulator while we're at it. These old ones have an unbalanced first stage. Gets too hard to breathe when the pressure drops." I put the regulator I'd been examining back in a nylon net bag and looked up. "And I'll need my own mask and snorkel. That should do it—depending upon how deep we go. If it's shallow diving, I'll go down without a wet suit."

"The sea's fairly shallow in the Malta channel. I doubt you'll be going below a hundred feet."

I perked up. The Malta channel. First indication of where we were heading. It sounded good to me. I tried to act as if I was pondering what he'd said about the depth. "Shallow? Maybe so," I said thoughtfully, "but if I go below fifty feet for any length of time—even in seas as warm as these—I may wear a jacket. Let me try on one of these."

I picked the largest wet suit top I could find and struggled into it. The sleeves fit fine, but the beaver flap was fairly tight. I pulled it through the crotch and then could barely get the buttons snapped.

Preston Blike saw me grimace and laughed. "That'll raise the voice a notch. Won't have to worry about having kids."

I paused. "Yeah. I think we'd better buy a bigger jacket. Wouldn't be too comfortable working underwater in this."

"Sounds like we're outfitting you from scratch."

114

I grinned. "Close to it. I'll be willing to chip in some of my salary. For the mask and snorkel. I'll keep that when the job's done and the rest can stay with the boat."

"No. All expenses are on us. You get what we send you down for and you can keep the equipment as a bonus."

I peeled out of the wet-suit jacket, stowed the equipment, and asked to look at the dive compressor. I'd seen it sitting on the open-air aft deck.

"We'll go aloft in a second. Since you'll be helping Billy Wayne if we have any mechanical problems, let's take a look at the engine room first." He put his left hand on my shoulder and said, "Billy Wayne, you lead the way." I could smell Henderson's perspiration in front of me and Blike's cologne from behind. Maybe Blike wore it to drown out Henderson's stench. Why didn't he just ask the guy to shower?

In the walk-in engine room—the headroom was the same six feet four inches that held for the entire cabin floor—Billy Wayne's face lit up with pride. The engines sparkled. The tools necessary for maintenance and repair hung neatly arrayed and accessible near lockers holding spare parts.

"Twin, four hundred horsepower, turbocharged Volvos," Billy Wayne said softly. "We cruise at seventeen knots. Got over a two-thousand-mile range. Nine-hundred-gallon fuel tank."

I whistled. "What's the top speed?"

Billy Wayne snickered. "Ain't never tried. The bible says twenty-five knots."

Preston Blike said, "The way Billy Wayne's got these running I wouldn't be surprised if we'd top thirty."

"Yeah," Billy Wayne put in smugly. "I'd bet on that. Take you to China and back without a cough."

He walked beyond the engines and pointed out the

generators. "Twin twenty-one-kilowatt generators. Enough power to light a skyscraper."

I doubted that, but I nodded appreciatively. "Top shape," I said. From the looks of the engine room, he was a good mechanic. "You had a look at the dive compressor?" I asked.

"You won't have any problems with air," he said firmly. "You leave that up to me."

I bristled and before I could control myself I blurted out, "No one touches my air but me."

The room suddenly grew silent.

Before anyone could say anything I apologized. "Sorry if that sounded harsh, but I've had some troubles with air before and I like to check it out myself."

Preston Blike clapped Billy Wayne on the back. "Billy Wayne doesn't mind. One less chore, right Billy?"

Billy Wayne didn't reply, just glowered and led the way aloft.

11

WE'D HOISTED THE dinghy aboard with the radial davit and were preparing to weigh the anchors when a woman in tan culottes and a light blue blouse came on deck.

"Hi," she said brightly. "I'm Diane Walker, the ex-Mrs. Blike. Preston tell you what a creep I am?"

I laughed. For a mature woman she had a frisky, coltish look to her, with a freckled face and athletic body. Her sandy-colored hair was tied back in a pony tail, and the pink ribbon matched her lipstick. Her voice had a husky tone to it, as if slightly hoarse, and I wondered if she were a smoker.

I shook my head and said, "Not really. Just claimed you were a terrible cook." Blike hadn't said any such thing but I was getting hungry and I hoped someone on ship was a cook. "What's for breakfast?" Her tone made me feel impudent and she responded in kind.

"Hey, you have to work before eating. Besides, everyone's on their own for breakfast. You look awful skinny though."

I looked down. It was true. I'd lost weight. My pants and shirt were getting baggy.

She reached out and pulled the edge of my shirt sleeve. "If you'd like, later today, I'm going to do a load of laundry. We can put your things in. The *Nerina* has a small washer. We hang the clothes out to dry in the air."

"Thanks," I said. "I'd appreciate that. I've been on the road and haven't had much chance to take care of chores."

She started to ask me a few questions and I could see she was curious, but Billy Wayne called me away before she could ask much. I was perplexed by the fact that none of the Americans seemed to have been expecting anyone by the name of Gene Harrell to show up. They were looking for a diver and I fit the bill. Was that all Harrell had to go on? Advance notice that three Americans would need a diver? I didn't like it.

And what had Preston Blike said? That their salvage expert had had family problems and had to return to the States. I thought about that for a bit, wondering if that was what Harrell had planned on. It didn't seem likely, but considering the fact I didn't know who was working for whom, anything was possible.

Something Lucio Dalmoro told me came back about then, swimming out of the past like a diver rising to the surface. Dalmoro had suggested the Americans were go-betweens, possibly involved with the Libyans, in the theft in Italy. I had to find out more about my new American employers without letting them know why I was interested. They might know the people who killed Wanda.

And then there was Carlo Spugna. I was sure his men were behind the explosions on the jackup. Did he also have something to do with whatever was stolen in Italy? When I found out he owned MIO, I'd assumed he wanted to kill me and not Wanda. But she'd blamed MIO, she knew about the company, she knew they had a reason for getting her. I couldn't forget that. Still, if Spugna wanted to kill either—or both—of us, why destroy the whole rig?

But when I thought about that some more it made sense, too. He was taking vengeance not only on me because of what I'd done to his company but also on PetroCanada. They were competitors, and they had close ties to the Canadian SIS. For all I knew it was the company in the first place who suggested that the SIS attack Spugna through his oil ventures.

I had no answers, only questions. But the more I thought about it the more I felt Spugna was the guy I should be worrying about, not the three Americans on the *Nerina*.

About then, Billy Wayne Henderson and I finished stowing the anchor, and with Preston Blike at the wheel, the ship got under way. The sun was close to straight overhead and my stomach was growling with hunger.

When Billy Wayne went below to the engine room, I stopped in the galley and looked around. The lockers, a small freezer, and the refrigerator were all well-stocked, and I helped myself to some cold cereal and milk. I was still starved, so when Diane joined me I offered to cook us some sausage and eggs.

We were eating when she said, "Tell me a little about yourself."

"I was about to ask you the same thing."

She tucked a wisp of loose hair behind her ear and fixed her hazel-colored eyes on me without speaking.

I pointed to the fork in her hand. "I notice you're left-handed. That goes with a well-developed right brain. You must be creative."

She nodded slowly, a small smile tightening the corners of her mouth. "And you're tricky."

I laughed. "Not really. I'm just tired of telling everyone what I do. I spent a week on Vignetti trying to do that—and Preston and Billy Wayne grilled me this morning. To be honest, I don't know what I am anymore. I used to be a petroleum engineer. And then I worked quite a while as a commercial diver. Offshore oil exploration mostly."

"You divorced?"

I shook my head. Diane's attentiveness had made me

unusually talkative but I didn't feel like mentioning Wanda.

"How old are you?"

I laughed. Nothing like being direct. But I've never been one to hide my age. "When I hit forty, I decided to start over and count backwards," I said. "So a year later I was thirty-nine. Let's see, that makes me thirty-six now."

She laughed and wiped the corners of her lips with a paper napkin. "I just hit fifty last June. I'll have to keep that trick in mind."

"What do you do?"

"Preston didn't tell you anything, did he? I teach French. At Berkeley."

"That's right. He did say you were a professor. I speak Italian and a little Arabic myself. But I didn't learn them in school. I've been working and living abroad for quite a few years now."

"Where you from?"

"I . . . ah . . ." Shit. How long was I going to have to go on living Harrell's background? To hell with it. I didn't know anything about Australia. "I'm Canadian. Born in Saskatchewan. How about you?"

"Chicago. Lived there all my life until I met Preston."

"What's he do, anyway?"

She laughed. "Boy, he must have grilled you. Usually all he talks about is his own work." She paused. "Mind if I smoke?"

I hesitated and felt my head beginning to waffle back and forth like a top.

"Okay," she said in a mockingly peremptory tone. "I'm trying to quit anyway."

I felt chagrined at getting my way—it was her boat after all—and my cheeks reddened. "I used to smoke," I said, to make her feel better. "It wouldn't bother me but I've been getting a lot of headaches recently. Hurt my head in an accident and they just won't go away. I've noticed smoke really bothers me now."

She put the crumpled pack in the back pocket of her culottes.

"We could go on deck," I said.

"Forget it. Preston would find something for us to do."

I leaned back. If that was true, maybe I should be on deck. It wouldn't pay for a newly hired hand to be found gossiping over breakfast with the captain's ex. But at the same time I wanted to find out what she could tell me.

Diane sighed and looked down at the table. "Preston always was a workaholic."

"You were going to tell me what he does."

When she looked up this time her eyes had darkened. I could see a trace of weary bitterness flicker across her features and then disappear.

She clasped her hands and leaned on her elbows. "He works for IDC."

I shook my head. The initials meant nothing.

"The Industrial Development Corporation. They used to be headquartered in Chicago. Then they moved south to Tucson. He's been in Arizona five or six years now. I lasted one."

"You didn't like Tucson?"

She laughed softly. "It wasn't Tucson, it was Preston. He may strike you as amiable, but he's a secretive, suspicious, critical, calculating, inflexible bastard. It took me a while to work those adjectives out, but that's what he is."

"Anything good about him?" I hadn't meant to be snide, but Preston Blike had struck me as a nice fellow and I didn't like seeing Diane's harder side.

She paused and stared blankly at a spot over my head. "I must have thought so once. We met when I was at Northwestern. He was studying law at Loyola and happened to be in our library doing some research. I thought he was handsome. Hell, he is handsome. But . . .''

Her voice dropped away and she shook her head slowly. ''He'd been to Korea as a marine when he was only eighteen. Saw most of his buddies die at Inchon in September of nineteen-fifty and at the Chosin Reservoir a few months later. That was all he could talk about.'' She laughed bitterly. ''You'd think he'd hate war.''

Her tone was remote and I was sorry I'd brought up the subject. But I didn't know how to get off it.

She shook her head and frowned. ''He was really angry when Jeffrey used a student deferment to keep from going to Vietnam.''

''Jeffrey?''

She wiped a tear from the corner of her eye. ''Our son.''

I nodded, puzzled at the display of emotion, and let her compose herself.

''I suppose I felt sorry for Preston.'' She paused reflectively and then pursed her lips. ''We got married on September fifteenth, 1954—the anniversary of his landing at Inchon Harbor—and he went to work as a patent lawyer for Borg Warner Corporation. Jeffrey was born the next June.''

Her voice choked up and she swallowed hard. I was feeling uncomfortable. This was too much emotion for me to take. I'd struggled too much over the last three months myself.

''Jeffrey had just celebrated his thirty-first birthday.''

My brows furrowed. Past tense. I was afraid to ask.

She wiped her nose on the napkin and looked at me and then her eyes widened in surprise. ''Didn't Preston tell you?''

''Tell me what?''

''Damn him!'' Her voice was unaccountably harsh. ''That's why we're out here.''

"For your son?" I was confused. What in hell was going on?

Her lips tightened. "You'd better go on up and see if Preston wants you to be helping with anything."

I stared at her face suddenly gone hard. "Okay." She didn't want to tell me about her son and I didn't think I wanted to hear about him. When the time was right, I'd ask Preston to tell me what was going on.

We passed through the Strait of Messina in midafternoon. I was in the wheelhouse with Preston, who wanted to show me how the boat handled.

"We may be needing you to stand a watch," he said. "Know anything about following a course?"

I shook my head. "Not really."

"It's pretty simple with the equipment we've got. Let me run over a few things with you."

He gave me a crash course on operational procedures when underway and then had me take the helm for a while. I stood at the wheel and tried to remember what he'd told me. To my left were the port- and starboard-engine clutches, and to my right, the two throttles. There seemed to be two of everything: tachometers, engine oil-pressure gauges, gear oil-pressure gauges, water temperature gauges, bilge and fuel alarms, voltmeters, trim tabs. Thank God there was only one wheel and one compass.

"Rough crossing through here," Preston said. "I'd hate to do it in a sailing yacht." He shook his head. "Some pretty strong tidal runs to contend with. They say the different levels of salinity are responsible—the Tyrrhenian meeting the Ionian. Glad we're powered."

I nodded, my eyes focused intently on the traffic. The strait was crowded with sea-going yachts, small pleasure craft, large passenger and train ferries, hydrofoils, freighters, container ships, seagoing tugs towing barges, and other commercial shipping. Overhead a steady stream of helicopters traversed the passageway from Sicily to the mainland.

Preston gestured toward a helicopter passing across our starboard bow. "Probably coming north from the Italian naval base at Augusta. One more hazard. At night, there's so many lights out here, they say some navigators even get confused by low-flying helicopters."

Billy Wayne popped into the pilothouse.

"We're putting in at Syracuse," Preston told him. "Gene will talk to the harbormaster and arrange for provisions and fuel. You and Diane can go ashore for a few hours when things are taken care of. I'm taking Gene to a chandlery to see what we can get as far as scuba gear. Why don't you show him how to work the radios. See if we can get us an updated met report. I'd like to ship out later tonight."

Billy Wayne's hard eyes caught mine. I wondered if Preston knew his engineer carried a gun.

Billy Wayne stepped over to the navigator's table and stared at the chart. "You've already plotted the course?"

Preston turned around and frowned when he saw Billy Wayne's hand on the chart. "It's all taken care of. Show Gene the radio controls."

Billy Wayne, his jaw set stubbornly, took one last look at the chart (if he worked for me, I'd've fired the intractable bastard), nodded, and then turned to me.

"You ever work a radio before?"

I stared back at him and took my time answering. "Yes," I said sarcastically, "I used to be a disk jockey."

After an early dinner, Diane Walker offered again to do my laundry. I changed at my berth, hiding my wallet in a footlocker, and put on a swim suit I'd borrowed from Billy Wayne. Unfortunately, Preston's waist was several sizes larger than mine, so I had to make due with Billy Wayne's clothes. Given his boils, which I was sure covered his entire body, I didn't want to wear any more of his stuff than I had to.

My freshly washed clothes were dry and it was dark by the time we cleared customs and were moored in our berth at Syracuse, lying stern to the quay with the bow lines made fast to a buoy forward, and our fenders set out. I was relieved to learn that under international law, customs required only that the captain present the ship's registry papers with the crew manifest form. I showed the *capitano di porto* the *costituto* Blike had picked up at the *Nerina*'s first Italian port of call and talked to him about facilities for fresh water and tax-free fuel, then explained the procedures to Billy Wayne, who listened with an irritable look to his face. It took all my patience to put up with his moodiness. I supposed he didn't like a paid hand telling him what to do.

We left Diane aboard the *Nerina,* reading, while Preston and I walked from the old city on the island of Ortigia into the larger, newer section across the low bridge. Multihued fishing boats were laid up in the small inner harbor, where several crusty seamen sat under a pole-supported string of bare light bulbs, repairing their nets.

The streets were deserted. "Dinner time," I told Preston. "I hope some of the shops are still open." The harbormaster had given me the address of a marine supply business on Via Eucleida.

We took our time since the air was muggy and walked all the way to the chandlery. The owner was just padlocking the retractable metal grating protecting the door and display windows, when we hailed him from across the street. He was reluctant to reopen until I mentioned everything we needed.

"If you've got it, we'll buy it," I said. "We're shipping out late tonight."

The Italian opened the metal grate, leaving room for

us to slip inside, and locked the door behind us. He removed a beret and slicked back his dark wavy hair.

"Scuba gear is not my main line," he said nervously. "But I've got some used equipment."

I frowned and snorted through my nose. "Damn! I wanted new equipment."

The Italian rubbed his hands apologetically. "I do have some new things—just a sample of items for ordering. If you'd like to look, maybe something will fit."

I looked at Preston, who was staring at me questioningly, and shook my head. "The guy hardly has anything in stock. Let's take a look and I'll get what I can."

We wound up buying everything we needed. The double-sealed mask and snorkel, flotation vest, and regulator were new, the clear silicon vented fins and wet-suit top used but in good condition.

Preston paid using traveler's checks. That was another hassle until I managed to convince the chandler that the checks were as good as cash. As it was, he charged us nearly five hundred dollars. Preston didn't seem to mind and I wasn't going to complain about the price. A good BC was worth three hundred.

We took a taxi back to the *Nerina*. Billy Wayne was still ashore, but Diane was sitting in a padded chaise lounge on the aft deck, engaged in conversation with two young Italian males who stood on the quay. Their English was quite good and Preston, in a jovial mood, invited them aboard for a tour of the boat.

I stayed on deck, since the temperature had become more comfortable, and dozed in the chaise lounge. I woke to hear Preston grumbling about Billy Wayne's absence.

"You told him he could go ashore," Diane replied sharply.

Preston's voice had a harsh tone I hadn't heard before. "Yes, and I told him we'd be leaving tonight, didn't I?"

126

I sat up and interrupted their squabble. "If it's okay, I'll go below to my berth. A little sleep will help me stand a watch later tonight."

They kept quiet until I disappeared down the companionway and then I could hear them start up again, their voices low but hard.

I don't know how long I slept, but when I woke I had another headache. I went to the head and then climbed the companionway to see what time it was.

The pilothouse was empty. I looked around, saw no one—even the quay seemed deserted—and my curiosity got the better of me. Preston still hadn't told me where we were going, other than the one reference to the Malta channel. If we were going to lay up in one of the harbors on the island of Malta, I planned on jumping ship. I didn't have much money and no papers, but getting Spugna didn't require either. If our destination was elsewhere, I'd take care of the salvage job as fast as possible, learn what I could about what these people were doing, and then either ask them to take me to Malta or, with my salary of four hundred a week, I could fly there.

Money. Shit! I slapped my back pocket. Just as I thought. I'd forgotten to put my wallet back after my clothes were washed. Preston had paid for everything ashore and it had never crossed my mind. I'd get it when I went below.

In the darkened wheelhouse, I found the light for the navigator's table without much trouble and switched it on. Great. They'd left the chart out. A dull glow spread over its surface, illuminating the penciled lines.

I stared at the course plotted by Preston. He'd drawn three connecting lines at nearly right angles to each other, leading first east-southeast, then straight south, and finally back toward Malta in a northwesterly direction. A roundabout route, but nothing too mysterious about that for someone who was afraid of scavengers following him to a dive site. But then the line died near the entrance to the Grand Harbour at Valletta.

I frowned and then shrugged. That was fine with me. I'd leave this crazy group at the first quay we tied up at. The harbor didn't matter—as long as it was on Malta.

Wait! The coordinates for the Maltese islands. I bent over the chart. Weren't those—

Suddenly a hand gripped my wrist and I jumped a foot into the air. I tried to turn, raising my hands instinctively to protect my face, and a fist slammed into my midsection. One blow was all it took. I doubled over in pain and sprawled to the floor, my body wretching with a dry heave.

I expected a knife to slash into me and I think I tried to say, "Don't kill me," in Italian.

And then I heard Billy Wayne's voice. "Shit, Harrell. It's you."

I rolled to my side, still holding my stomach and gasping for breath. I looked up through teary eyes. The bastard! He straddled me with fists clenched. If I could've moved, I'd have kicked him in the balls.

"Thought you were a fucking thief," he said. "What in hell are you doing up here?"

"What's it look like?" I muttered through clenched teeth.

"It looks like you're snooping. Got some friends you trying to help?"

It was none of his damn business but I sat up and said I didn't have friends. I just wanted to know where we were going.

"You won't find it on there," he said, his voice cold.

"What do you mean?"

"I mean we don't know where we're going yet."

I stood in a crouch and rubbed my stomach. I still felt like decking Billy Wayne. No way he hadn't recognized me. The light from the navigator's table wasn't that dim.

But what he'd said bothered me and I concentrated on that. What in hell were these people after? I was tired of letting other people's wills toss me about, tired of getting beat up.

"Are we searching for a wreck?"

Billy Wayne stared at me for several seconds. He rubbed his jaw, his fingers softly palping a fire red boil. "I don't know if I can trust you, Harrell. Preston will tell you—"

"Billy Wayne, damn your hide!" Preston's voice rumbled through the pilothouse and we both jumped. "I thought I heard you. Where you been all night?" His voice was angry and he stood in the door, his legs spread.

"I got lost in the old city—"

"Got lost in a bar, you mean."

"I—"

"Just shut your mouth. I don't want to hear your excuses. You think we've got forever?"

They stared at each other in silence. I cleared my throat but said nothing. I wasn't going to get involved in another fight. I'd learned my lesson with Cecco and Beppe. My head couldn't take another beating, and my stomach wasn't feeling so well either.

Preston jerked his thumb over his shoulder. "Gene, get below. We don't need you now. I'll wake you later."

I lay in my berth, fully clothed and unable to fall asleep, while they started the engines and prepared for our departure. Billy Wayne had been about to tell me something and Preston Blike had stopped him. How long had Blike been standing there listening to us? And the coordinates. Weren't they damn close to what Harrell had written down on the ten-thousand-lire note?

I opened the footlocker to get the wallet. In the dark, I swept my hand around. The locker was empty. I swore and groped my way to the light switch. Had I knocked the wallet out on the floor?

But the wallet was nowhere to be found. I ransacked my quarters and then sat down on the berth, feeling weak as the blood drained from my head. The skin on my neck and chest tingled and I looked numbly at my hands lying between my legs. I couldn't feel the fingers, but they were all curled up and shaking as if I'd suffered a stroke.

12

No one came to get me that night and I finally fell into a restless sleep just before dawn. When I awoke, we were underway into a headwind of about twelve knots. The *Nerina* cut smoothly through rolling three-foot waves, their glassy crests breaking under the wind. Scattered white horses appeared and disappeared. I wondered if we were in for a storm. It was that season. The hot winds off Africa would be sucking up water as they blew northward across the Mediterranean.

I undressed and took a shower, knowing I'd have to put on the same set of clothes. I was still angry with myself. I'd been letting others manipulate me ever since I'd washed ashore on Vignetti.

And why didn't I have Preston buy me some clothes in Syracuse? I hadn't been thinking straight. Not just about the clothes, about everything. They were going to tell me what was going on today or . . .

Or what? I couldn't jump ship in the middle of the Mediterranean—but I sure as hell would the first chance I got, Malta or not.

I confronted the three of them in the saloon, where Billy Wayne sat at the lower helm station while Diane and Preston relaxed on a blue velour built-in couch, drinking coffee. It looked like I'd interrupted a conference. There was an awkward silence that no one seemed disposed to break. So I broke it.

"My wallet's gone," I said, and then my mouth fell open. The wallet was lying in plain sight on the table.

Diane smiled. "Good morning, Gene. Sleep well? I found your wallet in your slacks when I was doing the laundry yesterday and forgot to give it back. Left it lying on the dinette table. I guess you didn't see it."

I didn't know what to say, the lie was so obvious—and she knew it. But did the others? Was she trying to tell me something?

With everyone watching, I didn't bother looking inside, just put the wallet in my pocket and sat down near a game table with built-in chess board. I was still peeved. "Where are we now?" I asked abruptly.

Preston spoke. "We'll sight Malta in an hour. Good weather all the way. We were going to anchor at Ta Xbiex, but I think we'll just skirt the coast and head straight for the salvage location."

"That's another thing I think it's about time you told me. What are we looking for?"

Preston turned to Henderson. "Billy Wayne, why don't you go up to the wheelhouse. I'll come aloft to relieve you in a while."

"Get yourself a cup of coffee in the galley as you go," Diane said. She seemed unusually cheerful, her pony tail bouncing as she spoke.

When Billy Wayne left, I focused my attention on Preston. "I want to know what it is you expect me to do. If you can't trust me, drop me off at the nearest landfall."

"It's not a matter of trust," Preston said. "We trust Billy Wayne, too. I just didn't think it was necessary to explain everything before now. But I understand your curiosity."

He paused as if searching for the right words and looked around the room without seeing anything. "You've probably wondered why Diane is here. We've been divorced several years now—and obviously none of us is an expert at salvage—but this is something that concerns our son, Jeffrey.''

"I'm concerned about Jeffrey," Diane said pointedly. "You're concerned about the cargo."

Preston frowned. "Jeffrey's dead and no salvage operation is going to bring him back to life."

"I want to know why he's dead."

Preston waved his hands in acknowledgment. "We all do." He turned toward me. "That's where you come in, Gene."

"I'm not a detective."

"No one's asking you to be a detective. But you might be able to tell why his yacht went down."

"You don't know what happened?"

Preston rubbed his beard. "We wondered at first if it might be sabotage." He cleared his throat and coughed nervously. "IDC has been involved in industrial espionage and we have a lot of enemies."

I narrowed my eyes. "What was Jeffrey transporting?"

"That's the strange thing. We hired him to bring some jewels from Rome to Vignetti." Preston grinned slyly. "I'm not so welcome on the mainland."

Diane interrupted him. "I was on vacation in Paris, so Jeffrey telephoned me and asked if I'd like to accompany Preston from Marseilles to Vignetti. Jeffrey and I hadn't seen each other in over a year. We planned on cruising together to the Greek isles. He was piloting a family yacht, a forty-three-foot Greek-made boat that belonged to my father. The *Kirke*. Preston and I used to do a lot of cruising when we were first married."

So now I knew what we were looking for. A sunken yacht with jewels. Why would the Italian intelligence community care that much about jewels? If they were stolen, that was a police matter. I wanted to hear more about the jewels, and Preston obliged me.

"The jewels were a miscellaneous lot, came out of Turkey by way of Yugoslavia and then into Italy. IDC had nothing to do with it—a private investment." He grinned, a venal look on his face. "The company provides the *Nerina* for executive vacations. I'm using it to make a little extra money."

The implication was clear. Stolen merchandise. The question was, from whom? And how did Preston Blike come into the picture? He was a patent lawyer working for an industrial development corporation, not a thief or a high-class fence. A collector of antiques, maybe? Were the jewels a museum collection?

Blike got to his feet and paced to the saloon door and back. "The Turks traced the jewels as far as Belgrade and then lost them. Jeffrey's job was to confuse them further if they managed to pick up the trail again in Rome. We'd arranged to meet him on the island—back at Vignetti. Only he confused all of us. He didn't show up. He radioed that he was altering course and couldn't give the reason over the air. And then he disappeared."

Diane extinguished a cigarette and exhaled a stream of smoke. "We thought his boat might have been hijacked. We knew we were competing with others."

Preston nodded and stopped in front of me, making his point with a raised forefinger. "We figured a competitor fed Jeffrey some bum dope—told him the area around Vignetti was dangerous, sent him off course where they could get to him easier."

I stared at Blike, my brows narrowed suspiciously. "Who's the competitor?"

Preston threw his head back and snorted. "That doesn't matter. The important thing is we know the guy never received the cargo either. Apparently Jeffrey's ship sank before reaching the man. We don't know if it was sabotage, a natural explosion on board—maybe from gas building up in the bilge—a fire, or a storm. They did have gale force winds and high seas when the ship sank.''

''When did this happen?''

''We were supposed to meet on the twelfth, a Tuesday. The boat must have gone down late that night or the next day.''

Today was Sunday, the twenty-fourth. Almost two weeks ago. What had delayed them so long? If others were after the jewels, they might be too late already. The jewels? I frowned. Or whatever the cargo was.

All told, it was as fishy a story as I'd ever heard. The hints of industrial espionage, that I could believe. But I'd seen through Preston Blike's story about the jewels. He'd provided just the right amount of venality to make me think the jewels were stolen. But the more I thought about it the more I realized I was being suckered.

Too many things didn't add up. First, the vague comment on ''miscellaneous jewels.'' Phony all the way. And then his son. So Jeffrey was supposed to meet him in Vignetti and his yacht winds up sunk off Malta of all places—two hundred nautical miles away. And I was supposed to believe either that modern-day pirates were involved or that a competitor had tricked his kid.

I recalled Diane's tearful reference to her son the day before. What was she along for? To convince me that all they cared about was finding out what happened to Jeffrey? That couldn't be right. They wouldn't go to all that trouble just to allay the suspicions of people like me—people they didn't even know they'd have as crew.

I caught myself. No need to be so damn suspicious of everyone. Maybe she was on board to meet her son for a vacation. Maybe she was only concerned about what happened to him. Most mothers, if their sons died, would like to know how and why.

But Preston Blike was a different story. He was involved with something illegal. I doubted it was merely for personal gain; it had to do with IDC. Billy Wayne was along to provide muscle if needed and . . . and what? To take care of me after I brought up whatever they were looking for?

The whole issue was too confusing to puzzle out. I didn't know enough about what was going on. I tried to think of questions I could ask to trip them up, find the chink in the armor, the broken link in the chain, the hole in the net. There had to be something that would help. I could simply tell Preston Blike I didn't believe his story. But what good would that do?

Silence had settled between us. I could see they were watching me think, waiting for a reaction. I decided to take a chance.

"Jeffrey was delivering the shipment—whatever it was—to Carlo Spugna, wasn't he?"

Preston's face froze for a moment and then the brittleness dissolved and he laughed, high-pitched and dry. He walked away from me toward the door—I enjoyed his obvious struggle to compose himself—and then he turned and came back to sit across from me. His silence was a better answer than any. He and Spugna wanted whatever had gone down with Jeffrey Blike.

"Do you play?" he asked, pointing at the chess board and then stroking his beard.

I nodded. "But not very well."

"Yeah, I bet. So you know Spugna?"

Small world, I thought. "Through the oil business," I said. "I've had contacts with Malta Independent Oil before, back when the company was called Spugna Oil Exploration. There's no one else on the island big enough to be involved with something like this." I pulled the lobe of my left ear. "I'm still wondering why you are?"

"It won't do you any good," he said. "Your only concern is recovering the cargo. It should be easy enough. A small safe. We won't even have to winch it aboard. We know the combination.''

Diane looked at her ex-husband and laughed. "So, Preston, that's why we headed east out of Syracuse. You're worried about some stupid oilman beating you to the scene." She turned to me and pursed her cheeks. "Preston thought we were being followed. We nearly went to Greece," she added sarcastically. "Otherwise we'd have been in Malta hours ago."

Preston gave her a dirty look but said nothing.

Suddenly, a flash of pain ran through my head and settled on the ridge behind my left ear. I moved my jaw and used two fingers to rub the area behind the ear. The skin felt swollen with blood.

Ignore the pain. Concentrate. "I suppose what's inside the safe is waterproof?"

He laughed. "Jewels don't melt."

Then, like lightning, a bolt of pain blasted through my head and I fell forward, collapsing on the chess table. Instant nausea coursed through me and for a second I was afraid they'd poisoned me.

Preston had his arm around me and helped me to my feet. My head felt like a resounding tunnel. Dizziness . . . the air turned gray, objects going out of focus.

"The head," I gasped, "I'm sick."

For a crazy moment I confused the nautical term with the anatomical and was afraid Preston had also. I wanted the toilet. I stumbled and tried to point toward the forward head. And then I heard screams as if from far away. Someone was being killed. *Someone was killing me!* Blackness closed around me. The last thing I remembered was my shoulder striking the coffee table as I fell.

I regained consciousness after what must have been just minutes. My head buzzed and pinpricks of white light flashed before my eyes. Diane was in the room, holding a plastic bag filled with ice against the back of my neck.

Preston's voice came from far away. "I'm going aloft to relieve Billy Wayne," he said.

"Help me get Gene to his berth first."

The voices. High and low. They swirled down a long, dark tunnel, striking my ears like . . . like the voices of angels.

In my berth, Diane put the ice pack behind my neck and went to get some aspirin from the medicine chest. When she returned, I chewed four of them, hoping the drug would absorb through the tissues of the mouth and reach my brain quicker.

Better off to be dead, I thought. I'd never been much affected by pain or illness till now. An occasional cold in the winter when I was growing up, the usual childhood illnesses—but not much else. I wouldn't have thought pain could be so devastating.

Diane handed me a glass of water, and I washed down the harsh taste and last hard bits of aspirin. I still felt nauseous.

"Feeling better?"

I took a deep breath. I didn't think I could answer that.

"Gene, I know you're hurting but I have to talk to you. We don't have much time alone."

Her voice was low and earnest. I nodded slowly, thinking, okay, get it over with. I swallowed hard. I wanted silence and darkness.

"I couldn't tell you in front of Preston, but I caught Billy Wayne going through your wallet."

I stared at her blankly. Was she still trying to pretend she'd found it in my slacks and had left it lying on the dinette?

"He didn't take anything," she said hurriedly.

"So? . . ."

"He was in your berth. I came here looking for you and found the door open. Billy Wayne was searching your locker."

I squeezed my eyes hard. "Thanks," I said. There was nothing I could do about it now, but I appreciated her telling me.

"I'll watch out for him," I said. "Did you know he carries a gun?"

She leaned toward me, frowning. "Are you sure?"

I nodded. "Pulled it on me the first day I came out to the *Nerina*. Looked like a snubby belly gun, only it was an automatic."

"I'll let Preston know. He's got weapons aboard for protection, but they're locked up. I don't trust Billy Wayne."

She paused but I said nothing, my eyes closed. I didn't trust any of them.

"I'll let you rest," she said.

I managed to nap awhile, and when I awoke the headache had subsided. I found the medicine chest and took two more aspirin for protection. I put the bottle in my pocket to have handy. I was getting paranoid about my head, using the pills prophylactically.

Just before going on deck, I heard voices from the saloon. Something about satellite precision. I stopped to listen.

Preston's deep baritone was clearly audible. "How long's he had it and who'd he give it to, is what I'd like to know."

Billy Wayne spoke and I strained to decipher his voice, which was higher and quieter. Something about Diane. The radio.

Preston asked, "When?"

I missed Billy Wayne Henderson's response and swore to myself. Speak up, damn it.

"Call her down here and we'll talk about it. Tell her to set it on autopilot. I'll control it from the lower helm station if we have problems."

I slipped away and watched from around a bulkhead as Billy Wayne bounded up the port companionway. In a few minutes he returned with Diane following behind.

They joined Preston in the saloon, and I crouched outside the door, my heart pounding in my chest. As an intensely private person, I'd always considered eavesdropping a crime. But it was high time to join my cohorts, who seemed to fit into that world just fine.

Preston waded right into Diane.

"I didn't know you knew how to use the radio, Diane."

"I watched Billy Wayne doing it," she said. "It's not that hard." Her tone was sharp.

"Who'd you talk to?"

"A guy at Radio Siracusa. Between French and English, I managed to get a met report out of him."

"Good. Did you write it down?"

She waited a moment and then said, "No."

I could imagine her face, probably pinched and tight. She didn't strike me as a woman who liked to be grilled by her ex-husband.

"I thought you'd want an updated one in the morning," she said evenly. "I was just bored and wanted to talk to someone."

I thought about my confrontation with Billy Wayne in the wheelhouse last night. And then Preston's arrival. Seems everyone had paid a visit to the pilothouse.

Preston's voice changed volume. "So, Billy Wayne, who'd *you* talk to?"

"Who says I talked to anyone?" His voice bristled

and I had no trouble hearing it now. He was just inside the door.

"Diane just said she watched you using the radio."

"Oh, honey," Diane said, her laughter ringing. "Not last night. Billy Wayne gets on the radio every morning."

There was a moment of silence and then Preston said, "Lot of good it does. Half the time he can't understand what the Italians are saying—and they're speaking English."

They all laughed at that.

"I'm going to take a shower," Preston said. "You take the wheel, Billy Wayne."

"Okay," he said. "I think I'll just stay at the helm down here."

I was afraid Diane might leave the saloon to go on deck, so I crawled away and watched the door for five minutes.

I couldn't hear any voices and no one came out. I moved back as close as I dared and heard a gasp. I held my breath and listened again. And then my eyes opened wide. I couldn't believe it. I raised my head and looked through the oval window in the door. Billy Wayne and Diane were on the couch, and they weren't engaged in conversation. At least not the verbal kind. They were having a go at it, with their clothes still on, and the only thing that came to mind was a memory from my days on the farm. They looked pretty much like pigs in heat.

13

You couldn't call it adultery. Diane and Preston were divorced. I guess I was just shocked that Diane saw anything in Billy Wayne. And his boils. How could she touch the guy? Maybe that's why they kept most of their clothes on—although I was more inclined to put that down to haste and passion rather than self-protection.

I needed a breath of fresh air.

I stood for a few minutes on the forward deck, staring at the horizon. A low land mass was visible two points off the port bow. The Republic of Malta. It wouldn't be long before the dark shadow separated into distinct islands. I'd made a similar approach years before. At our current heading we'd pass well to the north of land.

At midday, the cumulous clouds that had hovered in a line over the southern horizon since morning were beginning to pile up, growing darker and thicker. I wondered about the barometer and then swore at myself.

What was I wasting time for? No one was in the pilothouse. Get in there and see what you can learn.

I climbed the stairs and stepped into the wheelhouse. A soft hum filled the room. I glanced over the dials on the control console at the helm station and then casually turned and looked at the chart on the navigator's table.

Someone had erased the lines plotted the day before and had drawn in a new course skirting Malta and stopping at a small *x* to the northwest of Gozo. Geographical coordinates had been written in—N 36° 39′ 20″ E 13° 12′

47"—and I pulled out my wallet to compare them with what was written on the ten thousand-lire note.

Exactly the same.

But that was what I'd expected. That was why they'd dawdled in Vignetti, why they were originally going to Malta. They hadn't known for sure where the yacht had sunk until I—until the dead Gene Harrell, that is—told them. Who would they have met in Malta? And how'd Gene Harrell know the location of Jeffrey's yacht?

I wondered desperately who'd killed Harrell and who he was, his role in this confusing play. Somehow he'd been a piece in the jigsaw puzzle, a piece that someone wanted lost. He was connected to one side or the other. But how many sides were there?

I heard a noise and jerked around, expecting to find Billy Wayne or Preston.

No one was in sight. The wind rattled in the lines overhead.

I crossed to the barometer and checked the pressure. It read 29.40. Where was the log? Knowing the number didn't help if I couldn't tell if it was rising or falling.

I found the log in a drawer below the instrument console and flipped it open to the last entry, made at eleven A.M. The log was brand new, with only two pages of records. There were columns for time, place abeam, distance off, four subcolumns for charted course, engine r.p.m. readings, speed, wind direction and strength, current, state of sea, weather, visibility, and finally—to the far right—barometer and temperature.

The notation read 30.20. Shit. Falling rapidly.

I held my place in the log and looked up. The wind was driving dark, menacing cumulonimbus to the northeast, coming up on us across the port bow, but still some distance away. The land mass I'd seen earlier was lost now in the general darkness at the horizon.

Lightning struck—a jagged line that forked, died out,

and then blazed again along a new path. I listened for the thunder, counting seconds. Barely audible when it reached the *Nerina*. At the limit of its range. Eighteen seconds. Multiplying the interval in seconds by .2 gave the distance in miles. The worst of the storm was still nearly four miles away. A narrow curtain of rain fell from its center, dark in the middle and hazy near the edges of the vertical band.

I was about to put the log back and head below to warn Billy Wayne, when I noticed the flyleaf where the owner, captain, and crew were listed.

Log of Nerina *of Marseilles, France*

Owner	*International Development Corporation, Tucson, Arizona*
Trip No.	*16*
Master	*Preston Blike*
Crew	*Billy Wayne Henderson, engineer*
	Diane Walker, cook
	Gene Harrell, salvage operations
Guests	*None*

Blike, I saw, had added my name to the crew list. And then I looked at the date. *August 9, 1986.*

My heart skipped a beat, my breath suddenly ragged. I swallowed hard and stared at the log. I hadn't been aboard then. Was still somewhere in central Italy on the ninth.

The ink was the same color, the script by the same hand. Could Preston have added my name when I joined the crew?

I shook my head slowly. Impossible. Remember what he said? They'd lost their salvage expert. He had to return to the States. And where was his name?

It was staring me in the face.

*   *   *

144

The storm hit us then. The winds, shifting earlier, had grown steady about five miles ahead of the roll cloud, and when it passed over, violent winds followed, with strong downdrafts accompanied by heavy rain and some hail just abaft of the roll cloud.

Billy Wayne, wearing a wet-weather jacket over his red flannel shirt, joined me in the wheelhouse. We didn't speak. His attention was focused on piloting the *Nerina* and mine was wandering so erratically that I couldn't have made sense if I wanted to. I had storms inside and outside to contend with.

By two-thirty in the afternoon the core of the storm moved over, rain continuing, but no longer any hail, winds high. And then, an hour later, the downdrafts hit us again.

"That's the worst of it," Billy Wayne said. He nodded toward the window. "Lighter rain. It'll clear up soon. Be a little cooler. For a while at least."

I nodded, happy he hadn't bothered to ask me what I was doing in the wheelhouse. Now that they had the location of the sunken yacht it didn't appear to matter.

The islands of the Republic of Malta were clearly visible off our port side after the storm, first Malta itself, then the small stepping stone Comino, and finally Gozo.

As we drew abeam of Gozo I was filled with a vague longing, a desire to escape from the problems of the *Nerina* and recuperate on a sunny beach.

Donata was on that island, perhaps at that very moment looking out to sea. I laughed to myself. If she was, she wouldn't see us. San Lawrenz was too far to the south; her view would be due west. But I imagined her on a bluff, perhaps sitting under an olive tree, a book in her lap. Never mind that a storm had just drenched the scene. My imagination was full of sun.

"What's on your mind?" Billy Wayne asked suddenly.

I started. "What?"

"You looked out of it there for a moment."

I nodded. "I was. Thinking of someone."

He pulled a pack of cigarettes from his shirt pocket, offered me one, which I turned down, and lit up. I walked over and opened the wheelhouse door.

"You want ventilation?"

"Smoke's been bothering me, but I can go below."

"No, wait a minute. I'd like to talk to you. I'll turn on the air."

So Billy Wayne wanted to talk. Probably trying to find out what Preston and Diane told me. Good. I had a few questions for him, too. Might as well start myself.

"You been with Preston long?"

He exhaled toward the ceiling vent and squinted his eyes, his sandy lashes nearly closed.

"I don't work for Blike. I work for whoever happens to be piloting the *Nerina*."

Someone had to hire him. That meant he worked for the same corporation as Preston.

Billy Wayne swiveled the helm seat around and sat down, facing me. He'd rolled up the sleeves of his flannel shirt and I glanced quickly at his arms. Covered with scars so thick it looked like he'd been burned.

"I work for a yacht maintenance company. We're hired to keep the boat in shape and provide crew service when needed. I've been doing this for the last two years." He drew in a lungful of smoke and exhaled while he spoke. "Longest job I've had since Nam."

"Serve in the army?"

"Air Force. Master sergeant. Gunner on a C-130 gunship." He paused and then asked me if I'd ever been in Vietnam.

I shook my head. "Royal Canadian Navy. That's where I learned to dive."

"Diving ever give you claustrophobia?"

I was surprised by the question. "Can't say as it has.

Everybody's apprehensive at the start, but once you've been trained, there isn't much that can scare you.''

He grinned. ''Except sharks.''

I shrugged. ''Divers don't worry much. Most sharks are pretty timid. Unpredictable really. I've had a scrape or two. But, hey, let me tell you, you swim on the surface you've got more to worry about.''

Henderson pulled at a nostril. I could see it was inflamed. The guy must be a walking sore, I thought.

''Believe it or not,'' he said, ''I don't swim. Don't like the water. On top, in a boat, it's okay. Down in it, that's another story.''

''You spend much time on a boat and you might find yourself in it. I'd learn to swim.''

''Hey, I'm fatalistic.'' He waved his cigarette. ''Just like this. Cancer stick. If it kills me, it kills me. I do what I want.''

There's all kinds of fools in the world, I thought. We all have our moments of blindness.

Billy Wayne was opening up and I wondered why. Probably telling me about himself so he could pump me right after.

Billy Wayne took a drag and exhaled a cloud of smoke. ''I can't go back on a plane.'' He looked me in the eyes. ''Sounds weird, right? An Air Force gunner who can't fly. Form of claustrophobia, they tell me.''

I shrugged. ''Ships can sink, but you feel like you can still control your destiny. On a plane . . . I understand that.''

Billy Wayne tipped his head to the side, pensively. ''I got shot down in the Nam. In seventy-one. Fifteen years ago. Midair explosion. We had a crew of sixteen. Only three of us parachuted to safety. The rest went down.''

''How'd they get you out?''

''Fuck! We got ourselves out. Over a month in a Laotian jungle. Two of us made it. The other guy—''

He snubbed out the cigarette in an ashtray on the console. "He was pretty beat up. Couldn't take the pain. Shot himself through the head. I might have done the same in his situation. He was worried about slowing us down."

Billy Wayne Henderson's blue eyes stared vacantly as if he were seeing the scene again. He shook his head finally. "Too fucking stupid," he said scornfully. "I was too fucking stupid."

He picked at his forehead. "Joined up when I was eighteen, in sixty-nine. If I'd had half a brain I'd have gone to college like the rest of my classmates. Shit. I think about ten of us out of a graduating class of two hundred went to the Nam. The dorks and the gung-ho."

"What'd you do after your time was up?" I asked.

He raised one side of his mouth and snorted. "Nothing. Bummed around. I needed my freedom. That's one thing the military does for you. Makes you appreciate what you don't got."

Preston joined us about then, and Billy Wayne, after all his preparation, never did get the chance to ask me any questions. I stayed in the wheelhouse with the two of them for a half hour, until the islands of Malta were astern, fading back to an indistinct lump on the horizon. Finally, Preston said it was crowded in there and why didn't I go below and help Diane prepare dinner.

Working in the galley, lost in thought, I pondered the implications of what I'd seen in the log. I almost asked Diane about it and then decided not. She and Billy Wayne were too close. Let things roll, I thought. Don't mention the log. It wouldn't do me any good. They knew I wasn't the real Gene Harrell, but they didn't know I knew. Let them go on thinking I was a stupid sucker. Served me right. I was awful damn close to being one anyway.

*　　*　　*

148

After dinner, I helped clean up while Preston and Billy Wayne went aloft to prepare the *Nerina* for the night. We were going to anchor at sea, near the site where we'd begin our search the next morning.

"Shouldn't be hard to find," Preston had said at dinner. "The government did its job."

I'd frowned and asked which government.

"The U.S. of A.," he said with a big grin. "Spy satellite. IDC's got friends where it counts."

I had trouble keeping my eyes locked on his. Felt my cheeks redden for some strange reason—almost as if I'd been caught telling a lie when it was Preston who was doing the lying.

After I finished in the galley, I said I was going to my berth. Preston told me to rest up, that tomorrow would be a rigorous day of diving. I nodded but thought, *if* we find the wreck.

I lay in my berth for over an hour, unable to sleep. Friends in the government, Preston had said. And what about Gene Harrell? He had the coordinates too. Why didn't he pass them on to Preston? That I couldn't figure out. Unless . . . unless he was working for Spugna or some other group. He might have overheard a radio message to Preston, learned where the wreck was sitting, tried to pass it on to Spugna.

No, that couldn't be right. Preston hadn't received a radio message, didn't know the coordinates until someone found them in my wallet. They'd have been written on the chart. But in the end they got them from Harrell, so didn't that make him the government agent? Or was that just a lie from Preston to make me think no one on the *Nerina* had gone through my wallet. Of course they might even think I hadn't noticed the numbers. The possibilities swirled through my confused brain. For all I knew Spugna killed Gene Harrell before Harrell could get the coordinates to Preston Blike.

I sat up in the berth. Shit! Maybe Billy Wayne killed him.

Billy Wayne. He was a question mark. He'd opened up to me earlier, talking about Vietnam, trying hard to make me like him. Why the change in attitude? Was it just to pry into my own background as I'd thought? Maybe I was wrong. He didn't have to tell me as much as he had.

Someone knocked on the door and I said, "Who's there?"

"It's me," Billy Wayne said, opening the door. "Got a minute?"

Speaking of the devil. "I guess," I managed to mutter. I couldn't keep the reluctance out of my voice. I wanted time to think—time to plan what I was going to do to avoid the same fate as the real Gene Harrell.

Billy Wayne stepped in and sat down on the edge of one of the stateroom's two recliner chairs. "Preston thinks we've found the wreck site," he said. "You'll be going down first thing tomorrow to make sure."

"Fine," I said abruptly, thinking instead, Shit! Now I had a day, two at the most, before they'd decide what to do with me. But when they got what they wanted, wouldn't that be enough? Wouldn't they just drop me off in Malta? At Valletta? I hoped so. There was no reason to bother me. I couldn't do anything. But their logic might be different than mine. They might not want anyone to talk.

Billy Wayne stroked his chin, leaning forward to rest his elbows on his knees. "I'm curious about you," he said finally, breaking the silence that had fallen between us. "Who you working for, anyway?"

I stared at the top of his head, the red hair, just like that on his chin, looking like bristles on a sow.

Billy Wayne lifted his head and fixed me with a cutting

stare. In the dim light of the reading lamp at the head of the berth his eyes were dark and shiny.

My right hand closed over a knife that I'd secreted out of the galley and kept under the pillow. I didn't like this guy, but I doubted he'd try anything in here. Unless Preston had sent him. But I knew they needed me still.

"So?" he said.

"Same guy as you," I said calmly. "Who else?"

His voice hardened. "What the fuck, you take me for a blithering idiot?"

My jaw tightened.

He repeated my question rhetorically—"Who else?"—his voice low but harsh. "Lots of people. Why do you think his ex-wife is here?"

I frowned. "What do you mean? Her son asked her to come."

"That's what she says. Jeffrey never said a word about it to us."

So what? I thought. Did it matter? I stared at Billy Wayne's beady eyes and asked, "What are you trying to imply?"

"Simple." He opened his arms, palms up. "Someone else told her to be here. Someone who wanted information. Who wanted to know what we're doing and where we're going."

"You seem awful close to Diane to be questioning her motives," I said dryly.

"Self-protection. She's a wily bitch," he said, showing no surprise that I knew what he was doing.

I didn't like his tone. He balls her, I thought, and then calls her a bitch. "You don't seem such a high-and-lofty sort yourself."

He grinned. "That's my job."

"What is your job, anyway? I get the feeling engineering is just a sideline."

He laughed.

I kept at him. "Are you saying something's going on I haven't been told?"

He jerked upright and spoke with sudden vehemence. "Shit yes! You got the brains of a fucking titmouse."

We stared at each other and I let the knife slip from my fingers under the pillow and clenched my fist. It was time to shut Billy Wayne's foul mouth for him. I slid to the edge of the berth and Henderson straightened in the chair.

"She's just like you," he said. "I figure you're either working for someone else or someone's using you."

I swung for him then, but he was ready, ducking under the blow and shoving me to the side. I stumbled and caught myself against the forward bulkhead.

Billy Wayne sprang to his feet and blocked the middle of the room. "What I'm wondering is, who?" he said, his eyes intent on mine.

I glared at him and then my eyes dropped to his belly. A fold of his flannel shirt had caught on the automatic pistol tucked in his belt.

"I wouldn't try anything," he said, grinning. "You may have been in a few drunken brawls, but you haven't fought anyone like me. You might not be in shape to dive tomorrow."

"Get out," I said.

He raised a hand as if I were a dog he was shushing. "Take it easy. You're angry because you don't know what's going on. I'm trying to find out myself. Your life may depend on it, whoever you are."

My eyes narrowed. He knew I wasn't Gene Harrell. But that shouldn't have surprised me. Everyone on the *Nerina* knew. It was just that Billy Wayne was the first to hint that I was a fake. What was he suggesting? That I confess?

"Your concern for my life is touching," I said sarcastically.

152

He shrugged. "Have it your way."

I felt a sense of foreboding in the air. I knew I was just a tool, a diver whose usefulness ended once they got what they wanted. Better yet, I was a diver who was already dead. Gene Harrell had washed up on a beach in Vignetti and they knew it. Once I brought up the safe or what was in it, they could kill me with impunity. But maybe not before finding out who I was, if I was working for someone else.

"Preston send you to talk to me?" I said coldly.

He ignored me. "What do you know about Carlo Spugna?"

My cheek twitched. "About as much as I know about you and Preston Blike."

He didn't respond. Stood waiting.

"What's your interest?" I asked.

He pulled the skin over his Adam's apple. "I got the feeling you not only know Spugna, you work for him."

I laughed and shook my head slowly. "Bullshit. Let me tell you how I feel about Spugna. Spugna's a fucking cockroach spreading filth wherever he goes. The bastard killed my wife and you tell me I work for him." My voice cracked, I was so angry.

He raised both hands. "Okay, okay. You trying to tell me you're a disinterested party?"

I laughed in frustration. "I took this job to get out of a jam," I said slowly, enunciating each word for emphasis. "That's all it is, a job. I do what I'm asked when the time comes, and I scram afterward. I got other things on my mind."

"If what you said about your wife's true, you got Spugna on your mind."

"You could say that. I wouldn't consider you the most brilliant man on earth."

He grinned. "Damn lucky for you. You're in the middle of something that may just make your job easier."

"You know so much about what's going on, why don't you tell me? What's Spugna got to do with this?"

His face grew serious. "Maybe nothing, maybe everything. You'd have to ask Preston."

Ask Preston? I frowned. Was Billy Wayne trying to distance himself from Blike, just as he'd done from Diane?

Billy Wayne leaned back into the door, his hands behind him.

"It took me a while to figure out you weren't a professional," he said. "A plant."

My mind froze on the word *professional*. Professional what?

"Spugna's nephew got you on board the *Nerina*."

"What?" My brow furrowed, and then I shook my head. "Coincidence."

Billy Wayne shoved himself up and reached for the doorknob. "Think about it," he said. "Starting tomorrow, you're going to be working for someone. Better decide who. Can't stand on the sidelines now."

And with that he stepped out and left me to my thoughts.

Billy Wayne had asked if I thought he was a blithering idiot. I didn't know about him, but I sure felt like one.

154

14

WE WERE ANCHORED out of sight of any landmarks, in water that was about eighty feet deep. Two anchors were down, but both lines were only a hundred feet long, so the scope, or length, was insufficient for the anchors to hold well, and we'd drifted some during the night.

Preston wanted to move the *Nerina* directly over the object picked out on the seabed by the underwater detection equipment, but I convinced him I'd rather dive from the dinghy with Billy Wayne handy in case there were problems. The *Nerina* was leeward of the wreck and I could follow the anchor line down, taking a second line from the dinghy to tie off on the yacht—if what we'd spotted really was the *Kirke*.

I ate heavily for breakfast and advised Billy Wayne to do the same.

"Keep you from getting seasick in the dinghy," I explained. "And I'd take a couple of Bonine from the medicine chest if I were you."

He laughed scornfully, said he'd never been seasick a day in his life, and ignored both my suggestions. At least he won't be diving, I thought. All he'd need to do is take in a mouthful or two of salt water on the surface and he'd be sicker than a dog. We had a fresh breeze at eighteen knots and a moderate sea with waves cresting at nearly seven feet. I didn't envy Billy Wayne. I'd make sure he wore one of the old BCs for protection, although, when I thought about it, it wouldn't hurt to have him washed overboard.

We set up the equipment on the aft deck, while Preston paced anxiously and occasionally eyed the horizon with a pair of binoculars. We were in the general proximity of a sea-lane, and traffic was moderate to heavy, with ships steaming from Sicily to the African coast and back.

I told Preston that the first dive would be exploratory only—that I wouldn't try to enter the yacht if it was down there. On the second dive, I'd go down with a dive light and see what I could find inside. My intention was to do just the opposite. I wanted to stay one step ahead of them all the way. If I had to, I'd use my last dive to escape underwater. Either that or a late-night departure by dinghy. The important thing was to get the contents of the safe one dive before they realized I had it.

Before Billy Wayne and I cast off in the dinghy, I slipped into the water and checked my buoyancy. With the wet-suit jacket and buoyancy compensator, I needed quite a few weights. We added twenty-five pounds before I was satisfied. I wanted to be neutrally buoyant at about thirty feet. I'd have to descend against a slight positive buoyancy, but coming up, when I was tired, would be that much safer and easier.

None of the neoprene boots fit, so I wore socks to protect my feet from chafing against the fin straps and a pair of cloth work gloves with textured finger pads to protect my hands if I had to pull myself along the bottom. I had a dive knife strapped to the inside of my left calf, not a weapon but a useful tool—part saw, lever, hammer, pry bar, and probe.

Billy Wayne started the small Mariner outboard engine, and while he guided us into the waves to a location forward of the *Nerina,* his right hand on the steering and throttle arm, his left hand gripping the safety line along the top of the inflatable compartment on the port side, I tied off a quarter-inch line to the bow ring. We had a placement buoy in the dinghy to mark the wreck if I found it.

When we were about where I thought the wreck was, I gave him the okay sign. He cut the throttle so it was low enough to hold us in place and I dropped the line over and then did a back roll off the dinghy. I surfaced immediately to get my bearings. Strapped to my arm was a dive watch and a bourdon tube depth gauge with built-in compass.

I looked at Billy Wayne to give him the down signal and had to shake my head. He was going to have a rough ride. And the smell of gas exhaust wouldn't help. I couldn't wait to get underwater myself, back into a calmer world. In the last five or ten years, I don't think I'd been out of the water for as long a period—four months or so—as had just gone by.

Before letting the air out of the BC, I stretched my Eustachian tubes—holding my nose through the mask's nose pocket and blowing gently to force air into the middle ear—and then started my descent. Within eight feet the wave action disappeared, its underwater effect equal to the height of the surface crests.

On the way down, I equalized every five to seven feet with no problems. Scuba divers know that most ear squeeze problems occur within the first thirty feet, where changes in pressure are the greatest. Below that depth, I equalized every ten feet or so as needed.

Near the surface, the water temperature was bathwater warm, but at about forty feet, the temperature dropped noticeably. I was glad I'd worn the wet-suit jacket.

Below me, at about sixty feet, a school of bluefin tuna veered away as I kicked toward them.

My descent rate was close to a foot per second. I'd known some foolhardy commercial divers who claimed you weren't a pro if you couldn't descend at the rate of a hundred feet per minute. Personally I'd never let penny-pinching bosses put that much pressure on me. The risks were too great—anything from a possible fatal mask squeeze to sinus problems or a ruptured eardrum.

I'd planned a dive of thirty minutes, figuring that my maximum depth would be no more than ninety feet. I wanted to avoid decompression stops, and my maximum time at that depth was exactly thirty minutes. If something unusual should occur, I could stretch it to forty, with a seven-minute decompression stop at ten feet.

From translucent the water became first murky green and then gray, the colors of the various fish slowly disappearing as I descended. I lost sight of the dinghy at about fifty feet, and at eighty I was in a twilight world. Above me, my bubbles rose jerkily into a bowl of gray Jell-O. A school of pelagic fish, similar to the jack family, swam by, skirting me at a distance of ten or so feet. I hoped they weren't fleeing a larger predator.

The current at depth was fairly swift, and the silt in the water made me wish I'd brought along a dive light. Every time my fins struck the rocky bottom, I stirred up a swarm of obfuscating particles that turned the twilight to darkness. Occasionally I spotted other fish nosing around the clouds of plant life I was stirring up, mostly a few sea bream, some fleshy-lipped wrasse, and groupers.

I couldn't see any sign of the wreck, so I started a sweep, beginning at a large rock and using my compass for direction. I followed a shrinking-square search pattern, fifty kicks before turning, three turns at right angles before cutting the kicks by ten. By the time I spotted the wreck, fifteen minutes had passed since I left the surface and I wasn't happy. Almost no time for more than a cursory check.

The bow of the yacht was wedged between two large rocks. I tied off the rope I was carrying, two half hitches around the jack staff, and then started out slowly along the port side, moving against the current and intending to swim around the boat. For a while I was accompanied by a lone, blue shark, a good four feet in length, swimming leisurely to my right. The shark was an annoyance that slowed me down—forced me to focus my attention on two things at once. Made me wish I had a ski pole to whack across its snout. Anytime he disappeared behind me, I had to turn for fear he was coming up to attack. The blue finally left after sating its curiosity but, fortunately for me, not its hunger.

From bow to stern on the port side the yacht was intact, its name—*Kirke*—barely visible on the stern. But when I swam around to the starboard side I saw the damage that had sunk her. Just aft of amidships a ragged hole appeared in the keel, garboard strakes and bilge stringers jutting out like toothpicks. An explosion of some sort, from inside out. Not much fire damage, indicating a rapid and catastrophic sinking. I wasn't really qualified to tell if the explosion was natural or an act of sabotage, but I suspected the latter.

If the ship had been scuttled by modern-day pirates, then the safe would be either empty or gone altogether.

The current pulled me away from the boat and I saw that the yacht was about fifty feet away from a ravine that dropped precipitously into darkness. No telling how deep, but if the *Kirke* had lasted two weeks wedged where she was, she'd last another day or two.

I looked at my watch. Going on thirty minutes. Time to ascend.

On the way up, head back and arm raised, exhaling as I went, I felt a twinge of disappointment at not being able to begin my exploration inside the yacht. It looked like I was going to have to do some lying—and a few more dives—to get one up on the *Nerina*'s gang. I was thinking about my future as much as I was about the contents of the safe.

Suddenly I remembered I'd left the down line tied to

the *Kirke*'s jack staff. I didn't want to go back down, so I considered surreptitiously untying the line at the bow ring on the dinghy and blaming Billy Wayne for losing it. But I couldn't do that either. He'd seen me tie a good running bow knot. The fault would be mine.

Ah hell, I thought, as the circle of sunlight expanded above me, just tell Billy Wayne and Preston I set a rock on the bitter end. Nothing illogical about that. The simplest lie was always the best. I'd claim that I figured anchoring the line would make it easier to take up the search on the second dive.

I surfaced about fifty feet from the dinghy, inflated the BC, and swam over to Billy Wayne on snorkel. He didn't look too good, had his head hanging over the side of the dinghy, his blotchy, red skin pale.

I smothered a grin. "How you doing, Billy Wayne?"

He threw me a baleful look and said through clenched teeth, "I'm alive."

"Just barely," I said. "Let's get you back to the *Nerina*. A little food, some rest, and a few Bonine will do the trick."

He spoke with some effort. "Why don't we just go back and get another tank? Take care of the safe now."

The little bastard had guts all right. If I were in his shoes, I'd want to find the nearest berth and hide there.

I threw my fins in the dinghy and then the weight belt. "Can't do it that way, Billy. Need a surface interval or I'll start having problems with excess nitrogen." I tied my inflated BC with tank to the dinghy's painter and pulled myself in. "I go down too soon and you'll have my blood bubbling, like carbonated soda."

"Preston won't be happy."

I shrugged. "None of us are happy. That's life. If the boat's there, I'll find it. We got plenty of time today for another dive."

He closed his eyes and his face grew paler.

160

"Go ahead and vomit," I said. "You'll feel better."

He didn't respond at first, then whispered, "Nothing to vomit."

"Okay, you just lie there and I'll take us back."

I put the engine in neutral, moved forward, untied the line from the bow ring and attached it to the ring buoy. "I've anchored it with a rock," I said. "We can start at the same spot this afternoon."

Henderson said nothing and I wasn't sure he heard, but I wanted to practice the lie before telling it to Blike.

Halfway to the *Nerina* Billy Wayne took some deep breaths and managed to speak. "You said, *if the boat's there*. Didn't you find it?" He opened his bleary eyes, looking at me expectantly.

I shook my head. "Couldn't. Not enough light. I'll go down after lunch and look again."

"All this for nothing," he said weakly. "Shit."

I just grinned and cut the throttle, easing us up to the *Nerina*'s stern, where we'd moved the accommodation ladder. "That's the way it works sometimes," I told Henderson. "Not much visibility down there."

Billy Wayne was right. Preston wasn't happy when I said I hadn't seen the *Kirke*. "The damn thing's right there on the sonar," he growled.

I shrugged and peeled out of the wet suit. "I left a buoy out there. Rope's under a rock. We won't waste time covering the same ground twice."

"When can you go down again?"

I looked at my watch. "Let me check the dive tables. I want to get my residual nitrogen time down as low as possible. At this depth my total bottom time gets cut down if the surface interval's not long enough."

Preston Blike, his head tipped back and neck stiff, stared at me as if I were talking in Greek.

I went down to the storage locker and found a copy of the U.S. Navy Dive Tables, laminated in plastic. I'd stayed under the no-decompression limits, but having been at ninety feet for thirty mintues, I fell in group designation *G.* When I consulted the Residual Nitrogen Timetable for Repetitive Air Dives, I saw that I'd need a surface interval of at least three hours. That would move me up into group *C,* which meant that on a second dive to ninety feet, I'd go down having a residual nitrogen time of eleven minutes. In simple terms, that meant my maximum time down on the second dive would be thirty minutes less eleven, or only nineteen total if I wanted to avoid a decompression stop. Not the most favorable situation, but it would make it easier to lie. Preston would believe me if I claimed to have just had enough time to find the *Kirke.* He'd be happy that it was there. And I, in reality, would have already made my first inspection of the safe—provided *it* was there.

In the galley, over lunch, with all four of us sitting around the dinette, Billy Wayne having gulped a double dose of Bonine seasick pills and eaten a few saltine crackers, I asked Preston what the combination to the safe was.

He narrowed his eyes and then grinned amiably. "Aren't you jumping the gun, Gene?"

I shrugged. "Got to learn it sometime." I tapped my head. "Don't have the greatest memory. Start me now and maybe I'll have it down by the time I need it."

He laughed again and gave me a sequence of three numbers—37 right, 15 left, 24 right. I knew he figured he had nothing to worry about now. I repeated the numbers three times and then Preston added, "The safe's in the master stateroom, midcabin. To the port side of the ship. Let's just hope Jeffrey didn't hide the jewels elsewhere."

The mention of Jeffrey set me to thinking. No one on the *Nerina* seemed curious about him. There was no sense of foreboding, just eagerness to recover the safe. Had they grown that used to the idea that Jeffrey was dead? And what would I do if I discovered a corpse down there? The thought wasn't pleasant. In the absence of air, decomposition would be slowed down, but a body might not be a pretty sight after two weeks. I hoped Diane would be satisfied with a watery grave for her boy. But there wasn't much choice. We couldn't keep human remains on the *Nerina*.

I emptied my mind of the gruesome thought and said, "Well, if the *Kirke*'s down there. I won't have time to do more than a visual inspection this afternoon. Wish me luck. I'm going to go take a nap if I can. Wake me at two." I'd started my surface interval time at eleven-fifteen. "I want to be in the water around two-thirty."

Billy Wayne had recovered his complexion—bad as it was—by the time we were ready for the second dive. He took two more Bonine before we got in the dinghy.

"You'll sleep the whole time I'm down at this rate," I said.

He didn't appreciate the comment.

"You got nothing to worry about at my end," he replied impassively.

"Just joking, Billy Wayne. You won't have to worry about holding the dinghy over the site. We can just tie back up to the down line."

Ten minutes later, in the water, dive light hanging from a one-foot line attached to my left wrist, I checked my watch, gave the okay signal to Henderson, and went down. Once out of his sight, within the first ten feet, I kicked for the bottom, clearing my ears as often as I could while I plummeted down. I wouldn't have much time to get the job done. If I found the safe, whatever was in it would come topside hidden in one of the BC's pouches.

When I reached the *Kirke*'s jack staff, I swam imme-diately to the companionway leading to the cabin area, the dive light illuminating my way. Inside the yacht, it was pitch black and cold. I shivered, more from fear at what I might find than from the cold.

A few years ago, when I was on vacation in Italy, I saw the movie *Jaws* in a run-down third-class cinema in Milan. The Italians had retitled the film aptly—albeit generically. *Lo Squalo* they called it—The Shark—and I was mindful of the scene where the head falls out of the sunken boat when Richard Dreyfuss dives down to check it out.

I was expecting more of the same, but there wasn't a sign that anyone had gone down with the boat. No putrefying bodies, no corpses eaten to the bone.

The area forward of the galley was a mess—total destruction. This was no simple underwater explosion—unless the gas for the galley's stove had gone off, triggering somehow a second explosion in the engine compartment. But that seemed doubtful.

I looked at my watch. I had only ten minutes to find the safe, open it, and start my ascent.

I ignored the destruction forward and followed the beam of light through a door and into the master stateroom. I didn't expect to find the safe. The yacht looked to have been sunk on purpose and you don't destroy a fine boat without first getting what you want. The *Kirke* hadn't gone down in a storm, though I had to keep telling myself there was always a chance the explosions were of natural origin.

Find the safe, I told myself. And then open it, take what's inside, and get out of here. The bubbles from the exhaust ports of the second stage regulator roared by my ears, distracting me. I flashed the light upward, saw the bubbles flattening out and sliding out of sight toward the upper end of the stateroom.

The safe, to my surprise, was right where Preston Blike had said it would be. I glanced at my watch. Seven minutes. Time enough. I focused the dive light on the tumbler, spun it around once out of reflex, and was about to turn it to 37 right when I thought I saw lights.

I shut my dive light off, raised my head, and realized I could see out the port windows. My heart flip-flopped and my stomach felt suddenly hollow. I wasn't alone.

Two divers were approaching the *Kirke,* swimming fast. I could see the lead diver's spear gun in the hazy light of the following diver. It wasn't a reassuring sight. Armed men who knew where they were going.

Damn. I looked behind me toward the companionway. I couldn't see a thing. I'd have to use my own light to find my way out and I couldn't delay. If I was trapped inside . . . I didn't like the thought. These weren't two friendly divers out looking for amphorae.

In my panic, afraid to turn on my dive light, I swam into a forward bulkhead, knocking my mask to the side and breaking the seal.

Salt water hit my eyes, bringing sudden disorientation, the complete darkness adding to the shock. But the experience wasn't new and I calmed myself, cleared the mask, and tried to get my bearings.

I had to turn on the dive light then. I was sure the two divers had seen my bubbles anyway. It was me they were coming after.

With the aid of the light, I found the door leading into the companionway and started to move toward the port waterway when I realized I was too late. The two divers were swimming toward the hatch, cutting off my escape.

I looked around. Nowhere to hide. I bent my left leg, found the dive knife, and slipped it from its sheath. My mind narrowed down at that point, tuning out other stimuli, concentrating on the task at hand. A confrontation. Two against one. It didn't look good. I was a fish caught in its cave, I thought. But a fish with teeth. Let's see how well I could bite.

15

SOMEHOW I HAD to avoid the two divers and get out of the yacht. Inside the narrow confines of the sunken boat their spear guns would be of limited utility. Still, I didn't like the idea of facing their weapons—and two against one lessened my odds of coming out of this alive. My dive knife suddenly seemed puny. Hadn't I always thought of it as a working tool and not a weapon?

I turned and swam athwartships to the starboard waterway, and then toward the stern. As I moved aft I used the dive light to look for the hatch to the engine room. If I could find that, I might be able to make a getaway out the hole I'd seen in the starboard side. Wait until both were inside the cabin and then exit out the opposite side.

I heard a metallic clang echo through the hull. A tank hitting metal. They were moving down the port companionway ladder. I extinguished my light. I hoped they stayed together.

No such luck. One moved toward the bow on the port side and the other swam athwartships up the companionway toward the cabin door. I held my breath and prayed he'd enter the cabin. A few of my exhaust bubbles were still seeping out the door and finding their way to the top. It looked like I was inside.

My prayer was answered. The light disappeared into the cabin and I exhaled and took a deep breath.

I moved aft in darkness, feeling my way past three upright lockers. In the dark, it was easy to become disoriented.

In a few minutes, the diver inside would realize I wasn't in the cabin. Would he go forward to find his buddy before coming aft?

My first thought was a wish that he would. Let him go in the opposite direction. I'd have more time to find the engine hatch. But just as quickly I realized the advantages of him pursuing me by himself. One at a time. I would have a chance.

It's always dangerous underwater to hold one's breath. Scuba instructors tell you never to stop breathing. But if he came toward me and I expected to surprise him, I'd have to attack from darkness with no sign of bubbles.

Too many thoughts assailed me for clear thinking—strategy, options to consider, questions about the other diver's intent, fear. In the darkness, the fear was magnified until it threatened to suffocate rational thought.

It was time for me to use the light again. I switched it on and almost immediately spotted the engine room hatch. I kicked toward it and pulled on the ring.

The hatch was jammed.

A light stabbed up the waterway toward me. Had the guy seen my light?

I swore to myself and wrenched on the hatch. It budged but wouldn't open.

The knife. Pry the hatch open! I stuck the blade into the crack and pried.

The blade broke and I swore again—at the knife and at myself. I shouldn't have trusted the *Nerina*'s equipment. Should've bought my own.

I was just about to give up, had only a second before I'd have to turn and defend myself, when the hatch cover gave way.

Still gripping the knife handle, I thrust through the opening and pulled the cover shut behind me. I swung the light around the room, felt my eyes open wide to absorb the limited visual input.

There, the opening! Large enough for a man. I drove toward it, pushing my way through the jumble of shattered planks and skeletal timber.

Behind me I heard the shriek of metal. Light cascaded through the hatch. With my right hand I found the cord that attached the dive light to my left wrist and began sawing with the edge of the severed blade. The cord snapped and I tossed the light to my right.

It floated lazily, it's beam pointing upward.

And with that I kicked my way out of the *Kirke* and into the lighter twilight surrounding the ship.

The dive light would fool the guy for no more than five or ten seconds. I looked up, considered kicking for the surface, and decided I didn't know what I'd find topside.

I felt the current tug on me and remembered the ravine. That was my best bet. Draw them deeper. As long as my air lasted, I had a chance. As a commercial diver, I was used to depths far exceeding those of most sport divers, who rarely go below a hundred feet. At those depths, to anyone not used to the process, nitrogen narcosis sets in. Martini's law. I'd seen it do some strange things to divers.

As I scissor-kicked my way toward the dark gorge cut deep into the sea floor, I had the craziest memory—an Indian story that I must have first heard in the fifth or sixth grade in a two-room schoolhouse outside Regina— the story of the white man who challenged his captors to a race. The Indians forced the man to run barefoot. If he could outrun then, he'd be free, but the ground was covered with cacti.

As I recalled the tale, the barefoot runner out-distanced all but one Indian, the tribe's best runner. Finally, the white man stopped and faced the brave's spear. The Indian threw and missed and the white man killed him with his own weapon and then hid underwater, breathing through a reed, while the rest of the tribe looked in vain for him.

I don't know that I believe in prescience, but when I reached the gulf and started down the steep ridge, only one diver followed me. The other hovered at the top of the underwater cliff, waiting.

When I looked over my shoulder, I saw what I thought was the blue shark circling around the diver near the sunken yacht.

I felt a surge of exultation. I hoped the shark was starved, that the diver was stupid and scared enough to spear it. I knew that blue sharks were relatively harmless but a wounded one would attract others. "Get him, get him," I said to the shark and then forced myself to calm down.

Was I already feeling the effects of the greater depth?

I tried to read my depth gauge while swimming but couldn't focus on the dial. The light was fading rapidly, shrinking the perimeter of visibility.

I slowed my pace. Visibility was less than ten feet. If I had trouble reading my depth gauge, the diver chasing me would have trouble seeing me. Until he was close enough for his light to pick me out, I was one shadow among many.

I looked back. What I saw brought an involuntary giggle to my lips—the callous response of a drunk—and I choked and lost the regulator.

Breathing cold salt water sometimes has a salutory effect. In this case, it made me forget the diver spiraling above me, his spear gun hanging free from a cord attached to his wrist; it forced me to concentrate, made me realize I couldn't go much deeper without floating into that peaceful state where nothing would matter. My air would run out and I'd fall gently to sleep. Eternal sleep.

It was no consolation that the diver above me would soon join me on the bottom.

I found the regulator over my right shoulder, closed my teeth around the flanged mouthpiece, purged it, and coughed the water out of my lungs. My left hand found the BC's mechanical inflater and I gave the button a quick punch. At this depth, my wet-suit jacket had lost much of its buoyancy with the compression of the gas bubbles in the foam neoprene, and the weight belt was pulling me down.

The burst of low-pressure air drove me upwards and I let it carry me. As I came up, exhaling slowly, I knew I'd have to pull the dump valve or the expanding air in the jacket would launch me on an uncontrolled ascent. I'd been down far too long to rise straight to the surface without experiencing the bends. I needed to stay under, to keep the nitrogen in solution until it passed from the blood to the lungs and out of my body.

For the moment, I had only one concern. Would I be okay when I reached the surface? I'd seen what the bends can do to a careless or misfortunate diver. Bent-over was only the half of it. Nitrogen coming out of solution in the bloodstream could cause anything from itching skin, pain in the joints, labored breathing, and chest pain to blindness, paralysis, convulsions, and eventually death.

Bleeding a little air from my vest, I floated past the nitrogen-drunk diver, having decided not even to bother with him. He didn't have much time left. The mouthpiece hung slack in his lips. He didn't see me move past, and I knew he wouldn't make it any higher.

I looked up, saw the other diver still swimming at the edge of the ravine.

"Kiss your buddy, good-bye," I said to myself, thinking it was too bad the shark hadn't got the one waiting above.

As I approached the edge of the cliff, following the gently mushrooming bubbles, my ascent a steady foot per second, I looked at the pressure gauge, holding it to my face with my left hand.

I was down to seven hundred pounds. On scuba, in normal circumstances, I always began my ascent with a minimum of five hundred pounds. I never arrived back at the boat with less than three hundred in the tank. It was a small enough amount, but allowed for emergencies.

This, however, was an emergency. I'd have to act fast, run the tank dry if necessary. I knew I could abandon the backpack and make an emergency free-swimming ascent on one lungful of air if I had to. In the Navy, submarine training consisted in part of free ascents from depths deeper than two hundred feet. The air in a diver's lungs expanded as he rose, providing sufficient oxygen to make it to the surface.

Of course, I thought wryly, the Navy occasionally lost a few men that way, too.

I had one advantage, I realized. The diver waiting for me couldn't tell by the bubbles how close I was. For all he knew, his buddy and I were down another hundred feet.

For a moment, I regretted not stopping at the deeper diver. It wouldn't have taken much to strip him of his spear gun—or a knife at least. I had no weapon.

When you're underwater without a spear gun or a knife, there's darn little you can do from a distance.

You can't shout to distract your enemy, you can't throw a rock.

I had no desire to approach the diver unarmed, even with the shadows and poor visibility.

I looked down, saw the exhaust bubbles still rising from below and decided my best bet was to hold my breath, move horizontally just below the edge of the ridge, and come up some ways to the side of the diver standing guard over the precipice. Avoid him altogether.

As I swam away with forceful flutter kicks, I looked quickly over my shoulder. The diver hung suspended above the ravine, oblivious to my departure. A minute later, I expelled my pent-up breath and carefully pulled myself by hand up the rocky projections of the cliff face.

From my position on top of the ridge, I could barely make out the dim shape of the yacht in the distance. Suddenly lights appeared on the aft deck and I realized two other divers were manipulating a sling around a square object.

There goes the safe, I thought.

I strained to find the anchor line of the *Nerina,* while slowly swimming toward the *Kirke.* Gone. And wasn't that the down line from the dinghy trailing off the forward deck?

It was.

I was getting too close, couldn't risk them seeing my exhaust, so I turned reluctantly and swam with the current back to the drop-off.

From there, I watched them ascend with the safe, the third diver following a few minutes later, abandoning his buddy far below.

When they were indistinguishable shapes in the distance, I moved back toward the boat, keeping to the edge of the precipice, and saw why there was no effort to rescue their buddy. No exhaust bubbles.

I looked up, worried about how much time I'd spent on the dive and how deep I'd gone. I looked at the luminous dial on my watch. It seemed I'd been down forever, but only forty minutes total had gone by. Still, I was beyond the no-decompression limits and damn short of air. My agitated breathing, verging on panic, had drained the tank. If I couldn't pick up another tank on top and get back down, I'd be in bad trouble. The bends.

I checked my pressure gauge. Shit! Only two hundred pounds. That was nothing. I'd be breathing water in a few minutes.

I looked up again. I had to make a decision—easy, considering my limited choices. Under the circumstances, I had two options—ascend and be captured and probably killed, stay where I was and die of asphyxia, commonly but no more soothingly known as drowning.

Or was there a third choice?

Yes, I said to myself. There was.

I went down.

Could I find the dead diver before my air ran out? And if I did, would he have any air in his tank?

I'd better find him and he'd better have air, I thought.

I began searching along the ridge, dropping as quickly as I dared down the rugged slope. I knew as I went deeper, the air in my tank would shrink under the greater ambient pressure. It wouldn't last more than a few more breaths.

I found the guy at a depth of 160 feet, the regulator swinging free. His pressure gauge showed 1,200 pounds of pressure, and I fought a wave of exultation as I began to strip him of his gear.

Before I could get his pack off, my air ran out and I had to switch to his regulator, which made for some awkward maneuvering. A touch of light-headedness didn't help. Finally, I got it into my head to kick my way slowly upward as I worked.

When I had his tank pack free, I slipped out of my BC, released the regulator, and unsnapped the latch holding the tank in place. The tank dropped immediately into the darkness below, following the regulator.

By the time I loosened the pack straps and slipped the new BC and tank over my shoulders, I was exhausted. I hit the mechanical inflater button and pumped some air into the BC. It made for an uncontrolled ascent but I was too tired to kick my way up. The cold was beginning to bring on leg cramps.

I almost gave in to the impulse to fall asleep, but as I rose toward the one-hundred-foot mark, my mind started functioning again.

I bled a little air from the BC to slow my ascent and looked at my dive watch and then the pressure gauge. I still had just over a thousand pounds. By staying calm, I could expect to use the final forty-five minutes or so for a slow ascent. It was impossible to judge how deep I'd been and for how long, but there was no doubt I'd exceeded by far my safety limits.

My subjective time below a hundred feet seemed immense; I only hoped in real time that I'd spent five or ten minutes there. It wasn't going to do me much good to get to the surface if I suffered from the bends when I got there. I clutched the extra BC in my arms and thought, ironic to have struggled so hard to survive below only to die on the surface.

I relaxed as completely as I could and let my slight positive buoyancy lift me. My plan was to stay around thirty feet for as long as I could—until my air ran out if necessary. Then I'd drop my weight belt and ascend to the surface, where I'd have two BCs for flotation.

In fact, I spent thirty minutes at thirty feet, another ten at twenty, and fifteen more at ten feet before the pressure in the tank finally dropped away.

The current had continued to pull me along and when I surfaced, nothing was in sight. Where was the *Nerina*'s crew? At the bottom of the sea or had they made their escape?

Despite the warmer water, my legs were shivering. I manually inflated the extra BC and wrapped it around my thighs. I was floating on my back, the spent tank providing trim. I rested for fifteen minutes—trying to soak up some sun and stop my shivering—before I began to take stock of my situation. I had my whistle, but no flare. If I wasn't picked up soon, night would fall, lessening the odds of survival. Hypothermia would set in once the sun disappeared. I knew water absorbed heat twenty-five times fast than air. A diver at rest chills within one to two hours in water as warm as eighty degrees.

I checked the compass on my wrist. The current was bearing me toward the east. At some point, I'd be in the path of the ships plying the waters between Sicily and Malta. Might be able to spot a navigational buoy.

Every ten minutes, I raised up and tried to scan the horizon in a circle around me. The wave action made viewing difficult.

I spotted the fishing boat near four-thirty that afternoon. I started blowing my whistle and back-paddling toward the south, moving at an angle to the current. I didn't know what they were doing out here at this hour of the evening—usually fishermen were back in their harbors by ten in the morning—but I wasn't complaining. It took them a while to sight me and I was afraid for a moment they were all deaf, but they finally chugged over to me, their outboard motor trailing a plume of blue exhaust.

They gave me water and bread and then forced me to drink some wine. Two Maltese fishermen, father and son, both their faces leathery from constant exposure to the elements, their language difficult to understand. We made do with a mixture of Italian and Arabic. They would have understood my effusive thanks no matter what the language.

As we made our way south, the sun two hours above the horizon to our right, the old man tried to explain their problems. Engine trouble, he said. Took them most of the day to fix it.

They'd thrown their catch back into the sea. Then he grinned and said, "Lost it all, but caught the big fish, eh?"

I had to agree.

16

WE RAISED A landfall at dusk and by the time light disappeared from the sky we could make out the rotating beam of a lighthouse.

"Gordan," the older fisherman said. "Above Pinu Point." He spoke in Maltese to his son at the tiller, and the boat changed course.

I asked in Italian where we were going, and the son, who'd introduced himself as Pawlu and his father as Safiq, said, "Xweini Bay."

A moment later, Pawlu said, "We take you by mule to Zebbug."

"Zebbug," I repeated dumbly, to show I'd understood. Not that it helped. I hadn't had much time to think about what I was going to do on Gozo. Somehow, without money, I had to get across the Comino Channel to Malta.

The British High Commission in Floriana would be my first stop. They could put me in contact with the closest Canadian Embassy, which was in Rome. Using my real name, I shouldn't have too many problems getting a duplicate passport, as well as money from one of my Italian bank accounts. I'd been smart, I thought, to use Gene Harrell's identity on Vignetti. If the Italian police were looking for a fugitive, good luck to them. I was happy to be alive and rid of the *Nerina*'s crew—even if I'd wound up working for nothing. I had the feeling Preston never meant to pay me with anything but the contents of a gun. Better to forget them and their fate and turn my attention to Carlo Spugna.

As we approached the small harbor, I could see the lights of Zebbug, a long, narrow village high on what I would soon learn was a rugged hill. The bay itself was unlit and we put in by feel rather than by sight. Pawlu ran the boat up on the rocky beach and I helped the two men unload the nets. We worked in the dark for nearly two hours, hanging the nets to dry and clearing out the boat, which was one of the more crowded vessels I'd ever been in.

When the work was completed, we finished off a bottle of wine and then began a long hard climb from the bay to the top of the cliffs. There, a young girl was waiting with two mules and a small propane lamp. She embraced Pawlu and they talked animatedly while Safiq and I struggled to catch our breath.

Pawlu turned to me. "My younger sister, Teresa," he said. "She and I will walk. You and *Ic-Cappa* can ride." *Ic-Cappa,* as Pawlu had told me, was Safiq's *laqam,* his nickname. "We take a path and then a road," he added. "You will stay tonight with us and tomorrow . . ." He shrugged his shoulders and smiled. "Tomorrow will take care of itself."

I would have liked to have been magnanimous and offered one of the mules to Teresa, but I was so exhausted by then that I made no complaints. In fact, despite the mule's bony spine, I slept for the first part of the trip, awakening only when we reached the road.

Fifteen minutes later, we were on the outskirts of Zebbug, where we stopped at a humble cottage on a side road of packed dirt. Teresa put the mules in a small shed behind the house while the two fishermen and I went in to meet the mother.

The mother, stocky but pleasant-looking, was clearly happy to see both men home safely. They talked for a

178

while in Maltese but I was too dazed to pay attention—other than to note that the conversation was about their boat and then me.

Pawlu rummaged about in a large chest and brought out a pair of black cotton plants and a light blue pullover shirt with no collar. "You wear," he said.

I smiled appreciation. *"Grazzi hafna."*

I took the clothes and hesitated. Water was scarce on all the islands of the archipelago, but I wanted to wash the dried salt from my body before donning clean clothes. The air was heavy with humidity and I was sagging. A shower would do me a world of good.

"Skuzi, jekk joghgbok, ghandex una doccia?" I asked, trying to imitate falling water with my fingers.

The mother smiled at my mixture of Maltese and Italian. *"Iva, iva,"* she said, nodding her head emphatically. "Pawlu, take him to the shower and then we'll eat."

Pawlu picked up the propane lamp and we walked to a small concrete platform behind the mule shed. Ten feet above the platform, a water tower rested on four stilts, its black shape blocking out a patch of stars.

I stood in the middle of the platform, stripped, and left my shirt and the swim suit Billy Wayne had loaned me at my feet. When Pawlu opened the valve, a stream of warm water splashed down, the force of the blow draining the tension from my body. My head, utterly relaxed, wobbled on my neck. I wanted to stand there forever, but with a tremendous effort of will, forced myself to snap out of it. I didn't want to abuse their generosity.

There was no soap. I saw that the runoff was carried by trough to a nearby lemon tree. I ran my hands quickly over my limbs and then nodded at Pawlu. The water stopped almost immediately.

I stood outside for another five minutes, drying in the air and looking up in tired amazement at the tiny mother-of-pearl buttons stitched in random profusion across the sky.

This was the same sky Carlo Spugna would see if he stepped outside—and Donata. . . . A strange sensation overwhelmed me. I was alive and on land. With people I didn't really know. Tossed about like a piece of driftwood.

Back in the cottage, with me dressed in Pawlu's clothes, we sat down at a wooden table and the mother served the three of us dinner—a stew of boiled onions, potatoes, tomatoes, and small chunks of rabbit. The two men filled my glass with more of the coarse red wine, toasted what seemed everything under the sun, and when the meal was over, I was ready to collapse again—half drunk, and exhausted to the point of sickness.

The mother laid a thin mattress on the floor next to the table, apologizing for its shortness—at which I apologized for my height—and I fell asleep the second my head touched the cotton padding.

I woke instantly from dreamless sleep, wondering where I was and what had startled me. The air in the room was cool, the light pale. Dawn, no one stirring. And then I sensed a presence in the room and sat up suddenly. Three men stood just inside the door, none of whom I recognized.

I stared at them, my mouth open, no words coming out. Two of them exchanged a few words in a low whisper and then stopped uneasily as I got to my feet.

"Where's Pawlu?" I asked in Italian.

"I'm Pietru," one of the men said. He looked like a corsair, rough-shaven and surly of face. "Come with us." He spoke Maltese, but the meaning was clear. I didn't seem to have much choice.

I looked around the room, feeling a touch of apprehension run down my spine. I was getting tired of seeing people I didn't know and didn't trust.

"Pawlu's gone fishing," one of the other men said. "We take care of you. You come with us. We go by car."

I nodded. At least he spoke English. Was this more of the fabled Maltese hospitality?

"Where are we going?" I asked.

Everyone hesitated. I got to my feet and stared expectantly at the man who'd spoken English. "Nardu Azzini," he said, sticking out his hand to shake mine. A name. He hadn't answered my question; it was his own name and not a location he was giving me.

I could see all three waiting. They wanted to know what I was called.

I cleared my throat, clasped Nardu's hand, and said, "Jake Roberts." I couldn't think of a better name. Surprised myself even. I hadn't thought of Jake in a long time. But my old tender wouldn't mind me using his name. Texans were generous.

Apparently one formal introduction was sufficient. Without further words, the three men led me to a gray delivery truck the size of a small van. The name of a winery was painted along the side in red.

I got in the back with Nardu and Pietru, while the other man drove. The three of us in back sat on a bench running along the wall of the van to the driver's left. When they'd first opened the door and I saw the bench, I was sure Pietru and Nardu would want me to sit between them, so I scrambled in immediately and took the forwardmost position. No one seemed willing to ask me to move.

"Where did you say we were going?" I asked again.

"We arrive soon at the village," Nardu said curtly.

I sighed and lapsed into thought. I hoped the "village" meant Victoria, known to the Gozitans by its Arabic name of Rabat. Rabat was the chief town on the island, an administrative and commercial center with a population of nearly seven thousand. I could get help there.

I tried to keep my mind busy. I think I was afraid to admit to myself what my subconscious was screaming—that I'd fallen into the hands of Spugna's men—so I tried to think of other possibilities.

The three peasants looked like highwaymen, but any fool would know a man picked up at sea didn't have money. Not that they couldn't ransom me. Or try, that is. But there was no one willing to pay to free me.

The thought was discouraging until I realized I could ransom myself. I had money in Italy and plenty of it.

And then again sometimes the worst-looking men turned out to be the nicest. But until I knew for sure, I felt paralyzed.

We drove for what seemed about twenty minutes, our progress slow and laborious. I stretched my neck and tried to look out the front window but couldn't see much from the back. I kept slipping and sliding around on the bench, my shoulders jostling Pietru's.

We passed through a small village soon after leaving Zebbug. I didn't catch the name. Once we slowed down to drive through a herd of goats feeding on the verge at both sides of the narrow asphalted road. And then, after we came to a crossroad and turned right, a green bus with white top passed us going in the opposite direction. All impressions which I absorbed and cataloged.

As in Britain, driving was on the left. I missed the names on the front of the passing bus, caught only what looked like the number four.

But the next road sign was clearly visible. The road split into a Y, the branch to the right leading to Gharb, that to the left toward San Lawrenz.

We took the turn to the left.

I was growing more tense. Why am I so stupid? I wondered. Why can't I act when I have to?

182

I wanted to bolt for the back door but knew I couldn't make it past Nardu and Pietru.

Just wait and see, I told myself. Patience.

In the village of San Lawrenz the driver took a right turn down an unpaved road. We were heading west, toward the coast but away from habitation. My face muscles tightened with tension and I tried to relax my jaw before grinding my teeth away.

Suddenly the land split and fell from a narrow opening into a small *wied*. The driver turned into the valley following a road yet more primitive. Steep walls rose on both sides of the truck, the karstic terrain barren of vegetation. After a quarter of a mile or less, all in shade, the road suddenly climbed toward a plateau and we burst back into dazzling sunlight. In minutes we had a sea view. And finally, on top of the mesa, a beautiful villa appeared, a three-story building surrounded by a stone wall.

We drove through a gate and pulled to a stop in front of a massive entrance portal. The blocked-stone arch stretched fifteen feet above the ground. On both sides of the arch, each story of the villa had an elaborate balcony with panels that looked more like wood than stone. The balconies rested on four corbels carved in the shape of falcons.

The large front door swung open and a dapper man with a big smile stepped out onto the driveway, his hand extended toward me. He wore a pair of dark slacks and a white dress shirt embroidered with lace, the top three buttons undone. A medallion of the Virgin Mary hung on a gold chain over his hairy chest.

I took a hesitant step forward, feeling awkward in my peasant clothes.

"Well, Mr. Henderson," the man said. "Pleased to meet you." He spoke with a British accent, but it seemed a second language, the intonation not quite right. "We thought you might show up. I'm Carlo Spugna."

I stared at the fellow, frozen for five seconds that seemed an eternity, and then I burst into uncontrollable laughter.

They thought I was Billy Wayne Henderson!

Fear does strange things to a man. In my case it left me a little unhinged, a state in which everything seemed funny. I felt as if I were drunk.

I shook the man's hand and snickered like a crazy man. "Since we're friends, call me Billy Wayne," I said.

And then I swayed dizzily, and Carlo Spugna grabbed my arm and led me inside.

We stepped into a hallway lined with framed photos of family members. I thought about what the old man Safiq had said out on the boat. He hadn't been joking. They had caught the big fish. I couldn't wipe the crazy grin off my face, but I was sick with apprehension. A heavy ball of nausea settled in the pit of my stomach.

This weaselly old man was Carlo Spugna! Carlo Spugna—the guy responsible for Wanda's death. And now I was dangling on his hook.

"Billy Wayne, may I offer you a glass of Maltese wine?"

I nodded, my mind swimming in emotions too strong to understand. Might as well be drunk in reality. I couldn't get a grasp on the situation.

I drank half the glass, the same coarse red wine offered to me by Safiq and Pawlu, and choked. Spugna patted me on the arm in a fatherly gesture.

"Our Maltese wines require acclimation, Billy Wayne."

I nodded again, suddenly mind weary, and then slowly said, "I'm not Billy Wayne."

"Oh come now, Mr. Henderson. It's no use at this point to dissemble. We all know who you are."

I stared at Spugna's smile, trying to gauge his character. He glistened like a snake, his thinning black hair combed straight back off his forehead and hanging just below his collar. He was a short fellow, his features like his name denoting an Italian origin.

Spugna sat down across from me, relaxing into a high-backed chair upholstered in a teal blue fabric. He took a sip of his wine. "What happened to the dinghy? My men said they found you floating at sea."

I shrugged. "What's it matter?"

He grinned. "Don't be surly. I'm interested in you."

"Yeah, I bet."

Spugna jumped to his feet. "Come with me, Mr. Henderson. Let me show you the view."

We walked through a sumptuous dining room and out to a patio overlooking a kidney-shaped swimming pool.

"For my children," he said.

My heart skipped a beat. Donata Pellico had to be here somewhere.

"Where are they?" I asked.

"They've just started school this week. They're studying. Come, I want to show you my gardens."

We walked down a winding path lined by prickly pear and dead tamarisks. Suddenly a narrow side valley opened up to our left, some distance below. I could see workers in two terraced fields marked off by drystone walls. Limestone tablelands rose around the valley.

Spugna pointed. "Cotton in the summer," he said. "Early potatoes in the winter. For export. For ourselves we try to grow a little of everything—figs, pumpkins, tomatoes, onions, barley." He paused and sniffed the air. "Smell that sea breeze? The other side of the valley leads to a plateau. Just beyond that, cliffs three hundred feet high fall away to the sea."

He paused again, apparently to let that sink in. He was standing uncomfortably close. I smelled not the breeze but his strong cologne. I nodded and moved away a step, my hands in my pockets.

He followed me. "Farming, fishing, and tourism—twenty-six thousand of us Gozitans make our living at it."

I pursed my cheeks and said dryly, "Only you're not one of them."

He chuckled. "Now, now, Billy Wayne. Don't be snide. You don't make your living so honorably either."

"How *do* I make my living?"

Spugna roared with laughter—a chesty rumble that turned into a shrill nasal bark as it tailed off. He spoke over his shoulder in Gozitan and I turned, surprised to see Pietru and Nardu behind us.

They laughed at his words—to humor the boss it seemed. Neither spoke.

Spugna glanced in my direction. "We'll discuss what you do at the villa over lunch. Like civilized men," he added. "I think you'll be surprised at our guests."

No, I thought, I won't. I expected to see Preston Blike and Diane Walker there—the whole crew of the *Nerina,* except for Billy Wayne of course. Unless he was pretending to be me for some reason. That thought left me in a state of confusion and I barely heard Spugna's next words.

"What?"

"I was saying, ah, how I wish we had more time. Time for a drive to Rabat. From the citadel you can see the whole island." Spugna clasped his hands, his smile containing little humor. "Too bad you won't be alive in a few weeks."

So he was planning on killing me and not worried about hiding his intentions. He thought I was Billy Wayne Henderson, and Billy Wayne, for some reason, was his enemy. I found that ironic. Spugna probably had more cause to hate the man I really was, but I wasn't ready yet to tell him he had Derek Stone in his hands.

Spugna was enjoying himself. Playing with me, reeling me in and out like a fish. He wanted me to ask what would happen in a few weeks. What I would miss. But I wouldn't give him the pleasure of a response.

He let his words die away into silence, while I made an effort at studied nonchalance, and then he said, "The first weekend in September we have a beautiful regatta to commemorate the Grand Siege of 1565 and the bombing of World War II. Everybody goes to the Grand Harbour at Valletta." He looked up at me, his face quizzical. "Perhaps even the *Nerina* will take part."

"You're a bastard."

He laughed and took my arm, which tensed. "They told me you were vulgar, Mr. Henderson. Try to be civil at lunch."

I pulled my arm away and the two thugs stepped forward. Spugna waved his hand impatiently to dismiss them.

"I wanted to show you my falcons, Mr. Henderson."

I shrugged. "So, where are they? Little black statues sitting in an alcove?"

Spugna looked bemused. "Ah, the famous Maltese falcons. Humphrey Bogart. Everyone has seen the film." He pointed to our left and stepped in front of me. "This way."

Within fifty feet, around a bend, we came upon a clearing cut into the side of the limestone cliffs.

"A small quarry," Spugna said. "Globigerina limestone. The blocks of the villa came from here."

To the side of the clearing, back up against the hill, stood a wire-enclosed habitat. Inside, three bright-eyed falcons stared at us from their perches.

Spugna said, "I'm somewhat of a historian by hobby.

You might not know this. The Knights of St. John paid an annual tribute of a Maltese falcon to Charles V, King of Spain and Holy Roman Emperor. Back when Malta was granted to the order in 1530." He smiled grandly. "Let's say I continue the tradition."

"And who gets the tribute now?"

He looked surprised. "Apparently I didn't express myself well. I play the role of Charles V, my workers offer the falcons to me. We feed them petrels captured on the island of Filfla. Sometimes we go rabbit hunting with them. And for special occasions we give them a treat of human flesh."

An evil glint crept into Spugna's eyes. He pointed to the piles of bird droppings on the ground below the falcons. "Look well, Mr. Henderson. For you, it's not dust to dust and ashes to ashes. It's dung to dung."

I raised my hand to hit him then and felt a harsh jab in the back. I turned to see first Nardu's snarl and then a black 9mm pistol in his hand.

"Put it away, Nardu. Mr. Henderson knows we're just having fun."

On the way back up the hill, we trudged in silence, but when we reached the top, Spugna stopped and faced me, his dark eyes glinting.

"We in Gozo and Malta have a glorious history, Billy Wayne. A very advanced civilization. Even in antiquity. At Gigantija we have the world's earliest monumental architecture."

I stared at him with cold eyes. I couldn't care less about Malta's past; I was worried about my own present. If Pietru and Nardu weren't there, I would've strangled the bastard.

He waved his arms in an expansive gesture, oblivious to my anger. "When the Egyptians began building those crude pyramids for the Pharoahs, in Malta we already had the great temple complex at Tarxien. A work of art, built with a technical virtuosity far surpassing our contemporaries.''

He paused, as if overcome by emotion, and took a deep breath. And then, with his eyes fixed on the horizon, he said softly, ''A small island—but great people . . . great deeds.'' He was nodding to himself. ''The big powers have forgotten us, but they'll pay.''

Suddenly he laughed harshly and held out his right hand. ''Balls,'' he said. ''Russia and the United States are balls in my hand.'' And with that he squeezed his hand into a fist.

I snorted and shook my head, listening in exasperated silence to his mad ravings. Spugna struck me as a little Maltese Napoleon. I was tired of archaic pride, tired of jingoistic egoism, tired of little republics trying to regain their prestige on a global scale. It was bad enough having the French around thinking they were the center of the world. We could do without Spugna. Given half a chance I'd kill him without a qualm. Wanda deserved as much. And so did I.

And if his thugs managed to stop me afterward, fine. Let them feed me to the falcons.

17

BY THE TIME we reached the villa, Spugna's jovial mood had dissipated. Instead of being served lunch, I was taken into the cellar and thrown into a hole, an empty storage bin cut into the rock. Behind me, they slammed and barred the door, a heavy cast-iron plate that looked like it belonged to a furnace. There were no windows and no lights.

I crouched on the stone floor, unable to stand or stretch out, and tried to calm my mind. I was too scared to do much constructive planning. And that left me confused and angry.

What was happening to me? Ever since my failed rendezvous with the real Gene Harrell, from the moment I gave up my own identity as Derek Stone, I was a different person. A person I didn't like. My decisiveness had turned to hesitation. The future—the unknown that I used to welcome so gladly as a source of new experiences—now paralyzed me. My ability to suppress fear had fizzled away. Was that the result of trying to be someone else? Of wearing a mask that didn't fit? Or was it because of losing Wanda?

I thought of the weeks I'd spent wandering aimlessly around the Mediterranean. In a daze like now. Only now I knew that Spugna held the key to my uncontrollable emotions. The solution was simple. I'd suffered a relapse, my mind wasn't functioning right. I was sick again. Killing Spugna would be the cure. That was all I could afford to think about. No matter what effort it took—if it was the last thing I did—I had to kill Spugna. I let the hatred burn inside me, forming a core, giving me something to hang on to.

Time passed in utter blackness, unmeasurable. Occasionally, in an effort to calm myself, I slowly counted out a minute. Tried to figure out how long I'd been lying there. Sixty seconds seemed an eternity.

Some time later, the door swung open and rough hands pulled me into the light—a single bulb, but it still stunned my eyes. I stood erect for the first time in what felt like hours, stretched my stiff muscles. And then one of the men shoved me in the back, and Nardu led me up the stairs and into a den on the first floor of the villa. Three people were waiting, Spugna's men, all armed. I looked out the windows to the north and saw a guard with a rifle. Nardu took up a position by the door, his pistol clenched in his right hand.

Spugna was sitting behind a desk, his hands clasped in front of him, a small smile on his face. He gestured to a chair. I sat down and another man tied my wrists behind me and then to the back of the chair.

Spugna played with his gold wedding band for a few minutes, staring impassively at me, and then spoke.

"Well, Mr. Henderson, I'm sure you're a fine man and did your job to the best of your abilities. Unfortunately, your abilities were insufficient to the task, wouldn't you say?"

I didn't like the superficial summation. It sounded too much like an epitaph. Had he made up his mind to get rid of me?

I'd had plenty of time to think about methods of delaying Spugna from killing me, but I hadn't expected to need them so soon. I looked up at a corner of the room as if pondering his statement, tried to compose myself, and then said, "I'm not so sure I did fail, Mr. Spugna."

I dropped my eyes suddenly and tried to muster a shrewd look.

He waved his hand as if brushing away an annoying gnat and then cast a bored look in my direction.

"Come on, Mr. Henderson, the time has passed for games."

My lips tightened. In an icy tone I said, "Mr. Harrell doesn't think it's a game." Which was true. In a way I was still Gene Harrell and I was deadly serious—even if I didn't know what I was doing.

Spugna absorbed my statement in silence, the only indication that he'd heard me a slight flicker of his eyelids.

He breathed heavily through his nose and finally said, "Mr. Harrell? Who's he?"

As he spoke, a puzzled look flashed across his face, and I laughed. "Well done, Mr. Spugna," I said. It was as good an acting job as I'd ever seen. Nonchalantly bewildered. He'd heard about Gene Harrell all right.

I bobbed my head knowingly and let the silence ride. Make him come up with something now, I thought. My lips were sealed. I hoped he couldn't resist the smug look on my face. I kept staring into his eyes, which had gone opaque.

Spugna slid back his chair and got to his feet. "Mr. Henderson, Gene Harrell is dead."

As he walked around the desk toward me, I shook my head slowly, my lips curling up in a tight grin. "You'd like to think so, wouldn't you? He's very much alive."

"Impossible!" he almost shouted, spitting in my face in his vehemence. "He drowned."

Despite the exclamation, I could sense Spugna's doubt.

"Not only is he alive," I said flatly, "he knows what you're trying to do. And he has the resources to stop you."

Fury danced in Spugna's eyes. Before I saw it coming his right palm caught me across the cheek.

I went down—not that I had to but for effect—tipping over my chair and hitting my head on the floor. I twitched, fluttered my eyes, and then let my mouth go slack. A good imitation of unconsciousness. I'd had enough practice recently.

I heard Spugna stomp back and forth, his feet inches from my head. I tried to brace myself without appearing to do so.

He kicked me in the ribs then and I came close to passing out for real. The collision with the Italian when I was fleeing down the mountain path on Vignetti and Billy Wayne's fist in my stomach on the boat had already left me battered. My breath exploded out of me, and I curled up, groaning, wishing my hands were tied in front and not behind.

I moaned and went limp again.

Spugna moved away and called, "Pietru."

The door opened.

"Take him back," he said with obvious disgust. "Throw him in with Blike."

Blike! They had Preston Blike. But I should have known that. Hadn't Spugna talked about the *Nerina* taking part in the September festival?

Pietru untied my hands, rolled me over on my stomach, grabbed my legs, and slid me toward the door. My head skidded across the wood floor.

"We'll talk to him again later," Spugna said. "It may take a little persuasion but he'll tell us what he knows."

Preston Blike was surprised to see me, kept exclaiming, "I thought you were dead, damn it. I thought you were dead."

I nodded. "Me too." I don't know if he understood me. He didn't laugh. I guess I was trying to say I was

surprised both of us were alive. I sat up and grimaced
from the pain. I was in what looked like a bedroom—
only the furnishings had been removed, except for a
bunk, on which Preston lay, and one chair.

"Where in the hell did you guys go?" I asked.

"We didn't *go* anywhere. We were *taken*. They caught
us by surprise. Jumped me on deck and Diane in the
stateroom."

He paused and then looked at me with a frown. "What
happened to Billy Wayne?"

I put my finger to my lips. *I* am Billy Wayne," I
whispered.

Preston gaped.

I scooted over to where he was lying on one elbow and
said, "They think I'm Henderson, so don't say anything.
I thought Billy Wayne was with you guys. You didn't see
what happened to him?"

He shook his head. "He disappeared. I was too busy
to see what was going on. I thought Spugna's men took
him out too."

I paused. "They might have. The down line from the
dinghy was on the bottom when I came up. None of you
were in sight." I rubbed my chin, puzzled. "What about
the safe?"

Preston looked aggravated. "They winched it aboard
the *Nerina.*"

"Where is the *Nerina,* anyway?"

"I'm not sure. They bought us in from the yacht by
dghajsa. No harbors big enough for the boat on Gozo."

"The safe's probably off by now, too."

He nodded. "Probably."

I reached out and grabbed his arm. "Preston, you've
got to tell me what's in the safe. What're you involved
in, anyway?"

"You tell me who you really are and maybe I'll tell
you," he said gruffly.

I decided to play stupid. "You knew I wasn't Harrell?"

He wagged his head as if I were dumb. "Of course. We all knew. Billy Wayne killed Harrell."

The news came as a shock. I swallowed hard. Billy Wayne? "Why? Who was he anyway? Harrell, I mean."

Preston shrugged. "Billy Wayne thought he worked for Spugna. Caught him on the radio and Harrell wouldn't say who he'd been talking to. Billy Wayne shot him before I could do anything. We might have been able to get something out of him otherwise. We tossed his body overboard."

So that meant Harrell had been in touch with the *Nerina* from the start. He was on board as their salvage expert from the day they left Marseilles, just as I'd thought once I'd seen his name on the original crew list.

So why had Dalmoro told me Harrell was supposed to meet the three Americans? Damn him. That was either fucked up Italian intelligence or—or what? Were they trying to get me killed?

Nothing added up right, and Preston was still holding out on me. I wanted to know what he was after.

"What did Jeffrey have to do with this?"

Preston took a deep breath and sighed. "You might as well know. Jeffrey was transporting stolen microprocessors. Chips with military secrets. From a Russian missile guidance system. The whole operation was a government job. He was supposed to deliver them to me."

I frowned. "Jeffrey worked for the U.S. government?"

"Jeffrey worked for me. I work for the government."

I tried to mask my surprise. "Where'd the chips come from?"

He looked embarrassed. "Some Yugoslav scientists. They told us the Russians had made a breakthrough on a new system of vital concern to the West. A threat to our security unless we could prepare countermeasures."

He raised his hands. "So we paid them off. They gave

us two duplicate chips—each one a complete micro-processor. Trouble is, we couldn't use our own agents. We used Spugna's men. He had close contacts with the Yugoslavs.''

I wondered if Blike was spinning another fairy tale. ''If Spugna's men were working for you, why's he competing to get the chips?''

Preston's face darkened. ''Spugna's a greedy bastard. A lot of people would pay big bucks for the information on the chips. We knew he'd cause trouble, so our agents took the chips off his men in Rome. They were passed on to Jeffrey. He was supposed to bring them to me, I'd take them to Spain, and they'd be flown back to the States.'' He paused. ''Spugna will sell the chips to the highest bidder—and that might mean back to the Russians.''

''Do you know what happened to Jeffrey?''

He shook his head. ''Not for sure. Harrell might have been involved in feeding him bogus instructions. I suspected he might have been on the radio to Jeffrey. Told him we had a new rendezvous off Malta. Sent him where Spugna's people could recover the chips. They sank the *Kirke*.''

I thought about that. It made some sense, but not much. There were still too many holes. Too many contradictions. I didn't think Harrell had ever worked for Spugna. Spugna had gone crazy when I'd suggested that Harrell was still alive.

I said, ''Why would Spugna's men sink the *Kirke?* Spugna didn't have the chips. The safe was still in the yacht. And why attack us?''

''You got inside?'' he asked, surprised.

I nodded. ''That's where the divers jumped me.''

I was about to tell him I saw them removing the safe when I realized he'd told me the same thing. He'd just said Spugna's men winched it aboard the *Nerina*. I

196

frowned. Too big a contradiction to ignore. "Your hypothesis about the sinking of the *Kirke* doesn't hold," I said. I paused, lost in thought.

He shrugged. "Got anything better?"

I ignored him. "Spugna's men didn't sink the *Kirke*. They didn't know where it was until we found it. And we found it because of Harrell."

He tried to mask his surprise.

I said, "I know you found the coordinates on the bill in my wallet—in Harrell's wallet. And he couldn't have gotten them from Spugna—Spugna's men would've beaten us to the wreck."

"Okay, so he worked for someone else."

"Back on the *Nerina* you said you received the coordinates from the U.S. government—from a spy satellite."

He shrugged. "I lied. I had to say something."

"You may have thought you lied, but I doubt it. You knew the coordinates were too precise to be derived from anything other than satellite intelligence. The question is, if you're working for the government and the information came from them, why didn't *you* get it rather than Harrell?"

"Maybe he was on the radio when the information was sent to the *Nerina*."

"That I can't believe. No one would pass on information without some certainty that it was going directly to you. And wouldn't it come ciphered?"

Preston didn't say anything. He stared at me, stroking his beard, and then nodded. "Good point. Did it ever occur to you that Harrell was working for the Russians—trying to recover the chips?"

My voice hardened in frustration. "Are you fishing again, or do you know?"

Preston sighed, looked at the ceiling, and scratched his neck under the beard. "I'm guessing—but it's an informed guess," he added quickly when he saw my anger. "You got a better one?"

I sat there, breathing heavily, angry that no one had the answers. I had to tell myself to draw back, ask myself why I cared? This had nothing to do with me.

Trouble was, it did—against my wishes.

Preston Blike had used me, and Spugna thought I was Billy Wayne Henderson. Telling him who I really was would be a form of suicide. I grimaced. It didn't much matter if I was Billy Wayne, Gene Harrell, or Derek Stone. Spugna had a reason to kill all of us, especially Derek Stone. I'd done a lot to hurt him in the past and he was as bent on vengeance as I was.

And that brought to mind the puzzle of Wanda. She'd mentioned MIO. She assumed Spugna's men were out to get her. Why?

Did Spugna have something going with Gadhafi or his henchmen? I tried to remember what Dalmoro had told me about Wanda back in Messina. She'd learned something the Libyans didn't want her to know and she'd passed it on to Italian intelligence. What she found out must have implicated Spugna and MIO. His men were involved in the theft of the microprocessors—and it cost her life. That was something I couldn't forgive.

I didn't care about the microprocessors or military secrets. Let the chips fall where they would, I thought grimly. What I wanted was Spugna.

A while later I asked Preston a question. "What's Spugna aiming to do with you, anyway?"

"I don't know," he said. "What do you think?"

I didn't answer.

They came for him later that night. He returned just before dawn, unconscious and badly beaten. I listened to his labored breathing for a long time. I knew why

Spugna had done this—the bastard! He didn't have anything to beat out of Preston. He was working on me.

Sometime after dawn, Preston's raspy breath quieted.
I thought he was sleeping. It took me a good hour before
I realized he was dead.

$$\underline{}$$

18

$$\underline{}$$

"What time is it, anyway?" I asked Spugna.

He looked at a flashy gold watch on his left wrist. "Nine-thirty."

"Morning or evening?"

"Morning."

"Ah," I said, as if that explained everything. "I'm a slow starter. Lot on my mind but not much comes out of my mouth. You'll have to wait until after lunch." I tried to smile. Spugna's men had been beating me all morning. "You promised me a lunch . . . yesterday, wasn't it?"

After Preston's death, they'd taken me back to the underground storage hole. I wasn't sure how long I'd been kept there. They hadn't fed me.

"Very funny, Mr. Henderson. Maybe we'll have to see if we can't loosen your tongue." Spugna held up a pair of pliers. "Simple instrument, but effective."

So far, he'd left most of the dirty work up to his hirelings. I said, "Do we have to? I really can't tell you anything of significance. They say torture only tells you what you want to hear. Not the truth."

He grinned. "Billy Wayne, why do you make me suffer?"

My mouth fell open. "Make *you* suffer?" I laughed bitterly. "You look like you've suffered a lot, all right. Life's been rough, hasn't it?"

He shrugged. "You think I enjoy torturing people?" He tugged on his chin and then shook his head emphatically. "No, Billy Wayne, no."

He turned to the side, a pensive look on his face, while I stared up at him, growing angrier. He had no right to look distracted when I was in pain. Talking about suffering. I gritted my teeth. "You bastard!"

He didn't seem to hear me.

I let my head fall and breathed heavily through my nose and mouth. I was gagging on blood. An acrid chemical smell prickled my nostrils, reminded me of those few times as a kid when I'd come down with bronchitis in the cold Canadian winters.

For a minute I thought the smell was that of burnt rubber and raised my head in alarm, thinking they were warming up some other machine of torture.

Spugna spoke, his voice coming from far away, his eyes focused on an invisible picture in the middle distance.

"I was a young soldier in World War II," he said. "Stationed by the British at Fort Ricasoli at the mouth of the Grand Harbour. My parents were Italian expatriates, living not far away in Cospicua. Churchill called us his unsinkable aircraft carrier. But we were horribly bombed by the Germans. Both my parents were killed in the air raids of 1942. At the time I felt my life was a plaything of other forces. I survived by using my wits, but more than that through blind luck. I still pray in thanks at every mass."

He licked his lips, his face dark and serious. "We Gozitans are very religious. More so than the Maltese. Both islands are fervently Roman Catholic. We put Rome—the Vatican even—to shame." He paused reflectively. "You know how many churches and chapels there are on Gozo?"

He didn't wait for a response.

"Forty-three! We have the highest church attendance of any Catholic country in the world."

"Praise be to God," I muttered sarcastically.

Spugna glanced at me and snorted, but said nothing.

"You know what I believe," I went on. "I believe that old adage—worse things have been done in the name of religion than for any other cause."

Spugna waved his hand impatiently. "Religion has nothing to do with this. This is a private matter between you and me."

He rubbed the corners of his mouth, his mind apparently elsewhere, and then said abruptly, "Tell me, who do you work for?"

I raised my head slowly. It seemed to weigh a ton. "I work for Dwilley Yacht Maintenance Company," I said in a monotone. "The Industrial Development Corporation of Tucson, Arizona, hired us to service the *Nerina*. My immediate boss was Preston Blike, the ship's master."

Spugna's voice hardened. "Dwilley Yacht Maintenance. A front for the CIA."

I shook my head. "I'm not even an American."

"Don't lie, Billy Wayne. You were born in Portland, Oregon, on December second, 1951."

"Was it a hard birth?" I asked.

He slapped me across the face with the back of his hand, one of his rings cutting into my lip. I spit blood and then closed my big yap. Impudence didn't pay. He'd already tried to teach me that lesson once. But I was a slow learner when the teacher reminded me of my father. I think I was trying to reignite my old irascibility. I didn't suffer fools gladly, and Spugna was a fool if he thought I wanted to hear him narrate my life story—or anyone else's.

Spugna rubbed his hand and went on talking in the same tone, as if he hadn't been interrupted. "Your father worked as a insurance salesman and your mother was a bookkeeper in a bakery. We know all about you, Mr. Henderson. Have you read your Homer lately?"

The *non sequitur* baffled me. "I carry a copy in my back pocket," I said.

He laughed. "Then you'll be interested to know that Gozo is Calypso's island."

So what? I thought.

"We still show her cave to tourists," he added, clasping his hands primly across his belly.

I still didn't follow him.

"It's just above the northern end of Ir-Ramla I-Hamra beach. I hear you love caves, by the way."

"I prefer the beach," I said, and he laughed again.

"One sunburn is not enough for you, eh?" He pointed to my arms.

I looked down and back. I'd grown used to the mottled skin. I'd peeled badly after my excursion off Milazzo.

Suddenly I realized what Spugna was doing and why they'd stuck me in the small, enclosed basement cubicle. Billy Wayne had been to Vietnam. Got shot down. Spent time in a V.A. hospital. Spugna knew all about his claustrophobia.

Blood began to trickle out of one of my nostrils, running down my chin and dripping onto my chest. I let it flow, too tired to breathe in and hold it. With my hands once again lashed behind my back, I was helpless.

Spugna stopped his demonstration of how much he knew about Billy Wayne and gestured to Nardu, saying something in Maltese I didn't catch. Nardu grabbed my shirt, which was lying on the floor, and tore a strip of cloth from the lower edge. He rolled it into a small ball and stuffed it up the bleeding nostril.

So Spugna didn't like the sight of blood, I thought. It was okay for his bullies to beat me—as long as it didn't show on the outside. I could feel the swelling in my lower lip. Before long I'd look like a Ubangi.

I had to breathe through my mouth. I dropped my head in apparent exhaustion, partly in an effort at self-preservation, partly because they'd beaten the shit out of me and I couldn't take much more. Spittle and blood dribbled down between my legs. The next time he sicced his dogs on me I was going to fake unconsciousness at the first blow. It had worked before.

I tried to look groggy.

An uncanny silence settled over the room. Spugna had given some signal I didn't see and everyone was waiting. A minute later they wheeled a hospital trolley into the room. Out of the corner of my eye I saw two black boxes that looked like transceivers sitting on the top shelf. This was going to be music I didn't want to hear—on the order of electrical currents dancing through my testicles.

I lifted my head and looked at Spugna.

"You know," I mumbled, "I have a few other names beside Billy Wayne."

Spugna's eyes narrowed in interest. He took a step toward me, breaking out in a self-satisfied smile. "Ah, finally, code names. Good. I thought you might be ready to talk." He looked at his watch. "And it's only ten o'clock in the morning. Very good."

He eyed me speculatively and then said, "So, your employer sent you to monitor Blike. Did they tell you why?"

I sighed. Would it hurt to go along with the guy?

"We thought he might be involved in something illegal."

"Yes. Like what?"

I shrugged. "Industrial espionage. He said the safe held jewels. I didn't believe him. I wanted to see for myself."

"And then what were you going to do?"

I frowned and concentrated a minute. "I'm not sure. I hadn't figured that out. I was thinking about saving my scalp."

"You had the radio in the *Nerina*. Why not call for help? I can't believe they'd send you in on your own."

"Call for help?" I repeated dumbly. "The wheelhouse was off limits. I didn't have a chance."

"This Gene Harrell. What was he doing aboard?"

"He was a diver. A salvage expert."

"You believe that?"

"Why not? He did the diving."

"Gene Harrell worked for the CIA. We know his mission was to stop Jeffrey Blike and recover the . . . cargo. But he made a mistake. He destroyed half the goods in Rome when he tried to recover them, and Jeffrey got away with the other half. And when Harrell found out, he assumed Jeffrey was meeting his father in Vignetti to hand it over to him."

I'd noticed the pregnant pause. Why didn't he just say "microprocessors"? I knew what Jeffrey was transporting.

"So what did Jeffrey do?" I said. "Did he meet Preston off Vignetti or what?"

"That was Jeffrey's original plan, yes. Harrell knew it and that's why he tried to make it back to the *Nerina*. Harrell's people wanted the whole cargo. But you see, I was in control of the situation from the start. The cargo was supposed to be mine. I'd already sold half to someone else—for a lot of money—and was prepared to sell the other half to Blike's company for less. But once Harrell destroyed half, I needed the other for the higher-paying source. I had to order Jeffrey to come to Malta."

So far, some of what Spugna had said fit more or less with what Preston had told me. Only there were still too many missing pieces. I said I didn't understand.

"Yes, it is confusing. You have to understand who worked for whom. Jeffrey Blike and Diane Walker worked for me. It wasn't hard to buy her services. She hates"—he flashed a quick grin and changed to the past tense—"*hated* Preston Blike. Jeffrey was easier—money's the only thing that mattered to him."

He brooded a minute and then began pacing back and forth in front of me. "Preston—we worked together when we had to. I sold him part of the cargo, but when I lost the other half, I needed the . . . material in the *Kirke*'s safe."

I decided to spill what I knew. "Preston said the cargo was two duplicate microchips—microprocessors for a Soviet missile system."

Spugna laughed and shook his head. "Preston wouldn't tell his best friend the truth. Let's just say they're microprocessors with scientific documents encoded on them. It doesn't have anything to do with the Russians."

That set me back. I'd begun to believe what Preston had told me. I said, "Preston claimed they were stolen from the Russians. Said the Yugoslavs passed them on."

Spugna raised his eyebrows in surprise. "You got it backward. The Russians have never seen the microchips. They want the information on them as bad as the Americans. Who do you think sunk the *Kirke?*"

I was too tired to absorb that, just shook my head numbly. He expected me to figure out the answer and I couldn't even get the story straight. "You said you needed the material in the safe. So you let Preston find it and then took it away?"

He nodded. "Yes. You see Preston had access to data provided to Harrell by the CIA. Harrell had learned where the ship lay. Satellite surveillance. Once Preston got what he needed out of Harrell, Diane radioed it to me."

They didn't get it out of Harrell, I thought. He took the secret to the grave. It was fool me who gave it away—not that I did it intentionally.

I looked at Spugna's face, his forehead sweating, his

cheeks starting to show the puffiness of a man who eats too much. He had round cheeks that could shine with innocence. If I had met him in a bar I might have liked the guy. But only for the first half hour. Only until I learned what he was really like. Oh, he knew how to smile, apple-rosy and honey-sweet, but the amiable smile hid rot.

"What's the big secret with the scientific documents on the microprocessor?" I asked tiredly.

Spugna, standing in front of the desk with his butt on the smooth surface, leaned forward, both hands gripping the rim. "You don't want to know."

I tried another tack. "Didn't Diane tell you Billy—" I stopped, started over. Spugna still thought *I* was Billy Wayne. "Didn't Diane say I'd killed Harrell in Vignetti?"

Spugna looked puzzled. "You killed Harrell? He drowned."

My head bobbed back and forth indecisively. Finally I said, "I thought he worked for you." By he, I meant Billy Wayne but Spugna understood Harrell.

"I told you, he was CIA."

I was getting confused—playing the role of Billy Wayne and trying to step out of it at the same time. Any minute and Spugna would be probing into my activities again. I was afraid of that. How could I tell him what I didn't know?

But Spugna merely eyed me inquisitively and said, "If you killed Harrell, who dived for the safe?"

"A replacement. Someone we hired."

"His name?"

I paused. "We didn't know for sure. There was a mix-up. Apparently the guy lost his ID and the police on Vignetti confused him with Gene Harrell."

Spugna's frown deepened, but I rushed on before he could say anything. "The guy thought we didn't know.

He said he was Gene Harrell and we played along with
him.''

''And Diane knew this?''

''Of course she knew.''

Spugna turned to one of his men and gave an order.

What now? I thought. Was there any way I could save
myself by talking? I couldn't take much more.

I was struggling to understand what was going on and
I couldn't think straight. There were too many people
involved and I—shit, I was three of them myself! I
would've laughed if my body didn't hurt so much.

Suddenly the door opened and Diane Walker bounced
in. She was wearing a full-length silk evening gown and
smoking a cigarette. ''Carlo, Nardu said you wanted
me.'' And then she stopped in shock at the sight of my
battered body. Her jaw dropped. I tried to give her a sign
but it was a waste of time.

''That's not Billy Wayne,'' she exclaimed. ''Carlo,
that's the guy who said he was Gene!''

Thanks a lot, I thought. I looked up at Spugna,
shrugged, and raised my eyebrows. ''See, what'd I try
to tell you yesterday?'' I said. ''You wouldn't listen.''

They tortured me after that. I think Spugna was angry
I'd deceived him as long as I had. Whenever I passed out
from the pain, he revived me with cold water and started
in again. I tried to blurt out the truth, tell him whatever I
could without revealing my real name. I told him I was
Jake Roberts, but I was too dazed to manufacture a story
to explain why I was in Vignetti without ID in the first
place. He didn't believe anything.

More than once I wished I were dead. I think the only
thing that kept me alive was hatred. I cried tears—not of
pain but of frustration. I wanted to get my hands on
Spugna's throat and rip it out.

They finally gave up. On the way back to the basement

cubicle we passed a young woman, who gasped and fell pale, a stricken look on her face.

I glanced at her through bleary eyes, my vision hazy, my mind dazed and uncomprehending. I'd seen her before, somewhere. And then it hit me. Donata Pellico. The bitch who'd sent me to the *Nerina* in the first place. She was working for Spugna all along.

"Gene," she whispered, "is that you?" Her eyes were frightened.

"Thanks to you," I hissed, my voice rough from screaming. If my arms were free I would've hit her. I wanted to spit in her face, but before I could, one of Spugna's thugs grabbed her arm and hustled her away, speaking in a gruff voice. I tried to spit at her retreating figure, wrenching my head around to do so and hitting the guard at my side. He swore and gave me a quick chop to the neck that left my whole body tingling. I collapsed, trying to bite the guard as I fell, and that's the last thing I remember.

Much later, in the cramped darkness of my stone-walled cell, blinking back tears, seeing Donata once again as she stood on the windswept shore at Porto Metello, I wondered if it had all been a dream.

19

IN THE MIDDLE AGES assassins were sometimes executed in a very peculiar manner. The executioner dug a pit in the ground, next to which a scaffold was erected. The condemned man was led to the scaffold, but rather than being hung by the neck until dead in New World fashion, his feet were tied together and he was suspended upside down with the upper three-fourths of his body in the hole.

And then the hole was filled with dirt, suffocating the offender.

One of the pleasures of the method was that it allowed the spectators to see the spasmodic jerking of the criminal's feet.

The Spanish preferred the garrote—an iron collar tightened with a screw until the intended victim strangled to death.

Sometime in the next day or night I thought about the various ways of dying violently. Not that I would be given my choice. But I tried to imagine what Spugna's sadism would find most appropriate. Several forms of execution, mainly the judicial type, were too rapid and too pain-free—the firing squad, electrocution, chemical injection or inhalation, hanging, the guillotine—although anticipation from my point of view was in all cases sufficient punishment. Spugna, however, would delight in the more primitive methods of killing.

They must have left me huddled in my stone-box prison for hours—for hours that seemed days. I slept long enough at any rate to begin remembering my dreams.

One dream repeated itself like a loop of film running through a projector. Four men in a car drove down a winding road into an open gravel pit. At the bottom, rusting equipment sat next to a rainwater pond. The pit had long ago been abandoned. The dream was layered with a sense of foreboding so thick it hung in the air like fog. I was one of the men in the car and the others intended to kill me. Each time, as the dream wound down to its conclusion, my mind refused to finish it off—to live through the murder. And so the dream began again, endlessly running.

At one point I managed to snap out of my drugged condition and ponder my fate. It was then I began thinking of how I would die.

I wouldn't go without a struggle. I resolved that the next time the door was opened and I was dragged out into the light, I would fight before letting them tie my hands behind my back. I had no other choice and no other chance. Each time Spugna interrogated me I was helpless. The only time my hands were free was when I was left in this cubicle cut into the stone. And escape from the hole was impossible. The cast-iron door was too heavy, even though secured on the outside with only a simple sliding bolt. I'd already kicked it a few times as hard as I could from a sitting position without so much as getting a rattle out of the thing.

I slept again, lying on my back with my knees bent. When I awoke—once again as always in absolute darkness—I had a moment of disorientation and panic. I'd lost feeling along my back and wasn't sure if I was sitting up against the wall or still on my back. I had to force myself to breathe slowly. I was afraid I'd use up all the air before they came for me again.

I understood then why the thoughts of death by suffocation had filtered into my mind earlier. My subconscious fears were one step ahead of me.

I tried to think of pleasant scenes from my childhood. I relived every moment of my time with Wanda. When I realized I'd been trying to forget everything about her because of her death, that I'd been repressing my feelings and that it wasn't necessary, that I could remember the good parts without concentrating on the bad, I found tears streaming down my cheeks, tears of forgiveness for myself.

I'd taken the blame for having Wanda on the jackup in the first place; I'd accused myself of murder. I'd felt I was the cause of the explosions.

In my prison cell I forgave myself for everything I'd ever done—all acts whether intentional or accidental—and for the first time in my life I came to peace with myself.

But that didn't mean I gave up and prepared to accept my fate. It meant the opposite. I was a good person and I didn't deserve to die.

I must not have been the only one who thought so, or my thoughts must have been powerful enough to magnetize help, because suddenly the door to the cell creaked open and when I stumbled out, ready to grab for the gun that would be pointed at my chest, in one last desperate bid for freedom or at least revenge, I saw Donata.

Or rather heard her voice and saw an indistinct figure in a dress. Light from the single bulb overhead cascaded down, stunning me, and I had to squeeze my eyes nearly shut to bear what for Donata was weak illumination.

Her first words were, "I didn't know, Gene. I'm sorry."

I mumbled something incomprehensible and she grabbed my hand.

"Hurry, Gene. We have less than five minutes. The men are in mass."

My limbs refused to move, my mind not yet accepting what was happening.

"What? In mass?" I shook my head. Nothing made sense.

She slipped her arm under mine and we started toward the wooden stairs leading to the first floor.

"Dun Farrug is here for the weekly Friday mass. *Zi'* Carlo has all the family and men attend. I said I was sick."

Mass. The only good thing religion had ever done for me.

I missed the first stair and fell. The tread's metal nosing cut into my shin bone and I let out a sharp gasp.

Donata helped me to my feet, her eyes wild. "We can't make a sound," she said. "The chapel's just up the hallway from here."

I nodded, feeling my face shrivel with pain, and limped up the stairs with my left arm around her back. I wished I had a cane.

At the top of the stairs Donata paused and held her breath, pressing her ear against a narrow vertical sidelight built into the casing next to the door. Nothing showed through the dark blue glass.

She put her finger in front of her lips and then whispered, "To the right. Follow me."

I nodded and took a deep breath, wondering how fast and how far I could move, beaten as badly as I was.

As we crept down the hallway I could hear the *kapillan*'s voice, speaking in Maltese of the Sacred Heart of Jesus.

We had to pass through two other rooms, each carpeted with oriental rugs, before we could reach an outside exit. Each step sent a jolt of electricity flashing up my spine and into the back of my head. Beads of perspiration broke out on my forehead and involuntary tears formed in the corners of my eyes.

"Is there a car we can use?" I whispered to Donata just before she opened the outer door. "I can't make it over rough terrain."

She looked at me, her eyes tender yet sad, and shook her head. *"Zi'* Carlo and his men have the keys. We may be able to find a mule if we can get far enough away from the villa."

I grimaced. Okay, freedom had its price. One step at a time. At least she wasn't leaving me on my own. I needed someone who knew the quickest route to safety.

I followed her without speaking. The quickest route— was that the road leading to Victoria or to the coast? If we made it to the main road, we might be able to catch a bus. Or stop a vehicle. If instead we headed to the coast, there was the possibility of finding a tourist boat at Dwejra Bay. But how accessible was either route on foot?

We crossed a patio, dashed through a garden, and hurried down a path that led to another running along the inside of the stone wall surrounding the villa. When we reached the wall, we stopped and caught our breath.

"How are you doing?" she asked.

"So-so. It hurts to move." She looked at me anxiously and I took a deep breath and added, "It'll be easier when my muscles warm up. I've been cramped in that hole."

"I'm sorry, Gene. I didn't know what they were doing."

"You couldn't have done much to stop them."

She squeezed my hand. "Wait here. I'm going to bring a ladder from a shed. We can't go out the front gate."

I nodded and then, as she turned to go, asked if she had any money.

She turned back, startled, an anxious look creating

ridges below her eyes. "Money? I . . . I didn't think."
She hesitated. "Shall I go back?"

I shook my head vehemently. "No. Too risky. Get the
ladder. I'll wait."

After she left, running along the wall in a direction
opposite the main gate, I looked around for a weapon,
wishing I'd had the strength to go with her. A shed. That
meant tools—maybe a knife or a scythe. I should have
asked her to look. As it was I had a profusion of rocks to
hurl at men who'd be wielding rifles and pistols.

A few minutes later, Donata reappeared, breathing
heavily and dragging a stepladder behind. I placed the
ladder against the wall and told her to go first.

"Stay on top of the wall. I'll pull the ladder up after
me and we can use it to get down the other side."

She slipped up the ladder, her skirt billowing in the
light breeze from the west, and awkwardly straddled the
summit. In seconds, I was perched beside her and we
pulled the ladder up and slid it down the far side. The
ground dropped away rapidly, and as I was trying to
position the ladder in the rocks, I lost my balance.

Donata reached for me and I twisted around and
grabbed for the top of the wall. My hand missed. As I
fell, I instinctively clawed the jagged rock surface in a
desperate attempt to break my fall. I bashed into the
ladder and lay there stunned, the wind knocked out of
me.

Donata gasped, looked quickly back toward the villa
and then down at me. She opened her mouth to speak
but didn't say anything. I saw her concern and tried to
shake my head, squinting as I looked up at her into the
sun, which blazed down from straight above us. She was
suffering for me, and it wasn't like Spugna's suffering, I
thought. Hers was genuine and gave me strength rather
than taking it away.

Droplets of blood had sprouted on my right hand. I

wiped it on my shirt and looked at the ladder. The pail rest and several of the cross braces on the back rail were busted, but the front side was still serviceable.

I propped it against the wall and held it in place while Donata descended, then laid it down so it wasn't visible.

We were both breathing hard. Donata's blouse had come out of her skirt, and the hair over her forehead was plastered to the skin with sweat.

My heart filled with gratitude. She'd risked everything for me—not only her reputation but maybe her life. Spugna wasn't the type to forgive anyone.

I looked down the hill, its bouldered slope cut by ravines where the winter rains ran off into the dry riverbed at the bottom.

"Can we get out that way?"

She shook her head. "I don't know. We could hide there and try to make it out at night."

"Come on. We can't stand here."

We started down the slope, sliding through rock fragments, holding hands at first for support and then one following the other.

Suddenly I heard a horn blare and looked up. Above us to the left, a white Mercedes-Benz had stopped on the dirt road that led to the villa. Four men piled out of the car and I recognized Spugna. He pointed to one of the men and appeared to say something. From where we stood we heard nothing. The air was deathly still.

The man Spugna had spoken to raised a rifle and aimed in our direction.

"Down," I yelled. "They're going to shoot."

Donata slid beside me as a bullet whined over our heads. I thought of the mountain slopes of Vignetti, the man shooting at me and Giacomo. I rolled over into a shallow ravine and Donata scrambled in beside me.

I could feel her heart beating, her breath ragged on my cheek. "I can't believe he'd have his men shoot at you,"

216

I said, incredulous. "His niece! You could be a hostage
I took."

Another shot rang out, the echo of percussion following soon after, and then silence. I eased my head over
the edge of the ravine. A second car was tearing down
the road from the villa, a black sedan. It slid to a stop in
a cloud of dust behind the Mercedes.

"Quick," I said. "They can't see with the dust." I
pointed just below us and toward the side of the valley
where the road descended from the mesa. "Below that
cliff."

Along that area of the hill the slope angled down from
the road at a steep pitch, falling away into fifty feet of
sheer cliff before leveling out again. We scrambled toward the base of the cliff, moving closer to the men up
above but cutting down the angle.

We reached the protected spot before the dust cleared
and threw ourselves into the shade of the overhang,
gasping for breath and hoping the men hadn't seen us
flee.

It was my turn to ask if she was okay.

"I think so," she said, plucking at her blouse.

It was then I saw the dark stain below her left arm, a
stain that slowly spread down her side.

"You've been hit," I said.

She pulled the blouse away from her body, her face
pale. "I'm not sure. I didn't feel anything—a sting
maybe."

"Here, let me see."

I moved around her and lifted her arm. She was sitting
with her legs tucked up against her chest. The bloody
spot began on her arm, not her side. I pushed the short
sleeve up on her shoulder and saw a jagged scratch
running about two inches along her biceps. "Looks like
a rock chip. A fragment kicked up by the bullet. I'll
bandage it."

I took my shirt off and tore a strip from the bottom edge where Nardu had ripped it earlier to stop my nose from bleeding.

While I was working, Donata closed her eyes and a few seconds later spoke softly. *"Zi'* Carlo said you were working against him, that you'd tried to kill him. He said you weren't who you said you were."

I was too preoccupied to respond. I wrapped the strip around her arm three times and prepared to tie it off.

She opened her eyes and said, "I can't believe that, Gene. You aren't, are you?"

I supposed her question meant any of three things: Was I working against Spugna? Was I trying to kill him? And, was I not who I claimed to be?

All three were true. I nodded reluctantly. "Yes," I said. "I am."

What little color remained drained out of her face and she dropped her head between her legs and refused to look at me.

"Donata, it's not what you think," I said earnestly. "Your uncle is planning to kill *me*—" I cut myself short. I was about to say, like he killed my wife, and then realized that might be dangerous. "I'm not an evil man, Donata. You've got to believe me."

I pulled her sleeve down over the dressing. Crude, but it seemed to have stopped the bleeding.

I put my hand on her knee and added, "I'm just a person who came along at the wrong time."

She lifted her head slowly as if its weight was more than she could bear and looked at me with veiled eyes. "What is my uncle involved in?"

"I was hoping you could tell me."

I saw a strange look flash through her eyes and then she ran her hand across her face wearily. "He never talks to me about business. Just about Vanni and Franca. He's a good father, Gene."

218

I pursed my lips. She'd told me that before—the day she and Giacomo first picked me up on Vignetti—and I didn't like hearing it again. At least she didn't sound so confident now.

Neither of us spoke for a minute, and then she said, "I didn't like how I was treated after I saw you in the cellar—I didn't like how they'd treated *you*. I couldn't believe that." She shook her head in sorrow. *"Zi'* Carlo has never laid a hand on his kids."

"He's laid his hands on plenty of his enemies," I blurted out angrily.

To my surprise she absorbed that without defending her uncle. She sighed. "After they sent me away and wouldn't let me speak to you, I listened to *Zi'* Carlo talk on the phone."

My ears perked up and I nodded encouragement.

"He was talking long-distance to a man in Libya. The man wanted *Zi'* Carlo to deliver an item in Tripoli— something the guy had ordered—and my uncle refused. He said the Americans were putting too much pressure on him here in Malta and that any delivery in Libya was out of the question. Too dangerous. So then they asked to meet his representatives in Tunisia."

I was listening attentively, my eyes locked on her face as she struggled to get the words out. She was speaking so slowly that I tried to rush her along. "And what'd he say to that?"

"He said it was impossible. He asked them to pick up the material here."

"At the villa?" I asked, surprised.

She nodded. "From Tunis, they fly to the airport at Luqa, then here by helicopter."

"When did you hear this?"

"Last night."

"So they're flying in today?"

"I think so but—"

Suddenly Donata gripped my hand and pointed back the way we'd come. ''Men,'' she gasped. ''They've seen us.''

Three men were moving down the slope from the villa, one of them clearly armed with a rifle and the others, I thought, probably with handguns.

I groaned. ''Come on. We've got to find a hiding place.''

We moved along the cliff face, looking for the best place to continue our descent. The heat was taking its toll on both of us. I was dying of thirst, couldn't remember when I last had anything to eat or drink. And the headache was back, pounding away at my temples.

If we could only find a cleft in the rocks or a cave—somewhere where we could disappear. They didn't have dogs. If we could last till nightfall. . . .

Donata stopped and I bumped into her. ''My arm's killing me now,'' she said. ''Why don't I wait here? I can stop them. Delay them at least. Give you a better chance to escape.''

I didn't like leaving her alone, but I thought about it, not because I was selfish—hell, I was better off with her—but for her sake. She'd helped me escape, but that didn't mean Spugna would harm her intentionally.

And then I remembered how callously he ordered his henchman to fire at us. They weren't aiming just at me: both of us were targets.

I shook my head and said, ''We're safer together.'' And when she hesitated, looking back at the men, I added, ''I need you. I can't make it alone.''

The men were gaining on us and I pushed myself faster, trying to break through the threshold of pain. I needed a hospital bed and rest, not a violent excursion in the hills.

Ahead of us the path cut around a corner and disappeared. ''There may be a ravine there,'' I said. ''If we

220

can find a hiding place off the path . . .'' Donata stepped ahead of me and my voice trailed away. There was no time for useless words.

Twenty feet beyond me, Donata reached the turn in the path and disappeared. I thought I heard a muffled cry and sprinted to catch up. When I rounded the corner I saw why she'd tried to cry—to warn me. Pietru had one arm around Donata's waist and the other over her mouth. He was grinning as if oblivious to her efforts to kick and bite him.

Beside Pietru stood Nardu and another man I didn't know. They all had rifles and they were all pointed at my chest.

20

Fifty feet beyond Spugna's men sat the Mercedes-Benz, Spugna leaning on the right front fender. The path we'd been following led straight to the road. We'd never had a chance.

When we reached the paved road, each of us under the watchful eye of one of the men, I looked at Donata and tried to give her a sign. I wasn't going to go peacefully, but I wanted to protect her if I could.

"She had nothing to do with it," I said to Spugna as he approached. "I forced her to lead me."

And then, just when he began to smile, I snapped around and grasped the rifle in Pietru's hands, left hand finding the barrel, right hand the stock, jerking as hard as I could and then twisting the rifle in hopes of snatching it from him. But the sudden movement failed to catch him off guard. The rifle barely twitched, his hands gripping it like iron.

I raised my right knee and slammed it into his groin, heard him grunt, then I let go of the stock with my right hand and hit him with a slashing uppercut.

The rifle was free. I swung around toward the car. Blow his fucking head off! my brain screamed. My right hand slid down the barrel, found the trigger guard. The safety catch! For an infinitesimal moment I wondered if it was off and instinctively knew I had no time to check.

My finger hit the trigger and there was a tremendous roar. Glass shattered. Damn! I'd pulled the trigger too soon. A hole appeared in the window in front of Spugna.

His face registered shock but he still hadn't moved. His men were just beginning to react.

Frantically I worked the bolt, snapping it up and back, ejecting the empty cartridge and drawing a new one into the chamber. I was slamming the bolt forward when a shot blew the rifle out of my hand and sent a nerve-stunning blow up my arm.

"No," Spugna screamed. "I need him."

Mistake, I thought. He should let them kill me. A vision of Wanda's bloody chest passed through my mind and a guttural cry of rage burst out of me. I lunged for Spugna and he jumped back, but not far enough. My hands found his throat and I jabbed both thumbs into his windpipe, trying to crush the life out of him. His red face was twitching and his eyes bulging in front of mine, when everything suddenly disappeared.

I woke in the black sedan. Two men were taking turns slapping me. My back was on the seat, my feet bent over the edge. Pietru yanked me upright and then jerked my head back sharply. The other fellow splashed water from a canteen into my face. I gasped for breath and choked as some of the water ran down my nose and into my lungs. They slammed me forward and then upright again, my spine whipping at the neck.

I absorbed their blows, punch-drunk, not feeling much of anything, conscious of insignificant details. The leather upholstery on the back of the front seat behind the driver was stained with blood. Mine? The air was heavy with the smell of perspiration. Spugna sat in the passenger seat in front, his arm stretched along the headrest as he watched his men pummel me. He'd lost his smile. Around his throat I could see nasty red marks left by my fingers.

"That's enough," he said finally, his voice hoarse. "He's awake."

He stabbed a finger at my chest. "Three hours from now and you're dead. I won't need you anymore."

My head fell forward in exhaustion and I closed my eyes. "Need me?" I heard myself ask, barely aware that my mind had formulated the question. "Why?"

"Why?" He rubbed his throat. "Because of what you know. And who you know. I have to be sure you haven't told them about the safe. Once the contents are gone, you're expendable."

Told them? Who was them? Did he think I worked for the government? I had no one to tell. I shook my head, wanting to sleep but aware that I didn't have much time now. I struggled to order my thoughts, questions rising from a haze of confusion and dying away before I could put them into words. "You could've killed me when I arrived."

"Sure, and we'd never know who might come down on us. Until this afternoon you would have served as a good hostage if your people tried to stop us. It's too late now. The shipment will be out of Malta in a few hours."

"Tunisia," I said quietly.

Spugna chuckled. "You have sharp ears—or Donata does. But she won't be helping you anymore. I hope you said good-bye to her."

I was afraid to ask what he meant to do with her.

The driver pulled through the gate to the villa and drove toward the large garage behind the house.

"Throw him in the trunk," Spugna said. "And I want a guard over him." He turned to one of the men who'd slapped me around. "Vasco, you watch. We'll be through in a few hours."

Vasco pulled me out of the car and produced a piece of rope that he bound around my wrists, leaving one end about two feet long. He gestured toward the open trunk and I crawled in, worried about how much air there was to breathe. When I was inside, with my hands in front of

224

me, he tied the free end of the rope around my ankles. I felt trussed up like a rodeo calf. It'd be hard to kick now.

Vasco grunted and pointed to the rifle in his hands. "I'll be right outside," he said in a guttural Maltese dialect.

I said, "Where's the bathroom if I need it?" and he slammed the trunk lid on me, cutting off the light and all sound.

A tomb. Thank God I wasn't Billy Wayne, I thought. He'd have died already from claustrophobia. Not that I was doing much better. As the quiet settled over me and I began to think with some degree of clarity, my fear grew. I was conscious of my heart pounding, but felt strangely detached from the sound. It was as if a machine that didn't belong to me was working in my chest, its beating out of my control.

Time passed. Once I thought I heard a throbbing sound. I finally figured out it was a helicopter. The air grew stuffy, my breathing a little raspier. My wrists were burning as a result of my efforts to work the rope loose. Some time later the copter started up and left.

I heard loud voices for the first time and the trunk lid swung up, light stunning my eyes. The white Mercedes-Benz with its shattered front window sat next to the black sedan. Spugna was leaning on the fender.

"Left my mark on you and your car," I said. A kind of crazy bravado had come over me. Sign that the end was near I thought.

Spugna said, "That's it, George. I'm afraid your vacation is over."

I twisted around and glared at him. I had nothing more to say. A surge of pride ran through me. He still didn't know my name. And he wouldn't find out now. His jocular use of George was as good as any.

"I just wanted to see you one more time," he said.

"You'll be joining Jeffrey Blike somewhere on the bottom of the Mediterranean. Give him my greetings."

"Rot in hell," I said.

They slammed the trunk lid and a moment later we were bouncing down the road, leaving the villa behind. We drove for what seemed about an hour, picking up speed at one point. A major road, I thought, and then, to confirm my speculation, I heard the horn of a bus as it passed us going the opposite direction.

A while later, we left the paved road and traveled over rougher terrain, the car jolting over numerous rocks. We stopped and they let me out, cutting the rope around my ankles but leaving my hands tied. We were on top of a rocky plateau overlooking the sea to the west. The sun hung above the horizon, an hour from setting. I looked around. Only two men.

A small peasant's hut perched on the edge of the promontory. I wondered if they were going to toss me from the cliff on to the rocks below. I could see a path leading off the edge of the plateau, presumably dropping down to a beach.

Vasco jabbed me in the back with his rifle. "Down the path," he said. I walked toward the hut, my mind working furiously.

I could take off at a run, dodging around the hut but risking a bullet in the back, or I could jump from the path into the void below. I hadn't seen the path's route, didn't know if it would allow for a drop to the sea. I didn't want to land on rock.

Before I could make up my mind, the door of the hut burst open and a shot rang out, whistling past my head. Vasco screamed and flew backward, his rifle clattering on the rocks at my feet. In front of me, Pietru swung around, ready to fire. I flung myself forward and caught him behind the knees, changing the trajectory of his shot, which blasted through the roof of the hut. And then

I rolled away, flinching, as another shot rang out from the door of the hut.

Pietru bounced, gasped once, and I looked over to see what remained of his head, a sight that left me shaking. I lay there with my face down, unable to move from the shock. I expected another bullet to rip through my skull but I couldn't get up.

This was it, I thought. I was through. *Finito*. I couldn't take any more. I'd reached the limits of my endurance and sanity.

I heard a hiss, repeated three times before I realized what it was. A whisper came out of the silence and penetrated my consciousness.

"It's Billy Wayne," I heard. "It's me."

I shook my head in confusion. "I'm *not* Billy Wayne," I said. "I'm nobody."

He giggled nervously. "Damn you, I'm Billy Wayne. Look up, you idiot."

I raised my head in a daze. "You're not dead?"

"I could ask the same of you."

I nodded numbly. "I'm dead," I said. "I'm dead."

Billy Wayne laughed, walked over to me, and tucked a pistol into his pants. "I had to wait until they were right on top of me," he explained. "Not much range with this."

He bent over. "Here, let me help you."

When I got to my feet, my hands still tied, he led me back to the hut, where a shriveled old man with black skin and white hair crouched in a corner. "Ask him for a knife," Billy Wayne said. "He hasn't understood a word I've said yet."

A minute later I was rubbing my chafed wrists and trying to figure out what had happened. Billy Wayne materializing out of the blue—something strange was going on. No way this was a coincidence. A ploy of

Spugna's? An attempt to learn my name and who I worked for? Ingratiate Henderson so I'd trust him?

I realized I was thinking like a crazy man, but that's what I'd become for a moment. Things were happening too fast. Events were beyond my control. But I was alive. That alone was cause for sanity.

Outside the hut, breathing in the fresh sea air, I looked around for a second vehicle, wondering how Billy Wayne reached the hut. "Billy Wayne, how in hell did you know I'd be coming here?"

He laughed. "I knew two days ago. Hear that?"

I'd hear it, a mule braying.

"Brought me out from Gharb. I'm surprised these guys made it all the way. It's a pretty rough track after the road ends."

Two days ago. I frowned. "Are you in with Spugna or what?"

He looked at me, his eyes amused. "You're the dumbest fucker I've ever met."

My fists tightened. I'd told myself the same thing once or twice recently but I didn't like hearing it from this pimple-faced prick.

He raised both hands placatingly. "Calm down, calm down. Just joking." He paused. "Let's just say the government's got an inside source. Spugna's been penetrated for over a year now and doesn't know it."

We took the car Spugna's men had been driving, a black BMW Bavarian sedan, Billy Wayne at the wheel. "We'll abandon the car in Rabat," he said. "Catch us a bus to the port at Mgarr and then the evening ferry to Valletta. I've got a friend waiting to help us."

I absorbed that in silence, still numb. But a few minutes later, I said, "All the time I thought you worked for Spugna."

"What'd you think I thought about you? Shit! You

228

could've been working for anybody. I couldn't tell you who I worked for. I'm with customs.''

''Customs?''

''U.S. Customs. Undercover. I've been with the *Nerina* for a long time—trying to catch IDC. They've been heavily involved with industrial espionage. Shipping information both ways, in and out of the country. Shit! Preston Blike sure pulled the wool over your eyes. Him and his granddaddy look.''

I didn't care about Preston now. He was dead. ''Preston's dead,'' I said.

He nodded. ''I thought so.''

I had to get something straight. ''Why'd you kill Gene Harrell?'' I asked.

We'd reached the road leading from Gharb to Rabat, and Billy Wayne turned on the headlights. He looked over at me thoughtfully and then said, ''I didn't.'' He shrugged. ''I saw it happen but I couldn't stop it without breaking my cover. Even then I'd have been too late. Preston caught him using the radio, took him on deck, and blew his brains out.''

I frowned. Preston Blike had blamed Billy Wayne and Billy Wayne was blaming Preston. Maybe at this point it didn't much matter. But I wanted to believe someone.

Billy Wayne sighed. ''I was pretty sure Harrell was government. I couldn't ask. My contact in Valletta confirmed it. CIA. Harrell was trying to track down the material Carlo Spugna's people stole from the Italians.''

He paused. ''Apparently Spugna sold one microchip to Blike and was going to sell the other to the Libyans, I think. Harrell managed to take care of Spugna's man and destroyed the chip that was supposed to go to the Libyans. And I think he managed to plant a bomb on the *Kirke*, trying to destroy the chip going to Blike. Only it didn't go off when he thought it would.''

His brow furrowed in thought. ''Jeffrey got away with

the chip for Blike. I guess Harrell thought Jeffrey was coming to meet the *Nerina,* so he rejoined us. You see, Harrell was on board when we left Marseilles, but Preston had sent him to Rome to help Jeffrey.''

I nodded. "I know all this. Preston told me before they killed him.''

Billy Wayne snorted loudly. "You don't know everything. When Harrell came back to the *Nerina,* Blike caught him using the radio. Talking about the bombing of the *Kirke* and surprised to find out where it lay. Spugna was behind that—bribed Jeffrey to return the one remaining microchip. You don't cross the Libyans. Spugna was trying to save his own skin.''

I was stuck on something Billy Wayne had said about Jeffrey's boat. Everything else was slipping over me in confusion. I stopped Billy Wayne with a wave of my arm. "You're saying the CIA sunk the *Kirke?*''

"Who else?''

I'd heard most of the other stuff before, more or less, but this was new. I was tired of trying to figure out who was doing what. "Everybody tells me a different story,'' I said. "I don't know who to believe, and I've decided I don't care who's telling the truth. It's got nothing to do with me.''

"I'm telling you the truth. Believe me. Did any of the others try to spring you?''

I stared out the front window, watching the eastern sky grow darker. We were climbing slowly, the lights of Rabat visible in the distance. We'd be approaching the Old Town along St. Ursula Street.

"You know what happened to you?'' he asked.

"Huh?'' Now that was a weird question. Who would know if I didn't?

"When we found out someone was trying to contact Harrell, we arranged to meet the guy at night off Vignetti. Blike ran the *Nerina* right over the launch. Figured he'd kill anyone who might know what was going on. Some guy called Rocco and a Canadian agent. Rocco must have shit in his pants when he saw us loom out of the night. He thought he was setting up the Canadian, never dreamed Preston would take him out too. Blike tossed Harrell's body overboard to join the other suckers.''

I was staring at Billy Wayne in open shock, my ears roaring, but he didn't take his eyes from the road. Just shook his head and said, ''Took me a long time to figure out the Canadian was you. You're one hardy bastard, I'll say that for you. We circled around, didn't find a trace of life. When you showed up at the *Nerina,* I don't think Preston or Diane ever knew you were the guy in the boat. They thought for sure everyone drowned. I think they figured you were some beach bum who stumbled on Harrell's identity and decided to have some fun. All they cared about was finding a diver.''

I couldn't believe what I was hearing. Sat there silent, overwhelmed by it all. His words washing over me like a wave.

Shit! The voices of my mad dream in Rocco's launch. So I was right! That revelation had been nagging at me ever since hearing Diane and Preston's voices—back when the crushing headache hit me on the *Nerina.* Only I hadn't wanted to admit it. Diane and Preston! They'd tried to kill me. Didn't even know who I was, for Christ's sake. Talking on deck while I was struggling to cry for help, drowning in the sea.

I was stunned by the enormity of it all.

Billy Wayne, lost in his own thoughts, shook his head and said, ''We couldn't believe it when that Giacomo kid mentioned Gene Harrell's name. Diane and Preston about croaked.'' He snorted. ''Two Gene Harrells. Say, what's your real name anyway?''

I pulled at my ears, trying to stop the roaring. ''You

met me as Gene," I said, my voice coming to me from far away. "Just call me that."

I started to tremble and had to take several deep breaths to get control of myself. I didn't know how much to believe. But more and more made sense. I still didn't trust Henderson. Knowing he was a customs agent didn't make me like him any more than I had before. For all I knew he was out to save his own neck and I just happened to be standing in the vicinity.

"So I got to call you Gene." He shrugged. "Have it your way. Don't forget I saved your life."

"I was just wondering why," I said drily.

"Simple. I need you."

"I've heard that before. Sounds just like Spugna. And what in hell do you need me for?"

"You speak Arabic, right?"

I stared at him. "So?"

"So we're going to Tunisia. I need someone who speaks the language."

"I'm not going to Tunisia," I said flatly.

"Harrell, you're so fucking stupid." He was angry. "I'm a U.S. Customs agent and I'm asking for your help." He shook his head. "And here I once thought you might be CIA, too. Only you're too fucking dumb to be CIA."

"I'm too dumb to be anything," I said. "I'm a private citizen, for Christ's sake."

He looked askance.

"That's the truth. I'm not even American. You know that. I'm a Canadian national. I've been working as an oil-field diver. I don't have anything to do with what matters to you."

Billy Wayne laughed. "Yeah, you're Canadian. And Harrell said he was Australian. What a cover! The guy had the worst fake accent I've ever heard."

232

I shook my head helplessly. I didn't have anything more to say.

Billy Wayne slowed down—we'd reached the outskirts of Rabat—and turned toward me. "We've got to stop Spugna's intermediaries from handing the microchip to the Libyans."

"No way. Not me. I've had enough. Spugna's got a woman who needs my help. Giacomo's sister. Donata. She's saved my life too—and tried more than once. When she's free, I go after Spugna. You take care of the blasted microchip."

Henderson leaned over toward me and gripped my arm with his right hand. "Gene, you don't understand. Donata's with the chip."

My eyes flashed with anger. "Don't try to feed me that shit. You don't even know her. No way she's working with Spugna—she never knew what he was doing."

Billy Wayne drove through It-Tokk Square, where the local bus service originated, and pulled to the side of the road just beyond the main post office on Republic Street. We parked behind an old rusty Morris Minor not far from the bus station, which was around the corner on Main Gate Street. When the motor died, Billy Wayne turned toward me earnestly. "Gene, I'm not saying she's working for Spugna. I'm saying he's sending her as a hostage."

I was too weary to argue. I said, "I don't see the point."

"She's his niece. He can't kill her himself. The family would never accept that. But if he sends her as a hostage and she's killed at the other end, he's off the hook. She's not going willingly."

"How in hell do you know all this?"

"I told you. I've got contacts. Now listen. Spugna's given the chip to some Arabs who flew in from Tunisia. Just intermediaries as far as we can tell. So they've got to pass on the stuff to someone else. They've taken a commercial flight to Tunis. I have someone following them on the plane. My guess is they'll go from Tunis south along the coast toward the border with Libya. The transfer will take place somewhere in the desert.''

I stared at Billy Wayne's ravaged face, a boil with a whitehead full of puss protruding from the side of his nose. Why didn't he squeeze it? But that wasn't what I wanted to ask. I was thinking about Donata. I still didn't understand.

"You said a hostage.'' I lifted my shoulders in frustration. ''It doesn't make sense.''

"Come on,'' he said, opening his door. ''We've got to catch the bus or we'll miss the last ferry.''

Billy Wayne left the keys in the car, and we both looked around when we got out. None of Spugna's people were in sight. With luck, he might not yet know his men had been killed.

Billy Wayne grabbed my arm and we walked to the station. ''Listen,'' he said. ''These Arabs from Tunis don't trust Spugna any more than you and I do. All he has to do is plant a bomb on the flight they're taking and they're dead. Spugna's already paid off. What's he care?''

I interrupted. ''That doesn't make sense. That's not the way to do business.''

"Okay, it doesn't make sense. But who can figure out the mind of these people? They asked for a hostage— someone in Spugna's family. He sent the girl. They don't know he planned on getting rid of her anyway.''

I turned on Billy Wayne. ''Damn it. Following that logic, maybe there is a bomb on the plane.''

"I doubt it. Remember Spugna's not an Arab. He's not out to screw up the deal. But what happens to Donata once she's in Tunisia . . .'' He stopped and waved his hands. ''You're dealing with people that don't like

Spugna. If you're worried about the girl's safety, you come with me. It's as simple as that.''

From Valletta we took the number thirty-six bus to Luqa airport several miles south of the capital. On the way, I told Billy Wayne I didn't have a passport. "I'll never make it on the plane," I said.

He laughed and said, "We got us our own jet. Private pilot even."

But at the airport, when Billy Wayne went to a small Quonset hut near the main facility for Air Malta, he heard the bad news. His private pilot wasn't available.

"What happened?" I asked when he came back out to where I was waiting on the oily strip to the side of the hangar. A faded advertisement for Farson's Kinnie, Malta's brand of soda pop, followed the ripples of the corrugated iron as it curved from the ground up.

Billy Wayne shook his head angrily. "Fucking asshole broke his leg today." He picked absentmindedly at a pimple on his forehead.

"What do we do?"

He stared at me and narrowed his eyes. "You fly?"

I shook my head.

"Well, I do," he said, pursing his cheeks. "After a fashion."

He turned and looked over his shoulder. "Come on. I'll show you."

When I stepped through a side door at the back end of the Quonset-hut hangar, I saw the gleaming torpedo-shaped snout of an old jet airplane, the canopy set far back on the fuselage. A mechanic in striped overalls stood next to the pull-down boarding ladder in front of a stubby wing. I couldn't tell the plane's age, but it was old. Still, someone had taken good care of it. "What is it?" I asked Billy Wayne.

He grinned. "A beauty, huh? She's a P-80 Shooting

Star.'' We walked over to the plane. ''Built by Lockheed back in the late forties. Served in the Panama Canal zone in 1948 and then in Korea.'' He ran his hand along the fuselage. ''This was the first jet plane used operationally by the Air Force.'' Pride burned in his voice. ''Known as the F-80 in Korea. Could've used it in the Nam.''

''What's it doing here?''

''She hasn't been flown much recently. After Korea, most of the Shooting Stars went to air national guard units. But not this one. She was sold and wound up in private hands.''

I looked at the sleek body, thinking about Billy Wayne's claustrophobia. ''You sure you know how to fly this?''

He shrugged. ''I think I can get us up in the air and back down.''

I didn't like the sound of that.

''It's either you or me,'' he said and grinned. ''Flight plan's been filed. I say we go.''

I didn't want to stay on Malta, and for some reason I'd convinced myself he was right about Donata. Sending her along as a hostage sounded like something Spugna would do. This was my chance to repay a few favors.

''You have money?'' I asked.

''I have everything we'll need. Money and weapons. You think of anything else?''

''Information.''

''Hell, I got that too,'' he said. ''Coming out of my ears.''

21

"Tower, Four Nine Shooting Star. Think you can work me in for a takeoff after the Alitalia?"

"Four Nine Shooting Star, stand by." Fifteen seconds of radio silence passed and then the crisp voice returned, the accent faintly British. "Will squeeze you onto the schedule."

A moment later, the voice broke in again. "Four Nine Shooting Star, taxi for takeoff."

Billy Wayne spoke into his radio microphone, "Roger, tower, taxiing for takeoff," and we moved down an arterial runway to the south.

When we were first out, the guy in the tower repeated our call numbers and said, "Cleared for takeoff, wind from the north at seven knots."

We used the newest runway at Luqa—thirteen thousand feet long—and pulled up well in advance of the threshold, swinging around to the left and leaving the visual-approach slope indicator lights behind us off our port wing.

After we were in the air the Control Tower left us to our own devices. We were sitting fore-and-aft with Billy Wayne in the pilot's seat and in a moment his voice filtered into my headphones. "We're supposed to set down at the main international airport outside Tunis—at Al Uwaynah. Tunis-Carthage they call it." He lapsed into silence.

I'd caught the smug tone to his voice. "Supposed to— meaning we'll land where?"

He was waiting for the question, turned, and grinned. "Sfax. Slight variation of the flight plan."

I frowned. "Is that okay?"

"Shit. Flight plan's just a formality. Help 'em find us if we go down." He lifted his head and turned toward me, glancing back out of the corner of his eye. "Might help us avoid customs. I'll just mention, very casual like, that we're coming out of Tunis-Carthage."

"*Gomrick—Douane.*"

"Huh?"

"Customs. You work for them, you ought to know their name. Father's birthplace? mother's maiden name? length of sojourn? hotel? currency?"

"Hey," he shouted, his voice blasting into my ears, "you forgot 'cigarettes?' 'drugs?' 'weapons?' "

"How about passports?"

He laughed. "I got mine."

That sobered me up. After a moment of silence, he jumped ahead, saying, "We waylay them along the road from Sousse."

It wasn't hard to follow him. I just wished we had a better idea of who "they" were. I said, "What makes you think that's the route they'll take?"

"Ain't much else, is there?"

I had to admit that was true. It was the most direct route. In Tunisia, of the six thousand miles of paved roadway a few led westward from the interior mining cities to the coast, but the rest ran along the more populated areas—the northwestern region and the Sahel or "shore," the narrow strip of heavily cultivated land following the s-curve along the coast from Nabeul to Gabes. From Sousse south to Sfax, however, there were two main roads, one running along the edge of the coast, the other following the railroad tracks, which cut straight south along an inland route.

But that was in the future and I was still concerned

about the present. "What about Tunisian Air Control?" I asked.

"They haven't picked us up yet." He paused. "You know why?"

When I didn't say anything he pointed to a dial on the console just to his left. I leaned forward and looked over his shoulder.

"Radar altimeter," he said. "We're skimming over the waves at about three hundred feet."

"You better know what you're doing," I said.

He shrugged. "To tell you the truth, I'll be flying by sight. Once we hit the coast, we'll just head south until we see the runway at Sfax. Shouldn't miss it."

Shit! I thought. Flying by the seat of his pants. He'd be going through commercial air space all along the coast. Depending on how far north we were, we'd have the airport at Sousse to worry about. And if I wasn't mistaken there was a military airstrip just outside Sfax, too.

"You're going to get us shot down if you're not careful."

He laughed. "Tunisian Air Force has about seventeen hundred men all told. That leaves damn few fighter pilots."

He seemed to know more than I would have expected, but he could have been lying for all I knew. I said, "What are they flying?"

After a moment his voice clattered in my ear. "As I recall, North American F-86Fs. They may have some Northrop F-5E Tiger IIs also. I know they had them on order several years ago. But flying them's another matter. Anyway, they don't care about us."

He lapsed into silence and then out of the blue he said, "If you want, worry about the Hughes Mavericks and the Raytheon Sidewinders. I think they've got both for the F-5Es now."

Great, I thought. Why can't this guy do anything right? Was it that tough to change a flight plan? Or was he trying to fool someone in Malta?

Suddenly he jerked forward. "Oh shit!"

"What now?" I said anxiously.

"Radio compass. Give me a minute."

He leaned forward, speaking to himself. "Resetting the circuit breaker." He clicked the control from ANT to LOOP to COMP and then sighed. "Life in the needle."

"What's that mean?"

"It means it's working." He grinned. "Sit back and relax. We should sight the coast near Mahdia any minute now."

Mahdia. That was south of Sousse. I sighed. One less airport to worry about.

So, I thought, back to Sfax. It wasn't my favorite city, but I'd spent time there more than once. Was there anyone I'd want to look up at PetroCanada's district office? I thought not. The company seemed part of another life.

Sfax was Tunisia's second largest city, but it lacked the charm of some of the smaller towns with Roman and Arabic antiquities. Not that it wasn't old; it originated as a Punic trading post over a thousand years before Christ, but the town had suffered badly as a result of numerous bombardments. The French Navy nearly razed the town in 1881 to repress a revolt after the Bey had signed the Treaty of Bardo that made Tunisia a French protectorate. And more damage resulted from the air raids conducted by the Allies in 1942-43 during the battle for North Africa. Still, for a newcomer or tourist, I supposed the Old Town would have its charm.

But new Sfax was now a great commercial center, the finest port in the country. Most of Tunisia's exports passed through Sfax—olive oil, salt, phosphates, which were mined a hundred miles to the west, and small amounts of esparto grass, a base material for paper and cordage, which the nomads brought in from the steppes when they could find it.

I looked up at Billy Wayne, his hand on the control stick. "Better not miss the airport," I said. "South of Sfax, you got thirty-some miles of olive groves. All the way to Gabes."

"There's always the desert beyond," he said cheerfully. "Soft sand."

"Yeah, die of the heat or run into a military post. And you'd better hope it was soft sand and not *reg*. Endless plains of black rock the size of your fist or bigger. Rip this thing to shreds."

He shrugged. "You worry too much. I've got everything arranged. Ain't nothing going to hurt us—man-made or natural." He spoke in an intentional drawl that brought to mind Jake Roberts, my tender on the Al-Qabisi jackup.

His comment about man or nature made me wonder about the canvas grip Henderson had thrown into the cockpit just before we left Luqa. Looked heavy and sounded like metal.

"What's in the bag?" I asked.

He looked back, his face beaming. "Guess."

"Come on, Billy Wayne. I don't have the energy to fool around."

"All you been doing the last three days is sleeping, far as I can tell."

"Fuck you."

"Okay, man, don't be so touchy."

I glowered at his back and he gave me a few more minutes of silence before speaking.

"I'm sure you've heard of UZIs, but you probably think of the submachine gun. I've got an UZI auto pistol—fits in the palm of your hand and takes a twenty-round magazine, although they say it'll accept the twenty-five- or thirty-two-round magazines the carbine uses. Plus there's a good ol' Colt .45, Model 1911A1. You know your guns?''

I shook my head even though he couldn't see me. "Don't like them."

He laughed. "Depends which end you're facing. The U. S. Army's changing from the Colt to a Beretta—the 92F Parabellum."

He paused, shaking his head regretfully, so I decided to humor him and asked, "Why's that?"

"Lot of reasons probably." He shrugged. "It's a 9mm handgun, same round used by our NATO allies . . ."

I waited, but he seemed to have run out of reasons. "So what else's in there? Is that it?"

"Hell, no." He slapped his stomach. "Got my belly gun—"

"What is that, anyway?" I interrupted.

He pulled it out and held it over his shoulder without looking back. "This?"

When I reached for it, he pulled it back as if he hadn't seen me. "It's a Coonan Model B .357 Magnum. Got a bit of recoil but it's a damn good defensive weapon."

"You must be into guns," I said somewhat disdainfully. "A gun freak."

"It's part of my profession," he observed without rancor.

I was surprised my tone of voice hadn't set him off. "So that's it?" I asked again. The bag looked awful heavy.

"Gee," he said facetiously, "you're never satisfied, are you? Well, let's see. I think I threw in a Mossberg Persuader."

Now there was an effective name. "What's that?"

"Pump-action shotgun."

"Well, I guess we're all set then," I said, unable to restrain my sarcasm.

"You're just mad we don't have a submachine gun."

Despite my misgivings, we had an uneventful approach to Sfax, following a Tunisavia jet, and making contact with the tower when we were still fifteen miles to the north.

When we climbed out of the plane at a small hangar, an Arab driver and a guide were waiting for us, standing next to a battered, four-door Saab sedan. "Hey, what'd I tell you?" Billy Wayne exclaimed. "I took care of everything. And no customs. You lucked out, Gene."

He stepped away from me, walked over to the car, and shook hands with the men. "Come here, Gene. You can translate. The guide knows about two words of English."

I followed him to the car and said, *"Essalam alaikum,"* bowing slightly.

"Wa alaikum essalam," they both replied, bowing in unison.

I introduced myself, and the two men nodded respectfully, surprised at hearing more than two words of Arabic.

I'd never studied Modern Standard Arabic—the formal language used by educated Arabs around the world—but then neither had Mustafa, the driver, nor Larbi, the guide. Larbi, in western dress, was a short, stocky fellow with light hair and blue eyes—a Berber from Gafsa and thus Caucasian in origin—and spoke a Tunisian form of Arabic, which was different from the Gulf dialect I'd picked up working in the Middle East. I supposed Mustafa spoke the same dialect as Larbi, but it was hard to tell from the little he said. A laconic native of the Saharan deserts in southeastern Tunisia, he looked to be over six feet, with a swarthy complexion and surly manner. Except for his shirt, which was a cool linen, loose-sleeved *gondourah,* he too wore westernized clothes but seemed uncomfortable with the pants, as if he'd just given up the traditional *djellaba.* Both men wore flat cotton caps, once white but now sweat-stained and gray.

When Billy Wayne and I were together in the back seat of the car I asked him if he knew these guys.

"Not really," he said, hunching over as if to pull up his socks. He gestured for me to lower my head. "Mustafa comes highly recommended. The other guy—what's his name, anyway? He's a replacement for a guy I've worked with in Africa before, named Hassan Fouad. At least Hassan spoke English. This guy . . ." He shook his head. "Probably didn't make it through the first grade—or whatever they got here."

I didn't like the sound of the word *replacement.* "A replacement? Why?" I whispered.

Billy Wayne pulled up his pant leg and adjusted a knife in a sheath strapped to his left calf. "He's dead," he said simply. "But don't start worrying on me. Larabe—"

"Larbi," I corrected, wondering how long we were going to sit with our heads between our legs.

"This Larbi's okay. Ignorant as all hell, but he's been checked out."

Billy Wayne pulled down his pants leg, and I straightened, hoping that his knife had a better blade than the dive knife Preston had loaned me.

Billy Wayne sat up and looked at his watch, squinting in the dim light. Dawn was still a few hours away.

I decided to change the subject. "You hungry?"

Billy Wayne looked at me in surprise. "What we had didn't last?"

I shook my head. The night before, after our arrival in Valletta, we'd stopped at a food stand near the City Gate Bus Terminus, a large roundabout just outside the walls, for a quick snack—a slice of *timpana,* the Maltese version of marcaroni pie, washed down by a bottle of pale

244

ale. But I was famished again after being starved by Spugna.

"Well, let's eat," he said. "Tell these jokers to get us to a restaurant."

"It's pretty early," I said. "I know of an all-night café on the waterfront. Want to try it?"

"Fine with me," he said. "I knew you'd come in useful."

I asked Mustafa if he knew where the Napoli café was and he shook his head, so I gave Larbi directions and settled back for the ride. The Napoli café was a place I used to frequent because the food was good and the owner was Italian, a cheerful little guy from Naples who knew me by name and always greeted me with a big smile and arms spread as wide as Bernini's colonnade. I was always afraid he'd hug me for some reason. I didn't mind affection, but Luigi's apron invariably looked as if it had a week's worth of food plastered to it.

We parked outside the café, a rectangular building just off the docks near a narrow-gauge railroad line that ran into a large warehouse used for loading phosphate into cargo ships. The café was frequented mostly by sailors and stevedores.

Mustafa and Larbi weren't hungry, so Billy Wayne and I left them to watch the car and went in. The place hadn't changed. Three or four small groups of men sat in the main dining room. At the back, near the kitchen, a counter ran along the wall for people in a hurry. Takeout service.

Suddenly I realized Luigi would blurt out my name when he recognized me. At least four months had passed since he'd last seen me, but Luigi didn't forget a face. Not many foreigners talked to him in Italian, and he'd always appreciated my efforts to carry on a conversation. I didn't want Henderson to learn I was Derek Stone. No telling who'd find out and what might happen.

I turned to Billy Wayne. "Why don't you find us a table. I know the cook. Let me round him up and get him to fix us something besides coffee and rolls."

Billy Wayne looked around the room. There were empty tables everywhere. I pointed toward the front door, said, "Take that one," and strode quickly toward the kitchen. I'd never gone behind the counter before, but I stepped around the end and through a door hung with rows of plastic beads. Luigi had his back to me, a burgundy fez with black tassel perched on his head. I almost laughed. He'd finally gone native. Even if it was Turkish. Next he'd be wrapping a *chechia* around his head.

"Luigi," I said, *"sono tornato!"*

He swung around, surprised to hear a voice in the kitchen, and then burst into a big grin, his arms flying out in a gesture of welcome. "Derek, *caro mio. Tanto tempo che non ti vedo!"*

I put my finger to my lips and lowered my voice. Billy Wayne didn't know Italian, but I was taking no chances. "Listen, Luigi. I'm with a friend, only he's not so friendly, if you know what I mean."

Luigi's eyes looked puzzled and I hurried on in Italian. "I don't want him to know my real name, okay? Can you call me 'Gino'?"

His eyes widened. *"Ho un figlio chiamato Gino."*

"That's good," I said. "You won't forget then." His having a son named Gino was a happy coincidence.

"We're out front," I added, "and starved. Fix us a meal, okay? Something solid. And a *gazeuse* for both."

"Certo, Signor Stone, subito!"

I grimaced. "And don't use my last name, okay? *E' importante!"*

He nodded vigorously, and I said, "I'll make it up to you later."

I rejoined Henderson and we sat without talking, waiting for our food, our elbows tented on the circular wood table.

Smiling broadly, Luigi appeared a few minutes later with two steaming plates. He'd fixed an omelet, what the Arabs called *shakshouka,* eggs cooked in olive oil with a filling of tomatoes, onions, green peppers, and spices. To cool the palate, chunks of melon accompanied the dish.

"Ben fatto, Luigi," I said and was about to mention the coffees when he said they'd be coming right up.

It seemed Billy Wayne and I were talked out. We ate the entire meal without saying much, each lost in his own thoughts. When we'd drained the last of our third cup of coffee, Billy Wayne pulled out his wallet, stuffed with currency.

"How about lending me some of that?" I said. "I'm getting tired of walking around like a pauper."

"Hey, pope or no pope, what d'ya need money for? You're with me."

I nodded, my cheeks pursed. Right. I was with him and he wanted to make sure I stayed that way.

I put my hands on the table, about to shove my chair back and get up, when Jake Roberts walked through the front door. My jaw felt like it dropped a foot. Billy Wayne saw my expression and jerked around, his hand falling to his waist.

"Derek!" Jake looked stunned. "Holy criminy," he said, which, along with "Holy Moses" and "Holy Toledo," was about the extent of his swearing. "I thought you were dead!"

I glanced at Billy Wayne, who was staring intently at both of us, and looked back at Jake. I didn't know whether to strangle him or kiss him.

"Jake!" I pushed myself to my feet and he rushed over to pump my hand.

"Doggone! The company wouldn't tell me anything. I spent two weeks in a clinic in Garbes before they even

told me about Al-Qabisi.'' He shook his head. ''I
couldn't believe it, Derek. Terrible.''

Suddenly he stepped back and whispered, ''Wanda . . .
Did she make it, too?''

Either he was a good actor or he'd prepared his role
for a long time; when I told him Wanda died in the
explosions on the jackup, Jake looked genuinely
stricken. ''I'm just awful sorry for you, Derek. I wish I
could've taken her place.''

I nodded, and then Billy Wayne cleared his throat, so
I introduced him and after we'd all sat down he looked
at me with a question in his eyes.

''Jake was my tender on my last job,'' I explained. ''I
was diving for PetroCanada off a jackup in the Gulf of
Gabes. Lost my wife in an accident.''

Jake grabbed my arm and said, ''Derek, I heard it
wasn't an accident. That rig was sabotaged.''

I looked him straight in the eye. ''Yeah, but who did
it?''

22

JAKE'S THEORY WAS that the Libyans were right. An underwater team of saboteurs had planted the explosives. When I said most of the explosions were on the rig and not underwater, he guessed the team had had inside help.

"Jake," I said carefully, "the extra set of tanks you set up for me, remember them?"

He nodded. "Sure."

"They went off first."

He looked surprised. "You sure?"

"Positive."

His face darkened. "Derek, you're not saying you thought I had something to do with it, are you?"

I stared at him a moment and then said, "Yes, I guess I am."

He shook his head emphatically. "Derek, I swear on the Bible, no way, absolutely no way. I can't believe that."

"It's the truth. Tank pack went up like a bomb. Snapped that leg like a toothpick."

Jake rubbed his forehead, his face grim. "Those tanks sat there all night," he said finally. "You think of that? Anyone on the jackup could've planted explosives." He looked offended. "It wasn't me. I swear to God. What more can I say?"

We chewed the topic back and forth for a while, with Billy Wayne absorbing everything, but came to no resolution. I could sense the coolness that slowly settled between Jake and me. Sure, we talked about the oil business and what Jake was doing. PetroCanada had found what Jake called a fairly sweet crude and was reevaluating their decision to pull out, talking about resisting government pressure.

I understood the temptation. Most Middle Eastern crudes are sour—they've got a high sulphur content and it takes a special refining operation to remove the sulphur compounds. From what Jake said, this oil was much lighter.

"The only drawback, Derek, is it's a bit waxy—pretty high pour point."

I shrugged. "Still, compare Saudi Arabia's Safaniya crude—two-point-eight percent sulphur—to this. What is it? About point-two or point-four percent, I bet."

"Yeah. It's as good as what they found at Brega or Es Sidr."

Brega and Es Sidr were fields in Libya.

About then Billy Wayne jumped in with a few questions, and I talked about the oil business—partly to lessen the underlying friction between Jake and me, partly to drown out thoughts of Wanda.

"You'd be surprised what they're doing with petrochemicals," Jake said to Billy Wayne, interrupting my exposition of oil grades and refining procedures. "You ever hear of protein production?"

When Billy Wayne shook his head, I took the words from Jake's mouth. And probably fancied them up— that's what a college education does for you. "The microorganisms living in the hydrocarbon mixtures produce protein concentrates. They're more or less analogous to animal proteins and they're even rich in water-soluble vitamins. From a ton of normal paraffins, technically it's possible to obtain a ton of protein-vitamin concentrate."

Jake said, "There's a plant in Sardegna been process-

250

ing over a hundred thousand tons a year. And that's since 1975. Lot of things seem new but aren't. Heck, the Italians were distilling oil from shale as far back as the late seventeenth century. Produced enough to light the streets of Modena.''

Billy Wayne seemed interested. He asked what a Texan was doing here in Africa that he couldn't do in the Gulf of Mexico.

Jake grinned. ''A major discovery in North America usually offers you about twenty-five to fifty million barrels of recoverable oil reserves. Sound like a lot?''

Billy Wayne said, ''Sure.''

''A typical Middle East oil field yields ten times that,'' I put in. ''A billion barrels. Course that's the American billion, not the British.''

''Is there a difference?''

Jake smothered a grin as I said, ''For the Americans that's only a thousand million. For the British a million million. Anyway you look at it, it's a lot. There are at least a hundred and fifty accumulations like that in the rectangle between Turkey and Dhofar.''

I could see Billy Wayne thought about asking where Dhofar was but didn't. So Jake and I had something in common after all, and I suppose that should have made me feel better, but it didn't.

Jake told me he was due for a vacation and going to be spending a few weeks in Malta and another in Sicily.

''Malta?'' I said, trying not to frown. ''Why Malta?''

I avoided Billy Wayne's piercing eyes, angry that I'd let my emotions show for a moment.

Jake shrugged. ''Never seen it. I'll be staying at the Marina Hotel in Sliema. They tell me it's on the sea.'' He tried to grin at me but I guess my face was pretty hard. ''Much as we need to see the sea, huh?''

I didn't say anything. The memories were too painful.

"If you're up in that area, drop in and see me," Jake said. "We can rent us a boat and go fishing together."

I had a hard time nodding but did so.

When Billy Wayne and I finally left, and Jake stayed to eat breakfast, the distance between us hadn't closed any. It hurt to lose a friend but I couldn't make myself take that extra step to heal the mistrust I felt.

I was morose most of the eighty-some-mile trip north along the inland route to Sousse. I was oblivious to the scenery, having seen it on several other trips. Six miles out of Sfax the olive groves thinned out and we crossed the low-lying area just before La Hencha, most of it open country, and then picked up the olive groves again near El Djem.

Billy Wayne sensed my inner turmoil and didn't bother me, not even when the Roman amphitheater at El Djem rose up from the plain, an immense ruin rivaling the Colosseum in Rome. But finally, twenty-some miles from our destination, he caught my eye and broke the silence.

"So your name's Derek. Mind if I call you that?"

I glared at him and said coldly, "Call me what you want."

He shrugged. "Fine, I think we can bury Gene Harrell then."

Bury Gene Harrell. I thought about that and sighed. Perhaps it was time. All in all he'd served me well and I was grateful to him. But the guy was dead and I was alive. Let him rest in peace; and it was time I took care of my own business. I brooded a moment and then met Billy Wayne's eyes. "You're right," I said finally. "You can call me Derek Stone."

"Pleased to meet you, Derek," he said, his blue eyes steady.

I tried to read a hidden message there, but his eyes stared back at me like deep, calm pools. I hoped my face looked as impassive as his, but I doubted it.

We saw an inordinate number of police. The *Garde Nationale*, a rural force, was in evidence along the way. We spotted their cars three or four times parked at the side of the road behind a string of trucks. They were busy harassing commercial traffic, it seemed, and left us alone.

Between the olive groves, which stretched for miles in monotonous regularity, lay watery sheets of *sebakhas,* shallow lagoons where salt was harvested through evaporation. I was glad when the high tower of Sousse's Kasbah appeared in the distance.

When we reached the crenellated walls of the Medina, or old town, with their bastions and square towers, Henderson told Mustafa to turn right and we drove on into new Sousse, stopping first at a petrol station near the Quai Est and then at a hotel along the Boulevard Armand Fallières. Behind the boulevard, to the east and our left, rose the hill on which sat the Kasbah, Sousse's citadel, and to our right and much closer, the Ksar er Ribat, a large square building, once a Byzantine fortress, then a monastery, and later yet, a *medersa* or Moslem college.

I stayed in the car and admired the view while Henderson stepped into the hotel to make a phone call about which he'd been purposefully enigmatic.

Ten minutes later, Billy Wayne came charging out of the hotel and cut across the street, dodging traffic on the run. "Pile in," he shouted, and I gave the order in Arabic to Mustafa.

"Where to?"

"Just tell him to get us out of town—the road to Tunis."

I relayed the message to Larbi, and he told Mustafa to take a left after the Ribat and to follow the railroad tracks leading away from the Quai Nord. It took us a good half hour to get out of the city, with Billy Wayne fretting the whole time.

"They've already left Zaghouan," he explained in clipped tones. "Should be reaching Enfidaville on the coast soon."

"That route has some pretty steep gradients," I said. "Should slow them down."

He didn't appear to have heard me, his mind locked on its own track. Frowning, he consulted a map he'd picked up in the hotel. "I figure we'll stop them somewhere between Enfidaville and Kalaa Kebira." He stabbed his finger on the map. "Out here where it's more isolated."

I was beginning to get nervous. The canvas grip with our weapons was still in the trunk. "What are they driving?"

Billy Wayne folded the map and stuck it in his back pocket. "A white Citroen. Should be easy to spot a mile off. We'll have Mustafa park facing south. If we can get out on the highway in time, they'll have to pass us. Ping! I take out a tire or two."

"They'll be armed, too, you know."

He grinned. "Scared, huh? I'll give you the Colt .45. How's that sound? Nice hefty feeling in the hand. Make you feel better."

"Wouldn't it be easier to follow them and catch them when they've stopped? Get the drop on them?"

"Get the drop on them?" He laughed. "Hell, man, where you think they'll stop? Out here in the tooliberries? They'll stop in the middle of town."

I rubbed my hands, feeling edgy. "I may not be of much help."

A wide grin split his face. "Don't worry, ah—" He started to say Gene and corrected himself, "—Derek." He slapped me on the knee. "Our two companions here will help."

I hesitated. "You sure?"

"That's what they've been trained for."

Twenty or so miles north of Sousse, Billy Wayne found a spot he liked and had me tell Mustafa to stop and turn around. Out the back window, we had an unimpeded view north and a small clump of olive trees to hide the car behind.

Billy Wayne opened the trunk and brought the grip to the back seat, where he opened it and began handing out weapons. "To you, the Colt," he said, handing me the gun and three extra magazines loaded with cartridges.

I looked the gun over while he passed Mustafa and Larbi their firearms. Along the barrel it said Government Model and below that and just above the trigger was a serial number—FG389207. Made by the Colt Manufacturing Company in Hartford, Connecticut, U.S.A. I hoped I didn't have to fire it.

We sat and waited under the hot sun for nearly two hours. "Lazy Sunday afternoon," Billy Wayne commented once, and I thought about how, for me, time had lost its relevance. Minutes and hours passed like plastic ducks floating by in a carnival booth. The stream of time. Every now and then I'd reach down and pluck out a minute or an hour, win or loose a prize, and then back to the monotonous passage of time. Days merged into each other with a natural rhythm that had nothing to do with a calendar. The number of the day didn't matter. What mattered was that it was summer and hot.

Mustafa had just passed around his *djerba*—a goatskin bag filled with water—to quench our thirst, when Billy Wayne spotted the Citroen. In the distance, in glimmering heat waves, it looked like a white pellet.

"What's that in front?" I asked, staring at the black lump gliding along the highway a short distance in front of the Citroen.

Our Saab, with Mustafa behind the wheel, was on the

highway, moving slowly toward the south—ahead of the Citroen—by the time Billy Wayne swore and said, "Looks like a military truck."

"Think they're traveling together?"

He hesitated. "Probably."

"This changes things, right?"

I was afraid he'd still go through with his crazy plan but he nodded grimly. "I'll say it does." He paused. "Tell Mustafa to slow down and let them pass. We'll follow them at a distance. I've got to do some thinking."

Ten minutes later the vehicles pulled around us and I glanced over casually, trying to spot Donata.

The military truck had a canvas covered back but I could see soldiers armed with heavy weapons sitting on both sides. The car held five people, two in the front and three in the back. They whipped past before I could pick out the faces, but I looked at Billy Wayne and he nodded, reading my mind.

"She's there," he said. "That was a woman in the middle."

"They've got her wrapped in a white *ha'ik*, Arab fashion," I said. "Hard to tell for sure who it is."

"I didn't forget you, Derek. My man in Tunis said she was still with them." His eyes hardened. "What he didn't say was that they'd picked up a military escort."

"Maybe that happened after they left Tunis."

"Could be. I had the car followed as far as Zaghouan. Told my men I'd pick it up from there."

"That's a lot of ground with no one watching."

"Where else could they go?"

I snorted. "We'd have missed them completely if they'd taken the inland route from Enfidaville to Kairouan and then cut back to El Djem and Sfax."

"Unlikely," he said. "My map shows that road from Kairouan to El Djem as a track. Why go out of their way to take a slow dirt road?"

He was right, but his approach still didn't seem professional. I asked him how many people he had on this job and he laughed.

"We had a guy on the flight to Tunis and two men in this country—along with Mustafa and Larbi of course. It's up to us now. By tomorrow Spugna's intermediaries will be at the frontier with Libya."

With that pleasant thought we lapsed into silence.

Mustafa followed the two vehicles through the rest of the afternoon. Billy Wayne and I took turns napping, our eyes red from lack of sleep and the dry heat.

Spugna's Arab connection—his intermediaries as Billy Wayne put it—continued on past Sousse without stopping. Three hours later, they gassed up quickly on the outskirts of Sfax and, with night falling, headed south through the olive groves toward Gabes, eighty-six miles away.

At each town that passed, Billy Wayne swore. We rolled by Nakta first, then Chaffar, and then Mahares. At Mahares, the road left the railway and followed the coast, running through plantations for twelve miles or so and then through steppe-desert before rejoining the railway at Achichina. And after Achichina, La Skhirra. We were more than halfway to Gabes and I could tell Billy Wayne didn't know what to do, was hoping the men would stop for the night to give us time to plan something.

None of the occupants of either vehicle seemed to notice we were following, but just in case, at sunset we passed them south of La Skhirra and waited off to the side of the road a few miles short of Gabes near the Wedd el Melah, a dry riverbed debouching into the gulf.

The olive trees had given way to a more rugged terrain—bare hills and empty plains, both brooding bleakly under the harsh glare of the moon. Heat radiated from the earth, which had baked all day under a ferocious sun. We sat in darkness, wilting, with the car windows open, until finally an evening breeze gathered strength and washed over us, bringing relief. "A *gharbi,*" Mustafa said, speaking for the first time in hours—a cool wind from the west.

We passed around the *djerba* again, munched on dried figs, and Billy Wayne got out to pee. When he returned, I looked at him, sitting in profile to my left, and said, "We're in trouble if they keep going all night. They'll cross the desert and reach the frontier by dawn."

He didn't reply, just grunted and continued to stare out the back window, looking for the distinctive headlights of the military truck and the Citroen.

A while later, he muttered, "Can't let the Libyans get their hands on it," and lapsed back into a glum silence.

South of Gabes, once again on their track, our luck changed. The road from Gabes to Medenine runs forty-five miles along a narrow strip between the coast and the Ksour Mountains to the east—the desolate Plain of Arad. Somewhere in that desolate wasteland before we reached the village of Mareth, the truck pulled to the side of the road, steam pouring from the hood. We were too close to stop in time, so we passed them and pulled away into the darkness, with Billy Wayne whooping for joy.

"Tell Mustafa to pull off the road when he can and we'll wait," he said. "They're closer to Medenine than Gabes." He chortled. "I bet the Citroen comes on alone to get help." He punched me in the arm. "What say, Derek? The gods are looking after us."

"Maybe," I said grimly, wondering what was happening to Donata. In my tiredness, I found it difficult to fight my fears. I felt sick, and the task ahead of us did little to calm my nerves.

The lights of a bus coming our way from Gabes appeared in the distance, grew brighter, and then sped by.

Mustafa suddenly grunted and hit the ignition. The Citroen had flashed out of the darkness, its headlights extinguished, slipping by us like a ghost in the wake of the bus. Following the taillights.

Larbi turned, a startled look on his face. "Madmen," he said. "That speed at night."

"Mustafa, get going!" Billy Wayne yelled.

A translation wasn't necessary. Mustafa already had the car in gear and we spun from the rocky gravel on to the pavement. In the distance I could see two pinpricks of red. The Citroen was passing the bus, its headlights flashing on as it pulled out ahead.

"They've turned on the lights," I said, pointing. "Damn! They must've known all along we were following."

The wind roared into the car and the tires whined as the gas pedal hit the floorboards. Mustafa was equal to the challenge, and the Saab, for all its rattles, ran like a bullet. Within minutes we'd passed the bus and the taillights of the Citroen were growing in size.

"Tell him to hold it there," Billy Wayne said. "No closer for now. They'll have to stop in Medenine." He squeezed his lips between forefinger and thumb, musing, and then asked himself quietly, "Will they come back with help or send someone out?"

"Or go on?" I added. "It's just over a hundred miles from Medenine to the border."

He looked at me. "What do you think?"

I shook my head. "I don't know. What are our options?"

Billy Wayne scratched his head and then sighed. "Let's follow them into Medenine. I think they'll stop for the night. They've had a long trip. They've got to eat sometime." He took a deep breath and exhaled slowly. "Probably arrange for someone else to go out with a mechanic. If we're lucky, they'll leave the girl and one or two of the guys in town. We'll hit them in their room."

"And if we're not lucky?"

"Come on, Derek." Billy Wayne punched me in the arm. "Don't be so negative. At worst they get a mechanic, turn around, and go back. If they do, we catch up and hit them on the road like we were going to do the first time. Pass it on to the guys."

So I translated and sat back to wait. I didn't have long. It seemed like only minutes and we were in Medenine, parked across the street from the Citroen, which had pulled up in front of the Hotel des Palmiers, a three-story, Moorish-looking place with an entrance flanked by green-and-red-striped pillars and capped by a white dome. One taxi was drawn up at the side of the building, its driver not in sight.

We watched as the two khaki-clad men in back entered the hotel with Donata between them, followed a moment later by one of the men in the front seat, who carried a suitcase and small traveling bag and wore a pair of what looked like black bloomers and a white *gondourah*.

I could feel a sudden spurt of energy, repressed excitement in the air. We sat in tense silence, waiting to see what the driver would do.

The man who'd carried in the bags returned without them and got in the car. The two men lit cigarettes and then the driver pulled away from the entrance.

"Let them go," Billy Wayne said. "Jesus, we got 'em now. Five of us against two of them."

I looked at him puzzled, thinking *four* not *five* and wondering where he'd learned to count.

He saw the look and grinned. "The girl's on our side, right?"

We ate in the hotel's restaurant, a large room to the left of the registration desk. In the middle of the room, a black-hued *karoub* tree grew toward a domed skylight. Across the room the three people we were following sat in a small alcove, its Mediterranean arch decorated with hand-carved wooden arabesques. The woman had her back to us, and it was impossible to see if it was Donata.

"It's her," Billy Wayne kept whispering to me. "Let's eat while we have a chance. When they leave to go to their room, make sure she sees you. But be subtle about it," he added, and I frowned. I didn't like taking instructions on how to act.

I cut in impetuously, in a burst of bravado. "I say take them here in the restaurant. Why wait?"

"I don't like it here. Too many people. We follow them up to their room and do it out of sight of the others."

We ordered—the food wasn't cheap but then Billy Wayne was paying and that made everyone happy—and while we waited for the food, drank lemonade in glasses with silver cuffs. When our dishes arrived—tabouli salad, couscous, roast lamb, and chicken breasts stuffed with almond paste, accompanied by a sweet mint tea— we ate in a hurry, not doing the food justice but ready to leave at a moment's notice.

Mustafa and Larbi finished first, and Billy Wayne sent them out to the front desk. "Tell them to book a room for two. And then go on up. They can wait in the halls, one to each floor. Tell them to watch where our friends go. We'll be at the bar."

The bar was in a small side room, overlooking a paved courtyard with intricately carved white marble columns, potted fig trees, and a fountain that trickled with recirculated water.

The threesome in the alcove were in no hurry, and Billy Wayne and I had finished our meal and a dessert of fresh figs with wine, when they were still on their main course.

Billy Wayne cleared his throat and told me he had a phone call to make. "Wait for me in the bar and keep an eye on them," he said. "I'll be back in a few minutes."

From the bar I couldn't see the threesome in the

alcove, but I kept a sharp eye on the doorway. They'd
have to walk past it to get to the stairs leading to their
room.

Several people came and others went. A few Europeans wandered into the bar, ordered sweet after-dinner
drinks, and talked at the far end of the bar, their voices
reaching me as a low murmur. I was beginning to wonder
what was taking Billy Wayne so long when I heard loud
voices from the dining room. Arabic, but spoken with a
strong foreign accent. A word I was sure was Slavic.

Russians! I'd heard them speak Arabic before. Knew
the accent.

I stepped to the door in time to see two men at the
alcove, both dressed in business suits, guns in their
hands.

Shit! Russian agents had beaten us to it. Where in hell
was Billy Wayne?

And then I saw the two men with guns grab the woman
in the *ha'ik* and turn to leave. The suitcase and bag were
still at the feet of the two men in the alcove. Why were
the Russians taking the woman and not the
microprocessor?

I stared in shock as the gunmen rushed by, dragging
the woman with them, one of the men stifling her cries
with the folds of the cloth that veiled her face.

Was it Donata? Had Spugna freed her, after all? Used
his Russian contacts for help?

I couldn't tell if she'd seen me, but I'd been standing—
frozen by the suddenness of the event—just inside the
dining room, in plain sight.

I'd left the Colt .45 under the back seat of the Saab
and swore at myself while I looked around desperately
for Billy Wayne. He had the keys to the car.

He was nowhere in sight and I couldn't wait. Donata
was slipping through my fingers like sand through a
clepsydra.

I stumbled through the entryway, galvanized finally into action, prepared to fight with my bare hands if I had to, when a figure stepped from the side of a palm tree and jammed a gun into my neck. "Where are you rushing off to?"

I swallowed hard, turned my head slowly, stared at the man. It was Billy Wayne.

"Damn you!" I screamed, knocking his hand away. "They've got Donata, you fool."

I ran to the side of the hotel, where the taxi driver, back at his vehicle, stared at me.

"A car," I shouted in Arabic. "Did you see a car?"

He raised both hands in a gesture of ignorance. The men who'd taken Donata were nowhere in sight and I hadn't even seen what type of car they were driving.

Billy Wayne joined me then and I swung wildly, catching him just under the right eye. His head snapped back, but before I could swing again he dipped away and raised the gun.

"You fucking calm down," he said through clenched teeth, "or I'll put you on a slab. I thought you were running out on me."

I glared at his splotchy face, at his piercing blue eyes, which stared back at me like flint. His cheeks were red with anger, a mouse already forming under the right eye.

In an even tone he said, "Someone's as much a fool as you. We get the chip first, then the girl."

23

LARBI CAME OUT of the hotel then, gesturing wildly. He rushed up to me, words spouting like bullets from a machine gun.

"What the fuck's he saying?" Billy Wayne demanded, interrupting.

"I caught about half. Mustafa's waiting on the second floor. The men that had Donata have gone up to their room. With the suitcases. Just a minute."

I turned to Larbi. "Did you overhear them talking? Anything about the woman?"

"No woman," he said.

"I know, but didn't they talk about her."

He scratched his head. "Perhaps Mustafa . . ."

Billy Wayne was pestering me again, wondering what the conversation was about. When I told him, he asked me in an aggravated tone if I couldn't forget Donata for a while. There were more important things to worry about.

I could have strangled him then.

Billy Wayne looked around as if deciding on a plan of action. Behind us we heard another babble of voices near the entrance to the hotel. We turned to see a waiter chasing off an itinerant carpet seller.

Was he involved? I could tell I was grasping at straws. I couldn't concentrate. I didn't have a clue in the world and the lack left my mind in a black daze. Was there any way now for me to find Donata? I couldn't think of one, and Billy Wayne obviously didn't care. All he thought about was the missing chip. A heavy weight settled in the middle of my chest.

Billy Wayne paced back and forth in front of the hotel, stroking his chin. I wondered what was going on in that mind of his. We were getting to that stage of tiredness where the brain ceases to function with clarity. I found my own thoughts locked in a tight circle, running the same ideas over and over in an endless cycle—an annoying lilt, like the repetition of a broken record.

"So, what do we do?" I asked. "Give them some time to fall asleep and then break in? Surprise them?"

Billy Wayne swung around, his eyes narrowing as he squinted at my face. "I don't like what's going on around here," he said. "Too much happening we don't control. We hit them now and get the hell out of here."

Maybe that was best. The sooner we snatched the chip, the sooner we could look for Donata. And maybe the two Arabs who'd lost her could provide a clue.

I turned to Larbi and started to ask him in Arabic what he thought.

Billy Wayne grabbed my arm before I could utter more than three or four words.

"What the fuck you think you're doing?"

I bristled. "I'm just going to ask Larbi what he thinks."

"The hell you are. These goons work for me. They do what I say. You don't go around asking them what they think. They ain't paid to think. They're paid to obey."

"You make a great boss."

"Yeah, so you want to take over?"

"Just remember I'm here 'cause I want to be. I don't work for you and I don't work for any foreign government—and that includes yours."

"How about we shut up and do something?" He looked back and forth between Larbi and me. Larbi's expression hadn't changed a tittle despite the anger in our voices. We could've screamed at each other and pulled guns and I don't think Larbi's face would have registered the fact.

"Derek, you tell Larbi to wait out front here in case they get by us. We need Mustafa. I figure his Arabic sounds more authentic than yours, right?"

"He hardly speaks, but he's a native Tunisian."

"That's what I said."

We turned to go into the hotel, and Billy Wayne started to tell me what he wanted Mustafa to say.

I interrupted. "Wait a minute. I don't have my gun."

"What? Whaddya mean you don't have your gun? What in the fuck you do with it?"

"I left it in the car—"

"You left it in the car?" He stared at me with his mouth open, dumbfounded.

My jaw muscles tightened. "Yeah. All you guys had guns. I thought it might be good to have a backup gun— under the seat for emergencies."

"We got a trunk full of guns." He shook his head. "Derek, you're thinking too much. Come on, let's get it."

He started across the street and I followed. Billy Wayne unlocked the back door and I found the Colt .45 where I'd stuffed it beneath the seat cushion.

I straightened, stuck the gun in my waistband, and stepped aside as Billy Wayne locked the door and slammed it shut. The sound vibrated down the tight lanes of the village. Other than the lights of the hotel, the streets were dark, lit only by the moon, which bounced off the white surfaces of the apartment buildings with a cold, ghostly effect. Only the air was still hot. I felt gritty, in need of a shave and a shower, my eyes burning with tiredness. The energy provided by the meal was already dissipating.

I wanted to ask Billy Wayne who he thought took

266

Donata but didn't. The guy had one thing on his mind. As we crossed the street where Larbi was waiting, Billy Wayne said, "We'll knock on the door and have Mustafa tell them he's with the management. A mistake was made. They were given the wrong room. We're moving them to a better one, courtesy of the management. Something like that."

"And if they don't open the door?"

"We kick it down."

I shook my head. "There goes the element of surprise."

Billy Wayne didn't seem to care. He grabbed Larbi's arm and pointed to a group of date palms outside the hotel. "Derek, tell him to hide there—and shoot to stop them if he has to."

I translated and Larbi moved off to take his position.

Billy Wayne led the way into the hotel. We smiled and nodded at the night clerk and made our way to the stairs before he could speak. I saw the man's mouth open, and turned.

"Be right back," I said in Arabic. "We're just going up to visit our friends."

On the stairway, Billy Wayne said, "Just remember this. When we go in, I go in firing. So don't get in my way. I'm taking no chances."

I slowed down and thought about that for a moment. "What do you expect me to do?"

"If you're smart, you'll do what I do. These guys ain't the type to give in without a fight. I say hit first and hit hard—and maybe we won't get hit back."

He saw me hesitate and baited me. "You like Spugna?"

I glared at him. "You know I don't. What's that got to do with this?"

"These are Spugna's guys, remember. His intermediaries. They had your girlfriend."

"She's not my girlfriend. She's a woman who tried to save my life."

"Okay, but you get what I mean. You ought to hate these guys. Think of it that way. They probably hate you and they don't even have a reason. General meanness."

My mouth curled into a nervous half-grin. "Okay, but after we get the microprocessor we go after Donata, right?"

"I promise. But we got to have a lead, right?"

It was a stalemate.

Billy Wayne pointed to my belly. "Check your gun. Make sure you have a cartridge in the chamber and the safety off. You won't have time to think when it matters."

I could feel the tension hit me suddenly in the pit of the stomach. I checked the Colt and then looked up to see Mustafa standing on the landing above us. He flicked his head and I moved up, with Billy Wayne at my side, to see what he had to say.

"Room twenty-four," he whispered. "On the back overlooking the patio."

"Okay," I said. "Here's what Billy Wayne wants you to do." I told him what to say and what we'd do depending on the reaction of the men inside. Mustafa listened impassively, and when I'd finished he simply nodded and looked at Billy Wayne, waiting for the order to go.

In the hallway, I was happy to see that the doors had no peepholes. I was afraid the men had seen Mustafa in the dining room. Now we didn't have to worry about that. And his voice would be authentic. Mine would have been met with suspicion.

Billy Wayne took the right side of the door and I the left. The muscles in my face were tense—I think I was expecting a fusillade through the door and admired Mustafa's coolness. He stood directly in front of the door and knocked. Three times hard.

We waited. No answer.

Billy Wayne put his finger in front of his lips and leaned forward, his ear flat against the surface of the door.

He frowned and gestured to Mustafa.

Three more knocks, loud enough that I looked up and down the hall wondering if we'd attract the attention of other guests.

"Shit," Billy Wayne whispered. "I'm going in."

He gestured to Mustafa to move to the side, and the Arab did so, drawing the gun Billy Wayne had given him in the car. Billy Wayne stepped back and gave the door a tremendous kick near the knob. The frame shattered and Billy Wayne charged through, slamming the door open with his left shoulder. I swung around the frame a second later, aware that Billy Wayne hadn't fired.

No one rushed to stop us. The room was empty. Billy Wayne threw the bathroom door open, swearing softly. "Not here," he said, scowling.

I walked to the curtain and pulled it aside. "The balcony."

I slid the door open and Billy Wayne stepped out. I turned around to tell Mustafa to shut the outer door and saw that he'd already done so. "Wait here," I told him and joined Billy Wayne.

The balcony overlooked a patio with a small bathing pond surrounded by date palms as if the pond were a miniature oasis. At the far end, set in a massive stone wall, was a door.

Billy Wayne pointed and I nodded. "Looks like the side street," I said. "No trouble getting down from here."

Suddenly we heard what sounded like muted shots.

Billy Wayne turned and rushed back into the room. "Let's go," he yelled. "Larbi's got them."

But when we reached the street Larbi was nowhere to be seen.

"The taxi," I said. "It's gone."

Billy Wayne yelled at Mustafa and pointed to the Saab, then ran to the corner with me at his heels. A man stumbled out of the darkness, clutching his head and moaning. Billy Wayne raised his pistol.

"Don't shoot!" I screamed. "The taxi driver."

The man slumped to the ground and it was then I saw Larbi. He was lying behind a small ledge that formed a barrier between the taxi stand and the wall of the hotel.

"Shit! Larbi's been shot."

Billy Wayne put his ear to Larbi's mouth, shook him, and then stood. "He's dead. Ask the other guy where they went."

The taxi driver, still in a daze from a blow to the head, was unable to say much. He finally pointed to the road leading east and muttered, "That way."

Mustafa had the car waiting and we piled in, Billy Wayne in front and me in back. Mustafa looked back at me, a question in his eyes, and I shook my head. "Larbi didn't make it."

"The border," Billy Wayne said. "Tell him to take the road to Ben Gardane."

In a few minutes, Mustafa had guided the Saab out of the twisting streets of Medenine, and we were on the asphalt road leading east toward Zarzis on the coast. A few miles out of town we followed the main road, which cut south toward Oglet Nefatia.

"They could've gone to Zarzis," I said. "And gone from there by boat."

Billy Wayne bobbed his head curtly. "I'm sure. With the frontier fifty kilometers from here. Hell, they can make that in an hour on these roads."

At the rate the Saab was roaring over the road we'd

270

make it in less than that. I clutched the handgrip above the rear door to keep from being tossed around. Dust shifted down from the ceiling panel as we maneuvered over the slow rises and falls of the road. From Medenine to the border the road ran through the flat Djeffara plain, an open, featureless steppe with few oases and many dry wedds—riverbeds that were dangerous after a quick desert rainfall but dry otherwise.

Just south of Oglet Nefatia we saw the taxi ahead of us. Billy Wayne leaned out the right window, slapping the dashboard with his left hand in his impatience.

"Come on, come on," he said.

Slowly we overtook the taxi, an old Peugeot that didn't have nearly the power of the Saab. I looked over at Billy Wayne. From the side his face seemed glacial, a picture of intense concentration. There was no emotion in the eyes, not even excitement. He'd gone into himself, responding only to the darkness within—no light, no flicker of emotion, no response. He was a cold, hard block of granite.

Billy Wayne raised the UZI automatic pistol and leaned out the window, bracing himself for a shot.

The taxi's tires kicked up sand lying on the road, and Billy Wayne jerked his head in, swearing.

"Damn sand. Bites like needles."

The Saab surged for a moment and Billy Wayne leaned over to look at the gas gauge. My breath sucked out of me. The needle was in the red zone.

Billy Wayne swore. "Now or never," he said and leaned back out the window, shielding his forehead with his left hand.

I heard the percussion, ducked instinctively as if to avoid the spent cartridges that kicked away into the darkness.

At the second stream of bullets, the taxi swerved and left the road in a cloud of dust. Billy Wayne whooped and Mustafa hit the brakes, sliding to a stop with the Saab's headlights pointing into the desert to the south. A few scattered clumps of scrub brush appeared amidst the flat rocky terrain. No car in sight.

"Don't get out yet," Billy Wayne cautioned.

I leaned forward, my eyes straining, expecting to see a car surge out of the darkness toward us.

Billy Wayne finally leaned over and cut the ignition. We listened in the vast silence for sounds of the taxi. Nothing.

Billy Wayne whispered, "Tell him to cut the lights."

The darkness swallowed us up and then, moments later, as our eyes adjusted to the moonlight, slowly receded into the distance. Billy Wayne leaned over the back seat and smashed the overhead convenience light with the butt of his gun. The sound was deafening in the eerie stillness that surrounded us.

"We're getting out," he said.

I opened the back door and rolled out on to the rocky desert soil, my head near Billy Wayne's feet. Mustafa slipped around the back of the Saab and crouched near us.

"Tell him to circle around to the left. I'll go straight in and you can take the right. It's gotta be there somewhere. The motor's dead."

"Okay, let's just be careful we don't shoot at each other."

Billy Wayne ignored me. "Tell him to get moving," he said.

We split up, and in seconds I lost sight of both Mustafa and Billy Wayne. As I crawled through the desert, trying to keep the barrel of the Colt out of the sand, I wondered again about the men who'd taken Donata.

Was her kidnapping a diversion, a means of distracting us while the other two men—Spugna's intermediaries—made it away to the frontier?

272

Or were Spugna's men fleeing not us but whoever had taken Donata, fearing the same men would be back for the microprocessor?

I didn't have the answers, and for a minute I even considered again the possibility that Donata had been rescued by Spugna's people. That he didn't really want her to be killed.

I doubted that. Spugna wasn't the type to forgive—not even a relative.

No, for all I knew Donata had been taken ahead to the frontier. The Libyans might already have their hands on her. The Russians might have thought she was carrying the microprocessor. Or they planned on using her for something else. I couldn't figure it out. Were the Russians working for or against the Libyans?

And Billy Wayne. If we got our hands on the microprocessor, what was he going to do? He wouldn't help me then. The guy was a liar. The only thing he'd be worried about would be getting back to the plane at Sfax and taking off for safety. I'd be alone.

Somehow I had to make sure we didn't kill the Arabs in the taxi before we questioned them. They might know who took Donata. I only hoped when the moment came that I could restrain Billy Wayne.

I didn't have long to wait. A few minutes later, there was a clatter of machine fire to my left and a fireball burst upward. The taxi's gas tank had exploded.

I hesitated, wondering if one of us had done the shooting or if it were a trick. I didn't want to rush the car only to find the men at our backs.

Someone shouted in Arabic. Mustafa. He stood and waved.

"Billy Wayne," I screamed. "Don't shoot. It's Mustafa."

About twenty feet away he spoke. "You idiot. I can hear. You think I'm deaf."

I stood sheepishly. "Didn't know you were so close."

"Come on," he said. "Let's see what he's got."

We ran toward the car. In the light of the fire I could see Mustafa dragging a body from the front seat of the taxi. When we reached the scene, both Arabs were stretched out on the ground, each with a bullet hole in his head. I'd thought about restraining Billy Wayne but not Mustafa. Didn't think he'd be so ruthless. Damn! A dead end now.

Billy Wayne looked at the bodies, grunted, and then knelt quickly and went through their pockets. "It's not here. The suitcases," he shouted. "Quick, before they burn."

Billy Wayne rushed to the taxi and threw open the back door. The larger suitcase was already on fire. He grabbed the handle and half threw, half kicked the suitcase out of the car. I scraped sand over the case while he found the smaller bag and rushed away from the car, grimacing at the heat.

"Where's Mustafa?" he said.

I jerked up and looked around. "Don't know. Back at the Saab?"

Billy Wayne frowned, pulled his gun, and dropped into a crouch.

"I don't like this," he said.

I tried to restrain my breathing, listening for the sound of a footstep.

Billy Wayne whispered, "Get away from the fire."

I started to crawl away and he whispered, "With the case, damn it."

He grabbed the smaller bag and disappeared, slipping behind a clump of wild grass and scrub brush. I slid away in the opposite direction, pulling the suitcase behind.

Suddenly, out on the highway, I heard the Saab's engine kick into life. What in hell was Mustafa doing? He wouldn't abandon us out here, would he? Why?

274

I stood and looked toward the road. The Saab was coming toward us. I crouched, hesitating and then relieved. He was bringing the car to pick us up.

And then the UZI automatic pistol began spurting and I screamed ''No,'' and took off running toward the car. Billy Wayne, the bastard! He was shooting at Mustafa!

The car rolled slowly to a stop, and when I reached it, Billy Wayne had the driver's door open. I walked around to his side and looked down. Mustafa lay on the ground, half of his head blown away, his brain matter visible in the dim light from the burning Peugeot.

A picture of Wanda flashed into my head, and I turned away and vomited. It didn't help that Mustafa was a man I hardly knew and Wanda was a woman I loved. I'd seen too much violence. I felt sick, stretched to the limit, my mind in a frenzy. All the strength I'd regained since meeting Giacomo and Donata on Vignetti seemed to have slipped away. Regaining my identity had done nothing for me. I just couldn't take any more dying.

I shut my eyes and wished I were someone else.

24

"THIS IS IT," Billy Wayne exclaimed. "I've got it!"

I blinked to regain my night vision. I'd come around the front of the Saab and was still blinded by the headlights. I focused my eyes wearily on the object in his hand. I'd expected a small square chip the size of a quarter. This was a rectangular board loaded with what looked like small transistors and circuitry. A series of shiny, metallic chips reflected the light, each not much bigger than a good-sized piece of dandruff. The chips were connected by hair-thin gold lines, blue spaces scattered over the grid.

Billy Wayne looked at me and chortled, the microprocessor in his left hand, the UZI pistol in his right.

"Shit, I bet you don't even know what's on this," he said.

I leaned into the fender, too tired to care.

"You're a hotshot when it comes to oil but I bet you don't know shit about memory metals."

I ignored the sarcasm in his voice. "Why don't you tell me, if it'll make you happy, and then we can get out of here."

He snorted. "This board holds years of research. But that ain't what matters. What matters is it's got a breakthrough. Made by some wop scientists. Remember that bull Preston fed you?" He laughed. "About this coming from Yugoslav scientists?" He waved the board in my face. "This is Italian, man, Italian. A little red Ferrari. It's got something everybody wants."

"Fine. So you've got it."

"That's right, I've got it." He paused. "You want to know what's on this shit?"

He'd already asked me that once. "You're going to tell me, anyway, right?"

"Memory metals. Fucking U.S. guys been doing research on this for over fifty years. Now you got everybody jumping in—Belgians, Italians, British, Chinese, Japanese, Russians, you name it." He wagged the gun, its bore following a circular path that crossed my stomach and made me flinch involuntarily. With a sly look on his face he said, "All very innocuous, all very useful."

I crossed my arms and listened, noticing that he'd dragged Mustafa's body away and wiped up the blood in the front seat while I was throwing up.

"They tell me the technology has focused on titanium-nickel and copper-zinc-aluminum alloys," he said. "Shape-memory metals. When the temperature changes, the structure of the material changes. It's got something to do with what they call the crystal lattice structure of the alloys. Hey, don't laugh, the change can be lightning quick—thousands of feet per second—with the strength of a giant. A square inch of alloy moves a twenty-five-ton object."

Billy Wayne's spiel had caught my interest and I took a deep breath and asked him what the Italian breakthrough was.

"Be patient," he said, grinning. "I'll get to that. Good ol' Navy boys worked with memory metals in the sixties. In the seventies they were used in aerospace applications. You can make alloys that respond to temperature changes in a range varying from two hundred seventy-five degrees below zero to five hundred degrees above zero. Hey, you want to know some applications? They're as simple as slipping a supercooled metal sleeve around two pipe ends to bond them together when the sleeve warms, and as complex as using the metals to move robot's fingers when an electric current is switched on and off. They've done away with welding, no more screws and fasteners, fucking things replace motors and gears even—how do you think they reduced the weight in the Grumman F-14 fighter jet?—by using memory metals. They're in nuclear power plants, they reset circuit breakers when the wires cool."

Billy Wayne took a breath and rushed on. "Shit, they even have medical applications. They insert a small tube by catheter and it expands when it reaches body temperature—reinforces the walls of an artery. And don't forget solar energy. They got a process that produces electricity. On one side the metals face the sun and heat up. On the other side they have cool water, causes a type of continual motion. Whammo! Sparks."

He laughed, enjoying himself, and when he finally stopped, I said, "Billy Wayne, you sound like a salesman."

He grinned again. "I just wanted you to know before dying."

My brows furrowed. "Huh? You planning on dying?"

He raised the UZI and pointed it at my stomach. "Talking about you, man. You've served your purpose— just like Mustafa."

My mouth dropped, but I recovered in a hurry, afraid he was going to shoot that instant. "Wait, Billy, wait!" I chopped his name off, anxiety choking me, and raised my hands, palms facing him as if to ward off a blow.

My voice was hoarse. "You're joking, right?"

He shook his head, his lips parting in a smile.

"I don't understand," I said quickly. "I helped you. You were going to help me find Donata. Okay, we forget that. Just drop me off in Medenine. I won't talk. What does it matter anyway? You've recovered the microprocessor."

"The question is, who gets it from me?"

I stared at him, the barrel of the gun boring a hole through my midsection. I didn't care who got it.

"You might as well know that, too," he said casually. "I've been working for the Russians for the last three years or so. Very profitable. You know what this is worth?" He waved the board again. "A cool two million. Enough for me to retire on."

"Listen, Billy Wayne, maybe—"

I didn't have time to finish my statement. A tremendous roar filled the air and I clutched my stomach expecting to find it torn to shreds. Instead, Billy Wayne wavered and collapsed forward, his mouth open in shock.

I grabbed for him and he dropped the UZI, the board still clenched in his left hand. Another shot rang out, clanging into the Saab, and I gasped. Billy Wayne wouldn't be of any help now. He was dead.

I swept my hand around, trying at the same time to hide behind Billy Wayne's body. I couldn't remember what I'd done with the Colt—must've dropped it in the sand when I was vomiting.

I found the UZI and crawled under the car, pulling myself toward the passenger side.

The fire from the Peugeot had died down, a flicker of light occasionally visible off to my right, the smell of burnt rubber strong in the air.

I cut to the left, crawling across the ground, the rocks tearing the knees of the black cotton pants I'd been wearing ever since Spugna's men had captured me. I prayed the UZI pistol still had cartridges. What had Billy Wayne said it took? Twenty rounds? I wasn't sure when he'd slipped a fresh magazine in, but I hoped it was after he'd killed Mustafa.

Suddenly I realized there was a muted rumble coming

from the direction I was crawling. I raised my head slowly.

A motor. Whoever had fired the shot had come from the road. I was heading straight for them.

Libyans, I thought. They'd come to meet Spugna's men in the desert. Or could it be the same guys who'd taken Donata? How many were there?

I lay still and listened, afraid to continue, wondering where the bullet had come from? I tried to remember, to relive the moment, but I couldn't pinpoint the direction of the sound. The noise had been too much of a shock, too overpowering.

I looked back toward the Saab, its headlights still pointed out into the desert. If whoever shot Billy Wayne wanted the computer board, he'd have to approach the Saab, would step into the light.

And what about the car I could hear out on the highway? The driver?

Worry about the guy who'd shot Billy Wayne first, I told myself, and then the car.

I rose to my knees and was about to return to the Saab, intending to circle to my left and come up behind where Billy Wayne lay, when a voice no more than ten feet away said, "Don't move!" in Arabic. A flashlight went on, focused on my face, and without thinking I raised the barrel of the automatic pistol and squeezed the trigger.

Bullets sprayed from the gun, the quick spurt jerking my hand. Just as quickly the clatter died away, as the last cartridge was ejected from the chamber. The flashlight had shattered at the first spurt of bullets and I rolled to the right, praying the man was as blind in the darkness as I was.

The next bullet would be from his gun. I was out of ammo. I lay face down in the gritty sand, my shoulders hunched in expectation of a blow.

And then, piercing through the vibrating din in my ears, I heard a moan. And a second later, as if far away and disconnected from the scene at hand, the soft puttering of the car on the road.

I looked toward the highway. No headlights, no doors slamming, no sound of companions. The same soft puttering.

The man I'd shot was clearly wounded but not necessarily disabled. I took a deep breath and repeated the same words he'd said to me, told him not to move.

"Don't shoot," the man said, his voice full of pain.

I was afraid to stand. Didn't want him to have a good view of my silhouette against the sky. "Get up," I said. "Hands above your head."

He moaned. "I can't. My wrist is shattered."

I saw he'd sat up, a black shape slightly darker than the sky behind him, so I crouched and held my right hand out with the UZI pistol pointed at the shadow.

"You move and you're dead," I said. "Who's in the car on the road?"

"No one. I'm alone." He groaned and bent over, hiding his hands in his lap. I jumped to the side, expecting him to come up firing, took two steps toward him, and kicked for his head. My foot caught him in the shoulder and he screamed and rolled over on his back, his words a jumble of curses and cries for mercy.

I couldn't stand to hear him scream. If he was lying and he did have friends they'd know right where we were. "Shut up," I told him harshly. "I'll put a bullet through your brain if I have to."

His curses and groans dropped in volume, but he continued to thrash around on the ground.

I knelt and ran my hands over the rocky sand. Found first the shattered flashlight and then a gun. I dropped the UZI and took his pistol.

"Where's the computer board?" I said. He'd come from Billy Wayne's direction.

A groan answered me. I crouched over the fellow and grabbed his hair, shoving the barrel of his pistol into his cheek. "The board, damn it, or I blow your head off."

"I dropped it near the other car."

"On your feet." I stepped back and the man struggled to his feet. "Turn around."

When he'd turned, I took a step closer and put the barrel of the gun to his neck, my arm stretched out in front of my body. I leaned in and went through the outer pockets of his suit coat. Nothing—no weapons, no board.

"Okay," I said. "Over in front of the Saab. We'll see who you are and where the board is."

We walked fifty feet or so across the desert plain, the guy moaning at each step. His voice was beginning to wear on my nerves.

We approached the car from the left rear. I stopped where Billy Wayne's body lay and told my prisoner to stand in front of the Saab's headlights. He was a dark-skinned fellow of medium height, his hair, eyebrows, and untrimmed mustache all thick and black.

"What are you going to do?" he asked.

"That depends," I said. "You tell me the truth and you might live, you lie and you're dead." I paused, wondering how badly wounded the guy was. Blood smeared the front of his shirt and coat where he'd held his wrist. His head was bent to the right as he favored his wounded arm.

"Who are you?"

He grimaced and said, "Ahmed Dhaqui."

"Nationality?"

"Libyan."

"What are you doing in Tunisia?"

He raised his head. "We're neighbors."

282

I wasn't getting anywhere, so I asked him who he worked for.

He hesitated and then said, "Libyan Intelligence," in a soft voice, adding, "Can I sit down?"

I stepped toward the left front fender and nodded. "Go ahead, but back up a few steps first."

The Libyan backed up, but I noticed when he sat down he tried to sit between the two beams rather than directly in front of one.

"So you know about the microprocessor?"

He nodded, his head down, eyes hidden.

"What about the woman?"

He raised his head, his face mixed between a grimace of pain and a frown. "What woman?"

"The woman with the guys who had the chip."

He shook his head in ignorance and I studied his face cynically. Did he have any reason to lie about that? I said, "I might trade the chip for the woman."

He lifted his hands, the left one gripping his right wrist. "I don't know about a woman."

I paused and paced back and forth, rubbing my face thoughtfully. My whiskers felt like a wire brush. The strain of the last hour was beginning to tell. I was tired and my mind refused to focus on essentials. I wanted to find the board, get rid of the Libyan, and make my way back to a town where I could sleep and figure out my next step.

"I . . . I know you," the Libyan said and I looked up to see him squinting at me.

"You married that Italian woman. I met you at a reception one time. You were there for an oil company."

I stared at the Libyan. What was his name? Ahmed Dhaqui. I shook my head, frowning. "Did we talk?"

"No, but I heard you talking to the woman—the translater for the Italian ambassador."

I nodded. "Wanda Donati."

He shook his head emphatically. "Yes. Wanda Donati. We know her."

My heart skipped a beat.

"She worked for the Italians," he said. "You save my life and I'll tell you what I can.

I squeezed my forehead with my left hand, feeling a twinge of pain. My eyes were killing me and I needed water. It wouldn't take much before I collapsed in exhaustion. I felt limp.

Wanda. The guy knew something about Wanda. My head was in turmoil. I felt suddenly nauseous.

I swallowed and bent to one knee, my left hand splayed out on the ground.

The board—the microprocessor! There it was, lying in gravel near the left front tire. I slid forward and picked it up, shaking sand from the surface.

I heard a noise and looked up quickly, the gun in my right hand rising toward Ahmed Dhaqui. But he'd fallen forward in a dead faint.

I stood, walked back to the driver's door, and laid the board on the front seat. I rifled through Billy Wayne's pockets, finding his wallet—still thick with foreign currencies—and his passport. I slid behind the wheel of the Saab and tried to start the engine. The lights dimmed, the motor turned over, coughed, and died.

I looked at the gas gauge. The needle rested on empty. The Peugeot was a burned-out wreck, the Saab out of gas. I looked back toward the road and listened for the motor I'd heard earlier. Too far away now. For a moment, I worried about someone passing and stealing the vehicle. It was my only chance to get out of the desert.

As I started to slide out of the Saab, my leg brushed against an object. Mustafa's *djerba,* its skin damp to the touch. Water! I took a deep breath and began drinking, the warm liquid pouring down my throat like rain after a drought.

When I'd had my fill I squirted water on the Libyan's face. He was breathing erratically, moaned as he started coming back to consciousness. I lifted him into a sitting position and had him drink some of the water.

"We have to get to the road on foot," I said. "You can tell me what you know about Wanda once we're there. If I'm satisfied, I'll drop you off at a village. At Oglet Nefatia."

I pocketed the Libyan's gun and then remembered the bag in the trunk. I wanted a weapon with extra cartridges.

"Just a minute," I said. "I'll be right back."

I took the keys from the ignition and opened the trunk. The bag, zipped shut but looking empty, lay in the left corner. The trunk light had lost its power as the battery drained down. I took the bag to the front and unzipped it. There was one gun left. I pulled it out and held it up to the light. A Ruger Mark II .22 caliber auto pistol with a plastic grip and a long barrel that tapered down toward the bore. What had Billy Wayne done with the shotgun— or had he lied about that, too?

I felt around in the bag and found three magazines bound together by rubber bands. Looked like a ten-round magazine. All together, with the magazine in the gun, I had forty rounds. Not a lot of knockdown power with a .22 caliber pistol, but it'd be easier to aim than the Colt I'd been carrying and I knew a few well-placed shots could stop anyone. I didn't know what I'd run across on the road back to Medenine.

It took me fifteen minutes to shepherd the Libyan out to the highway where he'd left his car. The first thing I did after he was seated in the passenger seat in front was check the gas gauge. The tank was just under half full.

"What's this hold?" I asked.

Ahmed's head lolled on his shoulders. He needed medical attention, was losing too much blood. He opened his eyes weakly. "I don't know," he said. "I came from Tripoli through Rass Adjir on it."

Tripoli. That was at least 140 miles away. If the gauge was accurate, he'd made good mileage. I doubted the tank held much more than eight or so gallons. If he'd used five, that meant he'd got about twenty-eight miles per gallon. With three left, I had approximately an eighty-mile range. Enough to reach Medenine.

I started the car—a blocky two-door vehicle that looked like a Fiat but was of undeterminable origin—and found the headlights on the turn-signal arm. For the first time I realized my hands were shaking with the aftereffects of adrenaline shock.

I took a deep breath to compose myself. Three things to do, I told myself. Find out what Ahmed Dhaqui knew about Wanda, take him to a village with a doctor, and get the hell away. I didn't want to be around him or anyone else when the police found the cars in the desert.

I looked at Ahmed. His face was pale, his eyes shut. "You'd better talk fast," I told him. "Your life depends on it."

He opened his eyes a moment and then shut them. "Wanda Donati," he began, his voice drowsy. Every few seconds he took a shallow breath and in a raspy voice told me what he knew. Which was something, but not enough. Still, I listened intently, my concentration divided between his Arabic and the road. We talked for what must have seemed a long time to him, but for me was a fleeting moment—a moment, however, that replayed itself over and over again in my mind as we rode along in silence toward the village of Oglet Nefatia.

The sky was beginning to lighten as we approached the first signs of habitation—scattered date palms outlined against the horizon. The village was situated at a crossroads, around a small oasis with a dirt track leading

286

north toward the coast at Sidi Chemmakh and south toward Tatahouine in the Ksour Mountains.

I left the paved highway and drove down a narrow side road, looking for a clinic. We passed a turban-swathed man leading two camels with full packs. As we moved by, the camels made a weird screeching noise and the driver swatted the lead beast across the nose with a stick. No one else was in sight.

I turned a corner and came upon a bus stop near an open-air market just beginning to come to life.

Ahmed Dhaqui said, "Here."

"No," I said. "There's no one to help you."

He sat up in the seat and stiffened. "Here. Let me out. I did what you asked." His voice was panicking.

"It's okay," I said. "I don't plan on killing you, but letting you off here is about the same thing."

He shook his head. "I can get help. I can't go any farther. You're going to Medenine, right? Too far from the border. It's dangerous for me. Here in the village I'm okay."

I stopped the car and was about to say I still didn't like it, when he reached across his body with his left hand and lifted the door handle. He swung his legs out and I stared at his back feeling helpless. And then we both said, "Thank you," at the same time. It was an awkward moment. I guess he was thanking me for saving his life and I was thanking him for what he'd told me about Wanda. All in all, I had to admit, it was a fair trade.

25

It was dangerous to return to the Hotel des Palmiers, but I had to start where I'd lost Donata. If anyone asked me about Larbi I would have to lie. He was a driver hired by the red-haired American; they'd picked me up in Sfax, given me a ride south. I didn't know who they were or where they'd gone.

But no one asked a question. There was a new clerk at the registration desk in the hotel—the day man. And no evidence of either the national police force—the *Sûreté Nationale*—or the rural gendarmerie provided by the *Garde Nationale*. I booked a room using Billy Wayne's name and paid for one day in cash, hoping to alleviate any concerns on the clerk's part. I figured I looked a mess.

After he handed me my room key, I pulled out a few large *dinar* notes and said, "Can you send someone to see about a razor and shaving cream?" I knew they'd have a boy to carry out errands for the tourists who didn't want to find the market on their own.

The clerk took the bills and said they'd take care of it immediately.

I took a shower, washed out my clothes, and hung them to dry over a chair on the balcony. It seemed I'd just fallen asleep when someone knocked. I struggled awake and took the toiletries at the door. The boy tried to give me several coins and small bills in change, but I waved him off. He thanked me, his serious face not changing expression, and then rushed off before I could change my mind. I figured I must have tipped him more than the supplies cost.

I fell back on the bed, slept for what seemed forever, and woke wondering where I was. Then the events of the preceding twenty-four hours swarmed back—all those dead people. And Billy Wayne? I shook my head, dumbfounded. Better him dead than me. The guy said he was working for the Russians. Would've killed me, too, if it wasn't for the Libyan Ahmed Dhaqui—an intelligence agent who knew Wanda. Everything was coming full circle.

I got up and shaved—a painful process given the length of my whiskers. When I finished I took stock in the chipped mirror with its dull-brass frame. My eyes were developing some good-sized pouches beneath them. And I could use a haircut. And new clothes. But other than that I didn't seem the worse for wear. Just felt it.

Near the bed was a small stand with a Koran in Arabic. I took one of the razor blades from the shaving supplies and cut out a rectangle from the middle of the book just large enough to hold the computer board. I'd been sleeping on it, but didn't want to leave it under the pillow when I was up and about. I tore the excised pages into strips and burned them in an ashtray.

Desecrating the sacred scriptures. Most of the Tunisians were Sunni Moslems, and the Koran was the basis of all Moslem law, studied by every child and a regulator of all relationships and actions—personal, social, and political. One of its strictures was that the book itself never be carried lower than the waist nor should any other book ever be placed upon it. But I guess they hadn't thought ahead to computer boards with microprocessors, and there was nothing in it about cutting out a hiding place.

For a moment I recalled a hotel I'd stayed at in Tripoli where next to the Koran they provided a copy of Moammar Gadhafi's *Green Book*. I'd always thought it was funny how a man like that could write that the sports of boxing and wrestling were evidence that humankind had not lost all vestiges of savage behavior, and then add that both sports will inevitably end as we ascend the ladder of civilization. How the mind could distinguish between violent sports—a scourge to be eradicated—and holy war—where what could only be called murder was sanctioned—was beyond me.

My stomach was growling so I gave up the metaphysical for the pragmatic and went down to the ground floor and into the restaurant.

While I waited for my food I tried to figure out what day of the week and month this was. I was getting tired of just drifting through time. I didn't feel like asking at the desk and making a fool of myself. Finally, according to my rough calculations, I figured it had to be a Monday, the first of September. I don't know that I felt much better, but I had to marvel how little time had passed since my trip from the harbor of Milazzo in Rocco's launch. It seemed a lifetime.

While I ate, I thought about my plan of action. I'd parked Ahmed Dhaqui's car near the hotel, but it was probably too dangerous to use it. And where would I go? Back to Sfax to seek help from PetroCanada? The company couldn't do much more than put me in touch with the Canadian SIS agent in Tunis, and I didn't think the SIS would want to get involved. And if they did, I wouldn't want them to have the microprocessor. I felt it was all I had left to tie me to the men who had Donata.

There was an embassy in Tunis: I could get a replacement for my passport there—I was tired of traveling as a fugitive—but going to Tunis would only take me away from Donata. Not that I could assume she was still in the area. For all I knew, she could be back in Malta—or somewhere in Libya by now.

290

Only Ahmed Dhaqui had claimed the Libyans weren't responsible for her abduction. He didn't even know who she was. So who did that leave? The Russians. But were they working through Spugna? Or by themselves?

I was lost in these thoughts when I realized a person was standing at my table. I looked up, surprised to see a woman in a skirt and blouse, with a *sifsari*—a white wraparound shawl—covering her face and upper body. The attire was becoming more common among Tunisian women, especially in the large commercial centers—western clothes and a native cloak—but I was surprised just the same. Most of the women in places as small as Medenine wore the traditional *ha'ik* or a *mellia* in combination with a *futa*. The veil covered all but her eyes, which were not dark but amber. I stared at her, aware she was breaking what amounted to a taboo.

"So you and your buddy had to go and fuck things up," she said.

I was taken aback—by her abruptness, the words themselves, and the language. She spoke in English. The broad vowels of an American.

I cleared my throat as she sat down opposite, and said huskily, "What are you talking about?"

"You're damn fucking lucky you're not dead. You should be, you know. We should have taken you out. You just cost us one hell of a lot of work and effort. Meddlesome pricks."

I flushed and laid down my fork and knife. If there's anything I dislike, it's a woman I don't know calling me dirty names. Not that I wasn't aware, despite my years overseas, that coarseness was now endemic to both sexes.

I was about to reach over and rip her veil away—an insult to an Arab woman, although this was no Arab— when she said coldly, "I wouldn't do that if I were you."

For the first time I noticed her left hand was in a leather bag lying open on her lap.

"It's only a .22 automatic," she said, "but I don't think it'd help your digestion if I pulled the trigger. Unless you want to start pissing through your belly. Make a nice hole there if I shoot."

A hole in the belly—I was thinking lower down. I said, "Oh, a .22 automatic. We must be soulmates, I'm using the same today."

I shoved my plate toward her. "Like to share some pita bread and *harissa?*" The *harissa* was a hot sauce of red peppers, garlic, and salt. I figured the sauce might clean out her mouth.

She didn't waver, her eyes boring into me.

I said, "Well, if you don't want to eat, why don't you take a message back to your boss. You can tell Spugna Derek Stone's coming to get him. Oh, and you might add that Derek was that guy he had his hands on for a few days. He always wanted to know who I was."

"Don't fuck around with me," she said. "I don't have time for this shit. I've done more to neutralize Spugna in the last two months than you'll do in your entire life. I just want to let you know what you've done."

"Yes, I'm a little dumb. I don't usually know what I'm doing," I said sarcastically.

Her eyes flashed and the veil dropped, revealing high, sharp cheekbones, a thin-lipped mouth, and a chin chiseled out of rock. "You think you're so fucking smart—"

"I said dumb, not smart."

She hit the table with her clenched right fist. "God, I don't know what keeps me from putting a hole through your gut."

"Good manners, I suppose," I said.

She was shaking in anger, her amber eyes brittle as dried pitch. "So you think you saved the free world from Russia, I suppose?"

''No, nothing so grandiose—just from the Libyans. But then I'm dumb enough that I can imagine a few terrorist applications of the technology in that microprocessor. Something military. I doubt the Italian breakthrough was a commercial application.''

She raised her eyes to the ceiling and back. ''Spare me.'' She shook her head as if she'd come to the end of her patience. ''You ever hear of dissimulation, disinformation?''

''Yeah, they come in the dictionary after deception.''

''It's amateurs like you who give the intelligence business a bad name. This so-called microprocessor you kept the Russians from getting happened to be something we planted. There's nothing on it we don't want them to have. Think about that, why don't you?''

I stared at her, a feeling of cold horror creeping over my shoulders. ''This . . . this whole thing was all a deception?''

She saw the look in my eye, narrowed hers, and nodded slowly. ''That's right.''

And then I was angry. ''Do you realize how many lives this stupid game has cost?'' My voice choked. I could've cried just thinking about the pain it had cost me. And the poeple I'd involved. I dropped my head into my left hand, rubbing my forehead, stunned at the enormity—at the waste.

''Billy Wayne,'' I said, ''I don't understand. Was he working with you?''

She snorted. ''Billy Wayne was set up—only you screwed that up, too. Not that having him dead hurts. But we could have passed more shit through him.''

''Did he know? . . .''

She shook her head. ''Of course not. If he knew we'd uncovered him, he'd have split long ago. The Russians would've found out before he did. We can only fool them so long.''

I rubbed the bridge of my nose and then my closed eyes. The pain had returned. I found it hard to think rationally, my emotions were so unsettled. "Jeffrey Blike," I said. "Your people killed him?"

She laughed. "Jeffrey Blike's not dead. He's working for us, always was. He hated his father as much as Diane Walker hated her ex-husband. She just chose the wrong side."

"Who sunk the *Kirke?*"

Her lips twitched. "Jeffrey. But not before we planted the false processor. We had to make Spugna work to get the thing. Hand it to him on a platter and he might start asking questions." She paused and caught my eye, her voice calmer but not friendly. "So you see. You step in and save us from ourselves. Cost us the time we needed to develop the work in secrecy. The false information on the fake board would've kept the Russians busy for a while. You can sleep on that when you're out to get Spugna for your own petty reasons."

I felt the hatred radiating from my eyes and she must have, too. She faltered for the first time and looked away. "I have to go," she said. She looked back at me, her eyes hard again. "Thanks a bunch."

"Wait!" I leaned across the table and grabbed her bag. "You haven't asked me about the chip?"

She frowned, pulling the bag out of my grasp. "What about it?"

"I have it."

Her eyes widened. "You have the board?"

"That's what I said. What'd you think happened to it?"

She took a deep breath. "We thought it burned up in the Peugeot."

I shook my head. "You wanted the Russians to have it?"

"That's what I've been saying the last five minutes—"

"Okay, they can have it."

She chewed on her lower lip, thinking, and then nodded. "The Russians have the girl—Spugna's niece."

"*They* have Donata?" I was right!

She nodded. "They thought they could bargain with Spugna's men. Her life for the chip. The Russians don't want the Libyans to get the board. We were depending on Billy Wayne to get it for his KGB contacts before Spugna's couriers could pass it on to the Libyans. But this might work." Her voice fell as if she were talking to herself. "You just walk in and hand it to them, it's as bad as handing it to Spugna, but a trade for the girl . . ." Her voice came back strong and she nodded again. "Yes, it just might work."

I had trouble keeping a semblance of calmness. Every nerve in my body was vibrating. "You know where Donata is, then. Can you set up the trade?"

She thought about that. "I think we're better off if you do it on your own. They have to be convinced you're not working for us."

I stared at the table, concentrating, a frown on my face. "How do I approach them? I mean, how do I even know who they are, let alone where they are?"

"Well, you can't say we told you."

"Who's *we*, anyway?"

"We is me."

"Brilliant. Three words and you rhymed two of them."

She didn't appreciate my sarcasm. She tossed me a dirty look and said, "Billy Wayne."

"Billy Wayne what?"

"You could say he told you—that just before dying he said where the Russians were."

"Hmm." I pursed my cheeks. "They'll know instantly if I'm lying. Maybe Billy Wayne didn't know where they were."

"He had to have some contact—a case officer in the

field. The same people. I doubt there're that many Russians in the area.''

I pondered that. ''He was on the phone several times.''

She absorbed that without saying anything, and I had time to worry about the calls. He'd left the hotel restaurant just before Donata was snatched. Maybe set the whole thing up. And Billy Wayne had made all those calls *after* he knew my real name. If the Russians knew who I was—and how much Spugna wanted me—I might run into trouble if I attempted a trade for Donata. The Russians could wind up with Donata, the microprocessor, and me.

It didn't take me long to make up my mind what to do. Donata was worth the risk. She'd risked her life for me. I said, ''Okay, tell me where they are before it's too late. If they think the board's been destroyed, they'll have no use for Spugna's niece.''

Her eyes focused on mine. ''You can leave immediately. They're near the frontier with Libya. In Ben Gardane. Holed up in the Hotel El Marsa.''

''Okay.'' I didn't want someone jumping me from behind, so I said, ''What about the other two Arabs— the guys who left in the Citroen? Did they go back to the military truck?''

''Don't worry about them. The truck's gone back to Tunis. I'll see that the men in the Citroen are picked up and kept out of circulation. They're waiting here in Medenine.''

I let my breath out slowly, feeling the tension in my body. That meant they were probably right here in the Hotel des Palmiers. But I doubted either of them had ever seen me. ''Do you think the Russians have anyone watching us?''

''They better not,'' she said.

I stared at her a moment and then said, ''I'm not taking a chance on who's around. I don't want anyone thinking I'm working for you. Working against you would be more like it. Maybe this will help.''

I stood up as she hesitated, clutching the bag, a puzzled look on her face. I leaned over the table as she lifted her head expectantly, and for the first time in my life, I slapped a woman across the face. The sound echoed through the restaurant, followed by a moment of silence in which I said loudly, ''No way. I'm going back to Tunis.'' And then I walked out of the restaurant to a murmur of shocked voices.

I was a heel, but it sure felt good.

26

I STOPPED AT the registration desk and asked about car rentals, having seen a small sign there earlier reading *AutoTunis*. There was no way I was going to use Ahmed Dhaqui's car to head back toward the frontier with Libya. Too risky.

The clerk told me they had one compact available, and I said that'd be fine. I'd need it for two days and could they see that the tank was full. I pulled out my wallet and started to pay when the clerk said that wasn't necessary. He pointed to one of the credit cards.

"We take an imprint, okay?" he said. "When you bring the car back, you pay."

"Okay." I handed him the MasterCharge card from the Pacific First Federal Savings and Loan Association. In Portland. Poor Billy Wayne had been an Oregonian.

"And we need an International Driving Permit."

"International? I'm from the States. I have a license from Oregon. Will that do?"

I'd gone through Billy Wayne's wallet in the room, marveling at how much money he was carrying—just under a thousand dollars in various currencies—and had found two credit cards, a driver's license, and other assorted cards, including a tattered Selective Service System Registration Certificate, a folded Discharge Certificate showing Billy Wayne Henderson had been honorably discharged from the United States Air Force on May 11, 1974, a Social Security card, and two doctor's cards—one a psychotherapist connected to the University of Oregon at Eugene and the other a doctor of chiropractic in Portland. Billy Wayne's life was carried in his pocket, but I'd noticed with interest there was nothing to show he worked for customs.

For a moment the thought flashed through my mind that I was having one hell of a time with my identity. Going through a lot of people. Oh, well, even Spugna had thought I was Billy Wayne Henderson at first. Might as well play another man's part. Without a passport or other papers, Derek Stone didn't exist.

The clerk accepted the Oregon driver's license, filled out a one-page form in French and Arabic, and I signed it.

I walked up the stairs toward my room on the third floor, filled with excitement and anxiety. For the first time I felt I was in control of what I was doing. I was acting alone and was a step closer to Donata—and to Carlo Spugna. Until I cleared that slate nothing else I accomplished had much significance.

The anxiety came from what faced me at the moment—confronting the Russians, convincing them to give Donata up to get the computer board. I tried to visualize that in my mind, tried to imagine the encounter. But I had difficulty in picturing the scene, in figuring out how best to effect the transfer.

Maybe on the drive to Ben Gardane I could figure something out. Some way of protecting myself and guaranteeing her exchange for the board. Perhaps somewhere in the desert—an oasis. A place I'd pick and get to first. I'd ask them to come, only one man and the woman.

I felt the long barrel of the Ruger .22 as I took each step, and wished I had the shotgun Billy Wayne had mentioned. What was it again? The Mossberg Persuader. I was going to have to do some persuading and I didn't have much protection to back it up.

I was walking down the hallway on the third floor with

my key in hand when I realized something was amiss. A blaze of light cascaded into the hall from a room facing west—my room. The cleaning woman or . . .

I dropped the key, pulled the Ruger from under my shirt, and slipped down the hall, trying to make as little noise as possible. From ten feet away I could see the doorjamb was shattered and the casing trim had given way near the hinges. Plaster chips and dust covered the dark tile floor.

My heart was pounding, my hand shaking. I couldn't hear a sound from the room. Had they already left? No time to delay.

I slipped around the door and was greeted by devastation. The room was a mess—the mattress ripped to shreds, drawers from a small European dresser strewn about, the table overturned, my toiletries on the floor.

My heart sunk. The table . . . I picked it up and looked for the Koran. If they'd knocked it off, the book would've flown open, the microprocessor clearly visible.

I was sick. The book was gone.

Who? I thought. Who did this?

I sat on the edge of the bed, dizzy. My plans, my plans to save Donata . . . shattered.

I took a deep breath and forced myself to think. The Libyans. There was Ahmed Dhaqui. Had he sent his men after me?

Or the woman—the American woman whose name and employer I didn't know. Had she delayed me in the restaurant long enough for her compatriots to ransack the room? My God, I thought. If she were Russian! What a fool I was. She could've been Billy Wayne's contact for all I knew. I'd accepted what she'd said at face value. But she might have been just another good liar. Like Billy Wayne.

I was stricken at the thought.

God, I might have cost Donata her life!

I sat there in a daze, overwhelmed by the futility of my efforts to help. I even had a moment of doubt about Spugna—was I letting my desire for vengeance overcome my ability to think clearly? Was I getting what I deserved for wanting to get even?

My temples were throbbing and I closed my eyes and saw sparks. And then the pain came, concentrated over my left eye.

I walked into the small bathroom and vomited the meal I'd just eaten. I wasn't having any trouble staying skinny but I was getting awful tired of throwing up every time I had a headache. I couldn't believe how sick I felt. Part of my mind was screaming for the gun, screaming to die—just as it had done every time before when these crushing head pains hit me.

But before I'd never had a weapon, now I was armed. One bullet through the head and that'd stop the pain. Only the other half of my brain kept repeating, no, no, no. I had unfinished business to handle. If there was anything I had to do now it was to face Spugna. Face that bastard and . . .

And what? I couldn't think of a punishment harsh enough. Death itself was too kind.

After a while I realized I had to *do* something. I couldn't let Donata go without some attempt to help.

The woman in the restaurant had given me a location, the name of the hotel where the Russians were staying. The Hotel El Marsa in Ben Gardane. It was either the truth or a lie. Either way I had to check it out. It was my only lead.

On the drive south toward Ben Gardane, at the wheel of a no-frills Yugo—a new-car import from Yugoslavia— I tried to think of my options.

There was a good chance the Russians still thought the microprocessor was in the hands of Spugna's couriers.

If the American woman in the restaurant was right, someone—she hadn't said who but I assumed the Americans—was trying to trick the Russians into taking a fake microprocessor. Maybe I could do something similar. I'd seen the board, I could describe it. Only a fool would meet the Russians with the board in his pocket. They'd believe me if I said a friend was holding it.

I still had a chance.

And if they knew I didn't have the board? If they already had it?

A chill went up my back and I told myself that that didn't mean Donata was dead. I said it twice but I still had a hard time believing it.

I drove through the heat of mid- and late afternoon, passing sights I'd missed on the first trip at night—the wells at the side of the road in the bed of the Wedd bou Ahmed, the gravelly fields stretching endlessly before me to the east, Oglet Nefatia again, the wells at Bir el Ouahmia and then bare sandy plains and just beyond them, the first plantations as the road approached Ben Gardane. Somewhere along the route I'd passed without seeing them the remains of the burnt-out Peugeot and the Saab I'd abandoned.

The town of Ben Gardane, the last settlement before the frontier, was situated in a large oasis surrounded by irrigated fields. Numerous tracks radiated from the village, including one that followed the boundary between Tunisia and Libya, passing through Khoui es-Saidane, Taguelmit, El Hamada, Borj Stil, Dehibat, and points farther south. To the north, only five miles away, at the head of Bahiret el Biban—a large but shallow lagoon—lay the fishing harbor of el Marsa, with access to the Mediterranean through the lagoon's narrow opening.

Under the *chehili* or *scirocco*, Ben Gardane has recorded temperatures as high as 127 degrees Farenheit. When I reached the outskirts of the village, with its endless rows of date palms, the road shimmered with heat. Sweat evaporated instantly in the dry air that had to be over a 100 degrees at the moment. The sun behind me was low on the horizon and cast a harsh glare in the rearview mirror. I turned left down the first tarred side road I came across and then cut east toward the center of the village, following smaller dirt roads marked by camel tracks.

It took me a half hour to find the Hotel El Marsa, a small block building only one story high. I drove by the hotel and parked up the street near a small square with a public well in the center surrounded by a low stone wall. I tossed a few coins at a group of beggars who I could see were going to pester me otherwise and then made my way back to the hotel's entrance.

The clerk, who turned out also to be the owner, was a wiry old man with a well-trimmed gray beard. He wore a suit that looked thirty years old, spoke Arabic with a French accent, and called himself Monsieur LeFeve.

When I asked if he had any foreigners registered at the moment, he waved his arms and said they were all foreigners.

"Europeans?" I asked.

He shrugged, said, "Many nationalities," and then brightened. "But no Americans." I wondered if he thought I was from the States. I had Billy Wayne's ID, but I was Canadian. Given the machinations that were going on around me, I was glad of that. I had the feeling the CIA wasn't much different from the KGB.

"I'm looking for two men and a woman," I explained. "The men were dressed in western suits, the woman wore a white *ha'ik*. They would have arrived yesterday. I was told they were staying here."

The old man closed his eyes as if in thought, opened them, looked at me doubtfully, and closed his eyes again.

I got the message, took out my wallet, and pulled out a note for twenty *dinars*.

The old man took the note, smiled indulgently, and said, ah yes, he recalled the group.

"Could you tell me what room they're in?"

Monsieur LeFeve frowned and went into his routine again. I made a mental note to come to the point quicker when I wanted information and dug into my wallet again. I handed him a ten-*dinar* note and he squinted, so I dropped a second one on top.

Monsieur LeFeve leaned over the counter separating us and whispered, "Room ten."

"Thanks, you've very kind," I said dryly.

Impervious to sarcasm, he beamed and ducked his head in embarrassed pleasure. "This way, sir." He took my arm and began leading me up a corridor to my left."

I raised a hand, was about to stop him, and thought, what the hell. Going straight to their room was about as good as trying to catch them in public. It didn't look like I could expect much help from the locals, anyway. Not unless my wallet were open on the table first.

He showed me the door, bowed, and then left. I waited until he'd disappeared, took a deep breath, and knocked.

I heard a chair scrape. Hurried movement.

Nervous myself, I stepped away from the door and drew the Ruger .22, holding it behind my back.

"Who is it?" someone asked in fractured Arabic.

"Uh . . ." I grimaced. I'd suddenly realized I didn't feel like saying I was Billy Wayne. I'd done that with Spugna and it had brought me nothing but bad luck. "An American," I said, figuring that covered Canada as well.

The door opened a crack and two beady eyes stared up at me. I looked down and forced a smile.

"What do you want?"

I had trouble understanding the fellow's attempt at Arabic. "Do you speak English?" I asked hopefully.

The head wagged and I heard, "Just moment, friend."

The door closed and I shrugged. Three words, that was a start. Was he calling me a friend or what?

A few seconds later a different set of eyes appeared. They were just as black and just as beady but they were at my eye level. So this was the first man's friend. Not me.

I nodded and tried to smile, my hands still behind my back. I switched the gun to my left hand, thinking the guy might offer to shake hands.

"You American?" he said finally.

"Yes, I have a message from Billy Wayne." The words sprang to my mouth as if unassisted by mental processes, but I realized immediatley that it was as good as anything. I didn't have the board. Let them think Billy Wayne had it.

To my surprise the door swung shut.

I frowned and stepped to the right, afraid they might shoot through the door. But in a minute the door opened and the taller man stepped out, dressed in tan slacks and a patterned shirt. He had a high forehead, his thinning brown hair combed backward.

When I didn't see a gun in his hand, I pretended I was tucking my shirt in and, with my hands still behind my back, slipped the .22 under the waistband of my trousers.

He shut the door behind him and said in English, "So, you have a message from a dead man?"

I looked at him in disbelief and swallowed hard. They already knew about last night's encounter. Now I'd have to pretend I had the board hidden somewhere.

"I, ah, I was with him just before he died," I stammered.

He stared at me, his face expressionless, waiting.

Were we going to talk right there in the corridor? I wondered. I looked around. "Would you like to have dinner and talk?"

He shook his head. "No dinner."

I rubbed my chin. I didn't think I was going to like this guy.

He said, "What's the message?"

At least they knew Billy Wayne, I thought. I said, "Billy Wayne claimed you had a woman with you—Donata Pellico. The niece of Carlo Spugna."

The Russian let my words hang in the air for a while and then cleared his throat. "So what?"

"So before Billy Wayne died he gave me a computer board—he called it a microprocessor. I'm here to trade the thing for the woman."

"Where's the apparatus?"

I studied his face and then suddenly grinned. "You don't think I'd walk in here with it in my pocket, do you? It's in a safe place."

He studied my face carefully and then reached into his shirt pocket and pulled out a pack of Tunisian cigarettes. I shook my head when he offered me one and waited while he lit his own. The cigarette was unfiltered and foul smelling. I crinkled my nose and took a half-step back.

He exhaled, took a deep drag, and began speaking, smoke drifting from his mouth as he talked. "You bring it here. Then we'll talk."

I shook my head. "No way. That's not safe enough for me."

"What's there to be safe about? We don't want the woman. She obviously means more to you than to us. We want the microprocessor."

My mind was working furiously. Take this guy to the car, I thought. It's getting dark. Kill him and come back.

No. Too dangerous, and I didn't feel like killing someone I didn't even know.

Take him outside, pull the gun, and force him to call his friend on the telephone. Have him bring Donata to the square.

306

But that didn't sound so good, either. They'd speak in Russian and I wouldn't understand a word.

He shrugged. "What do you expect us to do?"

"I want to see Donata, make sure you really have her, that she's alive."

He grunted, opened his mouth to say something, and then shut it.

I stared at him. "You don't have her, do you?"

A slow smile creased his face. "You won't tell us where the microprocessor is, why should I tell you where she is?" He paused and then shook his head forcefully. "She's alive and we have her."

I almost laughed. If they did have her, she'd be in the room.

"Let's go in the room and talk," I said.

He grinned again. "I'll tell you what—"

Suddenly I heard sounds from inside the room—a scuffle, a muted cry, and then silence. I reached behind me and found the Ruger.

"Go ahead," I said. "I'm listening." But before he could say another word I whipped my hand around. He started to duck but wasn't quick enough, and I caught him in the temple with the gun. He went out instantly. I grabbed for him with both hands, easing him to the floor, the gun still clenched in my right hand.

I heard the cries again, followed by sounds of furniture being slammed around. I stepped back, kicked the door as hard as I could, and stumbled off balance into the room.

The smaller Russian was on the floor, entangled in the folds of cloth around Donata. She was biting him on the hand and he was trying to gag her and look back at the same time to see what was happening.

I pointed the gun at his head, shouted, "Get off her," and tightened my finger on the trigger.

The effect was not what I'd desired. The Russian,

short but powerfully built, let out a roar, slugged Donata in the side of the face, and rolled around to face me.

That did it, I pulled the trigger. The gun popped once and the Russian stood up, his feet entangled in the cloth. Donata was stretched out, motionless.

"You fucking bastard!" I screamed and pulled the trigger again. The Russian winced, kicked his feet free, and lunged forward. I straightened my arm, pointed the gun at his face, and shot him at a distance of one foot.

He dropped on the spot.

I looked back into the corridor where the taller fellow was beginning to moan. I didn't want to shoot him in cold blood and didn't know if I could hit him again either.

I bent over Donata and touched her face. "Donata, it's me, Der—Gino. Gene Harrell," I said, not wanting to spring a new name on her.

She didn't respond.

I turned, saw that the Russian outside the door was starting to move, and grabbed one of the sheets, which had been pulled from the bed in the struggle between Donata and the fellow I'd just shot.

I tore a long strip from the edge and went out into the corridor. The taller Russian was sitting up groggily. I lifted my right foot, placed it square in the middle of his back, and drove him down onto the stone floor, ramming his face into the pavement. Rought treatment but better than a bullet through the head.

After I'd tied his hands behind his back, I dragged him into the room and tried to shut the door I'd kicked in. It wouldn't latch but I jammed it into the frame.

The Russian stirred and came to before Donata did. I double-checked the bonds on his wrists and then tore another strip of cloth as a gag, which I tied at the back of his head.

I made sure Donata was comfortable on the bed, her breathing clear, and then poured water over her temples.

It took her a good fifteen minutes before she regained consciousness. She was in a good deal of pain and I understood that perfectly. I thought of going back to the front desk to ask for aspirin, but I was afraid to leave her in the room with the one Russian. I was so nervous I found myself checking the knots I'd tied every five minutes.

When Donata opened her eyes, I smiled at her and felt her hand squeeze mine before it rose to touch her forehead.

"He hit you hard," I said. "Are you dizzy?"

She nodded, just perceptibly, and shut her eyes. I tore yet another strip from the sheet I'd been using, dipped it in water, and laid it on her forehead. "Sorry there's no ice," I said quietly.

When I looked at her lying there with her eyes shut in pain, anger coursed through my body. She'd been struck in the temple, could've been killed. Probably had a concussion as it was. I didn't want to move her but was afraid to stay in the room. No telling who might show up.

I refreshed the cloth on Donata's head every five minutes and let her rest for close to a half hour. Finally, I asked her if she thought she could get to her feet.

"We've got to get away from here," I said. "Find a safe place to rest."

She opened her eyes and looked at me with an expression so full of gratitude that my breath caught in my throat. I leaned over and kissed her on the forehead.

She tried to smile. "We're even," she said.

I understood—she'd rescued me from Spugna—and returned her smile. And then I said, "Not until I get you out of here."

Donata sat up slowly and saw the Russian. Her face hardened. "They were going to kill me."

I looked at the Russian, who stared back impassively.

I wanted to tell Donata it was her uncle who'd made this possible, shipped her off as a hostage knowing she wouldn't come back. But I think I realized she knew.

She looked at me, squinting, her hand to her temple, the deep green of her eyes, the gray halo around the green, barely visible. "I have so much to tell you," she said.

I nodded. "First, we have to get you out of here." I had a lot to tell her, too.

When we stepped out of the Hotel El Marsa, Donata having first removed the *ha'ik,* which had been wrapped around her skirt and blouse, the sun had set and the sky was dark, the brighter stars already twinkling. The moon had not yet risen.

I led her up the street and we got into the Yugo, which I saw by the light of a single street lamp had been washed by the beggars I'd given money to earlier. Four of the boys, none older than ten, stood near the car, watching to see that no one stole anything. I pulled out Billy Wayne's wallet and gave them a one-hundred-*dinar* note. The bill was over a month's salary for a Tunisian worker, roughly equivalent to a hundred American dollars. They were almost frightened to take it, stood staring at us with wide eyes and gaping mouths.

"Many thanks," I said in Arabic. "If anyone asks about two Europeans, tell them we're driving to Tripoli."

They nodded vigorous agreement and then, as we drove away down a dirt road, headlights picking out the way, shouted after us joyfully and waved until we disappeared from sight.

I don't think the joy in their hearts was any greater than mine.

310

27

WITHIN MINUTES WE were on the highway to Medenine, the far dark horizon kissed by a touch of blue, neither of us speaking.

I turned to look at Donata, her face barely visible in the lights from the instrument panel. She was leaning back against the headrest, eyes shut, hair bunched at the neck, and I remembered when it had been me in that position—the Fiat, her cool hand on my forehead and cheeks, the soothing voice.

Almost three weeks ago—but a past that seemed to belong to someone else. Another lifetime.

And for her?

She'd gone from Vignetti, where her problems now probably seemed minor—the breakup with her boyfriend, the successful attempt to free me from the Mirabella police—to San Lawrenz on the island of Gozo, where her world fell apart. *Zi'* Carlo had gone from benevolent uncle and loving father to villain—an evil man willing to kill not only his enemies but also his relatives if threatened by them. And from San Lawrenz into the hands of men she didn't know, dangerous men for whom she was a pawn. A hostage to be dispensed with when no longer needed.

I glanced over and saw she'd opened her eyes and was looking at me. I smiled. "How're you feeling?"

Her lips quivered. "Not so good."

"I was thinking you needed sleep, but I'm worried about that. I had a concussion when I was a kid once—a bicycle accident—and my mother had to wake me every few hours so I wouldn't fall into a coma. Maybe we should try to talk.''

''Can I just listen to you?'' She tried to smile.

''Sure. I'll talk a bit and then let you rest.''

''Oh, Gene! How could I forget?'' She sat up suddenly and grimaced, her hand rubbing the side of her head where she'd been hit. ''Bukov . . . Kolesnik.'' She shook her head, her voice soft. ''They were talking . . . We have to get to Malta.''

''We're going to Malta.''

She put both hands to her temples and squeezed her eyes shut. ''Wednesday morning. *Zi'* Carlo will be making the exchange then.''

I frowned. The road dipped down, crossing a dry riverbed, and the Yugo's lights picked out a single date palm growing in the middle of nowhere. ''Exchange? What exchange?''

''The microprocessor. Stolen from Italy.''

''You don't understand,'' I said. ''The guy I was with—you didn't meet him—Billy Wayne Henderson, he took the board from your uncle's couriers. I had it in my hands just today. It was stolen—by Libyans I think.''

She looked over at me and I could see her head slowly shaking, so I rushed on. ''But it doesn't matter, Donata. It doesn't matter. Everything we did was a waste. The board is a fake, it's all a deception, a trick to fool the Russians.''

''To fool the Russians,'' she repeated with a trace of incredulity. ''No, Gene. You have it backwards. To fool the Americans.''

''What?''

''Gene, I know the couriers were carrying a fake. Bukov and Kolesnik knew. They were here as a diversionary tactic. They want the Americans to think the CIA's successfully deceived the Russians.''

I rubbed my forehead, bewildered. "Wait. Let me get this straight. The Americans are trying to pass a fake to the Russians, right?"

She nodded, and I rushed on. "Are you saying the Russians know this? That they're just pretending to be duped. Why? It doesn't make sense."

"They want the Americans to give up, to get out of the area. *Zi'* Carlo has the real processor. He'll pass it over to the Russians once the Americans are out of the way. The Americans will never know the Russians have it."

I stared at her skeptically. "I'm not so sure about any of this. The American woman I talked to said the computer board's a fake. She didn't seem worried about a genuine one in Spugna's hands."

"Gene, he has it. I know. I heard the Russians talking."

"You know Russian?"

"No, but the tall one—Kolesnik—he spoke English to *Zi'* Carlo."

"The one who's alive?"

She nodded.

I felt a sense of despair. "He'll call your uncle, tell him what happened. That we're alive and coming after him."

"Maybe. But *Zi'* Carlo isn't afraid of us. The exchange will still take place. I'm sure of it. *Zi'* Carlo and the Russians think they've fooled the Americans—"

"They have fooled them."

"So there's no danger now. The Americans are satisfied. They think they've tricked the Russians. *Zi'* Carlo will hand over the real microprocessor the day after tomorrow."

"I still don't understand that," I exclaimed. "The CIA—" I caught myself and said, "The woman I talked to, anyway, must have it. Jeffrey Blike turned the original over to *them,* and they substituted a fake board.''

"Gene, *Zi'* Carlo was talking to Jeffrey Blike when you were in the villa. They were planning what to do when they sent me away.''

"Sure, but Jeffrey's working *for* the CIA. He's fooling your uncle. He's just pretending to go along.''

Donata laid her left hand on my arm. ''No, Gene. I don't think so. He mentioned the CIA to *Zi'* Carlo—that's all part of the plan somehow. Jeffrey's working *with Zi'* Carlo, not against him.''

"I'm confused," I said and shook my head. ''But I'm not the only one. There're too many moves and counter-moves. Too much trickery and deceit. It's a triangle—your uncle Carlo, the Russians, the Americans. I'm not sure who has the upper hand.''

"Gene, I know. It's Carlo. We have to stop him," she said. ''He's my uncle, but . . .''

Donata fell silent and a few seconds later I nodded. She was right. No matter how you looked at it, Carlo Spugna was at the eye of the storm. I thought about telling Donata my real reasons for wanting to stop her uncle but the moment didn't seem right. Instead, I said, "Donata, I have to explain something about my name. When we met I was using the name Gene Harrell.''

I looked over at her and saw she was staring at me intently. ''It's not my real name. It's a man who died when he tried to stop the microprocessor from getting to the wrong people. My real name's Derek Stone.''

I waited to see if it meant anything to her, if Spugna had ever mentioned me.

She took a deep breath. ''Derek?''

"Derek Stone. I . . . ah . . . I was married to a woman, an Italian. Wanda Donati.'' There was no response from Donata so I hurried on. ''She worked for the Italian

314

government—in Libya. She was . . . she died several months ago.''

She reached over and put her hand on my shoulder. ''I'm sorry . . . Derek.''

She'd paused before saying my name and it sounded strange even to me to hear it from her lips.

I said, ''There's something else you should know. I'm using another name now—out of necessity. I don't have my passport. I'm using papers from the guy I was with. Billy Wayne Henderson. He's dead.''

''You? . . .''

I shook my head. ''The Russian's the first guy I've ever . . . killed. Billy Wayne died in a shoot-out with a Libyan intelligence officer. I wounded the Libyan and took the microprocessor but I guess I made a mistake. He took it back. Or his men did.''

''So, stranger with no name, what shall I call you?'' she said in a deep voice, and I laughed. I could tell she was feeling better already.

''We'd better stick to Billy Wayne until we're out of this country.''

''We need to find an airport.''

I nodded. ''I think we'll have to drive all the way to Sfax.'' I paused and sighed. ''That's a long ways and I'm tired and you're not well enough to drive. I don't know. Maybe we should stop in Medenine and hire a driver. We don't have time to sleep.''

''We can catch a flight tomorrow morning. Tuesday. That would give us a day to get to the police on Malta and explain what's going on.''

''The police? I don't know. I don't have any papers. I'm in trouble with the Italian authorities. I'd just as soon leave the police out of this.''

''Gene—''

I interrupted. ''Better practice using Billy Wayne.''

She shook her head. ''I don't know who you are.''

"Well I can tell you about me on the drive, how's that? And you can tell me about you. That'll keep us awake until Medenine at least."

We lapsed into silence for a moment and then she said, "I'm worried about *Zi'* Carlo, about stopping him by ourselves."

"We won't be by ourselves." I'd been thinking hard about that. I was going to have to rely on Jake Roberts. He'd sworn he had nothing to do with the explosions on the jackup. But there was only one way to find out if he'd been telling the truth—and that was to trust him when it really mattered. I was prepared to do that, but I wasn't stupid enough not to protect myself at the same time.

I cleared my throat. "I have an old friend in Malta now. On vacation. We used to work together. He's a good man. I know he can round up some others—men who can fight. I've been in the oil business most of my life. They don't call the hired hands roughnecks and roustabouts for nothing."

I glanced at her and then back at the road. "Do you have any idea where the exchange might take place?"

"*Zi'* Carlo's warehouse, outside Luqa. It's three or so miles southwest of the airport, toward Siggiewi."

"You have good ears," I said. "That gives us a lot more time to line up help." I pounded the steering wheel. "We can do it."

Her only response was a sigh.

I let her sleep for a while, driving carefully so as not to awaken her. We passed a few vehicles, mostly commercial trucks, the only sound the wind rushing by the open windows. The moon had risen in the east behind us and shed a washed-out light over the desert plain.

I thought about what was ahead of us and suddenly realized I wasn't just chasing a stolen computer board with scientific secrets encoded on it. I wasn't just chasing the man who'd killed my wife and tortured me. I was chasing myself. Because of Wanda's savage death, I'd come undone at a certain point—I'd been cut off from the identity I'd spent over forty years building. I had to find out now who I wanted to be for the next forty years, or fourteen, or four.

I could be who I wanted to be. But what did I want?

I looked over at Donata again. She reminded me of a nocturnal jasmine, a flower, bruised at the moment, but a flower whose petals open in the dark, like a chalice, to receive the moonlight.

A jasmine. Fragrance rising in darkness to the stars. And perhaps only a late returning bee, left outside the cells, had a chance to savor the nectar.

We'd driven through Oglet Nefatia, across the Djeffara plain, and past the point where the coastal road from Zarzis joined in, plantations of date palms now to each side of us, when we ran into the roadblock.

I saw the lights ahead and slowed, at first thinking we'd come upon a wreck. A military truck blocked the road, with two cars of the *Sûreté Nationale* off to the side.

"Donata, wake up," I said urgently. "A roadblock."

She came awake slowly, groaning softly. "What is it?"

"The police. They're stopping cars."

"Oh, no."

"Remember my name, okay? Billy Wayne Henderson." We were being waved to a stop by a uniformed official. "We'll have to tell the truth as much as possible. Don't let them know—"

I stopped talking as the officer approached, thinking, she doesn't know what happened in Medenine, nothing about Larbi, nothing about Mustafa and the two Arabs killed in the desert, and hopefully the national police hadn't heard what happened in Ben Gardane with the

Russians. That thought was unsettling. Only, if Kolesnik had managed to work free from his bonds, I doubted he'd contact the Tunisian police. That thought, at least, was reassuring.

"Passports, please."

I reached for Billy Wayne's passport and then panicked. What about Donata? I hadn't even thought about her ID.

I looked over, my eyes wide, and saw with relief that she was pulling a passport from a slit pocket at the side of her skirt.

I handed both to the policeman.

"The car's papers," he said.

I pointed to the glove compartment and Donata handed me the rental form.

The officer glanced at the form and asked, "Car rented where?"

It was written right on the form but I said politely, "Medenine—the Hotel des Palmiers. We're on our way to take it back now."

"You were staying at the hotel?"

"Yes. That is, I was."

His eyes were fixed on mine. "And your companion?"

I looked over quickly at Donata and back. "No, she was visiting friends elsewhere."

"The dates?"

"Of what?"

"Of your stay in the hotel."

"Recently—the last few days."

"You've been questioned by us before?"

I hesitated, wondering whether to lie, and decided against it. "No."

The officer straightened and called to another man, who walked over, both men meeting about ten feet from the car.

They talked softly and my hands, gripping the steering

wheel, began to sweat. I shifted them nervously. The hot air visibly sucked the moisture off the wheel.

The officer who'd questioned us returned and said, "Please drive the car over there, sir." He pointed to the side of the road where the two police cars were parked.

I nodded calmly but my heart was beginning to pick up its beat. The man hadn't shown any signs of suspicion, but still . . . I squeezed the steering wheel hard to ease the tension.

I drove off the road and parked facing one of the police cars. A short, dark man, sporting a thick mustache and wearing civilian clothes, came to the window and said, "Step out, please."

I got out of the car and shut the door.

"The lady also."

Donata joined us.

"She's not feeling well," I said. "She tripped and hurt her head."

The man ignored me. "This way, please."

He took Donata's arm, led her to one of the cars, and opened the front door. Another man in civilian clothes, heavier and sleepy-eyed, was behind the wheel, looking through a thin sheaf of papers on a clipboard. He yawned, then glanced up, nodded, and turned back to the papers.

The short, mustached man turned to me and said, "The other car."

I walked over to the car, my thoughts in turmoil, opened the door on the passenger side, and took a deep breath to calm myself, exhaling slowly as I slid in.

The mustached official joined me a second later, turned on the convenience light and slid around, facing me. His sharp, black eyes belied the casualness of his manner.

"Cigarette?" he said.

I shook my head. "Don't smoke."

He didn't ask me if I minded, just lit one for himself and settled back, exhaling a cloud of smoke in my direction.

"Purpose of your visit to Tunisia?"

"Vacation."

He stared at me and like a fool I said, "And some business."

"Port of entry?"

I took a shallow breath, relieved he hadn't followed up on the business comment. "Sfax."

"Why is it not stamped in your passport?"

I swallowed with difficulty. "I arrived by private jet— a business jet. A customs official cleared me at the hangar."

"When did you arrive?"

"Night before last."

"Last night?"

"No, I wasn't counting tonight. Two nights ago."

"Where have you stayed?"

I paused. "I was on the road the first night, and last night—night before this one, I mean—I stayed at the Hotel des Palmiers." Which wasn't quite true. But I'd checked in and slept there most of the morning.

"What's your destination?"

"Sfax."

"But you arrived in Sfax."

I nodded. "Yes. We're leaving from there also."

His eyes narrowed. "Two days for business and pleasure?"

I shrugged. "I guess it's what we call a working vacation. My company has a branch office in Sfax."

"Your company?"

"PetroCanada. Oil exploration."

He reached beside him near the door and pulled out a clipboard jammed between the seat and a plastic support.

"You have a name and number where we can contact you?"

"Sure."

I heaved an inaudible sigh of relief and gave him PetroCanada's address on the old Rue Victor Hugo. The business office lay south of the main commercial district, which spread from the central basin toward the old city. The local company executives occupied a new building just beyond the power station and a large olive oil refinery, on the opposite side of town from the railroad station. I was glad I could remember both the address and phone number.

While the man wrote the information down in Arabic, I looked across at the car holding Donata. She and the man who'd questioned her were standing in front of the car, both talking animatedly.

"Oh, by the way," the Tunisian said to me, his tone unchanged, "do you know a man by the name of Larbi ben Hani?"

My heart skipped a beat. "Larbi what?"

"Larbi ben Hani."

I pursed my lips. "I don't think so. I meet a lot of people—mostly in the oil business, but I don't recall anyone by that name."

"What about Mustafa Ghelaby?"

I looked thoughtful. "No, not that I recall."

"A man of your description was seen with both of them in the restaurant of the Hotel des Palmiers."

"Really?" I shrugged. "It must've been someone else." I gave him a huge smile. "Sometimes we foreigners all look alike."

His features never changed, the eyes, dark and serious, fixed on my face. My smile became forced and then disappeared entirely.

"The woman, she's your wife?"

Damn, what would Donata tell them? The truth, I supposed.

"Not really."

He stroked his mustache. "What's that mean?"

I tried again, letting a sly grin ease over my face. "Don't tell her, but I'm going to ask her to marry me. She's a good friend, like a fiancée."

He held my gaze for another awkward moment and then slid the clipboard between the seat and the door. "You can return to your car."

I was afraid to ask if that meant we could also leave. Better to ask the police official who'd first stopped us.

But the man talking to Donata made it easy, telling us to drive carefully and to have a good trip.

In a few minutes we'd left the roadblock behind and were approaching the outskirts of Medenine. I turned to Donata, marvel in my voice. "What'd you tell your guy, anyway? He was in a great mood."

She laughed and nodded, the sound refreshing. "I told him we were lovers," she said, her voice clear and full of spirit. "That we'd come back soon for our honeymoon and stay longer next time." She blushed. "He melted. Told me everything we should see in Tunisia."

I looked at her in the dim light of the car, marveling that the encounter hadn't worn her down. In fact, she seemed stronger for it, closer to her old self.

"By the way," she said firmly. "I can't stand the name Billy Wayne. I'm calling you by your real name."

I grinned.

"Now, Derek Stone," she said playfully, "what'd you say about me?"

I smiled. "You must have read my mind. I told them I was going to ask you to marry me."

We'd just crossed the Wedd ben Djaballah, the lights of the hospital and a military garrison visible off to our left, and I saw the right turn up ahead that would take us across the Wedd Medenine and into the old city, which lay between the Wedd Medenine and the Wedd Herir.

"Derek," she said, "was that a lie?"

I pulled to the side of the road and swung around to face her, my heart full of longing. Words were inadequate, unnecessary. I leaned toward her and she was in my arms, her cheek against mine, bodies pressed tight, our hearts beating wildly.

"Derek and Donata," she said softly. "It has a nice sound to it." And then her lips found mine.

I RETURNED AND paid for the rental car at the Hotel des Palmiers and we hired a taxi driver with a comfortable four-door Renault sedan to take us north the 130-some miles to Sfax. We left Medenine just after midnight, having eaten a light snack of fruit provided by the hotel's restaurant, and slept fitfully in the car until our arrival in Sfax at dawn.

I shaved in the pilot's lounge at the airport and we sat for a couple of hours at the international gate waiting for a Tunisavia flight to Malta that was scheduled to depart at eight-thirty A.M.

We went through customs together, and I was worried they'd have something on Billy Wayne Henderson, but we were ushered through with no questions. I marveled at the ease, considering we had no luggage and I looked nothing like Billy Wayne, as well as being nine years older than the age shown in the passport. When I thought about the difference in our height—I was a good seven or eight inches taller than Billy Wayne—I was happy U.S. passports didn't require personal measurements. But like the passport officials in most countries, the Tunisians were more concerned with incoming visitors than with those departing, and I don't think they would've noticed anyway.

The rest in the taxi on the trip north seemed to have done us both good. Donata's head no longer ached, though the area around her left temple was sore to the touch, and I felt fine. As we walked from the gate to the airplane and up the boarding ladder, the heat hit us again, already close to eighty-five degrees. I hoped Malta was cooler.

The flight was uneventful—we were served a light breakfast of croissants, jam, and coffee, and then it was time to land.

In the airport at Luqa I asked Donata if she thought her uncle would have the arrival gates watched.

She shrugged. "I've been looking, but I haven't seen anyone I recognize. He may not have heard from Kolesnik."

I wasn't so sure. "Someone had to find the Russian by now. He'd call your uncle, right?"

"Probably. Unless he wanted to get the computer board first. Convince the Americans he was really after it."

"Through the Libyans?"

"If they were the ones who took it from you. It might have been an agent left at the hotel by Bukov and Kolesnik."

I considered that. "Strange that they'd go to so much trouble—and danger, really—for something they know is fake."

"It's essential to my uncle that the Americans think the Russians are fooled. The Americans won't be watching him so closely."

We walked through the airport and hailed a taxi in front of the terminal. Donata greeted the driver in Maltese and told him our destination. He was a deeply tanned, pleasant-faced man in his thirties, a bit too talkative for my taste, but I let Donata handle the conversation. I'd noticed that as I approached Malta and the encounter with Carlo Spugna my mind had begun to turn in on itself. My responses to others were clipped. Talking was a distraction that kept me from focusing in on what had to be done.

Donata and I had discussed in general terms what Spugna had planned and what we might be able to do to stop him.

First, we'd decided to stay not in Valletta, where Spugna's people might stumble upon us, but a few miles south of Qormi in a little town with a population of five thousand, Siggiewi. We weren't sure if they had a hotel for tourists, but we expected to be able to find a *pensione* or guest house.

The taxi driver, however, was responding to Donata's request for information by shaking his head. He didn't know of any accommodations in Siggiewi. He looked at us strangely, perhaps wondering why we couldn't go to one of the major tourist centers on the island.

Donata took my arm and whispered, "Don't worry, Derek. I'll talk to the shopkeepers. There's always someone willing to take in a few guests to earn extra money. We'll manage."

In the airport at Sfax, I'd told Donata more about Jake Roberts, my old tender, about meeting him in the Napoli café in Sfax, that he'd said he was vacationing on Malta and had left me the name of his hotel.

"We need a backup," I said, "and that's the only person I know on Malta. He can help line up some good men."

"I know people who can help, too," she said, with an odd cast to her face, but I shook my head and said no.

"I'm afraid anyone you know might get back to your uncle. Jake and I have had a falling out of sorts, but I'm sure he'll have contacts here. We can hire enough men to help."

We'd also talked about when and how to accost Spugna. Donata thought it might be easier simply to go to the villa on Gozo with the Maltese police. I listened to her but I was still reluctant to contact authorities who might be more interested in just who I was than in Carlo Spugna, important businessman and native son.

"We have to be there when the transaction is completed," I said. "If we don't get the real microprocessor, we're wasting our time." Which wasn't quite the truth. I had plenty of reasons for wanting to meet Spugna, but harming him in an important business deal, an illegal one at that, would give me added pleasure.

In Sfax, I'd noted with displeasure that the closer Donata and I became—the more I thought about her and not about Wanda—the less I felt the emotions that had motivated me for so long, my deep-seated hatred of Spugna and desire for vengeance.

In the taxi, thinking about the matter again, I realized that part of my displeasure was seated in guilt. It was as if I were betraying Wanda. Hadn't she died just four months ago? Yes, she had. The span of time was almost equal to the short time we'd been married and more than equaled the hours we'd spent together. It hurt to think that.

I even worried at one point that Donata was just a substitute for Wanda. That wouldn't be fair to either of us.

Finally, I told myself that if I didn't shut off my mind to those kinds of thoughts I'd be in trouble. Facing Spugna with divided thoughts would result in disaster. I had to prepare and prepare well. And I had only the afternoon and night to do so.

My last thought about Wanda, before I forced myself to focus on the task at hand, was this: At least I'd grieved for her; I'd wandered for close to three months doing only that, thought only of her and her loss, suffered to the point of contemplating suicide. But when I crawled onto the beach at Vignetti and took Gene Harrell's identity, I became a new man in part. A divided man, thinking not only about Wanda but also about myself.

And finally about others. Now I wanted to be whole again.

Siggiewi was a picturesque though unpretentious town, the home a few centuries earlier of the Secretary of the Inquisition. The taxi driver dropped us off near the parish church of St. Nicholas, and we looked around for a likely candidate for information.

Donata asked me if I wanted to eat first. It was going on eleven—and I said no, even though a meal together at a small café was tempting. I couldn't get enough of seeing her in the daylight, rich chestnut hair cascading over her shoulders, the startling green of her eyes haloed in gray, the still-innocent softness of her features—and the playful smile she tossed me when she caught me staring at her.

I kissed her impulsively and she blushed. "Derek, on the church steps!" But she kissed me back a second time, longer than the first, and then said breathlessly, "Stay here, I'll ask some of the women if they can help."

She walked into the church and came back ten minutes later with an address. The home, she told me, was an eighteenth-century mansion just off the country road leading southeast toward the huge Laferla Cross, visible in the distance on the plateau of Gebel Gantar, the highest point on the island.

"There's a sheer fall to the sea beyond that," Donata said, and I thought of the three-hundred-foot drop to the sea at the western edge of neighboring Gozo where Billy Wayne had saved my life.

We set off walking, Donata's arm through mine, the sun high overhead and hot. Along the way, we stopped at a small market and bought some bread, cheese, and sliced meat.

"We'll eat once we're settled in the room," Donata said.

I nodded. I had other things on my mind. When we

were on our way again, walking along a dusty path, I said, "I wonder where Carlo is. At the villa or the office in Valletta."

She considered that and said, "Probably in the villa. I think he has the computer board in a safe there. He'll probably fly in tomorrow by helicopter and bring it with him then."

"So he'll have to drive from the airport to the warehouse?"

She nodded.

"Is that far?"

"It's only about two miles. After we arrange for the room, we could go back by taxi or bus. Take a look at the scene. The woman I talked to said bus eighty-nine runs out here from Valletta, through Hamrun and Qormi."

"Is the warehouse along that route?"

She shook her head. "No, but we could come back that way."

"Good." After a minute, I said, "I think we should rent a car in the city. We'll need our own transportation. Could you do that this afternoon?"

I pulled out Billy Wayne's wallet. "Plenty of cash here. Won't even have to exhange any. He's got Maltese pounds."

"What are you going to do?" Donata asked.

"I'll go in with you by bus. I have some business to take care of. After that, I'll track down Jake Roberts, see what he can do to help. Line up some men. We'll need weapons also. That'll be hard."

I'd had to toss the Ruger .22 before boarding the plane in Sfax.

I took a deep breath. "After you arrange the rental, you can find a restaurant, have a better meal. We'll meet somewhere in the city later tonight. You pick the place."

"How long will you be?"

"I'm not sure. Several hours at least. Give me until around nine."

She thought for a moment. "I don't think I should stay in the city that long. I'll come back by bus, meet you at the room."

"What about the rental car?"

"I'll pick it up for you and leave it in the parking lot near the police station in Floriana, with the keys under the floor mat and a scrap of cloth tied to the antenna. You couldn't rent the car anyway. If you're not a local, you have to have an international driver's license to rent a car in Malta."

A mongrel lying at the side of the road watched us as we walked by. "Do you have one?" She couldn't fool me. She was Italian, not Maltese. As much a foreigner as I was.

She glanced at me with a sly grin. "No."

"No?" I stared at her. "What'll you do?"

She pursed her lips. "All I have is my passport. *Zi'* Carlo had to let me take that to get out of Malta. I guess I'll have to say I'm Carlo Spugna's niece. They'll know him."

I was aghast. "You can't do that! They'll call him. He'll know you're on the island."

"I'll say he sent me to rent it, that he's busy, he couldn't do it himself. Something. They won't call."

"I don't know. I thought you'd have it easier. Maybe I should do it. At least I have an Oregon driver's license."

She shook her head. "They'll send you to the police to get a signature. You have to have an endorsement."

"I'll risk it." After a moment of reflection, I grumbled, "I'm tired of being Billy Wayne." Not that I could do anything about it.

She smiled, said we had no choice, that she'd rent the

330

car, and then she changed the subject. "While you're in the city, maybe I can find you some clothes that fit."

I grinned. "These have about had it, haven't they?" I was still wearing the black cotton pants and blue pullover shirt given me by Pawlu the first night I arrived on Malta. I shook my head. "Wish I had the time to join you."

She nodded. "Just tell me your size. After I rent the car, I'll buy you something."

"They couldn't fit any worse than these."

She laughed, tugging on my sleeve with her left hand, her other arm through mine, and then a moment later said, "We're here. That's the house."

I looked up and saw a country home, built, we soon learned, in the eighteenth century for a church dignitary and then sold to a private landowner. The house, an elegant two-story building, was set a hundred or so feet from the road with a flagstone walkway leading from the driveway to the front door. A white sedan was parked to the side in front of what looked to be an old coach house.

The room itself, on the second floor, turned out to be an immense bedroom-sitting room with separate bath. The lady of the house, a widow in her sixties, opened the curtains and looked at us to see if the room was satisfactory. We had a view, toward the back, of a garden and barren fields beyond.

We told her the room was excellent and that we'd walk back into town and return later with our luggage, which we'd left at the airport.

Over lunch, which we ate sitting on the bed, Donata laughed. "Now I have to buy us both some clothes *and a suitcase,* or she's going to wonder what's going on."

"Yes, from the look she gave us, I think she thought we were eloping."

"Women her age recognize young lovers when they see them."

Young lovers. When I thought of Donata I felt young; when I thought of Spugna I felt old.

Two hours later, after cleaning up in the room and then catching the bus in Siggiewi, we arrived in Valletta, and I gave Donata some of Billy Wayne's Maltese currency, saving most of it for what I intended to buy. No reason to tell her what that was, I thought. She'd only worry.

We went over what she was to do with the car so I could find it when I was ready, and I said I'd meet her back in Siggiewi later that night. She'd have no trouble returning by bus, she said, once she'd done some shopping for us. I knew we were both afraid someone her uncle knew might spot her if she waited around for me. And I wasn't really sure how long I'd be.

In fact, I was busy most of the afternoon—making my own preparations, and then finding the car and loading it up with some things I'd bought—and only tracked down Jake Roberts around seven that evening at the Marina hotel in Sliema. He looked happy to see me and said he'd been on the beach all day. "Some mighty pretty tourists around here," he added, and we both laughed. I knew Jake was saving his heart for a woman he knew back in Houston. That was all he'd talked about on the jackup—and was why he envied me and Wanda so much. The woman he loved was tied down to a job in Texas, and he was stuck for the time being across the ocean.

We went into the hotel bar, Jake ordering a soft drink and I a beer and sandwich, and I told him as briefly as I could what I needed and why.

"Are you armed?" Jake asked.

"I am now," I said. "I bought a hunting rifle and a pistol at a gun shop in Valletta." I didn't tell Jake but I'd paid the shopkeeper a bribe to avoid registering the guns with the police. The owner, a tall, sloop-shouldered fellow with a bald head, bushy eyebrows, and mustache, only accepted the money after I explained I was leaving right off to go hunting with friends but would be back late the next day to take care of all the formalities.

I drained my glass of beer and ordered a second. "What do you think, Jake? Any trouble lining up five or six guys with weapons?"

"It's pretty late notice," he said, "but I'll do it. I owe it to you for leaving you on Al-Qabisi."

"Shit, Jake, you didn't leave me. You busted your arm. You needed help."

He looked down at his right arm and nodded. "Not a day goes by but my elbow lets me know that. But I won't let you down, Derek. You tell me where you want us and when, and we'll be there to help. It's the least I can do as an American."

I smiled at the patriotic note and told him where the warehouse was and what I wanted him to do.

"If all goes well," I said, "I should see you tomorrow morning when you get there. I plan on being inside by four A.M. You should be there just before dawn."

"Okay, we'll be there by five. You let us in and we'll be ready when the time comes."

It was already dark when I left Valletta and took the road south toward Luqa and Spugna's warehouse. I drove slowly down the left side of the road, about twenty-five miles per hour, so I wouldn't miss the place. Every now and then, a taxi carrying people to the airport would blow by me at forty miles an hour or so.

I was worried about Donata, hoping she'd made it back to the room okay, and wasn't worried about me. Originally, I'd planned on going back to the room first and then to the warehouse. But given the late hour I'd changed my mind, deciding to get things done and then return to the room. We'd only be able to sleep till around three-thirty and I didn't want us up all night running back and forth. I had a couple more preparations to make in case Jake screwed up.

The warehouse was right where it was supposed to be, sitting dark and silent off the side of the road. I pulled around to the back and parked and sat there a moment. There was no sign of guards or dogs, no unusual security measures. So this is it, I thought, unsure whether I was feeling anticipation or foreboding. Tomorrow morning I'm finally going to learn the truth. If my plan works, that is.

It was time to make final preparations to see that it did.

$$
\begin{array}{c}
\rule{3em}{1pt}\\[-0.3em]
\textbf{29}\\[-0.3em]
\rule{3em}{1pt}
\end{array}
$$

Donata was waiting up for me in the living room on the ground floor. We embraced and I told her I was sorry it took me so long, that I'd spent a lot of time locating Jake Roberts and arranging everything before going to the warehouse.

"Did the door code still work?"

I nodded. "Perfect." She'd given me the numbers that unlocked the warehouse's security door, and I'd punched them out on a setup that looked like a small digital telephone and was rewarded by the sound of the locking bolts snapping back into the striker plate.

"I spent a lot of time inside getting the layout down in my mind." I didn't want to tell her what else I'd done. Let her think I'd spent most of my time with Jake Roberts.

"I was afraid Carlo had changed the code," she said. "No problems, then?"

I shook my head. "What time is it, anyway?"

Donata looked behind her. An ornate clock, mounted in a case modeled after a classical temple with its outer columns supported by two volutes, sat on top of the mantel over the enormous fireplace. Reminded me of the facade for Santa Maria Novella in Florence. The gold-plated hands read one-fifteen, a small moon appearing just above the dial to show that it was night.

"I borrowed a travel alarm from the widow," Donata said. "We'd better get some rest."

I nodded. "Barely two hours before I want to get moving. How'd your shopping go?"

"Come see, Derek." She took my hand and added, mischievously, "I have some things on the bed for you."

I expected to see the bed covered with clothes but there were only two packages. She handed me one and I pulled out two shirts, one a casual pullover, the other buttoned up the front, and a pair of blue jeans.

"Work clothes," she said. "Made in Malta. The island's one of Europe's major suppliers of jeans." She blushed lightly. "There's a pair of cotton briefs in there also. And some socks."

Sure enough, they were folded in the bottom of the bag. "Thanks," I said. "These are perfect." I looked her in the eyes. "After tomorrow, if we're alive, we'll splurge—spend the rest of Billy Wayne's money. What there is of it. I spent quite a bit to pick up a rifle and handgun."

The mention of weapons caused a small furrow to appear between her eyebrows.

"Derek, after this is over, I have something to tell you. I did a lot of thinking while you were gone."

I stared at her, surprised, and then nodded. Fair enough, I thought. I had things I needed to tell her, too. We all had pasts, and sometimes there were things in there that needed to come out before one could go on with a clear mind and a free heart. I understood that.

"What's in the other package?" I asked her.

Suddenly, Donata turned shy, dropping her head and picking nervously at the bag. "It was foolish of me," she said in a soft voice. "I thought we'd have more time."

I took the package from her hands and opened it. My breath caught in my throat when I saw what she'd bought, a blue silk camisole. "It's beautiful," I said. "Will you put it on?"

"I thought we'd have more time," she said again.

I looked at her eyes and hesitated. I'd wanted the first time we made love, whenever it came, to be special, unhurried. Tonight we would be rushed by a timetable, our concentration marred by thoughts of what faced us in the morning.

That was what the rational part of my mind told me. The other side argued differently, and desire won. To-morrow was too uncertain, the outcome in doubt. The moment was all that mattered.

We made love with a passion that left me shaken, our desire to merge with one another so intense as to be almost desperate. The strength of our feelings, the depth of our urge, was overwhelming—passion inflamed by love. After Wanda died, the feeling was one I never thought I'd experience again. I was a lucky man. For the second time in my life, I'd found someone who meant everything to me. Someone for whom I'd willingly die.

The thought brought with it a moment of fear—not for myself, but for Donata. I knew she'd do the same for me, sacrifice her own life for mine, and I didn't think I could bear, a second time, the death of someone I loved so much.

Neither of us slept. Our lovemaking was a tonic that sparkled with renewed life the more it was consumed. Pleasure washed away anxiety. Loving touches, whis-pered words, the bonding of one body to another—with this our night slipped away. The alarm caught us still awake, Donata above me, her hands on my chest, legs bent, dark hair falling forward over her shoulders and around her breasts, sweat beading her forehead and mine, my hands caressing her bottom, our bodies joined.

I reached over and shut off the alarm.

Donata whispered, "Shall we stop now and take up later where we left off or . . ."

We both smiled. We knew the answer to that. It came after the *or . . .*

                              *   *   *

We arrived at Spugna's warehouse at four-thirty that morning, the sky just beginning to lighten in the east, no clouds in sight. It was going to be a hot day.

Donata punched the six numbers into the digital locking pad, while I took a look around to make sure no one was in the area.

The lock clicked at the conclusion of the sequence and she pulled the door open, turning to smile at me as she stepped inside. I had the rifle in my hand and the double-action .357 Magnum revolver tucked in the waistband of the jeans. Fortunately, the shopkeeper had let me practice in a shooting gallery beneath his store. I'd emptied two cylinders before I was used to the blinding muzzle flash, loud boom, and violent recoil of the gun.

It took us about fifteen minutes to verify that the warehouse was empty. I showed her where I'd hide the men Jake Roberts would be bringing by in less than an hour.

"And then we wait," I said. "I hope it's not too long. Feels like this place gets pretty hot."

Jake showed up ten minutes later with three men in a small jeep. "These were all I could get," he said. "Will four of us do?"

"Five counting me," I said. "What are they carrying?"

We went over the weapons and I gave one of the men the rifle I'd bought. He had a .22 rifle suitable for rabbit hunting but not much else. Everyone spoke English, and I told the men they'd better use the bathroom if they wanted to be comfortable because they might have to stay in hiding quite a while. I sent Jake to hide the jeep.

Donata wanted to stay with me, but I told her I'd rather have her wait up the road in the car.

"When you see your uncle arrive and go in, move on down but try to stay out of sight. We may need to make

338

a quick getaway.'' I took a deep breath. "And if things go bad, you can get help. I'm not sure how many men your uncle will have, but he'll have his backup and the Russians will have theirs, I imagine.''

I reached out for her hand and said, "Whatever you do, don't come inside the warehouse, okay? No matter what you hear. If your uncle gets both of us, we're finished.''

A few minutes later I was inside the warehouse, hidden near a pallet stacked with boxes of American-made dolls. I'd made myself a fort on my first trip to the warehouse, leaving an opening between piles of boxes which allowed me to slip into a hollowed-out space. The boxes weren't going to provide any protection. I didn't need that. My plan required me to face Spugna. I needed information from him and there was only one way to get it—put myself in his hands. Only I'd have to make him think I did it through stupidity.

I stripped off my shirt and for the next fifteen minutes I completed the preparations that I figured might make the difference between success and failure. And then I got dressed again and lay down to wait.

I had a lot of time to think and I found myself laughing at a story I'd once read. Nerves getting to me probably. My last-minute mechanical preparations had reminded me of one of my engineering courses at the Montana College of Mineral Science and Technology in Butte. Of a professor who had us look at the notebooks of Leonardo da Vinci. I'd gone beyond the diagrams and scientific discoveries to read one of Leonardo's tales, a story about a priest who went around on the Saturday before Easter sprinkling holy water on the houses of his parishioners.

Along his route, the priest walked into a painter's studio and started sprinkling the paintings. The artist, with some annoyance, asked him what he was doing and the priest said it was the custom and his duty to act thus, that he was doing a good deed, and for every good deed he did on earth, God promised him he would be rewarded a hundredfold from on high.

The painter waited until the priest made his exit and then from a window up above tossed a bucket of water on the priest's head and said, "There's your hundredfold reward from on high for having ruined all my paintings."

I guess I felt like Spugna was the priest and I was the artist—about to reward him for his *good deed,* and in just measure at that.

I napped fitfully for a while and woke about two hours later when Carlo Spugna arrived, the door slamming behind him. I was surprised to see he was unaccompanied. He walked into a small office, made a few telephone calls, and left.

I looked around for Jake. I wasn't sure where he'd hidden himself. I hoped the men were patient. I didn't want any of them stepping out until I gave them the sign. I'd had five minutes to go over the plan and I hoped they weren't too nervous to remember it.

The time began dragging and I felt a wave of tiredness wash over me. Tiredness and impatience. Everything depended on whether or not Donata was right about when and where the transfer of the microprocessor would take place, on whether Spugna would stick to his plan.

I tried to doze again, curled in a ball on the pallet, surrounded by Raggedy Ann-doll boxes. But now an undercurrent of tension made sleep impossible.

I was just beginning to doubt Spugna was ever going to return when he showed up with two men around ten that morning. Both of Spugna's men, dressed in work clothes, were armed. He himself wore slacks, a white shirt with no tie, and a light gray linen sportcoat. His gold chains

340

with the Virgin Mary medallion were visible around his neck.

We waited again, all of us, this time for his Russian contacts.

They arrived what seemed an eternity later but was only twenty minutes, just two men, both tall and slender. I didn't recognize either. They wore sportcoats that looked as if they concealed guns and one of them carried a suitcase.

I watched the transaction for five minutes, heard both tall men use English—the accent Slavic—to make sure Spugna had the microprocessor.

I saw the board come out, still in Spugna's hand, and knew it was time to act. I made a big deal of stumbling out of the boxes, tripping on the pallet, and falling on my face. The gun flew from my hand and I lay there as if momentarily stunned. When I looked up, faking shock, I found four guns pointed at me. Spugna stood there, unarmed, the microprocessor in his left hand, an amused smile on his face.

"Mr. Henderson," he said jovially. "Nice to see you again. And in such good shape. You must have come for this." He held out the board and then looked it over. "Looks just like the one you had, right?"

I got to my feet slowly, my face grim. I turned to the Russians and said, "I wouldn't trust him if I were you. That may be a fake."

Spugna laughed. "Mr. Henderson, I can see we have a lot to talk about."

A man stepped inside the warehouse and Spugna waved him over. "Just in time, Jeffrey. I'd like you to meet an old acquaintance of mine, goes by the name of Billy Wayne Henderson."

"No," I said. "The name's Derek Stone. You might've heard of me a few years ago in connection with some of the oil rig disasters off Malta. Back when MIO was known by a different name too. I hear the company—what was it called? Spugna Oil?—was pretty upset. Or maybe you know me as the man who married Wanda Donati.''

Spugna shrugged, the trace of a smile playing at the corners of his mouth, and turned to Jeffrey Blike. ''Jeffrey, meet Derek Stone. As I said, an old acquaintance of mine.''

Jeffrey Blike had the facial features of his mother, Diane Walker, and the build of his father, Preston. He was a stocky man in his early thirties, with close-cropped hair and a clean-cut, college look. He smiled congenially, but said nothing and didn't offer to shake hands.

Spugna calmly rubbed his chin with his right hand and then pulled the loose skin over his Adam's apple. His eyes took on a thoughtful look and he said, ''So, Mr. Stone, you're probably wondering what's going on?''

''I know what's going on,'' I said. ''I'm wondering about my wife.''

''Your wife's dead. We all know that.''

''I want to know why.''

Spugna shook his head tiredly. ''Such a stupid question. People die every day. Why make a big deal out of it? It was her time. She knew too much—like you. She snooped where she shouldn't have.''

''Who killed her?''

He sighed. ''Does it matter that much?''

''Yes, it does,'' I said coldly.

He paused and shrugged. ''Your wife found out about the plan to steal this.'' He flipped the microprocessor back and forth, holding it between thumb and forefinger. ''One of my Libyan contacts bragged too soon. So I had to silence her—it was that or no deal.''

He grinned. ''I told them what I was going to do. Blow up their rig. How's that for teaching them a little efficiency? Take out Wanda Donati, get even with Petro-

Canada, and punish the Libyans for talking too much. If they'd kept their mouths shut, they'd have one of these today.'' He waved the board again. ''You see, we only had two of them—duplicates—and once the Americans were on to us, we had to use one to fool them. We gave it to them as a gift.''

I frowned. ''The Americans destroyed the other one. Gene Harrell.''

He shook his head slowly. ''No, that's what he thought, but we had both.''

''Then how'd—'' I stopped, confused.

''You see, Jeffrey Blike was working with me from the start. He knew we couldn't get away with it once his government's agents were on to us. So we used a very simple stratagem. The Americans like to complicate things.'' He turned to Jeffrey. ''Why don't you tell him what we thought up.''

Jeffrey cleared his throat, his eyes blinking too fast, a nervous tic in his cheek. ''You tell him. It was your idea.''

Spugna nodded, smiling beatifically. ''That's true, it was.''

He was enjoying himself.

''Yes, my idea, but your action.'' He turned back to me. ''You see, Mr. Stone—may I call you Derek, by the way?—Jeffrey went to the Americans the second he had the two boards. Of course he claimed to have saved only one. It was easy to pretend a change of heart. You know. Working for me but suddenly realizing how evil I was. He simply said he hadn't known what I was involving him in until Gene Harrell destroyed the one board. Which Jeffrey'd hidden on the *Kirke,* by the way. The Americans had no way of verifying what Harrell had done. They'd lost contact with him. He didn't destroy anything.''

Spugna snorted and then rushed on. ''In their excitement, in their zeal to use Jeffrey, the Americans sucked in that line about him turning against me. Patriotic citizen seeing the light, you know. They didn't hesitate. Especially when Jeffrey provided them with a plan. They could give him a fake microprocessor and he'd pass it on to me. And from me it'd go to the Russians. The possibilities of that were exciting. Fool the Russians by passing on bogus information, slow them down, keep them occupied with misinformation, while the Americans worked with the Italian development."

He laughed. "That part was easy and so was fooling Billy Wayne. You see even the Russians knew the Americans had found him out. Billy Wayne's usefulness had passed. So, what did we do? We made Billy Wayne think he was recovering the original board for the Russians. The Libyans thought they were getting it. And of course the CIA thought everyone was after a fake."

He paused dramatically and then said, "And of course they were. But you see, I and my generous colleagues knew all the while that it was a fake. They pursued it only to make the Americans think they were taken in. And I might say you helped as well. The Americans thought you were working for the Canadians again."

My mouth dropped.

"Yes, I knew who you were. Near the end." He grinned. "I have resources, the same ones who found you in the first place."

I rubbed my chin thoughtfully, playing dumb to draw out Spugna. Let him gloat while he could. Soon it'd be time to signal the men to step out and it'd be my turn.

"And what happened to the *Kirke?*" I asked. "Was that the real microprocessor your men brought up?"

He laughed. "Of course not. We couldn't risk that. Jeffrey took it off the yacht himself. Took the dinghy and blew up his own ship. He's been waiting patiently in Sicily."

I frowned, aware for the first time that I hadn't seen a dinghy with the sunken yacht, and angry at myself for not noticing. For some reason it never crossed my mind to look for it, but had it been tied up off the stern, the dinghy would have sunk with the *Kirke*.

I said, "Did the Americans know?"

"About Jeffrey escaping to Sicily?"

I nodded.

"Yes. But not that he had the real microprocessor. They had one, they thought the other was destroyed. They knew the one in the safe was a fake. Jeffrey's escape was all part of their plan. They probably had a good time watching me try to recover the safe. Of course our effort was all planned to fool them. We did rather well, I'd say. The Americans have gone home happy."

"So you think you'll get away with this?" I said sarcastically.

His laughter was filled with incredulity. "You take me for a fool? You think you can stop me? Men like you deserve their fate." He snorted again. "Last time we talked, I said you'd be joining Jeffrey at the bottom of the Mediterranean, but of course we knew he wasn't dead and I wasn't ready to eliminate you."

He laughed. "Not that I controlled that question entirely. I wasn't sure if Billy Wayne could take out the two men I sent with you but I thought he'd probably handle it without my help. Cost me two men." He shrugged. "I couldn't tell them. The cost of business. All part of fooling the Americans. This time, though, I can tell the truth. I'm ready to say good-bye to you for good." He paused, and then, with contempt in his voice, said, "Say hello to your wife for us."

I could feel my jaws tighten and he grinned in satisfaction, an evil glint to his eye. It was time to act. I raised my hand and wiped my brow, the signal for Jake and the others to step out.

"You could tell her yourself," I said, "except you're going to rot in hell. I told *you* that last time and it's still the truth."

I looked around, expecting to see four men with guns pointed at Spugna.

Nobody in sight.

I felt my brows twitch nervously. Where were the men? "Jake," I called. "Tell Mr. Spugna what we have waiting for him." And with that I hit the floor, expecting to hear a fusillade of bullets.

What I heard instead was Jake's voice. He stepped out from behind a series of pallets stacked to the ceiling. "Sorry, Derek, but you were right the first time—about the jackup."

I sat up slowly, my face frozen in shock. Doing a good job of acting. I looked at Jake and shook my head, bewilderment showing in my face and then anger.

"It's business, Derek. You know I want to marry Charlene."

I rose to my feet and stood there with clenched fists, face drawn, my suspicions confirmed. I could still feel the hurt wrenching my insides. There had always been the hope I'd been mistaken about Jake.

Jake hurried on, as if his explanation would help. "Carlo's paying me enough to retire, Derek. I'm flying to Houston tomorrow. I won't have to work with Arabs and Dagos anymore."

I nodded, my gaze suddenly cold. I'd expected as much. It was good to know for sure. No time now to wallow in regret. Time only to prepare myself for what remained. The final confrontation. Me against Carlo Spugna. No, me against Spugna, two Russians, two armed hoods, Jeffrey Blike, and Jake Roberts.

I have to admit, it didn't look like I had much of a chance.

346

30

I CLEARED MY throat and took my time in the silence that settled over the warehouse. Jake's men had apparently left, probably when I was napping, so that meant I had fewer men to deal with before getting to Spugna, who I thought was probably unarmed. As usual, he left the dirty work to his hired hands. But I didn't think Jake would put up much resistance, and Jeffrey Blike, if I'd judged him correctly, would worry only about himself. The two Russians would try to get the microprocessor and leave; they had nothing to do with the feud between Spugna and me. If they got away, fine. If the Americans couldn't handle things any better than they had, this Canadian wasn't going to risk Donata's life helping them recover the stolen board.

"Jake," I said. "I never did trust you. But you see, I didn't have any way of figuring out if you were telling the truth. I guess you'd have sworn your innocence on the Bible. You sell out your country, you're going to sell out a friend."

Before I could finish what I was going to say, I heard a commotion. Spugna's men swung around and my heart fell. Donata had stepped inside the door, a man with a gun pointed at her head right behind her.

The effect was devastating. Whereas before I'd faked shock, now I was paralyzed. For a moment I couldn't think, frozen in horror at the thought that Donata might die. A vision of Wanda flashed before my eyes and I felt my mind raging. The top of my head felt like it had been blown off by a shotgun.

I couldn't understand what they said then. I looked instead at Donata, my face gone suddenly cold and pale.

They shoved her beside me while I struggled to collect my thoughts, Spugna's face leering grotesquely the while.

I hadn't wasted my time all afternoon the day before. I'd gone back to the same supply houses I'd used fifteen years earlier when I sabotaged the exploratory efforts of Spugna Oil off Malta, and I'd bought dynamite—supposedly for PetroCanada. I knew the system and the dealers knew me. They didn't have to have fifteen-year memories; five months ago I'd ordered the latest shipment of explosives for the Al-Qabisi jackup from suppliers on Malta.

And the night before I'd worked several hours in the dark before returning to Donata in Siggiewi. I'd set explosive charges at strategic points around the warehouse, all connected by a line of Primacord with delaying devices so I'd know when the explosions would occur and from where. I knew I'd be inside the warehouse with Spugna, that I'd have to put myself in his hands if I wanted to learn the truth, and that I'd need some protection if Jake turned out to be rotten. The timing of the explosive charges was critical. I had to know the exact sequence to protect myself and come out of this alive.

As part of my purchases, I'd bought a radio-operated detonator. All I had to do to set off the initial charge was touch my wrists. A line ran down both arms ending in a thin strip of metal glued to the skin. The radio was under my left arm, the battery my right. The signal would go off the second the connection was made.

I figured the system was foolproof. If they wanted to tie my hands together, boom. If they asked me to raise them, I'd join them behind my head and boom. Seconds before the first blast I'd hit the floor, the explosion at my back. Confusion would reign and only I would know where the next explosion, ten seconds later, would occur. And the ones after that. Enough noise and destruction, enough turmoil, to make my escape.

I should have trusted Donata, I thought crazily. How could I not tell the woman I loved what I'd done? She knew nothing about the explosive charges, would not know how to react. My only hope was to throw my body over hers before the explosion, move a few seconds earlier than I'd planned. That would give Spugna's men more time to react. A bullet could end our lives before the first explosion shook the warehouse.

No time now for talk. My words of vengeance died away.

I looked at Donata, said, "I love you," and crossed my wrists. And then I slipped a foot behind her and tossed her to the floor, falling on top of her as she gasped in surprise.

The next thing I heard was Spugna's mad laughter ringing through the warehouse and dying away finally with a shrill wheeze.

For the second time that morning, nothing had happened. The first time—when I called for Jake and his men—it didn't matter; this time it did. Suddenly the pain hit my head with the strength of a massive underwater explosion and I spiraled down, following the pain, like a diver whose destination is death.

It took me a while to absorb my failure. The next words I recall hearing were Jake's. He said them quietly, while Spugna stood sneering at us, shaking his head in amusement.

"Derek, buddy, you didn't think they'd be stupid

enough not to watch the warehouse, did you? Even without me.''

"Tell him about his suppliers," Spugna said in a mocking voice.

"Carlo never forgets, Derek. He learned a lesson in seventy-one. There's not a stick of dynamite sold in Malta without him being informed.''

Jake shook his head regretfully. "Sorry, buddy. God just wasn't on your side in this affair.''

I laughed harshly, still a little deranged by it all. "Bullshit! God doesn't take sides.''

"But people do," Donata said, interrupting me, her voice clear and firm, no trace of fear, no trace even of the anger I was feeling.

Spugna looked at her intently, his eyes narrowed. We were on our feet now.

"*Zi'* Carlo," she said. "You killed a lot of people in your organization trying to find out who was leaking information to the authorities. You never thought of me. You never told me—*your loving niece!*—anything, so how could I be the one? But you see, I was the one. I knew what you were doing was against everything our family has ever stood for. I heard enough long ago to despise you. I knew you were capable of killing one of us—one of the family—long before you ever tried to. So I listened and what I heard I passed on. You can thank me for that, just as you can thank Derek for destroying your attempts to find oil.''

The words had rushed from her mouth in a torrent. I stared at her in amazement. Here I was feeling bad for hiding the explosives from her and she'd hidden a whole past of trying to thwart Spugna's criminal activity.

She turned to me, saw the look in my eyes, and slipped her arm around me. "Sorry, Derek." She shook her head sadly. "On Vignetti I didn't know who you were. I thought you might have been planted by Carlo. Later, the police told me not to say anything until they had everything wrapped up. It's the only thing I intentionally hid from you.''

I opened my mouth to speak and a tremendous roar filled the warehouse. I was slammed backward, everything in slow motion. I recognized the sound before I hit the concrete floor. Someone had fired the .357 Magnum. I'd been shot, didn't know where. I stared at the ceiling of the warehouse, a red haze flooding over everything.

Donata, I thought. My God! Not again! Not after Wanda!

Suddenly the noise was deafening, shots thundering into the warehouse from outside, an answering roar echoing inside.

I tried to sit up and found Donata beside me. "Derek," she screamed. "They said they wouldn't fire.''

I pulled her down beside me, her mouth by my ear. "I've been shot. I don't know where.''

She wiped my forehead, her hand coming away soaked with blood. *"Madonna mia,"* she whispered, reverting to her native language. *"What have I done?"*

I looked over her shoulder, my eyes clearing. Spugna was screaming, standing over us with a revolver in his hand. *My .357 Magnum!* I saw his finger tighten, tried to rise, and found I was screaming myself.

The gun shook in his hand, his finger jerking on the trigger. Suddenly I realized there was nothing coming out of the barrel. The sounds were from other guns. The cylinder of the .357 Magnum had shattered at the first shot.

Donata rolled away and I came to my feet, rushing at Spugna with a savage snarl on my face.

He raised the gun, his face tight with fear, and pulled the trigger again.

And again nothing happened and for a crazy second I

was grateful that nothing I'd prepared had gone right. Not even the gun.

Spugna drew back to hurl the revolver at my face, and I grabbed for his arm, my crazy thoughts running on wildly.

Funny how all the weapons were mine, I thought, and as the gun dropped and my hands went for his throat, my mind said, maybe I wasn't meant to kill Spugna.

My mind uttered the thought but my hands didn't get the message. They closed around his throat with bestial fury. And then I lost all my strength and everything went from red to black.

Ascending. Smooth, rhythmic flutter kicks. The light above growing slowly brighter and brighter, expanding into a huge circle of light. The water slowly warming. The surface, just above me, waiting. Patiently waiting.

Coming closer and closer.

Twenty feet . . . fifteen feet . . . ten . . . five . . .

And then, like the first kiss after a long awaited reunion, I was breaking through, my lungs filling with breath after breath of fresh air, my ears suddenly able to hear, the light so bright I had to shut my eyes.

For a moment, I wondered where I was and then realized I was lying on concrete and someone was holding a wet rag to the side of my head. I opened my eyes, feeling strangely clearheaded, although the silence was dreamlike.

Donata was bent over me, tears in her eyes. "Derek," she said. "The police are here. They've got Carlo. He shot you in the head."

I tried to smile. There was no way I was going to die now. The emerald green of Donata's eyes—a sign of hope, of life.

"I may have been shot," I whispered, "but I've never felt so good in my life."

I paused, wondering if she understood, and looked up at her, opening my mouth to speak. I was suddenly very tired.

She was waiting—expectantly—and I gathered my strength for one last phrase and said, "Except making love to you."

They took me to the hospital then, and only later did I learn Spugna was still alive. His windpipe had been crushed and they'd had to perform a tracheotomy and remove his voice box, but he was going to live. In prison, of course. And for a long time.

My head wound required forty-two stitches—two more and they'd have matched my age, I joked—but I was going to live also.

"Superficial head wounds always bleed the worst," the doctor told me. "You'll be in fine shape when you leave here."

The doctor must have been clairvoyant. Not only was I in fine shape, I suddenly realized after two weeks had passed that I was also free of headaches.

I kept asking the doctor if that was normal and shouldn't I have headaches from the bullet wound, but he just smiled and asked if I was complaining.

Donata stayed with me in the hospital and when the two weeks had passed, we moved back to the room we'd rented from the widow in Siggiewi, while I waited for a duplicate passport to arrive from the Canadian High Commission in Rome and recuperated following removal of the stitches.

A journalist from the *Times* of Malta stopped by to interview us in Siggiewi, and I learned I was somewhat of a celebrity on the island. After thirty or forty minutes of questioning, the journalist, a serious young fellow who'd just graduated from the university, asked me in English what my plans were for the future.

I'd had a lot of time to think about that.

At first, before I learned I hadn't strangled Spugna to death, I'd wondered if I could live with myself—and, after a long mental struggle, came to the conclusion I sure as hell was going to try. And later, when I found out he was alive, I wondered about that. Could I bury Wanda and move on, or was I going to be locked in a vicious cycle of frustrated vengeance and hate for the rest of my life?

It was then I realized that Donata was my vengeance. Spugna's organization had been destroyed, his operation foiled. Even his niece had turned against him—and saved my life. If she hadn't ignored what I said and informed the police—told them the day before to be outside the warehouse that Wednesday—I'd have never made it out alive.

Yes, I thought, my love for her and hers for me was vengeance enough.

I looked at the serious face of the journalist and said, "Three weeks ago I nearly drowned in the sea north of Sicily. A lot has happened since then. I don't know if I can think about what's going to happen three weeks down the road, let alone a lifetime."

I paused and rubbed my chin reflectively. Donata was looking at me intently and I turned to meet her eyes. Our smiles were instantaneous, joyful. There wasn't a fiber of doubt in either of us. She wasn't waiting in fear to hear what I'd say, she was waiting with pleasurable anticipation.

I glanced back at the journalist, who was now scribbling in his note pad, and realized I was anxious to send him on his way.

When he finished writing, I caught his eye, put my hands on my knees as if to get up, and said. "But I'll say this about right now. Right now, if you'll excuse us, I'm going to make love to this willing and beautiful woman. And tomorrow I'm going to marry her.''

I looked over at Donata, as the fellow blushed and hurriedly closed his note pad. He shook hands with both of us, thanked us, stuttering in his haste, and we all wished each other good luck.

The widow accompanied him out of our room on the second floor of the villa, carefully shutting the door behind, and I waited until their voices faded away in the distance before I turned and said, "Donata, where shall we spend our honeymoon? I don't think we should go back to Tunisia.''

She laughed and I thought how appropriate her name was. *Donata,* feminine past participle of the verb *donare. Given as a gift.* Like a gift from the gods, I thought.

"Somewhere far off in Canada?" she said, and we could hear the widow ushering the journalist out the front door. "No journalists, no police, no doctors, no one but you and I.''

She slipped into my arms then, and I held her tight, feeling our hearts beating as one.

"No one but you and I,'' I whispered back to her, and a moment later, together in bed, with our bodies also one, I said again, *"No one but you and I."*

If you have enjoyed this book and would like to receive details of other Walker Adventure titles, please write to:

Adventure Editor
Walker and Company
720 Fifth Avenue
New York, NY 10019